BEFORE PITTSBURGH

BEFORE PITTSBURGH

KASIE WHITENER

Chrysalis Press
Columbia, SC

FOR JESSICA

VIRGINIA
FEBRUARY 18, 1995

*P*ower Hour: one shot of beer every minute for an hour. Six beers in one hour. A toast for every shot. It's juvenile, but gets you hammered. Tony and I sat on a dorm room floor at Radford University. Erica, a girl Tony knew who graduated the year before us, invited him down. I'd tagged along to wing man.

"Traditional first toast," I said, "To brothers."

We clinked the shot glasses. Tony's bore a Disneyworld logo and mine had a Redskins helmet. We took them from the shelf over the desk where they sat beside a snow globe from Philadelphia and a stuffed teddy bear holding a black rose.

Fifty-eight seconds later: "To road trips."

Drink.

'Plan A: Fraternity Keg Party' had been a bust. Radford is in the Blueridge Mountains, and the walk from campus to the party had been up a steeply inclined road lined with gravel that sloped off low on one side. When we arrived, knowing only the two girls we'd come with, and had to pay ten bucks each for a red cup, I tried to remind myself I wanted to be there. But by midnight, I stood on the back deck of the shitty rental townhouse smoking a cigarette and missing Kacie. When I looked down below, I saw Erica making out with some guy who wasn't Tony. She had been kind of drunk an hour ago but at midnight, the rugby-wearing blonde she was lip-locked with was just about holding her up.

Tony appeared as she turned her face away and Crew-Team-Ken tightened his grip on her waist. She squirmed and made a noise that sounded like resistance. I tensed.

"Let her go, man, she's pretty hammered," Tony said.

"Find your own pussy," the guy responded, groping Erica's ass.

Tony stepped closer. "I said let her go."

"Tony!" Erica squeaked at my best friend. "I wanna go."

"You're going home with me," handsy man growled.

"Nah," Tony said, "She's done."

The backyard seemed to still as the crowd sensed a controversy. The music got lower, conversations hanging in the air like cartoon bubbles attached to mouths. I looked around for how to get to Tony and, seeing a rickety staircase behind me, moved that way. It was still early by college standards, so not everyone was plastered. Except Erica, who couldn't be more than 110 pounds if she'd had an anvil in her pocket. Tiny frame, a boy's chest and narrow hips, red hair looped into a low-neck ponytail.

Tony was a decent-sized guy, but the bully holding Erica was obviously older than us.

"Go home, kid," he said. "The grown-ups are talking."

"Is that a euphemism for date rape?" Tony sneered. "Grown-up talk?"

Coming down the steps, I saw Tony's face and knew he wanted to fight. The last time I saw that look, he lunged at his brother Gavin and their dad had to break them apart. From the deck, the backyard sloped toward a wooden fence that separated the yard from the forest beyond. The house lights cast the shadow of the deck out five feet or so.

"Hey, Chad," a guy behind me called down. "Is there a problem?"

"Chad," Erica squeaked, "*That's* your name."

Rugby guy shoved Erica aside, and she staggered but didn't fall. I had just made it down to the yard and caught her as she sagged into my side. Tony watched her, saw me, and stood up straighter. In a cartoon frame, he would have been rolling his fists, eyebrows angling down in a V, readying himself for violence.

"Who the fuck are you?" Chad's face reddened, maybe anger but probably beer.

"Tony's a really nice guy," Erica slurred, nodding at me, like I didn't know.

"No means no, *Chad*." The sneer landed on dude's name and Tony might have wanted this, but I totally didn't. Bad enough we were the youngest people there. Still in high school. Oughta just be invisible, getting cup after cup of ten-dollar keg beer. Maybe a blow job later from a high school girl who mistook us for college guys. But come on. He's my best friend. So, I sat Erica upright against a post on the stairs and stepped closer to Tony, his mischief contagious like that time he stole candy from the 7 Eleven when we were nine.

Chad swayed a little, his Rugby stitching straining tight against the bulge of chest muscles, and glanced past us up to the deck, but no one seemed to be near enough to take his side.

Maybe Tony and I could get away with just backing out and urging Erica to flee with us.

"Hey, man," I said, "it's cool. We were just leaving."

Tony glanced at me, eyebrows knitted like he was surprised I'd try to talk us out of this. Seriously, though, a fight? I'd never been in one before and neither had he except with Gavin and fighting your brother didn't count. Brothers pulled their punches. Chad probably wouldn't. And was it worth it? I looked over to Erica, slouching against the rail.

Then Chad saw me, backing up Tony, and shoved his white cuffs up beefy forearms.

"Don't be an idiot," I said, maybe to Tony, maybe to Chad. "Just let us go."

"After this little prick called me a raper?"

Then Tony laughed because the word is ridiculous, and I laughed because he laughed and that just made Chad even more pissed. And he hit Tony. A wide swing of a punch, like a right hook, and it might have been in slow motion because we both just stepped out of the way and he barely made contact with Tony's shoulder. The momentum of the swing and the slope of the grass put Angry Chad off-balance, and he staggered toward Tony, cussing. With arms outstretched, Tony shoved him, and a Rugby isn't a parachute so Chad flailed backward and fell to the ground, somersaulting ass over elbows until the fence at the end of the yard, some five yards away, broke his roll with a thud.

"What the hell, man?" someone called down from the balcony.

"We're leaving," I called back, with a wave in the general direction of cartoon bubbles and muted music. "*What the fuck, man?*" I hissed at Tony.

"I barely touched him," he said. "Besides, some assholes think they can just have whatever girl they want. And they can't." He stepped past me, over to Erica, and helped her stand.

"This is *Chad's* fraternity," she said, and laughed maniacally. *Drunk chicks.*

Later, sitting on the floor below Erica's lofted bed playing Power Hour with a warm twelve-pack of Busch Light, Tony said he never wanted to do that again.

"Rescue a damsel in distress?"

"Fight a motherfucker."

"But he was a raper," I responded, eyes wide, mockingly incredulous. "And it was hardly a fight. More like gravity getting the best of Chad."

Another minute passed: "To college parties."

Drink.

Another minute passed: "To knowing what's yours."

Drink.

Another minute: "To knowing what's waiting for you at home."

Drink.

"You mean that?" Tony asked.

"I do."

"You and Kacie?"

I shrugged. "I love her."

"San Francisco is far away."

I had been accepted to Cal State and would be leaving in the Fall. Everyone knew I was going but no one knew what it would do to me. To us. I just knew I wanted out of Northern Virginia.

"To getting out."

Drink.

Tony dropped his head back on the loveseat he leaned against. "Shit. What a night." He had recently shaved his hair up the back and on both sides. The top was longer, spiky, and standing straight up after he'd run his fingers through it a thousand times.

"We should have gotten stoned before we went."

He hiccupped, blinked, and said, "Might not have been there for her if I'd been high. Then who knows?"

"To being safer with a couple of high school guys than with a raper."

Drink.

"I don't think Kacie expects you to be faithful."

"Why wouldn't she expect it?"

Tony shrugged. "She's going to college, too, ya know?"

"What did she tell you?"

"Nothing, man, shit. I'm just saying you should make it easier on you both. Just get the rules straight."

"The rules are straight. They are that I'm going to try to be faithful and she should, too."

"To trying to be faithful," he said and his voice had a tinge of bitterness to it.

Drink.

"What's with you?"

Tony shrugged which was one of the things he did that made me crazy. It wasn't indifference, it was him saying he didn't want to pursue whatever we were talking about because we would probably fight, and he didn't want to fight. Ever. Until tonight.

"You're pissed at me," I said. "So, spit it out."

"Just love her, man."

"I do."

"Then you shouldn't have to *try* to be faithful."

I stared at him, and he lifted his shot glass and we took the ninth shot without a toast.

We knew people who played Power Hour with one toast every ten-minutes, but we liked the challenge of thinking up sixty toasts. We'd toast *Animal Farm* and Alice in Chains and macaroni and cheese and all kinds of other stupid shit.

I still couldn't believe that asshole's whole fraternity didn't jump us. The only thing I could think was that he was a real dick and no one really wanted to fight. Except Tony. He seemed kind of disappointed it was over so soon. At least, until we got back to Erica's dorm and put her to bed and sat on the floor and got to the real binge drinking.

"I gotta piss," he said. "Catch up when I get back."

"Can't leave the room," I said. "Erica's not supposed to have male overnight guests." I burped. "Use the sink."

He looked over at it, toothbrushes dangling nearby, then stood and staggered closer, turned on the water and unzipped his pants. I refilled our shot glasses.

"It's weird in front of a mirror," he said after a minute. "Watching yourself piss."

"Just hope Erica doesn't get pissed," I said.

"Not like we had a choice. Anyway, she's out," Tony said, coming back to sit across from me and lifting his shot. "To getting pissed."

Drink.

"Think guys like Chad the Raper are at UVa?"

"Wondering who's gonna look out for Kacie next year?"

"Could be you," I said.

"Man, you know I can't get into UVa."

"But you could go down there. Work. Live nearby."

Tony's expression hardened. "I get enough of that shit from my parents, ya know? So could you not?" He gestured to the dorm room, indicating the college life. "This is not my future." He raised his glass. "To the working class."

Drink.

"You're more than that," I said.

"Do I have to be?"

But I didn't really know what that question meant, and I didn't know how to answer, so I just looked away.

A minute later he said, "To *Facelift* and the genius that is Alice in Chains."

And we drank.

BARCELONA
MAY 15, 1999

*E*ighty-nine days and 4,000 miles since Tony died.

My backpack rests at my feet in the courtyard of the Barcelona Museum of Contemporary Art, where I stand watching skateboarders have their way with an expanse of concrete. One guy in a Metallica shirt. One with a cast on his wrist. Two wearing shorts despite the chill and two with earphones hanging around their necks and bulges in their pockets, heads bowed over a nylon case of compact discs.

In forty-five minutes, I'll meet my landlord at the communal living building that's home for the next seven months. For a moment I'm homesick for San Francisco and my one-room flat. Then cast kid pulls a trick that lands him on his ass and I'm smiling. But it doesn't last. It doesn't feel sustainable. Eighty-nine days of unsustainable.

On day ninety, I'll go to campus and find out what's required to register. Then I'll get a job.

I'm smoking a cigarette. It's cooler than I expected as the sun sinks. Must be the onset of evening or the chill of familiarity that comes when I remember parking lot tricks set to the cadence of teasing voices.

Seven months in Spain if I have a job, enroll in school, see a therapist, and "show progress" in my "writing career," whatever the hell that means. Mom and Dad agreed to let me stay through the end of the year if I can demonstrate I'm healing. That I've dealt with my feelings about Tony's death. About that fucker killing himself.

Except right now all I can feel is the distance.

From everything.

June 3, 1999
From: captainlisto@yahoo.com
To: melisings@yahoo.com
Subj: Apology

Meli,

I know it's probably too late for an apology. I know you were really hurt in February. When you told me you loved me I didn't know what to say. And then dad called and Tony was dead and I had to get on the plane. Then all that shit in Virginia, Kacie and whatever. I know the drugs were part of it. I'm not myself when I'm stoned and drunk and whatever.

Jesus this apology sucks.

Just know I'm sorry and I hope you'll accept it. I don't know what to do without my friends and you're one of the few I've got left.

Okay. That's all.

- Brian

June 7, 1999

"**F**orgive me, Father, for I have sinned," I said.

Between the Port where I fulfilled the job requirement and the place I had been staying was a Catholic Church. I walked past it most days. On day 112, I went home to bathe then doubled back and went inside. The sun had come up and stretched itself across the sky, and the midday was fresh and cheerful. I walked directly East into the sun, feeling it wash over me with warmth and tenderness. All these years of San Francisco sunsets, I'd forgotten the subtle seduction of sunrise. Getting reacquainted with it in Barcelona had been bittersweet.

Inside the church, it was cool and quiet even in the height of summer tourism, and the smooth bannisters and pews felt slick beneath my fingers. It was early enough that no one knelt in alcoves under statues of the Virgin Mary and Saint Paul, but a few people prayed and lit candles against the wall in the narthex. Some murmured confessions to priests hiding in carved wooden cabinets. I was one of those.

"How long since your last confession?" The priest asked this question in Spanish, but I didn't have the vocabulary to respond in kind. I speak Latin American Spanish, according to my buddies, so I basically sounded like a redneck. They just laughed at me.

"The last time I confessed was in an email to my dead best friend. I'm not Catholic. But he was. I thought maybe." The words fell out and then stopped, clogged my throat, and tears welled in my eyes.

"Maybe I could hear your confession on his behalf?" His English was heavily accented, and he spoke slowly, as if he were translating as he went, searching for vocabulary as well.

"Does it work like that?" I wiped the back of my wrist against my nose.

"Not usually, my son."

Tears dripped down my cheeks. I pressed the heels of both hands to my eyes.

He shifted a little in the seat, the light through the shade between us flickered, and a knock on the wall might have been his elbow, or his knee.

"Why don't you tell me what you need to say? Unburden yourself. Then we can decide what you should do with that, okay?"

Thing is, I didn't really know which of my sins I should confess. I cannot even count them on one hand anymore.

"There are so many," I said in Spanish, "How do I know what matters to God?"

"Can you not believe that all of it matters?"

"I believe none of it matters."

"You have no faith?"

"Tony said I had none. But now he's dead and I find myself believing. Only that I miss him so bad. It's like I need to believe I'll see him again in some kind of afterlife. Catholics have that, don't they? An afterlife?"

The priest took a deep breath which I couldn't tell but might have been patience or frustration.

"Tell me what you wrote to Tony."

"That I was sorry for not returning his phone calls or emails. He tried to reach me, and I was angry with him and I ignored him."

"I'm sure he forgave you."

"He killed himself before I could apologize."

Another deep breath. Another shift on the seat beyond the wall.

"Does suicide keep him out of heaven?" I knew the question was childish, like my asking Chris about heaven on the day we buried Tony, and him saying, "A five-year-old could ask that question better than you." But I thought I'd heard something about suicide being one of those sins you can't be forgiven for.

The priest cleared his throat. "Well," he said, "The Catechism asserts that our life belongs to God and we are only stewards of it." This he delivered in Spanish, a slowly articulated interpretation that nonetheless pained me as I understood it. He was quiet for a moment, when he continued, his voice had a strain to it, as if he were fighting past his own emotion. "Because God entrusted this life to us, it is wrong to dispose of it."

Silence between us while we both seemed to be interpreting in our own heads.

Then the priest added, "But I believe when you ask, God forgives."

And I said, "So I apologized for all the shit that went down with Kacie and the drugs and the twins and how we were so dishonest for so long. With everyone." I felt the tears start again. "How we fractured our family, our friends, with our addictions and our lies."

"Addictions?"

"Drugs. Sex." The snot was coming now, so I leaned my face to my shoulder and wiped it away with my t-shirt.

"I see."

"Kacie called me a whore. She's right. It's one of the demons I need exorcised."

"Demons?"

"I must sound like a fucking lunatic." My hands in fists, I pounded them on my knees. The box suddenly felt too small, the air too old, the quiet too quiet. I couldn't breathe. It was a panic attack like the kind I had been having since February. The kind Dr. Moses gave me medicine for. Medicine he's refusing to send unless I find a shrink here. I used my tactics, though, the ones he taught me. I squeezed my eyes shut until I could see the water. I saw it calm and clear before me and my hands cutting through it stroke after stroke, pull, kick, flip-turn, push off, swimming laps in that calm, even way I remembered how to do.

Then the priest was saying, "Son?"

"Yes, father," I murmured.

"Are you okay?"

"Yes, father."

"Your friend, Tony, he was a good person?"

"Yes."

"And he loved you?"

"Yes."

"Then there is something redeemable about you." His English seemed less forced now and his voice was tender, deep with compassion. "We see the good in others and they see it in us. You miss your friend because he showed you the best of yourself. You need to find some way to see your best self without your friend reflecting it."

"Yes, father."

"Pray, young man, that relationships replace the high you get from your addictions. Let your friendships be your drug."

"Yes, father."

"God forgives," he said, for the second time, and it was a kind of blessing. "And you must, too."

The tears resumed then. That word – forgiveness – heavy in my throat and on my heart, felt not like freedom but like an albatross. Yet another demon I must exorcise. The list kept growing and I was not really making progress. Except against time. I was working against time and as the time passed, chunks and days and weeks, I expected to feel the healing salve of distance.

All of this I'd confessed before walking to the church, in spiral-bound pages of tightly scripted pencil scratchings:

Day 109, 110, 111, time and distance growing, and I am still the whore. Still the addict. Still the mess that withered in Virginia, flaked apart in California, and buried himself in Barcelona seeking new roots, new stems, new blooms. I look up and see the sunlight. I can feel its warmth. And the water its nourishment. But I am still those things I wish I wasn't. I am still me. And Tony is still gone.

I walked away from the church, the sun on my back, and the Mediterranean out in front of me, and I imagined walking straight off the dock and into the water and sinking to the bottom under all the flush of the boat wake and the fishing nets and the cargo ships and the cruise liners and the churn of water and sea weed. Burying myself.

Maybe that's how Tony felt when he looked at himself in the mirror that night, the blood dripping from his wrists. Like going under. Like not wanting to resurface. Like it was easier to just swim down.

After my visit with the priest, I begged Mom for another refill of the anxiety meds. I also found a pool in which I could swim some laps. I didn't go right then, but I got a student pass for when I needed it. Day 113, the visualization was enough, unsure how my body would react to the real thing. I didn't even have a suit. Or goggles.

I wrote to Kacie but I didn't send it. She made it pretty clear when I was cracking up in California that she didn't want to be part of my recovery effort.

I called her one night, like a Tuesday maybe, in March, and begged her not to hang up.

"What do you want, Brian?"

"You."

Motion on the other side of the phone. A shuffling, like maybe she was traveling from one room to another. Walking away.

"Wait. Wait. Sorry. Not you. I mean, yes, you, but just to talk. Just talk, Kace."

"Are you high?"

"Listen. I've been thinking maybe when I head to Barcelona I'll come through Virginia and maybe we can see each other."

"I can't see you, Brian."

"Why not?"

"Is she with you?"

"What? No. I wouldn't call you if she was here."

Hang up. Dial tone.

Then, the next day I called to apologize, and I got her machine.

"Kacie, listen, I'm sorry. I just called to say that. And to see if maybe you'd pick up. Which you didn't. And I understand. Maybe you're in class or something. But I'm not high now." That was a lie. "And I wanted to talk about February and what you said and tell you that you were right. But you know that and you know . . ." but then the answering machine beeped and clicked off and I was listening to a dial tone again, which was starting to sound like the tone of her voice—flat and cold and unemotional.

So, I wrote to her. She was the one I wanted to confess, even though when I was with the priest, I only talked about Tony. He's my big sin. Kacie's one, too, and Meli, and The Crew and my parents. So many of them. But Tony's my big one.

The priest said God forgives and that I had to, also. I would have to forgive. Myself, I guess. But I didn't know if I could.

June 16, 1999
From: captainlisto@yahoo.com
To: melisings@yahoo.com
FWD: apology

Meli,

Did you get my email from before? Maybe you got it and don't accept my apology? Not sure what I'll do with that. Kacie's not speaking to me either. So maybe you two have some kind of pact or something. Girl shit. Whatever.

- Brian

June 17, 1999
From: melisings@yahoo.com
To: captainlisto@yahoo.com
re: apology

Brian,

Of course I accept your apology. Everything that happened around Tony's death was just fucked up. But that doesn't mean we can get back together. I've got a lot of work I need to do on me. What I want, what I need, what I will and won't put up with. You're complicated and I can't really handle complicated right now.

And of course Kacie and I don't have some girl shit pact. Get over yourself. You must have been mad I didn't respond right away. I don't check this email that much. So. Anyway. It's fine right now how it is. You being away. Maybe I'll see you when you get back.

- Meli

June 18, 1999
From: captainlisto@yahoo.com
To: melisings@yahoo.com
re: apology

Meli,

I wrote that follow-up email drunk (of course). Just easily frustrated when I don't get a response. Sorry. I'm a jerk.

- Brian

June 22, 1999
To: mac.williams@turnerwatts.com
From: captainlisto@yahoo.com
Subj: father's day

Mac,

Thanks for being at my dad's yesterday when I called. It was good to hear your voice. Sorry I cried.

- B

June 22, 1999
To: captainlisto@yahoo.com
From: jlisto@aol.com
Subj: Father's Day

Brian,

Thank you for calling yesterday and for speaking with Mac. We were all pretty emotional but it's part of the healing process, I suspect.

Mac said Rhonda hasn't come back and he's not sure she plans to. They may be in for a long separation. He also said Gavin hasn't called in weeks. If you have Gavin's email, can you send him something? Just tell him to call his dad.

Be well, my love. We miss you and hope you're seeing someone. Grief cannot be postponed, Brian. Remember that.

Love,

Mom

June 22, 1999
To: captainlisto@yahoo.com
From: alisto@aol.com
Subj: Fathers Day

Brian,

Thank you for calling yesterday and for using the calling card. I thought you'd forgotten about it.

I've added more money to the account to get you through July. Thought you said you'd found work? If it's not enough to pay your bills, you need to find another job.

Heard from Dr. Moses regarding your prescription. He said he can't renew it without confirmation you're seeing someone in Spain. Are you seeing anyone?

Do you want me to get a referral from our insurance?

Your mother is worried about you. Also, change your email address to something respectable. All the resume tips say your email should be professional even if it's a personal account.

Stay safe.

Dad

July 3, 1999
To: ksoutherland@uva.edu
From: captainlisto@yahoo.com
Subj: Reminders

Kacie,

I know I never told you what I wrote about the way we made love. I know I made you think you were just one of many, that our times together blurred with all the others. But you weren't and they didn't.

Just finished reading the book The Hottest State by Ethan Hawke. Something about reading William's descriptions of being with Sarah, the way he talks about how she was all-consuming, reminded me of us. I couldn't put it down. To be fair, I was traveling and would have been staring at the back of someone else's airplane seat if I hadn't been reading it, but I also could have slept.

No, you're right, I don't sleep on planes.

Anyway, the book was really, really good and for the first time I've read a style that felt Hemingway-esque but new, like what I'm trying to do. It's the first book I've picked up where the voice sounded like me. Not just the character, but the writing. It made me want to write.

Since the airport had made my fingers itch with all the stories begging to be told, I just took to the notebook and sketched out a few stories. You know my stories always start with dialogue, a conversation I'm overhearing in my head. So I wrote the conversation I was hearing and then the story just kind of came from that. It's rough but I think I can do something with it, maybe workshop it at school and revise it for submission.

Coming to Spain, I had the plan to submit at least 10 stories to literary magazines and try to get published. Mom and Dad required a plan and lit mag submission was part of it. I can't truly become a writer without some lit mag credits. It's a thing. It's how agents find you. How publishers decide you're worth the gamble.

But first, first you have to have a story and until I got to Spain, I didn't think I had any. But this one came from me. Not the shit I made up in undergrad that didn't bear any resemblance to my actual life. But a story from me. Like peeling off the layer of skin around a broken fingernail. How the edge of it is hard and dry and then it pulls and the cuticle lifts and the skin breaks and that twinge of blood surges to the surface and it stings so you yank and rip it deeper than you'd intended.

That's how this story felt.

I'd forgotten, truthfully, all about it, until I started with the dialogue and the story unraveled and it hurt to remember. But I wrote it and I think it's something and I'll take it to workshop and maybe if it gets published, I'll send it to you.

You'll remember it, I'm sure. You remember all the shit that happened between us. You have some kind of scrapbook in your head with empty matchbooks and movie ticket stubs that helps you recall everything we did and were.

I've been trying to forget. For years.

Anyway, just thought I'd let you know I'm writing. I think Tony would be happy. I think Ethan Hawke better watch out. I'm gonna be a contender.

- B

July 8, 1999

On day 148, I got my ass kicked by a couple of Russians then had a threesome with two Lufthansa flight attendants. Here's what I can remember of it:

I'd gone out with Marco and Paulo, two servers at a coffee shop I frequented. They wanted to take me to a club, and I hadn't really been out in a long time, so I agreed. I dressed up, for me anyway, in a gray shirt and black jeans, both of which fit tighter than they had a month prior when I'd packed them. Even so, I was less conspicuous than either Marco or Paulo. They slicked their hair back, wore jewelry, and flashed rolls of cash when they paid cover charges and bar tabs. I wasn't used to paying cash and only a little bit more familiar with the currency than when I'd arrived. In the first week, I'd paid a cab driver by showing him a wad of bills and telling him to take the correct one from my hand. Probably overpaid for that ride.

Marco led the way, kept me close, and Paulo followed us both to keep me from falling behind or getting taken for another ride. Marco knew some girls at the first club but none of them spoke English. They were all excited to meet me, but my redneck Spanish didn't impress. Then we had about four rounds of shots and one of them stuck her tongue in my mouth and I felt like maybe we had gotten past the language thing. I begged off dancing but the making out was just fine. We left that crowd and went on to the next bar, Marco promising the girls we'd meet back up and then telling Paulo and me he had no intention of doing so. He reminds me a lot of me.

The next bar was one I'd been to before, but Marco knew the bartender and Paulo greased the door man, so we got in ahead of the line and only paid for about fifty percent of our drinks. We didn't know any girls at this place, but they found us, approached us, and introduced themselves. One of them, Anna, was an American. She was on exchange from a high school in Pennsylvania and when she said high school, I quickly put her on the do not touch list. It was nice to talk to an American, though, and since she'd just arrived, I could show off a little about what I knew of the city. I told her I'd missed the Fourth of July.

She asked why I was working on the docks if I was in college and I pretended I hadn't heard the question. *Punishing myself for my best friend's suicide* didn't seem like a night-out-at-the-bar kind of response. Especially for a high schooler.

Finally, Marco said the crowd there was too young and we left. I told Anna to come by the dock and we could get lunch sometime. I forgot how bad I smell after work, but I didn't expect she'd show up anyway. She knew I was too old for her and I think she got the sense that I was hiding something. A bad break-up, criminal record, panda bear tattoo. Could be anything, really.

The third bar was nearer to my house in Vila de Gracía, inland near the Avinguda Diagonal. I'd been staying there since arrival, and the communal courtyard, bath and kitchen facilities had grown on me. My roommates were all guys like me, working their way through studies, but of varying ages. A pair of guys from Saudi Arabia were in their thirties and two kids from South Africa were just out of high school. The bar teemed with foreign nationals, drawn to the area by the promise that it was full of locals. The primary language, though, was heavily accented English. I liked it, even if it was rather dim and dingy, less posh than the Olympic area and less flashy that the club scene we'd just left. It felt a little bit like what I imagined Seattle to be like.

Marco ordered our drinks and Paulo secured us a table. I hit the john. The single door had a hook-and-hoop lock and gave a few centimeters of visibility while I stood at the urinal. I looked at the wall above the porcelain commode and read some lyrics from an old Counting Crows song. They made me smile and then ache a little. I remembered them from the Tony's Green Velvet Notebook. Which Kacie still had. Because she took it back the morning I left. So very far away from Virginia and yet still haunted in innumerable ways by all that happened after December.

When I left the john, two girls were blocking my way out of the back corner of the bar.

"Hola," I said, a little drunk by now.

"Your friend said we should come get you," the taller one said. "He said you might get lost."

"Coming back from the john?" I asked.

The shorter one nodded. "Want to?"

I looked past them to Paulo who was grinning at me.

"What did you have in mind?" I felt flirty, a little drunk, and maybe open to suggestion.

"Maybe just a little kiss," one of them said.

"You know Lara, don't you?" the other one said.

I thought back to my first weekend here and the woman who'd shown me around Barcelona and introduced me to the dock manager. She was red-haired and creamy-skinned and I'd enjoyed her, but she'd been temporary, off to another adventure further south.

"She's not from here," I said.

"No, she's a flight attendant, like us. She told us to look you up."

"Surely not for this," I said, as the shorter one dragged her fingertips down my arm.

"She told us," the taller one leaned close to me, her breast pressed against me, her lips on my ear, "About the outdoor shower in the courtyard."

I closed my eyes and felt myself responding to the two of them, the touch, the warmth, the promise of something. I needed it.

"Move, *vyrodok*," someone grunted. I speak less Russian than Spanish, but the term was an insult, that much was easy to interpret. I looked up and one of the mean bastards from the docks glared down at me.

The girls shifted closer to me to get out of his way. I wrapped my arms around both waists and pulled them closer.

"You need two?" the Russian grunted. "Greedy American." Then he barreled his way into the john, and I let the girls kiss me.

The shorter one nipped at my neck, her hand on my ass. The taller one kissed my mouth, her hand sliding down the erection bulging in my jeans. *I need this*, I told myself.

Then, over the tall one's shoulder, as she kissed my ear, I saw the Russian pissing through the crack in the door; pissing and watching me with the girls.

"We should go," I said.

The door burst open and the Russian was there, and the girls had flinched back, and he had his hand around my throat, shoving me against the wall.

"Paulo!" one of the girls squealed.

My friends pushed their way into the darkened hallway and the Russian dragged me toward the back door. We fell through, his hand still on my neck, my feet barely on the ground. Outside a ramp descended toward the parking lot, and a railing stretched between the ramp and a closed dumpster. The Russian shoved me and let go and I tumbled over the rail, onto the lid of the dumpster. Turning a backwards somersault, I tried to focus on the light of the parking lot or the building's hard edges but rolled and then fell onto my knees on the asphalt, disoriented and more than a little drunk. The Russian leapt the rail, feet first onto the dumpster and then to the ground beside me as I was getting to my feet.

"Come on, then," he said, and then that same insult in Russian.

"Dude, wait!" I said. "I'm not gonna fight you."

"Yes, you are."

"Hold up. *Mis amigos?*" I looked up to the rail for Paulo and Marco.

"Woah, fella," Marco's smooth voice and accented English came through the noise bleeding out of the bar's open back door. "You don't want to fight," he said, jogging down the ramp and rounding the dumpster so he stood between us. "You're just drunk."

"Been need to kick this little shit's ass for weeks."

"The fuck did I do to you?"

"*Callaté*, Brian," Paulo snapped, still on the ramp above.

"You work but you don't need to. Fucking Americans taking jobs."

"From Spaniards. Kind of like you, *el culo*," Marco said. "Maybe I oughta kick your ass on behalf of all of Spain."

"*Bravo*," Paulo said.

"Fuck it, Marco. He wants me, let him have me," I said, a new bravado surging. Strange how quickly a hardon went to clenched fists.

The Russian pushed past Marco and charged at me. I took a left-handed swing as he came near and caught his jaw with my fist. The punch glanced off without making much of an impact other than to make him madder.

"Fucker!" he shouted in a voice that sounded like Schwarzenegger.

"Sergei!" He turned to the sound of his name and I threw another punch, this time on the other side of his jaw with my dominant hand. He reeled and stumbled back. His friends were on the rail now and they watched as he righted himself and came back at me. His eyes burned with rage, but I could see something else there, too, a kind of unfocused glaze that made me think he was drunker than he'd admit.

"Sergei," the friends from the railing called again.

"Now you pay," Sergei said. He took a swing, but I ducked and he stumbled into me. I turned and dug my elbow into his stomach, so he doubled over, falling to his knees.

Then his buddies were on the asphalt, too, and one of them had grabbed me and the other landed a punch across my face. Blood spurted from my nose.

"Hold the fuck up," Marco said, kicking Sergei in the chest and pulling on the shoulder of the guy who'd hit me.

I broke free from the one who was holding me, turned and swung wildly at him. He stepped out of the way then hit me in the stomach. Choking on the blood from my nose, I felt the liquor came back up as vomit surged into my throat.

"*Basta! Basta!*" Paulo was trying to get us to stop fighting without getting into the fray himself. But his efforts were wasted as Sergei stood back up and stalked toward me. His buddy had my arms again and Sergei landed another hit, this one a backhand across my cheek, that turned my head and sent another wave of nausea through me. My eye felt like it would explode.

Marco and the other Russian were in a bear hug of body blows spitting obscenities at one another in their respective languages.

Finally, the back door opened again, and the bar manager and two bouncers streamed out and down the ramp. Dude let me go and followed Sergei and the other Russian thug as they fled down the alley. Marco and I stood catching our breath and wiping blood off our faces while Paulo explained to the manager that we'd been brutally attacked. My face and shirt were ridiculous, swollen and covered with blood.

Looking up, I saw the girls in the doorway and waved at them, proud I hadn't puked, but tasting bile and blood. They came back to the villa with me and peeled my shirt off in the courtyard and walked me into the shower, lathered soap, and gently washed me clean. Then the three of us went to bed and I decided to work on that sex demon the next day. Along with the fighting demon. And the drinking one. It had been a long night and I'd earned this.

August 27, 1999
From: captainlisto@yahoo.com
To: melisings@yahoo.com
re: apology

Where have you been? I've been calling. Why won't you answer? When you said you needed space, what you meant was we're through. I get that.

I just need a friend, Meli, honest, I'm not trying to get anything else.

I mean, I'm in Spain. I just thought maybe someone who knew me could help better than these people here. My therapist, Jesus, she's useless. Claims I'm still in the anger stage of grief. I'm deep into the depression by now. I'm not mad anymore. I'm just really, really sad.

Just answer the phone, please, when I call.

- B

August 28, 1999
From: melisings@yahoo.com
To: captainlisto@yahoo.com
re: apology

It didn't have to be that way, Brian. You made that choice in February. You're not ready for a relationship like I deserve. You're too into yourself. I have needs, I tried to tell you, I have plans. I need to work on that. My space is just that, mine.

I didn't know how to tell you I needed space without pushing you away. But I guess they're the same thing. Maybe you're right about that.

- Meli

August 29, 1999
From: captainlisto@yahoo.com
To: melisings@yahoo.com
re: apology

That wasn't what I meant, but it should have been what I expected. Everything I say you make it about you. I don't know what any of this has to do with you. You barely knew Tony and that was years ago. If you're not going to help me with this then fuck off.

August 30, 1999
From: melisings@yahoo.com
To: captainlisto@yahoo.com
re: apology

This is getting ridiculous. Your therapist is right, you're in the anger stage and you're being a real shit. Just stop emailing me. It's over.

August 30, 1999

My therapist told me to call my dad. I said I called him on Father's Day. She said that was three months ago. *So?* *So call him.*

So, I did.

"What did you expect?"

"I don't know. I guess it just caught me by surprise." I had told him my professors all speak Spanish all the time.

"Should have taken business classes. Bet those are in English."

I had stared up the courtyard wall to the pale blue sky above. Some sheets flapped on a clothesline like flags of surrender. The payphone receiver was big, like really old or something, and it smashed my ear to the side of my head. I pinned it against my shoulder and continued to look up. Tears stung my eyes and I thought it must be the brightness of the midday sky.

"It's early in the morning, Brian. Did you know?"

"Were you sleeping?"

"No, I was leaving for the pool."

"Is mom there?"

"She went on an overnight spa trip. Yoga and massage and pedicures and stuff. It was her Mother's Day gift."

"From me?"

"Yes, but in English."

I managed a laugh. "Stupid, right?"

"I bet your Spanish is getting really good, though."

"*Por supuesto.* Sometimes it's nice to hear English. Without an accent."

"So, call more often," he said.

"Why are you swimming at five in the morning? You have all day."

"Habit."

And then a few more reminders, updates, and we hung up. I replaced the receiver on the payphone. Staggered across the courtyard, bone tired and stinking from a morning on the docks. Stripped down to my shorts at the outdoor shower, tugged the chain for the cold water, and rinsed off in the summer sunlight. A few hours' sleep and then a five-block walk to therapy. Notebook open in my lap in the waiting room, I had captured the conversation with my dad. Then, in my therapist's office, scrubbing my fist against an unshaven jaw, sitting upright on a leather chair, sliding my finger down the page, I wrote: *Do I still smell like saltwater now the way I used to smell like chlorine long after swim practice? Does Dad smell like chlorine? Why can't I remember?*

And my therapist said, "That sounds like progress."

"Toward what?"

"Understanding your father. Being less angry with him."

"I'm not angry with him. He's not the one who died."

"Brian, the anger stage of grief is not necessarily anger with the dead person."

"His name was Tony."

"See? That sounds like progress, too." She wrote something down on the pad of paper she kept in her lap. "You used the past tense when you referred to Tony." She didn't even have the decency to look up at me when she said it. If she had, she might have seen the way that realization decked me same as one of those Russian goons punching me square in the jaw. The way Kacie slapped me clear across the face that time. The way Meli told me to leave her the fuck alone. Past tense.

In my notebook, I scribbled: *Hear that, Tony? You're over.*

The thing is, I'm a writer so things like past tense really matter. I'm probably more sensitive to that shit than normal people. After she told me I'd used past tense about Tony, I thought about the last few times I had written to him and how I haven't really treated him like he's still here. And I wanted to grind my teeth, squeezing my jaw together so tightly the words would be crushed into never having been said.

Instead, I took a deep breath through my nose, exhaled through my mouth, and said, "Does past tense mean I'm out of the anger phase?"

"It means you're out of denial."

"Well, yeah, it's August. I've been out of denial."

Then she did look up, removed her glasses, and her face softened into compassion. Her voice sounded as if she were soothing a child.

"Brian, grief is not like college. It's not on a calendar where a certain number of instances or checked boxes determines moving from one stage to another."

"Okay. Great."

"And some people relapse into previous stages for a variety of reasons."

"Okay."

"How many days has it been since Tony died?"

"One hundred ninety-three," I said automatically.

"You're still keeping score, Brian. I don't think you fully understand what's happening to you." She had the slightest accent, a soft *th* sound to her *S*s and a British arch to her *A*s. I'd only ever heard language like hers in commercials and films. There's an authority to it, something trustworthy about it. This was our third month together and she usually led me down a path of realization, stopping to provide context when I struggled for it. Reminding me to breathe. Waiting while I gripped my pencil, scribbled my own notes, held my breath, and avoided eye contact. Challenging me to be truthful with her which was the hardest part about the sessions.

Telling the truth hadn't been easy for me.

I'd say not ever but I think it had gotten more complicated in high school.

"Of course I understand what's happening to me. I've lost my sense of home. Poof. Gone. Disappeared." My cadence was dismissive. Arrogant. The way I responded when challenged.

She knew it, too, and she didn't break eye contact despite my sneer.

When the silence between us lasted long enough, I had to breathe. I said, "Happens to everyone in college, right?" and added a shrug for effect and looked down at my notebook as if there were answers there.

She got frustrated with me, I think, when she tried to explain what I might be feeling, and I sat there refusing to take her seriously. She got this pinched expression, like she was holding back a sigh.

"Brian, the stages of grief are just a vocabulary. Some things you're feeling won't fit into any category. And it's okay to experience what you're feeling without naming it anything or trying to get away from it or over it."

"Isn't that the whole point of this? To get over it?"

She did sigh, finally, and lay her notepad aside. Folding her hands in her lap and crossing her legs at the ankle, she shook her head and let her hair flutter a bit around her ears.

"Would you have come to Spain if Tony hadn't died?"

"Why does that matter?"

"So, then this, Spain, is not about getting over Tony. This is the life you would have had anyway."

"Except Meli might be here."

"Okay. Let's explore that. Why do you think Melissa would be here?"

"Because the reason she broke up with me is because of what I did when I went home for Tony's funeral."

"Which was?"

I'd opted for upright in the brown leather chair and suddenly I wanted to be lying down on the couch. Folding my leg across my lap in a figure four, I tugged my ankle up, gripping it tightly, resettled the notebook on my knee, and gripped the pencil in my hand.

"Let's go back to February. What were you doing? What were you feeling?"

"Alone."

"And what did you do about that?"

"It goes back further than that. In December, I went home and Kacie and I broke up."

"But you'd been dating Melissa before that."

"Yes, but she didn't know Kacie and I hadn't officially split."

"And then on New Year's Eve?"

"I found out Kacie had cheated with Jason and I got pissed at her. So, I owed her a better goodbye than that, okay? And Tony's funeral weekend, she and I were feeling the same thing, I thought." I looked away, found something shiny and glinting on a bookshelf and focused on that. Remembered the drippy candles in Kacie's sister's room and said, "We went to bed together and had a better goodbye."

"It was one time. Unfinished business."

"Yes."

"So then why did Melissa break up with you?"

"For the same reason Kacie slapped me across the face."

And even though it was nearly 200 days ago, I could have been standing in my bedroom on that Sunday morning, five days after Tony died, watching Kacie recognize the guilt in my voice. I'd been on the phone with Meli and she came in and she'd known. Almost immediately but she'd waited a few minutes to confirm. Then she'd slapped me. Called me a whore.

"Why did Kacie slap you?" my therapist pressed.

"Because I fucked the bartender."

"A third woman?"

I looked away and grunted, "Nobody important."

"The day after reuniting with Kacie."

"I wouldn't call it *reuniting*."

"You cheated on Melissa twice in the same weekend." Though her voice had a sharp edge, when I looked, she was settled back in her chair, as if the entire conversation bored her. Painted nails on fingers twitched and the pen thumped the notepad. She watched me. Waited for me to tell the truth.

"She was right. Kacie. I was a whore." In my notebook, in pencil, I wrote, *I'm still a whore. One hundred ninety-nine days and four thousand miles later.*

"When you are with these women," she said, her tone more inquisitive now, leading, "How do you take them?"

"Excuse me?" I wondered if she thought I was a misusing the word 'whore.'

"Are you rough with them? Do you kiss them?"

I thought about Lara in the shower in the courtyard and Wendy and Sloan in my bed after the fight with the Russians.

"No," I said. "I am not rough. I don't want to hurt them. Yes, I kiss them." Releasing my leg to the floor, I folded the notebook closed, dropped it and the pencil between my shoes and settled back into the chair.

The therapist mirrored my shift, set aside her own notebook, closed her hands over her lap.

I let my shoulders and chest relax, dropped my arms to my sides. Things said were vapor. No notes. No evidence.

"The best sex is tender. Soft and slow. Sometimes more fervent, more intense, but never unkind." I closed my eyes.

"Or degrading."

"Never." I shook my head, rolling it side-to-side on the back of the couch.

"And why, do you think, are you so willing to have sex with these women?"

"Because they are willing to have sex with me." I opened my eyes, tilted my head to one side, still casually reclined, arms limp. Met her stare. "It's their desire that brings me in. Some of them I barely noticed before they noticed me."

The therapist stood then and walked to the window. She wore a business skirt, high heels, pantyhose, and a white blouse. She was older, maybe late-thirties and while she'd told me to be honest, I hadn't expected the afternoon to evolve quite like this. In San Francisco, therapy had been interrogation and judgment. It drove me deeper into my grief. But these explorations of my addictions had felt less invasive though not completely without judgment. Not without written record, either. Until now.

"Brian," she said, without turning around, "Before December, did you notice the women before they noticed you?"

I reached for the glass of water the therapist's assistant had left me on the small table beside the couch. It was slick with condensation and almost slipped from my hand. When I lifted it to my mouth, it dripped on my shirt.

"You said this is the life I would have been living anyway." I replaced the glass and wiped my lips. "But it's not, is it?"

She didn't turn around. She said, over her shoulder, "You know it isn't."

I mean, what the fuck was that? The door opened almost right away and it was time for me to go. Don't even know how

she could have signaled to her assistant to enter because usually she just tells me herself it's over. But this time, the assistant
opened the door and said, "Señor Listo?" and I left with the damp
drops still darkening my shirt.

August 31, 1999
From: captainlisto@yahoo.com
To: melisings@yahoo.com
re: apology

You're right, of course. I'm sorry. Again.

September

September 2, 1999
To: tonywilliams@yahoo.com
From: captainlisto@yahoo.com
Subj: what to do now

Dear Tony,

My therapist actually thinks it's good I'm writing to you. She says it's a way to keep you alive in my heart and memory. I don't want you there, to be honest. Get back in your fucking box and stay there. She says that's the anger talking.

"Stages of grief," I said, "I know." I thought I was a lot further along, honestly. I thought I'd gotten through to the cusp of acceptance.

But apparently my plan to be a better person, to stop all the casual sex, stop the drugs, be a good friend to Chris and Jason and Joel and even Tabby, to make amends to Kacie, apparently all that was first stages of bargaining.

"Tell me about denial," she said.

"Like when was I in denial?"

"Yes. It would have been recently. Maybe before you came to Spain?"

I told her that's when I started writing to you. Emails first and then a spiral notebook. I told her I let you know I'd be coming to visit and instructed you not to ask about Meli. She said I was treating you like you were still alive.

"Yes."

"Do you think he'll be there when you go home?"

"He is there," I said. "He's in the ground."

"But he's not really there."

"Look, I'm not religious or spiritual or whatever, so afterlife or what the fuck, he's there. In the ground, waiting."

"For you to come back."

"I always go back."

"But now your parents, they have moved away?" Yes. Tucson. A whole other set of baggage and grief and shit. I didn't respond to her, so she switched tactics. "You said you emailed Tony."

"Yeah, just . . ." I leaned forward, elbows on knees.

"Just what?"

"Nothing."

"Brian, you'll have to say something if you want to make any progress."

"When?"

"Ever. Just *what*?"

"A confession. I write Tony confessions. I told him I'd bring him along in Spain. I'd narrate it for him. Tell him what I saw, how it smelled and sounded, what he was missing."

"He's dead."

I glared at her. I might have reverted to denial.

But she told me to keep writing the letters to you. Really, this could be something, maybe a book or something someday. The stories are great, right? The bar fight and the sex after and all that. I could focus on those good things, maybe make the whole thing more cheerful for you, ya know?

I still haven't heard from Kacie. Just so you know. You should tell her to quit being such a bitch. Months now. Since February. And nothing.

The therapist thinks the Kacie conversation clouds the Tony conversation, so we don't talk about Kacie. Pretty much not at all. Whenever I bring her up, the therapist reminds me I'm still working on losing you. It's not time yet to think about losing Kacie. But I didn't lose her. I drove her away.

Not like you. You left.

She says I'm still pissed about that. Pissed at you. But that's fucking stupid. I was pissed at you before, but since you're dead now it's not worth being mad anymore. Might as well just try to learn to live with this new whatever it is we have now.

B

September 10, 1999
To: tonywilliams@yahoo.com
From: captainlisto@yahoo.com
Subj: what to do now

I gotta admit I'm struggling. I guess it was going to happen eventually. I knew eventually I'd have to say, "okay anger sucks," and "okay, I'm lonely." I just didn't know when.

I did know when. I knew it would be your birthday.

So we went out, me and my two Spanish buddies and the three American flight attendants who have made it a habit to come through Barcelona whenever they can. Yes, Lara and the other two. They're not all with me anymore. Lara and me and then Wendy with Paulo and Sloan with Marco and it's all just flirtation and good fun. Nothing serious.

Anyway, we all went out and I'd pretty much forgotten about your birthday. I woke up thinking about it, took myself to the priest and confessed about it. Prayed. For whatever fucking good it did except helped me forget for a while. And then we went out.

And I got drunk and I know I'm not supposed to. It just makes it worse. Makes it harder. But it's what I do. So, I did it.

We were in the place I'd met the Russians in the alley only we haven't had any more alley experiences there. The bartender is cool with us and the Russians haven't come back. We were in that place because they have a dart board and we know the bartender.

Anyway, it was the six of us and the girls were dancing, like girls do, and going to the bathroom in pairs and shit. And we were just putting back shots when they weren't there and smoking cigarettes.

Then they came back, and we ordered six shots and I thought about it and ordered a seventh. One for you. The Crew said anytime we ordered six shots (Joel, Jason, Kacie, Chris, me, Tabby) we should order seven, one for you. So, I ordered seven shots.

"Who's the seventh one for then?" Wendy asked. I know I said they're American, but Wendy grew up in England, so she's got a great accent. Her dad was some kind of foreign digni- tary. Ambassador or something. Anyway, she sounds really sophisticated until she starts drinking and every other word is the f-bomb. It's even sexier than the accent, truthfully.

"My buddy Tony," I told her. "Today's his birthday."

And then my chest tightened. I could feel my heart throbbing, not fast really, just harder, like it might come through the skin. My vision narrowed, like black shades clouding the edges.

"How old is he?" Sloan asked.

Paulo shook his head at the girls.

"Is he here? In Spain?" Wendy asked.

"He's dead," I said.

Marco's eyes widened, though he already knew it, I wonder if he was surprised I said it the way I did.

"When?" Wendy asked.

"In February," Lara supplied.

My throat had closed up. I could barely breathe but I shoved a cigarette between my lips anyway.

Paulo lit it for me. I tried to inhale but just coughed and my eyes watered, and I couldn't tell the difference between suf- focation and sadness.

The bartender delivered the shots.

I raised mine and said, "Happy birthday, Tony," at least I think that's what I said. Lara said I was crying pretty good by then. I took my shot and yours, too, and then I stumbled into the pisser and threw up everything I've ever consumed in my entire life.

Felt like anyway.

Marco took me home. Lara stayed the night. She said I slept like the dead. Then she regretted the phrase, I think, cuz she left not long after and didn't kiss me goodbye. But that could be because I'd puked and not brushed my teeth.

I'm a fucking wreck. I knew I would be eventually. I just didn't know when. I did know when. On your birthday.

You remember that year you had the pool party, and no one came, and we were kinda pissed about it, and then your mom found all the invitations, stamped but not mailed, and we realized no one had been invited? That was a long time ago.

So, what now? Now I've finally let it suffocate me. I've said it out loud. I need help. Work. Swim. Run. Something. I need to figure out what to do about this. I feel so sad. Worse even than February. Worse than ever before. I can't imagine how it will ever be anything but this.

Is this how you felt? Hopeless?

I know it's not. I know it's grief. Dad said it would come. Mom said I couldn't escape it. I just thought it would be like somewhere familiar, ya know? Like Herndon where you're buried or like San Fran where I was told. Not Spain. This was supposed to be something totally different. Something so new it doesn't have anything to do with you.

But here you are. Like you're sitting on my chest, pinning me to the floor. Like gravity has chosen you and I'm fucked for it.

Trapped under something heavy. That's me.

So what now?

B

September 17, 1999
To: tonywilliams@yahoo.com
From: captainlisto@yahoo.com
Subj: what to do now

Dear Tony,

Yesterday Marco and I went out for pints after work. After work and a shower. I stink off the docks, so I shower before we go anywhere. By that time, it's like 2:00 p.m. on Saturdays and the whole city has come alive. People flood in from out of town to listen to street musicians and patronize galleries and theatres. It's amazing the life that comes in here on the weekends, so different from the business crowds during the week.

The tourists are all but completely gone. Back to school time of year. All the Americans have gone home. I can remember the first days of school. After we knew who we had for teachers and after we bought new school clothes and as we rose through the ranks earning more and more seniority. The first day of third grade we rode the bus to school for the first time, do you remember? Until that point our parents had taken turns dropping us off.

Anyway, yesterday Marco and I were drinking on a patio in the arts district, away from the weekenders, where the locals hide on Saturdays, a back-alley beer garden with a tall fence they've grown moss and ivy on so that it's like sitting underground. The specks of sky you can see through the growth gives the semblance of being buried.

Marco knows this chick who waits tables there so we go there on Saturdays a lot and she kind of counts on us, I think, to make most of her money. We drink pints of warm Belgian beer and flirt with the waitress and her friends.

Yesterday a couple of guys from the soccer team came in. They call themselves FC Barcelona, or fútbol club Barcelona, and they compete in the same league as Manchester United and Real Madrid and all those clubs. Anyway, Marco invites them over to drink with us, says I'm an American and I don't know anything about real fútbol. I think he was pretending to get them to agree to hang out. They're like celebrities.

So anyway, one of them said he's never been to America and wanted to know where I'm from. I told him California and that set the other one off. They started in about 90210 and babes in convertibles and all the same shit Joel teases me about whenever I see him.

"No," I said, "Northern California. San Francisco. It's warm but not like SoCal. There's this crazy ass fog that hangs around a lot, chills everything off."

"Like where Alcatraz is," the other guy said. "The island prison."

"Exactly."

"What the hell is an island prison?" Marco asked.

"San Francisco sits on a giant bay and in the middle of the bay is this big island. Well, it's not that big, but it's big enough. So they built a prison on it and they'd send the worst criminals there. It was said to be impossible to escape from."

"An island prison?" Marco mused. "That's some literary shit right there."

"Yeah, it's definitely got some legend around it."

"No, I mean, a writer must have thought that up."

"Writers are not usually the cruelest people," I argued.

"No, but the most creative."

"Why are you giving writers such a bad time?" one of the footballers asked.

"Because this chump thinks he is one," Marco said, and punched my arm.

"No kidding?" the other footballer said. "Would we have seen anything you wrote?"

See, that's the shitty thing about professional athletes. They think everyone else has reached the top of their professions, too. There are, like, millions of writers out there and getting noticed by an agent or a publisher is so fucking hard. I've been writing query letters and I just keep getting rejected.

Which is what I was explaining to the football guys when one of them says, "Is it because you're not any good?"

And I said, "It's exactly because I'm not any good."

I know you thought I was, but you didn't know shit about writing.

I'm reading all this amazing stuff. Really talented writers. And

I'm thinking I cannot even begin to tell stories like they tell stories. I don't even have the stories to tell.

So then I drink more. And talk to more footballers. And throw more fish. And fuck more stewardesses. And I think the stories, they'll come. Eventually they'll come.

B

OCTOBER

October 23, 1999
To: ksoutherland@uva.edu
From: captainlisto@yahoo.com
Subj: Reminders

Dear Kacie,

The water cuts away as I glide through it. Stroke after stroke, I can feel it giving way and then filling in behind me as I move through. It's cool and clean and clear and I feel at once exhausted by the effort and exhilarated by the intimacy of it.

The new goggles and suit Dad sent me have the feel of familiarity and the water itself, the scent of it, the taste. But the facility is foreign and strange. My Spanish is much, much better now and I can read the warning signs and the rules list. The accents and ñs make me feel like I'm reading italics. The sounds of the pool are different, children at lessons, the elderly in water aerobics, their alternating squeals and murmurs a cacophony of delight and uncertainty.

But submerged I hear nothing.

For the first few workouts I had to swim backstroke. I wasn't able to breathe. Or, more accurately, I couldn't hold my breath long enough to keep my face in the water for more than a few strokes. Even today I breathed on every right arm. It's kind of embarrassing to be so out of shape.

That's why I'm swimming now. Every day. When I see Dad at

Thanksgiving he'll want to swim and he'll expect me to work out with him and he's good for at least 5,000 meters. So I need to up my endurance as much as possible before then. A month doesn't give me much time but I don't think I'm as out of shape as I thought I was.

My California therapist suggested I use the visualization of swimming to calm myself down whenever I feel anxious. Now that I'm actually in the pool, I feel only the anxiety of old ghosts. It's hard for me to swim without seeing the Herndon Community Center pool, thinking of those long hours of practice, Coach Joe stalking the deck shouting at me. I remember everything about those early mornings. How cold the morning air was. How it had the crisp scent of snow and the stillness of being empty.

I don't swim that early now.

The Herndon pool would part because I was the only one cutting a path through the water at 4:55 in the morning. But this pool is wild with activity. It's mid-morning and noisy. I'm intentional about it. Trying to dislodge the stillness of empty. Trying to fill the gap left by the early morning quiet.

Anyway, I thought you might understand. Or give a shit. Or something. I dunno. Hope you're okay. Wish you would write back.

- B

October 24, 1999

My therapist has been saying for months that I ought to get back in the pool and Dad sent me a new suit and goggles. Like that's not a hint. So not only did I go and sit on the side and watch the other people in the place, think about how different it sounds, and feel that tremendous sense of loss that comes when you realize a part of your life is over forever. But I actually got in. Slid down deep into the water. Let it surround me. Let it hold me up.

I positioned the Swedish goggles I'd assembled last night: two small, unpadded cups, a string through a plastic tube for the bridge, and double straps over the back of my head. There's something familiar about the way those cups dig into my eye sockets. Like they've always been part of my corporeal existence. Like I'm an alien in disguise and those are the lenses through which I actually view the world.

Dropping into a low crouch, I dug my arm in behind my head and shoved off the wall into a tight, well-practiced stream-line. The water broke around me, rushed over me, parted and re-pooled behind me. Stroke after stroke, long, controlled pulls, working my way through the surface, the long black line down the center of the lane guiding me. I could see the individual square tiles that composed it, their order and symmetry a stabilizing presence.

Into the flags, the line T-boned and I flipped into the wall, caught it with my feet, and shoved off again. My lungs just about exploded as I streamlined out past the flags, kicking. I broke the surface with my left arm, ending the streamline rotation with the bottom arm like I'd been taught. Took a breath on the right. Then another on the next right. And another on the third right. Flip turns would drown me. In all, I swam fifteen-hundred yards. Nothing. Less than a mile. Up and back and up and back. Flip turns, streamlines, third stroke breathing, steady pace. I did some kicking and some pulling and rested only minimally between 100s at the wall. It was brutal.

Brutal and beautiful.

No butterfly, no fast intervals, just long slow freestyle and backstroke with some breaststroke during the kick sets. Easy. Get-back-to-it easy.

When I go to Tucson for Thanksgiving next month, Dad will want me to go along on a workout or two. He'll know when I can't get past twenty-five hundred yards that I'm out of shape. I wonder what he'll say about it. For now, just gotta work up to twenty-five hundred. If I could get in three thousand with him, that'll be something. You never really lose it, swimming, but getting back to it is exhausting. I went home and napped. Later that same day I saw my therapist. She's agreed to sign my prescriptions, new ones, lower dosages. She was pleased I'd been to the pool.

"How did it make you feel?" she asked, of course.

"Lazy. Out of shape."

"It's visceral for you, swimming. I expect there to be some reflection or introspection about the activity."

"It's not meditation."

"Isn't it?"

The truth is that aside from kneeling in the confessional and blurting all my sins to a priest who may or may not have cared I'm not Catholic, swimming is the nearest thing I have to confession. Every stroke that hurts, every breath I can't catch betrays the condition I'm in. It's physical evidence of my failure. It's total honesty.

I've been running. Sporadically and with varying levels of intensity and success. But it's not the same. A good run through the streets of Barcelona on a warm summer evening is exploratory and vibrant. It's diverting.

Swimming is like climbing into a coffin and pulling the lid down and realizing I'm still breathing and being kind of pissed about it.

When you can't be what you used to be and you don't like what you are, what is there to do about it besides sulk?

Which is what I was doing when my therapist said, "You don't have to swim. You could meditate. You could Tai Chi. You could do martial arts or Pilates. Anything that connects that physical part of you with the mental. Anything that lets you channel the hurt you feel into something positive and energy-giving. Instead of channeling it into those things that take your energy and leave you depleted."

"Like drinking."

"And sex."

I looked away from her then. We've already talked about what I get out of sex. It sure as shit isn't inner peace.

"You own your body, Brian, and it's the only one you have. What you do to it and with it is up to you."

"It's not like I've been abused or anything," I said. "I'm not a victim or a survivor or whatever."

She didn't say anything to that. I know the pain is self-inflicted. A month ago, she told me to keep writing to Tony, which I've done. I filled the one spiral notebook and bought another one. This one has kittens on the cover because I thought it would be funny to write my gay love letters to my dead best friend in a kitten notebook. It's wide ruled even.

Eight months ago, Tony killed himself. Eight months and I'm still having trouble putting the pieces together. I can't exactly figure out how we failed him. I failed him. Our whole lives we were like mirror images of one another. Brothers. We did everything together. I just can't understand how we drifted so far apart.

And then I remember the drugs. I know it's cliché to say they changed us, but they really did. I know he used them to manage the imbalance within. My therapist says it sounds like he was bipolar, which means sometimes he was flying high and then, like flipping a switch, he'd be deeply depressed. I think he must have hidden the extremes from me.

I'm going to stop counting the days. Counting the days feels like watching myself smoke or clasping my hands around my throat and squeezing. Enough is enough.

From now on, I'll use months. Sum things up.

And maybe I'll allow Tony to become peripheral to me. Like, only remember him as part of something else. A co-star in some scene. Even when I write *to* him in the notebook. Or in email. In my head while I'm working, or swimming, or running, or listening to music, I'm always composing a letter to Tony. I might do this for the rest of my life. Memorize the moments. The details of each and every one. Live for him. Because he can't.

NOVEMBER

Dear Tony,

I'm going home. Well, not home, really. It's Oro Valley, Arizona and it's my parents' new house. Right now I'm sitting in the airport in Amsterdam making a list of all the places on the continent I need to see before I go home for good. This is just for Thanksgiving week.

The good thing about Oro Valley is it's not Herndon so it won't be steeped in all those memories that suffocate me every time I go there.

It's also a good thing that no one I know will be there. Since it's Thanksgiving, we'd usually all be home together and be drinking our faces off at Uno or Market Street or somewhere. But they'll all be going to Virginia and I'm going to Arizona.

I've never been to Arizona. We're going to take a day trip to the Grand Canyon. Mom and Dad have been waiting for my visit to go. The place they're living in is like a retirement village and they're playing a lot of golf and seeing a lot of movies. Hanging out with Uncle Kevin.

So at least this week there will be no sex. And very little boozing. Probably a good thing to take a break on both for a while.

The only things I know of Arizona I learned from watching Pump Up the Volume and Raising Arizona and so I have this vision of Mom and Dad's house carved out of some brown mountainside devoid of trees or shade. Maybe some trailers nearby with busted satellite dishes on them. Maybe they planted cacti in the front flower beds instead of the holly bushes we had in Virginia.

The airport makes my fingers itch. There are so many stories here. Every person moving through the terminal, perched nervously on a chair, or standing bored in a line has a story. Why they're here. Where they're going. Why they're going. Who waits for them there. Who's sending them away from here. All the characters of other people's lives crowd around me here, push their way into mine.

And the way people read in airports. It's second only to the library for the studiousness of the population. What is it about travel that encourages the perusal and purchase of new literature? I have two paperbacks with me but I've been unable to force them open. One is required reading for my mid-20th century dystopian fiction class. You wouldn't think there'd be enough of that shit to make a whole class, but there is. Most of the work is so bleak and unforgiving. It's all responsive to the tremendous shifts in society and global economics caused by World War II and the proliferation of weapons in the military industrial complex.

Can you understand why I'm not that excited to pick it up? Forcing yourself to read is the worst. Although, I am reading a helluva lot more than I did in San Francisco. Maybe I'm more disciplined now than I was then (ha).

The other book was recommended by my therapist of all fucking people. It's Fight Club by Chuck Palahniuk. Supposed to be a movie coming out. I haven't started it yet, but my therapist says she thinks I'll be able to identify with the main character. When I asked her how she'd heard of it, she said Brad Pitt was on the Today show promoting it. The fucking Today show. What the fuck.

So just gonna put that off for a while, too.

B

November 22, 1999
To: tonywilliams@yahoo.com
From: captainlisto@yahoo.com
Subj: hottest fucking Thanksgiving ever

Tony,

I went for a run this morning. I don't know why. Maybe because I didn't drink much last night and I'm still so jet-lagged I woke up at like 3:00 a.m. and by 4:30 had no excuse for just laying in bed.

"Wanna go with me?" Dad asked. Yes, he was going swimming at 5:00 a.m.

"No, thanks. Think I'll take a run instead."

He'd raised his eyebrows and said, "Watch out for rattle-snakes." By the time I came out with my running gear on, he'd left.

The neighborhood has more hills than I expected. It's bigger, too, than I thought. The streets twist and turn against one another and against the side of the hills. Not so unlike *Pump Up the Volume*. Not at all like *Raising Arizona*. I followed under the streetlights until I reached new construction that didn't have any lights. The sun came up early, tingeing the sky around 5:45. My legs were tired and I was starting to feel the fatigue of having woken so early, but I kept running.

The morning was so peaceful. I saw some rabbits and the neighbors' sprinklers were running here and there. Not sure what they were watering, most of the lots are decorative rocks. Nothing grows.

Poor rabbits must be starving. They were skittish and bolted when they heard my foot strikes. I didn't wear earphones, just listened to the morning sounds of Arizona and tried to feel familiar with it all. In the back and forth and winding of the neighborhood, an hour run probably took me about six miles. I haven't gone that far in a long time and I know I'll probably feel it tomorrow.

When I got back to the house, a full pot of coffee had brewed and quiet instrumental music was tinkling through the house stereo system. It was a builder upgrade, the speakers in every room, and mom loves it. She plays music 24/7. This morning it was a spa suite, some new age melodies that you'd hear in a yoga studio or a dimly lit massage room. I half expected rocks to be heating in a sauna therapy arrangement.

Mom sat on the back patio, the newspaper splayed in front of her, a small lamp on the table, the sun peeking over the horizon. She had her reading glasses on and her hair was still a little mussed from sleeping.

I walked around the table and sat in what I assumed was my father's chair.

She glanced over at me.

"You didn't go swim with Dad?"

I shook my head.

"How was the run?"

I shrugged.

"Get some coffee," she said. "After a shower."

I nodded and stood and went back inside.

I stretched in the bathroom waiting for the shower water to run hot. The old leather necklace with the clay stones I bought at beach week finally gave way over the summer, and I tucked it into my box with those things I like to glance at now and then. Now I wear a hemp necklace that has three silver cylinder charms carved with eyes and leaves. I got it in Montenegro on a weekend trip with Marco to see the fjord. Paid like $3 for it. It's tight on my neck, hangs inside my collarbone and seems like it could be the thing to decapitate me should it ever come to that.

My shoulders are broader than they were when I got to Spain, as if that were possible, I was always pretty broad from swimming but the dock work has filled me out even more. Makes me wonder why people waste time in gyms when they could get this by earning a living in the early morning light of the Barcelona docks. The idea made me grin and I felt a little like I missed the place which, of course, made me feel stupid. I'm a young man, I know, and old men can't throw fish every morning. Someday, I'll have to adopt a workout habit like my dad. But not today.

I got in the shower and rinsed off the sweat and crust of Arizona's outdoors. There's a grit to the atmosphere here. As if the desert dust is swirling in the very air I'm breathing. Showering helps.

When I got back into my room, the clock by the bed said 7:30. I remembered I was on vacation, dropped the wet towel on the floor, and climbed back into the bed. I slept until 10:30.

My parents were draped lazily over the living room furniture when I emerged. Dad had a book in his hands, his feet up on an ottoman, reading glasses on the tip of his nose, and a mug of something on the lamp table to his right. He left the recliner behind in Virginia and had adopted this two-part lounge posture in its replacement. Mom had the corner of the couch, her feet tucked up underneath her, and some printed computer pages laying over the wide arm rest. She was marking the pages up with what looked like a red felt-tipped pen. Her own reading glasses perched on the end of her nose, and her lips were moving slightly as she read and re-read a certain passage.

She looked up, squinted, then shook her head, removed her glasses, and smiled.

"Jet lag?" she asked.

I nodded. "What's on the agenda today?"

They looked at each other and shrugged, almost in sync, then Dad went back to reading and Mom smiled up at me.

They were different in Arizona. Calmer. They'd settled into a kind of lackadaisical existence that was completely devoid of errands or appointments or routine. With the exception of Dad's swim habit, I doubted there was anything they did every single day. After they'd been so regimented my whole life, this new floating life was exceedingly odd.

"Are you hungry?" Mom asked.

"Yep."

"There's a great bistro we go to sometimes."

"Yeddy's," Dad said without looking up.

I never understood how he kept reading when we spoke to

him. I always lose complete focus when people start talking. I typically read alone in my room because cafes distract me.

"Yeti's?" I asked. "Like Bigfoot?"

"No, Yeddy is the guy's nickname," Dad said, finally placing a bookmark to hold his page and closing the book. "An old hippie from California. Cool guy. You'll like him." He flipped his wrist, checked his watch, and said, "Wanna go over there?"

Mom nodded. "Dad goes more than me," she said. "Sometimes right after swimming."

"Sometimes," Dad agreed.

Like I said, weird. No routine. No schedule. No structure at all. Who the fuck were these people and what had they done with my parents?

The cafe was a hut. The back of the menu explained Yeddy had built the place after a little breakfast joint he'd frequented in Maui. None of the tourist Hawaii stuff, just genuine slacker style place: mismatched china, chipped coffee mugs with sayings like "World's Best Grandpa," and paper menus that looked like they were printed decades ago.

"Hey, Alan," someone said when we walked in. I glanced toward where the voice had come from, but three different tables were acknowledging Dad with head nods and small waves.

My dad was a regular here. The place might as well have had dirt floors. Paper fliers decorated the walls, the edges frayed and curling up. Guitar lessons. Lost cat. Roommate wanted. Concert in the park, July 14, 1989.

"This your place, Dad?" I asked.

He grinned. "Kinda, yeah. One of the guys I know from the golf club," he pointed at a skinny guy at a corner table with a pretty young girl, "Brings his daughter here every day. He's retired but she's still in school. They eat together before he drops her off."

The girl looked to be about 17. When she looked up and saw me looking at her, she blushed and looked down at her plate. I saw her dad glance over, see me, and laugh a little bit.

"I told him you were in town," Dad said, pulling a chair out of a table and waiting for Mom to sit in it.

"What else did you tell him about me?"

Dad shrugged. "Spain. School. Swimmer. The basics."

A pretty waitress stopped at our table with a coffee pot in one hand and a mug in the other. "Coffee for y'all?" she asked Mom and me while pouring Dad's. The mug said, "Swimmers do it in the water."

What. The. Fuck.

"Sure," I mumbled.

"Yes, and water," Mom said.

Dad drank his black, sipped a little, and said, "I've probably had enough. But it's nice of her to remember." He turned the mug so Mom could see, and she smiled.

You gotta know, Tony, that Mom and Dad are happy. They really like it in Arizona and they like spending time together and making it up as they go along. Mom does some work sometimes. She says she's on the payroll of some consultancy and they call her now and then and ask her opinion on stuff. She'll read proposals for them and offer responses. She says it's less than a few hours a week, but the salary is ridiculously generous and she kind of feels like she's stealing.

Dad says she's earned the position and that it's more than worth it for the consultancy to brag they've got her on the payroll.

We didn't talk about that at breakfast. She'd told me about it the first night I arrived. We didn't talk about why it was so important to them that I get back to swimming or whether I was going to need a new round of prescriptions. We didn't talk about much at all, really, just ate breakfast quietly, breathing and glancing around and feeling a small sense of relief that we were together.

It reminded me of the night I got home from California for your funeral.

Mom had found me in the kitchen, in the dark, drinking beer alone. She'd pressed her hand on my forehead and hugged me to her, breathing deeply and making me feel so secure. Despite the oddity of the shack cafe, Dad's status as a regular, and the void of schedules and requirements, these were my parents. I felt safe again. For the first time in a long time.

B

Nov 28, 1999
To: joel@planethack.com
From: captainlisto@yahoo.com
Subj: Thanksgiving

Hey, Joel,

Forgot to tell y'all I'm in Arizona for Thanksgiving. It's fucking hot here. Have a good weekend. Tell everyone hi.

B

Nov 30, 1999
To: captainlisto@yahoo.com
From: joel@planethack.com
Re: Thanksgiving

B—sorry we missed you. Hope Arizona was great. Give my best to your folks.

Joeler

Nov 30, 1999
To: joel@planethack.com
From: captainlisto@yahoo.com
Re: Thanksgiving

Not exactly. It's disorienting to see all of the childhood things relocated. They were incongruent with the landscape. Family photos and Mom's seashells that used to hang in the colonial-style kitchen in Herndon have a weird archeological look to them on walls colored like scorched earth.

Mom hung Tony's burning valley painting over the mantle and got two burnt orange leather couches that face one another. Not sure why there's a fireplace? I told her if she'd wanted to decorate like the Santa Fe Cue Club she could have stayed in NoVa. She just laughed.

Weird.

B

December

Dec 5, 1999
To: captainlisto@yahoo.com
From: joel@planethack.com
Re: Thanksgiving

Sorry, man. I know that must have been rough. Glad the painting found a place, though, and your parents sound happy. At least there's that. Mom sends her best. Hope to see you over Christmas.

Joeler

December 5, 1999
From: captainlisto@yahoo.com
To: ksoutherland@uva.edu
re: Thankfulness Day

Kacie,

Spent Thanksgiving in Arizona with my parents in their new house. Feel more disoriented than ever. Sense of home completely gone.

- B

DECEMBER 24, 1999

The semester ended. I packed my stuff. Spain was over. Almost.

Mom and Dad came to Barcelona and we did the Christmas Eve services at the Cathedral. They're not religious, really, so it was just kind of a dumb touristy thing to do. Then we had dinner at this fancy place Mom found in the Lufthansa magazine. Dinner was good. The red wine was exceptional.

Two years ago, Tony and I went to the services at Dranesville United Methodist with Kacie. It's such a tiny sanctuary that the Christmas Eve parishioners were crowded into the aisle and out into the narthex. I remember the poinsettias all over the alter and the choir wearing red robes and singing carols. They handed out candles with small paper discs and we passed a flame, turned down the sanctuary lights, and sang Silent Night. The Cathedral had poinsettias and candlelight, too.

There's a ritual to Christmas that feels forced. Like everyone's going through the motions and recognizes the dance, knows the duty side of it but no one really feels it. And I'm not sure what there is to feel on Christmas. I mean it's a birth, right? So, what does it really matter when we think of how helpless and useless babies are. Except we celebrate what this baby is ultimately going to become, right? The savior.

"For on this day a savior is born," they say in the pageants and plays and they remember the words and suggest the impossible. "For he will be unto you a savior." And really, what does that mean? Exactly how will he save me? I've gotten morose. I know. Cynical. I'm asking the same questions Biblical scholars have asked for years which is, "Why Him?"

None of this was a Christmas Eve or Christmas Day conversation. That was more Mom and Dad and me watching in awe as the Catholics walked through their ritualized version of Christmas. There was communion and singing, and people seemed moved by it all. But, really, it had the feel of a theatrical production, with timing and cues and people moving in a rehearsed and purposeful way without really knowing what they're doing or why. Without feeling it. Without feeling anything. But that might have just been me.

At this point in my grief, I was in depression, right? I asked my therapist, after Thanksgiving but before Christmas, and she reminded me the stages of grief weren't a college course syllabus. I told her thanks a lot and also, I'm leaving so she can fuck off. But not really. I thanked her for administering my care and asked her to send whatever she thought was relevant to my San Francisco shrink who would pick up where she left off, instead of where he left off last May because please, please, admit I've gotten a little bit better from the shitshow of last spring. She said she'd report my progress.

Mom said she could see my progress. Dad said he was glad I was swimming again.

I left Mom and Dad at their hotel after midnight. They said we'd have lunch together Christmas Day, so I wandered through the streets expecting to end up back in the courtyard staring past the light pollution to the stars. Instead, I stepped into Maddie's

Pub and had a pint. It's an Irish place on the corner between the hotel and my place, and it was pretty full for being after midnight Christmas Eve. A musician played acoustic guitar accompanied by a guy with a djimbe drum strapped around his neck. They played covers of Peter Gabriel and U2 and the Rolling Stones. I sat at the bar watching the scores of the U.S. football games flash on the TV.

The New Orleans Saints beat the fucking Cowboys. So, I ordered a shot. It wasn't my first time there, and the bartender poured his own, toasted mine, and grinned at me as we downed the vodka together. Got pulled into conversation with some other expats about the games on the screens and the general merriment of the holiday. One wore a Santa hat, the other a sweater with snowflakes on it, even though it was only in the fifties outside, hardly sweater weather.

Later, after the US football was over and the bar had closed and I was wandering —not exactly drunk but not fully sober— back toward my tiny apartment above the courtyard in the shit hole I'd been living in for seven months, I tried like hell to see the stars through the light pollution. I considered going down to the water to see them. I imagined the coastline in California and what it was like seeing the stars from the beach. I thought about how far away California was. I felt how far away from Tony I was. I had always expected him to be there, like another appendage, like a piece of yarn knotted on my wrist that chafes and weakens but doesn't actually break. But there I was, in Spain, and Tony had never been there. Would never be there.

We used to spend Christmas Eve talking about what Santa would bring us. Best gift ever was those walkie talkies we had when he lived nearby. We'd whisper into them thinking we could alert the other when Santa showed up. One year he asked if he could spend the night and his mom said, "Won't you want to see what Santa brought you?" and he said, "Whatever he brought Brian is mine, too."

Whatever Santa brought me was his, too. I wandered through the streets of Barcelona loving someone so much that whatever Santa brought me would be his, too. I don't think I'll ever love anyone that way again. And while that thought made me want to fall to my knees on the cobblestones and beg whatever God invented this Christ's birth miracle craziness to send Tony back, it also made me feel a strange sort of peace.

Like just knowing Tony would never be again.

Just knowing I would never have to do *that* again.

Whatever the outcome. I will never have to love like that again.

Relief.

I felt relieved.

December 24, 1999
To: melisings@yahoo.com
From: captainlisto@yahoo.com
re: Christmas in Spain

Yeah, my parents got here a couple of days ago. It's weird to see them here. I can't really take them to the docks or the bars, so I don't know what to do with them. Mom wants to be all touristy and see the Olympic village and museums and shit. Dad wants local places and keeps making us stop in street cafes so he can get a Hemingway view of the bull fighting arena. Fucking ridiculous. They're taking pictures of everything and insist on reading every goddamned historical plaque we pass. Tonight, it's dinner in some place they read about in the complimentary magazine on the flight over. Mom got me a miniature Christmas tree and a new watch. She and Dad both had these pinched looks of disappointment when they saw my room. It's brutal.

December 25, 1999
To: captainlisto@yahoo.com
From: melisings@yahoo.com
re: Christmas in Spain

You really can be such a shit. You know that don't you? Your parents love you. Why can't you share Spain with them? It's a big experience. Maybe too big to be locked inside your head and the letters you keep writing to Tony. Of all the things you've ever withheld, refusing your parents Spain is probably top 5 worst.

December 25, 1999
To: melisings@yahoo.com
From: captainlisto@yahoo.com
re: Christmas in Spain

That wasn't what I meant. I only meant to try to explain the dislocation of having them here. That's all.

- B

December 25, 1999
To: captainlisto@yahoo.com
From: mac.williams@turnerandgrace.com
Subj: A Very Different Christmas

Dear Brian,

Merry Christmas. I hope this email finds you well.

I am writing because I owe you an apology. I have been reading the emails sent to Tony's old email address. I haven't responded, of course you know that, but I have been checking them and reading them. I'm so overwhelmed by the grief and pain you're feeling. I don't even know how to respond. So I haven't.

At first, I thought I should just close the account. Or at least not log in. But your missives kept coming and I found they were so honest and truthful and so refreshing from the typical grief literature I've been given by my church and my support group that I preferred your emails to their interventions.

It was wrong. I know it was wrong to read them without you knowing. To choose to immerse myself in your pain rather than deal with my own. To stand by and watch you suffer without doing anything to help. I never told your mom or your dad what I'd seen. I only hoped, each time I logged in, that there would be another one, so I knew you were working through it all. Not giving up. Not giving in.

You've given me hope sometimes. When you wrote about toasting Tony on his birthday and about your parents' new life in Arizona and about being in school and writing. You're growing up and as you do so, you're healing and learning and changing and it's great. It's what I would have wanted for Tony. You've made me laugh sometimes. When you talked about the Russians you're working with pushing you around and about that pool party when Rhonda forgot to mail the invitations.

Goddamn but you're so young.

This Christmas has been so hard. Rhonda was home for about a week but then she went back to Stacey's and I tried to convince Gavin to go up there with me yesterday, but he said he didn't want to. He's with his girlfriend's family today and I'm home alone. The house is quiet except for the Grandfather clock, and I'm remembering when you kids were little and how much excitement there was around the new ball or Nerf gun or whatever you'd gotten that you could torture the dog with. And how she'd bark and chase you both around. Butterscotch. She was a good dog.

Anyway. I just wanted you to know those emails aren't going out unheard into the world. They've helped me sometimes. You're a good kid, Brian.

Merry Christmas. I hope to see you again soon.

Love,

Mac

December 26, 1999
To: ksoutherland@uva.edu
From: captainlisto@yahoo.com
Re: This Year's End

Kacie,

Top 5 Worst Things I've Ever Withheld

5. Spain from my parents

4. The truth about Meli from you

3. The truth about Tony calling me from Joel

2. The words "I love you" from everyone

1. Forgiveness from Tony

- B

December 27, 1999
To: captainlisto@yahoo.com
From: ksoutherland@uva.edu
Re: This Year's End

Brian,

Stop emailing me.

- K

December 27, 1999
To: mac.williams@turnerandgrace.com
From: captainlisto@yahoo.com
Re: A Very Different Christmas

Mac,

You don't owe me an apology. I owe you one. I shouldn't be rambling off in emails to Tony. It feels infinite, you know, like if I send them then he's there, somewhere, receiving them. I guess it's a little easier than the notebook writing my therapist suggested. Maybe it's the "send" button that makes me think I've done something with them. The pages in the notebook just stare back at me.

These emails have become something of a confessional and I know Tony's Catholicism (and yours) would be insulted by it. I doubt he'd even have the ability to absolve me were he actually reading this shit. Jesus. Sorry. It's late.

I'm just surprised. I think somewhere I'd hoped someone was reading them. But I didn't think it would be you. I'm sorry. I've just always been so, so sorry for not being enough for Tony. Not being good enough to save Tony. He wouldn't have let me down the way I let him down. I don't know what else to say.

Brian

December 29, 1999
To: captainlisto@yahoo.com
From: mac.williams@turnerandgrace.com
Re: A Very Different Christmas

Brian,

The hurt doesn't go away. Not exactly. But it lessens. I've been told it will lessen. This was our year of firsts, right? The first of everything-without-Tony. July 4th. His birthday. Football season. Christmas. Eventually, we'll run out of firsts and then we'll just be living without him.

Your friendship with Tony was a once-in-a-lifetime relationship. It meant the world to him. Whatever you think you know about his sickness and how it all ended up for him, you should know that your friendship was very important to him. You two understood one another in a way few men ever have the chance to. I think you'll find that it's very hard to get to that level of honesty with anyone else.

Mac

December 31, 1999
To: mac.williams@turnerandgrace.com
From: captainlisto@yahoo.com
Re: A Very Different Christmas

Happy New Year, Mac.

Maybe this year will be better than the last.

- B

SAN FRANCISCO 2000
WINTER

January and San Francisco was going about its business, working the widgets and wheels of other people's lives, bending time like the glass refraction of light. At home in my San Francisco studio, the only weight I carried I dropped, in a clutter of dirty laundry and souvenirs, at the door.

The light on the answering machine blinked, so I pressed play.

"You have thirty-two messages," the voice said.

I sat down with a notebook and started to record the details.

"Brian, it's Mom. Have you left yet? Call me if you haven't."

"Brian, David. Just heard about your trip. Call me before you go so we can send you off."

"Brian, it's Abbie. Melissa said you were going away for a while. Can I see you before?"

And more from the school and from friends wanting to say Bon Voyage. My first semester of MFA was over; six short stories and three notebooks of letters to Tony to show for it. Home felt different. I was different. Changed by my time abroad.

At last, message eighteen: "Brian. It's me. It's July and I know you're in Spain. I guess I just wanted to. I don't know. Check in or something." Then the line went dead.

It shouldn't hurt that much to hear her voice. I really thought I'd been gone long enough.

The messages continued: property management, financial aid, Joel once, maybe on New Year's Eve. And then the last one, from just an hour ago: "Brian, this is your father. Dr. Moses is expecting you to make an appointment within the week. Call us when you get home."

Closing my eyes, I heard the echo of "It's July and I know you're in Spain." Given the surge of tears that threatened just from hearing her speak, an appointment with Dr. Moses was needed. I called and set it, then tossed the notebook I'd been recording messages on aside.

It was late afternoon and the sun was melting into the sea beyond the window. Dad had never found a sublet, and the place had the stale scent and stillness of a crypt. I walked to the west-facing window and drew the curtains, let the burning sun wash over me, blinked into it. It's my favorite part of the flat, that big bay window that watches the sun set. At one point I moved my mattress underneath it so I could lay in the sun like a cat. And make love to Meli in the moonlight.

I wandered, dejected and a little jet lagged, between the window, the futon, and the kitchen bar and finally to the bed. The linens were stripped, washed and folded. I set about making it up, fitting the sheets around the corners, and shaking pillows into cases. By the time I draped the fleece blanket over the bed, I'd closed the blinds and stripped to my boxers. I crawled under the sheets and succumbed to sleep.

A pounding on the door pulled me out of heavy slumber. The clock read 4:12 and I thought it must be before dawn. But the loft glowed with afternoon sunlight, and the pounding on the door resumed.

"Brian? It's Abbie. Open the door."

I dragged myself off the mattress, scrubbed a hand down my face and went to open the front door. Twenty-four hours of sleep in the stillness of my own space; I felt grateful. And tired.

"It's about fucking time," Abbie said, pushing past me and into the loft.

David followed her, looking me up and down and grinning.

"You look awful," he said, folding his hand into mine and stepping in for a bro hug, which was only a little awkward with me in my boxers and bare chest and him fully clothed.

"You look like a rock star," I said, to which he curtsied.

"I told you we should have a key. We would have kept an eye on the place," Abbie was saying as she looked around. "The dust is ridiculous."

"Seriously, Bri, clean something will ya?" David's voice broke with laughter, and I grinned at him, closing the door and following them in.

"Let me brush my teeth and I'll clean up for ya."

"And put some pants on?" Abbie asked.

I scratched myself and shook my head at her.

"He's too sexy for his pants," David sang, and we both laughed again.

A few minutes later I was pulling bottled water out of the fridge while Abbie ran a dust cloth over the tables, shelves, and windowsills. My jeans hung loose and unbuttoned, but my face was washed and my teeth clean. I finger-combed my hair and offered David a water. We watched Abbie.

"You can thank that one," she pointed at David, "For not letting me disturb your sleep last night."

Abbie and David had been my best friends in San Francisco since our comparative lit class at Cal State sophomore year.

They'd dragged my drunk ass home. They'd read almost everything I'd ever written. They'd watched me downward spiral last spring after Tony. But they didn't know him. And they hadn't gotten anything from me since I'd left in May, until yesterday when I called David from the third of four airports to tell him when I'd be home.

"I want to hear all about Spain," David said.

"Because apparently you went there and forgot how to email. Or call. Or send a postcard," Abbie added.

I jerked my chin at the notebooks of letters and story bits I'd collected.

"It's all in there."

David pulled one out of the backpack. "Kittens?" he asked, frowning at the cover. "Definitely a story here. What will you do with it?"

"Construct a thesis I hope."

"Did Kittering approve the transfer credits?" David took a swig of water.

"He's on my list to visit this week." I handed the third bottle to Abbie.

"Classes start in two days," she said.

"Yeah, I'm enrolled. Just not sure at what progression."

"Think you have another year?" David asked.

"Or two." We had agreed on this plan in the spring, but I'd mostly be deranged, bereft, and high. Abbie and I would enroll at San Francisco State University for the MFA in literature, David would enroll for art. Having actually fulfilled the enrollment, we all stood for a minute looking around and drinking water.

"Will you stay *here*?" Abbie finally said. "In this loft."

"Yeah. My parents own it, so it's home."

She smiled with something like relief. "Good. Because David and I have a surprise for you."

"Get dressed," David said, with one last glance at my chest and arms. When I caught his appraisal, he smiled shyly at me.

"Six months of dock work," I said.

"Looks good on you," he murmured.

A shirt, some shoes, my keys and wallet and we were out in the hallway as I locked the door behind me.

"You know David's place was condemned," Abbie was saying, "And Arietta turned out to be a real cunt, so I had to leave. So, we got a place together."

"It's here," David added.

Abbie had opened the door across the hall and sure enough, they'd moved into my building.

"Cool?" Abbie asked.

"Or stalkerish?" David frowned.

I laughed and clapped my hand on his shoulder. "Cool, seriously. That's awesome you're so close."

"Like midnight stagger-home close." David grinned.

"Like early morning need-a-coffee-filter close." I followed him through the door.

"Like water-my-plants-while-I'm-gone-to-Spain close," Abbie said. "Just sayin'."

Having my friends nearby felt like the homecoming I had wanted yesterday. They each wrapped me in hugs, and we passed smiles between us standing in the very tight foyer of their apartment.

"Let's eat," David said finally, and we headed down into the San Francisco streets to find sustenance.

It was nearing five on a weekday, and the worker bees from the financial district were streaming into the streets to catch transportation out of the city. We navigated the sidewalks to our favorite diner, a corner set-up with a high pastry counter, vinyl booths, and chrome-rimmed tables. The place had always reminded me of Amphora in Herndon, but Abbie swore it was like the *Seinfeld* deli. Over an early dinner, Abbie caught me up on the demise of her relationship with Arietta. They'd been together for two years, and the pain in her voice when she described the last few weeks made David reach across the table and hold her hand.

I sipped my tea and nodded empathetically.

Then David talked about his new crush and his cheeks blushed when he described how they'd met. Apparently, the guy was a fan of David's art and had semi-stalked David by sitting near his favorite painting that hung in our coffee shop waiting to be purchased. David and Tony had that painting thing in common, but David's work was more people and animals than landscapes and dream imagery.

"It's the one Abbie calls Medusa."

"Because the girl looks like she has snakes coming out of her head."

"They're curls," David argued.

"Green and gray curls?"

"No, they're golden in real life," David said, and made eye contact with me, "But they feel gray now."

"Have I seen this painting?" I asked, sipping my tea and thinking of the girl I knew with wild golden curls. If I let myself, I could remember her bending over, combing them down over her face, and then flipping them back up like a mane of sunlight. But I didn't let myself.

"We can go by the shop."

"He didn't buy it?" I asked. "Some stalker."

"He's not rich," Abbie said.

"How much is it?"

"Six hundred dollars."

"Holy shit, David," I said. "Since when did your coffee house paintings go for more than a semester's reading list?"

"Since I sold one to Anchorage."

"No shit?"

He smiled with a kind of pride I hoped was contagious. Anchorage was a gallery in the arts district that David and I had discovered years ago on a walkabout. It was posh and polished, and David had set inclusion there as a personal goal. That he'd achieved it both stunned me and made me feel like I'd missed so much in their lives.

"I'm proud of you, man," I said. "Truly." And I bumped my shoulder against his.

"Thanks, Brian." He bumped me back a little and relaxed into the seat.

"Yeah, well it's all fun and games until they sell that piece for three times what they paid you for it." Abbie snorted. "Fucking art world."

"Fucking musicians," David said, "So cynical about everything."

Abbie was a guitarist, percussionist, and poet. She'd played a little here and there, sometimes with Meli, and just then it occurred to me I hadn't bothered to ask about Melissa since the two of them had shown up at my place. We'd been kind of a foursome for a while, before Tony died, and though David and Abbie had stood by me last spring, I knew they'd probably spent time with Meli since I left.

We ate quietly for a little bit until Abbie finally said, "She's fine, Brian. Moved out to Sacramento a couple of months ago."

The moment I thought had broken us took place two days after Tony's funeral. Sunday. I was expected to fly back from Virginia to San Francisco and collapse into her arms in a rut of caring and sadness and exhaustion. Except the night before, I fucked the bartender, and Meli had heard it in my voice when she called my parents' house Sunday morning. In all the time I was in Spain, a safe distance from her being naked and me being apologetic, we'd emailed in hurt and confusion and frustration and sadness. Until August, when she was finally done with me.

Abbie looked sad and then said, "You could have asked."

I shrugged. "Not sure I wanted to know."

"Of course you did," David said. "It's called closure."

January 31, 2000
To: melisings@yahoo.com
From: captainlisto@yahoo.com
re: Back in San Francisco

Meli,

Just wanted you to know I made it back. Same apartment and phone number. But anyway. I'm here. When you're ready.

B

I visited Dr. Moses just three days after returning from Barcelona. His office was not like the shrink in Spain. He had shelves of books, only about half of which were professionally relevant. One entire shelf was dedicated to World War II pictorial history books. Probably gifts he'd received that he didn't want in his personal library. Maybe from patients like me who'd shown their asses and needed to make amends. I came with a book about Spain's role in World War II. He flipped through it, sniffed and said, "It's in Spanish."

"I could translate for you."

We made eye contact. Moses took a beat, seemed to decide something, and then waved at a chair and said, "Take a seat."

"How involved has my father been in my care?" I asked.

"Financially, of course."

"Naturally."

"And as a concerned party. A parent."

"I'm twenty-three years old, Dr. Moses. When does he stop parenting me?"

"In some cases, never. In others, too soon. Have a seat, Brian. Let's talk about Spain."

"In English? Or *en Español?*"

I'd met Dr. Moses when I was downward spiraling and he had been like a match to dried tinder. I hated him. I fled San Francisco partly to get the fuck away from this guy.

Then my Barcelona shrink had helped me understand that weekly, habitual, focused contemplation was a path to healing. She was less bossy, less judgey, less Moses. And she had zero contact with my father. Moses had been recruited by him, and though my relationship with Dad was better, I didn't think that fixed my relationship with Moses. Both therapists knew I had a lot of work to do, and me and Barcelona shrink had done it. A good bit of it. But there was more to be done. I still felt broken.

In one month, I would be through the first year without Tony since we were eight and neighbors and best friends. Barcelona shrink had encouraged my writing to Tony. Moses would hate that. She had suggested I unpack the addictions I had to smoking, sex, and drinking. Recognize them as failed coping strategies. Moses would hate that, too.

He was less empathetic to what he called self-destructive behavior. More business-like. In the few appointments we'd had last spring, he'd kept an air of man-to-man objectivity. Like a job interview.

"Mac was reading the emails I wrote Tony."

"Mac is Tony's father?"

"My Barcelona shrink suggested I write to Tony as a way to process the grief. To shift my perspective from him existing still, just away from me, to being gone. For good."

"And have you made that shift?"

"When Mac said he'd been reading the emails I felt let down.

And guilty. It was like Sunday morning all over again." The weekend of the funeral, after I'd slept with the bartender, I'd stumbled into Tony's basement room in the pre-dawn Sunday morning and slept in his bed. Mac had found me there. After a tight hug, he'd released me to The Crew who had shown a spectrum of disappointment in my inability to get my shit together.

"He cares for you," Dr. Moses said.

"He misses Tony." I did, too. It wasn't every day like it had been. I was no longer a nail being hammered with "Tony is dead," every moment of every day. I wasn't even counting the days anymore. I'd stopped keeping score. But I felt an absence, like how in darkness we miss light, or in the water we miss air.

"When will I stop missing him?"

"You probably won't," Dr. Moses said, pushing his glasses up onto the bridge of his nose and jotting something on a legal pad. "But the pain will lessen. That's the course of grief."

"In the beginning, I didn't want it to get less. I wanted to feel it all."

"You felt guilty."

Now I did sit down. The stiffly upholstered chair barely made room for me. Staring over Dr. Moses's shoulder out the window, I saw the courtyard and two heavy-branched trees that sagged in the afternoon light. I'd brought my notebook with me, turned to a clean page, but had yet to write anything down. This wasn't exploration, it was interrogation.

"What's next for you?"

I shrugged. "I'm in school. I'm writing. I'm submitting. Working toward the MFA. Dr. Kittering asked me to be a graduate assistant, but I think that's too much right now."

"Why is it too much?"

"Undergrads are needy."

"You know this how?"

"I was one."

Dr. Moses let that one go. His sweater vest had a pattern of repeating diamonds that looked like strands of DNA in alternating navy and forest green. I let my eyes blur so the sweater looked fuzzy and cozy, but really it was a façade. The whole thing was a façade. Corduroy pants, sleeves rolled up, hair slightly mussed as if he'd been napping when I arrived. Moses wasn't a hippie; he was a scientist. His inquiry wasn't curiosity and it sure as shit wasn't compassion. It was study. I was less an individual experiencing grief and more a single point within aggregated data.

"My parents moved to Arizona."

"I remember."

"I went there over Thanksgiving."

"How was it?"

"Brown. Dry. Nothing like Virginia. And they love it." Mom and Dad's easy Arizona existence had felt like a strange new chapter in a book I couldn't decide whether I wanted to keep reading. They'd established something that seemed comfortable to them, but I'd had trouble reconciling it with the regimented people I'd grown up for.

"They have this looseness to them. It's weird."

"Retirement."

"More like they're unburdened somehow."

"And how does that make you feel?"

"As if I missed the opportunity to have the same peace. Like someone handed them quiet. Acceptance. And I was sleeping or had my back turned, and I didn't get it." I suddenly recognized what I'd been feeling with them in Barcelona at Christmas. Resentment. They were so well-adjusted. They'd gone through the same year of firsts I had, but it hadn't broken them. They seemed tranquil. Experienced.

"What can you do about that?"

I shrugged. "It's their life."

"I meant what can you do about being denied peace?"

My eyes blurred again, this time with tears. My jaw clenched. "I don't want peace."

"Why not?"

"It's a grave in Northern Virginia. It's giving up."

"Peace is death?"

I wrote in my notebook: *Peace is a myth. There is only the pulse of persistence. The constant forward motion of gravity and the rotating earth.* Some days the only thing I could feel was the prose. It bubbled up behind my lips all the time. I couldn't stop it.

"You've been writing?" Dr. Moses nodded at the notebook in my hand and rolled his own page over, tucking the full one between his knee and the legal pad.

"Can't stop. I bleed on the page." Flipping back through the first third of the notebook, seeing my frantic script describing Montenegro and Serbia and the Adriatic Sea glistening in the sunlight. "But it's no good. It's all hurt and anger and loss and devastation and the kind of guilt that only the unredeemable can understand."

"You said you went to confession and that you prayed in Barcelona."

A dip of the chin, the slightest nod that the Barcelona shrink, who watched her notepad and listened, would have missed. But Moses watched me, and he saw it and he said, "Why not try prayer now?"

I wrote: *Fuck me but he's still completely useless.*

But, okay, I should take that grad student job. Make progress somewhere at least.

February 2, 2000
To: graduateschool@sfsu.edu
From: kitteringja@sfsu.edu
cc: captainlisto@yahoo.com
Re: Graduate Assistant Placement

Please accept this email as confirmation that Brian Listo, graduate student in the Master of Fine Arts program, concentration Creative Writing, will serve as graduate assistant to myself and Drs. Watts and Gladstone for the duration of his program. He should receive tuition and stipend accordingly. Any concerns can be addressed to me.

Sincerely,

Kittering

Carrying two bags of heavy books that banged up against the door as I tried to open it, I pushed my way into the apartment. Boxes of memorabilia, picture frames, incense holders, and other remnants of a past life gathered dust against the wall. I had a stereo near the door, scratched from dropping my keys on top of it every time I entered. A small table held it up, a drawer beneath it bulging with mail that needed sorting. Since I'd been gone, my mail had been collected in a bin downstairs that sat next to the door, as well. Not quite full but full enough to stoke procrastination over emptying it.

Banging the books against the door must have alerted my new neighbors to my return because their door flew open, and David said, "Sweet! You're back."

He followed me in and watched me sort the books out on the kitchen bar.

"So ya wanna go somewhere with me?"

"Where?"

"It's kind of a surprise."

I shrugged. "Why not? It's either that or take on that pile of mail. Where's Abbs?"

"Working. Bring that." He pointed at the Santa Cruz skateboard wedged into one of the boxes against the wall.

"What for?"

"Firewood. What do you think?"

It had been two years since I rode that board. The last time was the summer before Melissa and I started hooking up. It was 1997 and The Crew was all in Herndon. Before Jason dropped out of Frostburg to play hockey. Before Joel started his company. That might have been before Tabby even. Tony and I were coaching the summer league swim team, and we would mess around in the parking lot outside Chris's summer job at Baskin Robbins killing time until we could all get stoned again. Once we got stoned, we didn't skate. More and more we got stoned. Less and less we skated. Then the board went back to San Francisco, got stuffed in a box, and never got on another plane.

If David thought I would question the request, he didn't show it. I lifted the board and did a cursory inspection of the bearings and deck. Blowing some dust off the trucks and wheels, I smacked the board and grinned at David. He held the door open and I closed it behind us, locking it and dropping the key ring in my pocket. A short walk later, and we faced a pop-up skatepark. About a dozen riders slipping across handrails, popping over steps and rolling around curved concrete.

"What are we doing here?"

"You used to be pretty good. Melissa said you went to the xGames."

"A qualifier. And I failed. And it was a half-pipe, not this park stuff."

"What's the difference."

"Should I list them alphabetically?"

"No," David said, and his gaze landed on someone about thirty yards away. I watched the rider and board go blunt-to-fakie on what looked like a mini ramp, but David was watching the skater, not the tricks. Thick hoodie sweatshirt, splayed fingers while he cruised through the park, smiling at what was probably his crew, the object of David's interest was about our age. He had dark hair and eyes, and when he saw us, he lifted his hand in acknowledgement.

"You brought me to a skatepark to scam on dudes?"

"Maybe?"

"Is this like bringing a dog to the dog park to meet chicks? Am I the dog in this scenario?"

"Yep. So, do some tricks so he'll notice and come over to talk."

"Who is he?"

"Medusa stalker."

"Thought you guys were dating already?"

"Less talking, more skating." David flipped his hands at me, shooing me away.

I grinned. "Did you bring treats for me?" Then I dropped the board, stepped on and rolled away. The Crew had skated for twelve years, from age nine until twenty. We'd spent every waking minute on our boards over the summers together. Every driveway, cul-de-sac, parking lot, and swimming pool was fair game. One summer Tony convinced his parents to keep their pool empty so we could skate. His older brother, Gavin, skated, too, so that meant all the boys were at Rhonda's house. She liked knowing where we were, so she'd agreed. The next year, though, Gavin had grown out of skateboarding (replaced it with recreational drug use) and so they'd taken the pool back.

At the park in San Francisco, it didn't take long to warm up and remember how to kick flip, ollie, and grind. The park was tight but had a good variety of obstacles. I got kind of lost in playing and watching until a while had passed, and when I looked back at David, remembering he was there, the Medusa stalker was standing beside him chatting.

They both watched me. I lifted a hand and they waved back.

I couldn't remember the last time I'd been so consumed by something that I'd lost track of everything else. Maybe writing, except that was bleeding, opening a vein so it all leaks out. Maybe running, except most times I did that, my whole body hurt. Maybe swimming, except it was still too tightly connected with achievement and my father's expectations. Skating, I'd forgotten, was pure pursuit of the trick, feel of the board, visualization of what I wanted to make happen and then making it happen, or bailing before I fell. Freedom. It felt like freedom. From everything.

Three weeks into the term and I finally made it to the library. It was time to start submitting to journals, and I needed to know which journals were good fits for my work and how they wanted their submissions. I pulled a dozen from the shelves and started reading, sorting the issues into yes, no, and maybe. The nos went back on the shelf. The yeses had their submission details recorded in my spiral notebook. The maybes I took back to the shelf where I pulled two more issues down to get a better feel for the work they published. In the end, the submissions list had three dozen entries with varying submission deadlines. Later, I organized them by deadline in another document to begin submissions.

After Spain, I had six stories ready to be workshopped and submitted. Only one of my graduate classes had a workshop format and we read in rotation. With nine students, it would take weeks to get through my work. To make these deadlines, I needed to find some other readers to provide feedback. Abbie's mom was a working author in Oakland, and part of a critique group that I thought might have a chapter closer to me and campus.

Part of my deal with my parents on the work study in Barcelona was that I actually work and study. So, I'd had the dock job for cash, but I was constantly writing, too. Dad didn't know what a career path for a creative writer looked like, so I had to research the various jobs available and the requirements for each. He'd been peppering me with marketing copy writer jobs, but I told him I thought I was better suited for a teaching role. I could almost see his eyes rolling over email.

The library has study tables by floor-to-ceiling windows that, when I sit close to them, make me feel like I might just fall over into the parking lot. Whenever I got distracted by the activities below, I would squeeze my eyes shut and repeat a mantra I'd learned in Barcelona for concentration: *Words on the page. Words on the page.*

It's not particularly poetic or inspirational, but it would create a rhythm for me that helped with the reading that came afterward. In one of these squeezed-eyes moments, I felt the light touch of a hand on my shoulder and looked up to see Abbie.

"Hey, pal," I said.

"Hey, pal," she replied, setting her books on the table. Glancing over the titles, I frowned at her. "Whatcha workin' on?"

When we were in undergrad, Abbie had written some challenging and emotive poetry that I didn't fully understand. In our finer moments under influence of wine or weed, we'd discussed the existential crisis of *The Wasteland* and some other canon texts. I'd convinced her to read Sylvia Plath's *The Bell Jar* and she'd instructed me on some Shelley and Byron.

Abbie was from the Midwest, led to San Francisco by her mother's career as a women's empowerment author. She had terrible things to say about the patriarchy and homophobia-driven literary norms, the likes of which had championed Hemingway and Fitzgerald but ignored the homoerotic undertones of Jake's travel companionship with Bill and Nick's affection for Jay Gatsby. Abbie had a square jaw and furry eyebrows, and she exuded confidence that was sexy and asserted herself in any conversation whether she knew what she was talking about or not. On more than one occasion I told her it was very masculine of her to do so, but she'd balked and said shit-talking was a genderless art.

"I haven't had sex in weeks," she said, collapsing into the chair next to me.

"Because Arietta turned out to be cunt?"

"Exactly." She sighed heavily. "Your dick available?"

"Not to you."

"Because you don't want to ruin our friendship?"

"Because you wouldn't know what to do with it."

"Burn. Good one. But burn nonetheless." Abbie had also been a lesbian since puberty, and her mother had rejoiced in her daughter's otherhood. The idea that she'd managed to birth a person of such variety and nonconformity was a genuine source of pride for Margo, who had joined PFLAG almost immediately and become chapter president before they moved to California where *everyone was special*. Or so Abbie liked to sing-song whenever she told the short story of their West Coast migration.

"When I'm a published author," Abbie said, a game we played a lot, "I'll submit to contests I know I can't win just so later I can taunt the people who rejected me."

"When I'm a published author," I said, "I'll sign books in tiny independent stores in places like Bangor, Maine, and lie to the buyers about the characters and story so they'll think they're interested and pay for copies."

"Of course, this is a pirate story," Abbie said.

"It's all about the Penobscot River." I laughed.

"The what?"

"It's a real thing."

"How do you even know that?"

"Been there once." My mother's brother had died there, and Dad had sent me as her funeral companion to punish me for some minor infraction, probably related to skipping school or swim practice.

"Say it again?"

"Pen-OB-scot," I annunciated. "Freezes solid in the winter. Probably frozen right now."

"Take me there." Abbie grabbed my arm and stared me in the eye. "Take me there in January. I want to see a frozen river."

"That got weird," I said, looking around.

"Brian!"

"Fine, okay, fine. Stop squeezing my arm, Abbs, shit."

She threw my arm back at me and I rubbed the skin where she'd clutched it. Abbie hadn't wilted in the anonymity of everyone's specialness. She continued to find ways to stand out. Today she wore a skater skirt and knee-high socks with chunky boots and a rock band t-shirt.

"I really wish David would make more progress with the Medusa stalker. Then he could get laid and I could live vicariously through him."

"He's made some progress. Dragged me to the skate park on a date."

"Oh, trust me, I know. It was all 'Brian is amazing' and 'did you know he could insert-skate-trick-lingo-here?' You turned him into a fan girl." She settled back in the chair and tilted it on its back legs, balancing and rocking.

"You know I want you both happy," I said. "If you're happy, I'm happy."

"Is that true?"

"Why wouldn't it be?"

She shrugged. "You haven't been happy in a while."

"I'm past hanging in there but not quite to thriving. Spain was good for me."

Abbie tilted her head at me, her hair falling over one cheek.

"Make promises, Brian," she said. "That's how you build a life.

You make promises about what the future will bring. You. Me. Penobscot River. Bangor, Maine. Done."

"Done," I echoed. But sometimes we need more than the idea of what we should do. Sometimes we need the how.

There were six stories I felt ready to get feedback on, but the group Abbie's mom recommended for me wouldn't let me read the first time I attended. I got the page of rules (submissions were limited to six pages, double-spaced, 12-pt, Times New Roman font) and listened to what the other writers had prepared.

One reader, a professor of philosophy that I'd never met but whose office was in the same building at Kittering's, distributed copies he'd made of the three poems he wanted feedback on. I don't know shit about poetry, and my concentration in creative writing for the MFA wasn't changing that so far. But my comments were about imagery and word choice—that's the bit I do know—and I could tell he appreciated the remarks; he was open and didn't respond, argue, or justify the work in any way. He was professional and everyone else was, too.

Another reader brought pages from a memoir she was writing. The topic was sensitive, a time in her early teens when she'd been sexually abused by her stepbrother, and the room was still and quiet as she read through the work. Afterward, the philosophy professor, who I learned was named Ed, thanked her for trusting us with something so personal. The readers all acknowledged her bravery in sharing, and then remarked on the writing itself, structure, vocabulary, and pacing. I took my cues from the others, thanked her for allowing me the privilege of reading such a work. She nodded in acknowledgement.

"Your perspective is that of a woman your age looking back,"

I offered. "Maybe there's some strength in that, but the vulner-ability of being that age, while it's happening, and not knowing what to do, might be more compelling."

"It would be a challenge," Ed said, "But Brian's right that being that close to the circumstances might be very rewarding, not only for the reader but also for you."

"Yes," an older woman, whose tone didn't sound like she really agreed, "Get closer to your pain. It would make for great literature."

Sarcasm. It was sarcasm.

The writer winced, but her eyes met mine and she smiled. "Thank you," she said in a near whisper. She was in her thirties probably, soft voice and pensive expression. She took copious notes as the others spoke to her and brushed her hair from her face before making eye contact with me. She seemed fragile, and it wasn't just the content of the piece.

Sarcasm lady read a poem about a cat who stalked birds in her owner's garden. It was pithy and clever but lacked emotional depth. But it was a welcome respite after the quiet writer's mem-oir.

As the session broke up, Ed pulled me aside and asked what I thought.

"A lot of talent here," I said. "I'm anxious to bring my own stuff and see what you all think."

"We've been together for a while," he said. "Know each other pretty well. Don't let our familiarity with one another fool you. We take the work seriously, but we care for one another. All criticism is wrapped in kindness and a genuine desire to see the writer improve."

"Understood, sir."

"Good. See you in two weeks?"

"Count on it." I grinned at him wondering, not a little bit, what they would think of the stories I brought in. Probably best not to start with the drunken post-bar brawl hook-up in Barcelona.

Out on the sidewalk, the sarcastic lady and the quiet writer were saying goodbye as I started to pass them.

"Thanks for coming," sarcasm lady said, sounding genuine. "Will we see you back?"

"Next time, sure," I said.

"Are you going this way?" The quiet writer tucked a lock of hair behind her ear and pointed toward the stoplight at the next block. "Would you walk me home?"

"Yeah, sure. Whereabouts?"

Her name was Sara and she lived a block from me. After we said goodbye to sarcasm lady, AKA Bethany, Sara and I walked toward the intersection. When I told her which building was mine, she smiled.

"I dated a guy that lived there a few years back."

"Who was he? Maybe I knew him?"

"Calvin Paine?" she said it like a question.

"Tall, glasses, wouldn't know a good thing even if the lenses were clean?" Yeah, it was a flirt and yeah, she liked it. She blushed and smiled.

"We had irreconcilable differences."

"Such as?"

"I thought he should be faithful. He disagreed." Again with the hair tuck behind the ear, and I found myself smiling at her in that way I sometimes smiled at bartenders and baristas.

"One of those, huh?" I said, as if I wasn't one of those, too. "One of my best friends, Chris, dates a Sarah. Are you Sarah with-an-h?"

"No, just four letters. S-A-R-A." She shifted her backpack from one shoulder to the other as we neared the intersection and had to stop to wait for the light.

The group met from 5:00 p.m. until 8:00 p.m., so the sun had set and the winter's evening was cool with an aggressive wind blowing down the hills into our faces.

Sara blinked against it and her hair blew back from her face. She was plain, wore no make-up, and some early grey in her hair betrayed her age.

"How old are you, Brian?" she asked, as if she knew I'd been eyeing her grey.

"Twenty-three."

"Are you from here?"

"Northern Virginia."

"You say that like it's its own state. Virginia is one state, right?"

"Well, there's West Virginia, which is a totally separate one, but yeah, Northern Virginia is part of regular Virginia. Except it's pretty different than Richmond or Norfolk or Roanoke."

"You know I have no idea what any of those are."

"Richmond's the capital. You have to know that at least."

She shrugged. "There's just so many states over there. It's hard to keep them all straight."

I laughed. "They were the original thirteen colonies. Doesn't every year in elementary school history begin with colonization? The revolutionary war? Or did your school just start at Westward Expansion?"

Now she laughed. "You're impugning my public education and I should be pissed, but the truth is you're right. I know embarrassingly little geography and even less history."

"So, what do you know?"

"I'm a programmer. I write code. Build websites. Internet stuff."

"No kidding? One of my best friends, Joel, runs an internet company. Maybe you could meet him when he comes."

"How many best friends do you have?"

"Four. Well, three now. Tony is dead."

She stopped walking. We were on the sidewalk three blocks from where the group met and two blocks from my building. She stood still and stared at me until I realized what I'd said and then I stopped, too, and turned back to her. A space of a few paces had opened between us, and the streetlights glowed above her like a halo.

"Who was Tony?" she asked.

"My best friend since we were little kids. He killed himself."

"When?"

"A year ago. Why?"

She shook her head and started walking again. "It's nothing. It's just that was my stepbrother's name, too."

"Is he dead?" I asked.

"Yes." There was steel in her voice, and I thought I'd like to ask how he died but then maybe I didn't want to know. Or maybe her memoir would get to that part of the story. I fell in step beside her and we were quiet for a while.

"Do you believe in destiny, Brian?" she asked. "Fate?"

The answer was no, but I thought maybe she did and since she was a new friend, I didn't really want to alienate her. So, I said, "I believe friends come into your life for a reason or a season. Think I might have read that on a Hallmark tchotchke or something."

We had passed my building and approached hers. She stopped outside the tall stoop and looked me in the eye.

"Which will I be?"

I tilted my head as if considering the answer, though it had come immediately to my head. "You're a reason. You have something to teach me, Sara. I can feel it."

Her eyes were green and they glowed under the street light. "Maybe it's you who will teach me," she said.

"Come on. I'm just a kid."

"No," she said, and her voice had gravity to it. "You're not a kid anymore." Then she was gone, up the stairs and into her building without looking back.

I walked home thinking about that. Tony's dad had told me I was just a kid only one year ago. When had that changed? And how?

One Sunday morning in February, I woke early and decided it was a good day to try church again. Years ago, I'd gone a few times with Kacie and her family. That was mostly because she carried some guilt around what we did together not being married and all, and I wanted her to believe what we had was real, was love, and was okay to be expressed physically the way we did. Not sure I'd ever been able to fully rationalize it for her, but she'd found a church in Charlottesville. She told me the weekend of Tony's funeral that she'd been going, and it had helped her give up the cocaine.

My own search for forgiveness was nearly a year old, and while I was headed back to church, I wasn't thinking about Kacie much on Sunday morning. Or at all lately, actually. I was trying to focus on the memories I had of worship in Barcelona. Christmas Eve service with my parents. All those candles. The narthex of the Cathedral of Barcelona. The confessional which I visited more than I ought to have, not being a Catholic. The priest who told me that Tony must have loved me and been hurting in a way that was completely separate from me.

The truth was, Tony had only been dead for a year, but he'd been separated from me long before he'd killed himself. And that wasn't just on me, it was part of his illness. And part of the distance, and part of growing up. In any case, he was gone. Buried. And I still felt that. Sometimes like I was buried, too. Like the depth of my own grief could be six feet of mud and grass in the shadow of a headstone that read "Anthony Michael Williams." But mostly I felt like moving on. So, I went to church Sunday morning.

Holy Trinity services had not yet begun, but the organ was playing, and people were filing in, greeting one another, smiling in a gentle, friendly way. Dr. Moses had suggested I go back to church. A month ago. So, there I was eight rows back, middle of the pew, clutching the bulletin and reading the news as if realizing for the first time that there was a separate rhythm to life that I was not part of. Someone would serve as acolyte and someone would be an usher, names I didn't know acknowledged like actors in a play. Prayer breakfasts and circle meetings, youth fundraisers and Sunday School meeting times—all evidence of the life of the church, a life that looked familiar, as if I were seeing it through a window. The ritual, the habit, felt rehearsed and performed, just like on Christmas Eve. As if the smiles were part of the show. Until the music began. The organ player moved to the piano and sat quietly as a trumpet player appeared and began a slow, calm fugue that pulled at a place I'd forgotten all about. In an instant I was in Tony's basement, him playing a disc he'd just bought for five bucks.

"Study music," he called it, but I knew he bought the classical for two reasons: They were the cheapest discs at Sam Goody, and he need it when he was in the moods he called headaches.

In my memory, he tore the packaging away, slipped it into the player, and paused, hands midair while the trumpet filled the room. There was a low tone that climbed over several measures. Sitting cross-legged on the floor in front of his stereo, Tony flipped the disc case over in his hand, muttered, "Telemann. And a trumpet." And we listened, we breathed, we felt the emotion of the piece. He may have played it again. He may have insisted I listen, that I feel it, and I may have told him to shut the fuck up and let me. In any case, when the trumpet finished, the full symphony kicked in.

At church on Sunday, the trumpet player arched his back as the piece climbed, the depth of the solo digging into me. The ache of it. The need. A keening sound that made my hands want to fold in prayer. That blinded me with the memory of the burning valley and Tony's outstretched arms and the sense that greatness, majesty, divinity, was nearby, was accessible. We need only be willing to see it.

Then the piano joined the performance and the two musicians brought everyone in the room, even me, closer to God through Telemann. And the tears were on my cheeks before I knew they were, and I felt myself opening up, like stretching my chest open, facing the sky, and there was sunlight somewhere and I blinked into it, feeling its warmth on my cheeks. Remembering that New Year's Eve dinner at Joel's when Tabby told us about the CDs she'd been buying: *Mozart for your Morning Workout, Debussy for Daydreamers, Bach for Breakfast.* We had all added our own silly titles to the conversation: *Haydn for Hangovers, Tchaikovsky for Chocolate Lovers.*

Now, amid my tears: *Telemann for Telling Him.* Telling him you loved him. You wanted him to stay. You needed him in your life. *Telemann for Being Too Late.* I pressed the heels of my hands to my eyes and took several deep breaths as the music ended.

Dr. Moses had been right (though I'd never in a million years tell him that). Going back to church gave me a chance to reach for peace and maybe—even just during a three-minute piece of music that I had known once in a different capacity and heard there, in a new way—earn forgiveness.

The service progressed in that familiar weekly habit way. The minister was Latino, smallish with wire-rimmed glasses and a wide smile. He looked parishioners in the eye as he preached and raised his hands to the heavens when he declared the gratitude

he felt. The structure of the sermon had the feel of classic ora-
tory: an opening story, a biblical parallel, a lesson, and an appli-
cable resolution to the story. Enjoying the minister's enthusiasm,
tone, and delivery, I lost track of time and space and relaxed into
the pew, as if attending a lecture at school or a workshop at a
conference, something anonymous but familiar. As the service
wrapped up, I filed out with the rest of the congregation. The
minister stood at the door shaking hands as people exited.

"You're new," he said, but it wasn't an accusation. "What
brought you to us this morning?"

"Woke up before noon. Remembered it was Sunday." I
grinned and he did, too. "The trumpet was spectacular."

"Taylor is very talented," the minister said, and nodded
toward the back of the narthex, where the player in question was
accepting compliments and smiling at grateful patrons.

"Does he play every week?"

The minister shook his head. "Not here, no. But he has a few
different musical pursuits, so he's in various locations around
town. Perhaps you'll catch a different project of his sometime?"

I saw Taylor handing flyers to the patrons and nodded at the
minister.

"I also enjoyed your sermon. Thank you for the message."

"That *is* a weekly feature." His eyes squinted with his smile.

"So maybe I'll come back?"

"I'd like that. I'm Thomàs."

Detecting the slip of an accent in the pronunciation of his
name and I responded, "*Mucho gusto.*"

Surprise lit his features, and he replied, "*Igualmente, mucho
gusto.*"

We conversed for a moment in Spanish, his Latin American
accent and my own mixed pronunciations. Barcelona had
affected my delivery more than I'd realized. Telling myself the
weekly visit with Thomás would give me a chance to keep my

Spanish fresh, I walked away from Holy Trinity feeling like I might become part of that world, that image through the window, that life someone else had built and made available to me. It was only a block or so later that I wondered how long the peace I achieved there would last and if I would find myself in a different kind of addiction visiting just for what Holy Trinity gave me, not necessarily giving back anything of myself. I wasn't sure what I had worth giving anyway.

I started with another email. Cowardly, I know, but it was the best way to get everything I had to say out to Melissa. She'd likely hang up if I called. Besides, I didn't have her phone number, but I knew her email address. I'd harassed her through it from Spain. Daily, at first, and then sporadically until she stopped responding all together.

Her last reply was back in August, and I'd followed that up with a groveling list of the top five things I'd withheld. My Barcelona shrink said I was still in bargaining and my efforts to keep Meli engaged were part of that. I didn't email her again until January. Just to let her know I was back. Kind of a "be seein' ya?" inquiry. Pathetic. She'd ignored it.

I'd been so deep in self-destructive patterns a year ago that I had actually been outraged when Tony told Kacie about me and Meli. I felt betrayed, like Tony should have kept that secret, that if he'd loved me, he would have protected me. Instead, his honesty with Kacie revealed me as the demon who lied to and used both women. He was right. I was out of control, unfair and deceitful. Greedy and unkind. My Barcelona shrink provided that vocabulary, too.

Turns out Tony had loved Melissa and was hurt that I'd

formed a relationship with her. First because I was already in a relationship with Kacie, whom he also loved but in a different way, and second because he'd figured Meli for himself. Even though he didn't live in San Francisco. And hadn't seen her since he'd been out to visit over a year before he died. She had a right to move on, didn't she? Did he really expect she was waiting for him? Why hadn't he come back to California and committed to her if he loved her so much? But I knew the answers to all of those questions. I'd asked them in therapy. The relationship with Melissa was a construct Tony used to imagine the future. And I took it from him.

The day my father called to tell me Tony was dead, I'd made love to Melissa in my bed under the late-afternoon sun. Her skin warmed to a golden hue, her red hair softly feathered over my chest and neck. She'd let me kiss her small breasts, grip her narrow hips as she ground down on me. She'd smiled at me and when it was over, she asked, "Do you love me?"

The phone rang. I answered it. Tony was dead. And nothing else mattered.

It had been a year almost to the day. I emailed her something lame about hearing she'd stayed in Sacramento, and would she be back around here anytime soon? She called me.

"This is my new number," she said. "I'm living in a three-room above an art gallery. If I'm not home, leave a message with Shawna."

"Who's Shawna?"

"Drummer. She and Nix own this place. He's our bassist."

"You're in a band?"

"You're doing okay?"

"What kind of music do you play?"

"How are David and Abbie?"

"They live across the hall." Then silence. It didn't stretch the three thousand miles from San Francisco to Herndon, not like a year ago, but it felt that far.

"My parents are settled in Oro Valley." But she had only met them once, and she probably didn't care much about that. "I went to church yesterday." But she was more spiritual than religious, and she probably wouldn't know what to ask about that. "And I joined a writing group. To get feedback and critique and stuff."

"That's great, Brian. Feedback is crucial to art." She thought what I wrote was art?

"Tell me about the band."

She said they formed last spring in San Francisco, but the scene was hard to get paid gigs. They'd gone to Sacramento for studio time and found a few local places to play regularly. It paid, she said, but not that great. She'd gotten a job in a coffee shop.

When was she coming back?

She shrugged. I could hear it over the phone. I could hear it when she said, "I don't know," a kind of practiced indifference.

"Are you happy?" I asked.

"Mostly. Are you?"

"A little bit. Now and then. Until I remember. Then I'm sad again."

"I'm sorry, Brian." More apologies. She'd littered her emails with them. It seemed to be the only thing she could say between that afternoon in my bed and the morning I took that flight to Virginia. She was sorry. She hurt for me. She wanted me to know she was there for me.

"David took me out to skate. He was trying to pick up some dude. A grad student."

"He took you out when he was trying to pick someone else up?"

"He needed an excuse to be at the skate park."

"And you skateboarded for him?"

"Like a trick pony."

She laughed then.

"Comes right back, ya know? Like muscle memory. Think I'm going to keep doing it."

"I think you should."

"It's easier than swimming. Less baggage."

She didn't respond to that. Maybe I'd never told her about swimming. I couldn't remember.

"I'm working with Kittering on my thesis," I said. "Collection of stories. Submissions."

"Any acceptances?"

"Not yet."

"Well, stay hopeful. I had a poem accepted to a journal at Utah State."

"Really? That's awesome. Will you share it with me?"

Another audible shrug. "It was good to hear from you, Brian."

"Wait, Meli, don't go. I'm sorry."

"I know you are, and I'm not gone," she said. "Call any time you want."

"Do you *really* know I'm sorry? If you did, you could forgive me, right?"

"I don't think knowing compels further action. And anyways, there's nothing to forgive."

"Mels, please," I hated the way my voice caught, and it sounded like I was begging. Was I begging? Wasn't I doing okay? I had David and Abbie here. Mom and Dad were close, just a short trip away. I'd met Sara at the writers' group and Thomàs at church. I was building a support network. I didn't need Melissa.

Needing her was never the thing, though. Not really.

"Not forever. Just for now." And she hung up. The last time she'd said that to me, she'd climbed into my lap, wrapped her arms around my neck, and pressed her cheek to my forehead. It had been a gesture to draw us closer. It was a promise that commitment could wait. We could have each other. I could have her. For now.

As the dial tone reached my ear, though, the words were different. They meant she was gone. Not *gone* gone. Like never coming back gone. Like Tony gone. But gone just the same.

February 18, 2000
To: captainlisto@yahoo.com
From: theargonautslit@uidaho.edu
Re: submission

Thank you for submitting your work to The Argonauts Literary Journal. Although it was well written and entertaining, it does not meet our needs at this time. Please resubmit.

Best,

Editorial Staff
Argonauts Lit Journal

February 18, 2000
To: abigailnichols@sfsu.edu
From: captainlisto@yahoo.com
FWD: re: Submission

Rejection #9. See below.

B

February 18, 2000
To: captainlisto@yahoo.com
From: abigailnichols@sfsu.edu
Re: FWD: re: Submission

Stop counting that shit. It's their loss.

Come over. Let's get boozy.

You meet my needs at this time. Bring the story.

Abbs

Spring

Two weeks until Spring Break. I had to hang in there until then. The schoolwork was piling up. Kittering had given me every fucking undergraduate assignment to grade. He had ninety students and they'd all written five-page research papers. I had to read the shitty things, check citations, and make recommendations on grades. Kittering said he graded them himself. He didn't. He looked them over after I marked them up. Five marks meant a C, six marks a D, more than 6 was an F. The Bs had four marks or fewer. There were no As. Then his fiction workshop students turned in their try at short story writing and I wanted to burn the pages myself.

Until one. One story peeled off the page. It wasn't the contrived child-abuse-date-rape-drug-addiction drama. It was about a cemetery bench and the view of a stone angel monument. The narrator was trying to read the inscription but would need to get closer, and refused to get off the bench. It was fascinating. More so for the colors the author used to describe the trees (yellow), the sky (green), the grass (red like lava), as if the cemetery existed in the pages of a child's coloring book and not in real life.

Though the writer never explicitly said it, it brought to my mind funeral homes giving out coloring books to bewildered,

red-eyed children, exhausted from witnessing others' grief, not quite sure what life would look like on the other side of loss. *Scenes of Death: A Child's Coloring & Activity Book.* There would be word finds with vocabulary like urn, wake, cremation, and bereavement. Color-by-numbers with just two colors, black and gray. Rainy funeral scenes with umbrellas and galoshes. Flower arrangements in team colors and the darkest, most tragic red-black roses, deep green stems and thorns, ribbons that curled and cascaded but not with joy, not like Christmas presents or front-door wreaths. Sensible, dignified curls and cascades, ribbons that said, "We're so sorry for your loss," and "He'll be missed." And those children—the weepy, stunned, and bewildered ones—would scribble their purple wax crayons across the pages, coloring the casket yellow and putting the mourners in stripes and polka dots. Hand-drawing dogs and other pets curled on laps and seated at ankles.

I read the story four times. Made my own extensive notes. Found the specific vocabulary of grief the writer had leveraged and then grinned at the effort. Heartbreaking and brilliant and so, so moving. Then I carried it down the hall from the grad students' shared office into Kittering's.

"Got a minute?"

He waved me into a leather C-shaped chair.

"This story, man, it's brilliant."

He took the pages from my outstretched hand and looked at the top of the page.

"Jada," he said, approval in his voice. "She's good."

"Have you seen this one before?"

He skimmed the pages. "Not this particular submission, no. But the stuff she brings to workshop is always strong. Great voice."

"She's a freshman?"

"No, no, she's a senior. Been in the program for a while."

"And this is the first time she's taken workshop?" The class was a 100-level, meant for rookies and freshmen.

"No, she's taking it a second time. She dropped out last time."

"Why?"

Kittering shrugged. "Not sure. Something family related, I think. It's been a few years." He shook his head dismissively. "What are you working on?"

"I'm visiting a workshop off campus," I said. "I've been taking pages every two weeks."

"Any good writers in there?"

"A few. Good feedback on my work. It's building the calluses." He'd once told me I needed to get over my critique phobia and develop some thicker skin. The work, once it was on the page, was no longer about me, it was about the organization of letters and words. Hearing what readers thought of it—making adjustments—was part of the process. The real work of writing, Kittering always said, was revision.

"Got anything ready yet?"

"Maybe."

"Bring it to workshop. 4:30."

I frowned. "You want me to bring my story to your freshman workshop?"

"Why not?"

Good question.

"All right. I'll be there. How many copies do I need?"

"Thirteen."

Six hours, a lunch break, a trip to the copier, and a call to Abbie telling her I'd catch up with her later, and I was seated in one of the L-shaped wooden desks in the classroom.

And in walked Jada. Ebony skin, braided hair, wide sable eyes with long feathery lashes, and a tiny sparkling nose piercing.

Kittering started the class by introducing me as his graduate assistant. He said I'd been working a story with some readers off campus (true) but needed additional input (not true). He told them I wanted this story in *The Missouri Review*. Of course, I did. I wanted all of my work in *The Missouri Review*. But I'd settle for Sarah Lawrence's *Lumina*. Hell, I'd settle for *Westwind* out of UCLA. But, sure, *The Missouri Review*. Why not?

I told him to let the others read first. And they did. She did.

Jada read a piece of flash fiction. I saw Kittering frown and when she'd finished, he started asking questions about exposition. Stakes. We need more, he said, to care. To be interested.

But I didn't need more. I loved every concise word of it. I thought the reader could fill in what was missing and, in that participation, become more invested in the work. Which is what I wrote on the back of the copy she'd given me.

Out loud, I said, "Nice stab at the iceburg theory. The reader fills in the un-given details. Hemingway favored that style." That earned me a frown from Kittering.

A week later, after I'd read my story in Kittering's undergrad workshop—his students had been polite and useful but not too critical—he called me and said he was sick and would I please lead the workshop that day. He gave me the names of the two students assigned to bring pages. Reminded me of the criteria we used to evaluate the work. Coughed a few times into the phone for effect. Wished me luck and hung up.

I wore a Van Halen t-shirt and a flannel. She wore a turtleneck sweater and jeans. Her hair was a messy pile on top of her head and a ring, not a stud, curved over her nose. As her classmates read aloud, she marked frantically on their pages, circling whole passages and scribbling in the margins. But when it came time for verbal critique, she was subdued. Kind and complimentary.

"I love the conversation on page four," she told one writer. "There's a real desperation here. Maybe just clip the words they exchange so we can feel how uncomfortable they are?" That slight up-tick at the end, as if she were asking a question, made the critique sound gentler, suggestive instead of instructive. I doubted the listener, a sophomore who'd written the driest, dullest exchange I'd ever read between a mother and a teenaged son, would be able to make the change.

"Like Jada," I said, "I think the dialogue is the most important part of the scene." *The only part worth saving.* "Maybe when you reduce their words, remember to only leave the impactful ones. For example, 'I'm leaving.' could become 'Gone.' and 'Call me when you get there.' could become 'Call?' Readers know the procedural stuff. Only use what you need to tell the story, I guess is what I'm saying." *Or don't tell the story at all.*

The author nodded appreciatively.

Later, outside the building, Jada was smoking when I walked by, and she called me over and said, "I like that you know how."

"Pardon?"

She took a drag and blew out the smoke and smiled. "I like that I tell them to do something, but you know *how* they can do it. So, you teach them."

"Just following Kittering's lead." I reached into my shirt pocket for a half-empty pack of smokes, took one out and lit it, and we stood there for long enough that I wondered if I shouldn't have walked away instead. But I was committed now. We both knew it.

I wanted to tell her about the coloring books idea I had after reading the story she submitted but decided I would wait and get to know her better. If she'd let me.

"Your story. From last week." She spoke with the kind of inflection that made sentences out of fragments. "It's missing something."

"No shit." Except she was a student, and so I recoiled a bit until she laughed, and I shook my head and said, "Sorry."

"I'm just telling you what you already know. It's missing the truth."

"If I just put in the truth it'd be better?" I asked. "Any idea *how* I should do that in a work of fiction?"

She rolled her eyes and took another drag, shook her head so that messy bun shivered a little. Then she grinned at me, deep rose lips, squinting onyx eyes that saw right through me.

"Get *real*, Brian. Somehow I don't think I'm the first person to tell you that."

She wasn't much younger than me. A year maybe. But somehow, she felt older. Maybe like she had her shit together. But everybody felt that way to me. Everybody but me.

By the third time I saw Jada, it was on. I knew she wanted me. She was single. I was single. She was hot. Hotter every time she spoke to me.

I'd gone to see a band she recommended. I took the BART down to meet her. David went, too. It was an hour trip, but since we were high when we got on and drunk by the time we got off, it was the right thing to do.

Jada ribbed me about slumming it in Haywood.

I told her San Francisco was as much a collection of boroughs as New York and Haywood was one of them.

She asked how I got to California to begin with.

I told her it was the furthest from Northern Virginia I could get without leaving the continent.

David said strictly speaking that wasn't true, that I could have gone to Alaska, but they wouldn't accept me because my poetry was mediocre.

I said he was being kind. My poetry was shit.

A band played. It was loud and I got to lean in to Jada a lot and talk right in her ear. Then she leaned in to me and she smelled so fucking good. I cursed the idea of leaving at 9 p.m. for an hour

BART ride home and wondered if she'd invite me to stay at her place.

Then I wondered if she lived at home with her parents.

Then I thought about Tony's basement room at Mac and Rhonda's.

Then I thought I must be drunk and decided to pay the check and go before it was too late to get out with my dignity intact.

David let me pay the check.

Jada confirmed we were just friends, David and me, and then she kissed me good night and it was on. Fucking on. Her lips were soft, and she pressed herself against me and I wanted her like I hadn't wanted anyone, not really, since before Spain.

"When can I see you again?" I whisper-shouted into her ear over the band.

"I'm off work all weekend."

"Come to my place," I said. "I'll send you the address."

"On a flyer stapled to a pole?"

"The Want Ads," I joked.

"A fortune cookie?" She grinned.

"Email," I said, tipping my forehead against hers in that move I know girls love because they think it's sincerity, and maybe it is. "I'll email you. Tomorrow."

"Tonight."

I kissed her.

"G'night, Brian," she said, her lips against mine.

The whole way back to San Francisco I thought about that kiss, the words inside it, the forehead thing, and the intimacy that was possible with someone who might get you. I wasn't playing her. This wasn't a game. Not like any of the others, the ones I wanted who wanted me, they were like popcorn. Shape or weight or feel or sound variations aside, the popcorn is the popcorn. It's an accessory. It's about flavor and enjoyment, taste and texture. It's physical. Not cerebral. There have been the brick wall alley encounters, the bathroom stall connections, the back row (kneeling) exchanges. But few women have been the show. The show itself was only Kacie. And Meli. But Jada could be.

All the way back to San Francisco, David explained why Latino men were reluctant to come out and how he'd been fine getting some closet dick in East Bay but he wanted a commitment now and he didn't think Romero? Claudio? Whoever was going to commit. I asked him about Medusa-stalker Alec, and he smiled that silly in-love smile and said yeah, he was glad he hadn't hooked up tonight. Alec might be someone. He might be the show.

I didn't tell him I thought Jada might be, too. No reason to jinx it. But the next night, when she showed up to my place, I was pretty sure I'd irrevocably crossed that popcorn line.

And then we were alone.

And I couldn't wait to get her naked.

And it occurred to me that I was more dangerous than I thought I was. I had a clear advantage on my turf. And she was trusting me.

I was trusted.

And that's how we ended up unpacking a bunch of dusty boxes.

I always thought of those boxes as used-up stuff. Things that I no longer needed or wanted. Picture frames and trophies and memorabilia from a life I couldn't really remember living. Not that it had been so long ago, although it had, but because I spent most of that time high. High with Tony, granted, but high, nonetheless.

Jada reached deep into a box and withdrew the scrapbook Kacie had given me for Christmas our freshman year in college. We'd been apart at the start of term for our longest separation ever, seven weeks, and I'd ached for her. Thanksgiving was a blur, and then I was home again for Christmas. By then, though,

I'd cheated on her with my roommate's girlfriend and though Kacie didn't know, she knew things were different between us.

"She collected all these things about you?" Jada asked, flipping the pages. She stopped to squeeze a clear plastic baggie with cotton inside and looked up at me.

"The American History Museum in D.C. had an exhibit about the cotton gin and Eli Whitney, and you could grind the cotton. It was one of those kid-interactive things. Kacie got a kick out of it."

"And this is the cotton you ginned together?" Jada's grin was bright.

"Fucking stupid?"

"Fucking great," she said. The next page was ticket stubs. The page after that had a dried boutonniere from prom, the broken rhinestone choker she'd worn, the hotel receipt, and the after-prom party photo booth trio of pictures, the fourth one torn off for her to keep.

"Looking through an ex-girlfriend's scrap book isn't exactly the best first date activity," I said, reaching into the box for a yearbook and setting it aside on the floor.

"She's really pretty."

"Yeah. So, pizza?"

"Who's this?"

And it was me and Kacie and Tony, arms slung around one another, in a polaroid from the all-night graduation party.

"That's what happened to me," I said.

Jada tilted her head.

I took the scrapbook from her and said, "Let's order pizza and I'll tell you about it."

Ten minutes over the menu, a knock on Abbie and David's door to see if they wanted any, a call to the place on the corner, and Jada and I were sitting across from one another, cross-legged, on the floor with a different box between us. One I hadn't opened yet.

I'd poured us some red wine. Just one bottle for the two of us. No one was getting hammered.

"Mac sent me this while I was gone," I said, staring at the box between us.

"Who's Mac?"

"Tony's dad."

"Who's Tony?"

"The guy in the picture." I used the wine tool's label-cutting knife to slice through the packing tape and peeled back the flaps.

"You loved him," Jada guessed.

When I looked up at her, the softness in her expression made me grin.

"Yeah," I confirmed. "Like a brother."

"Oh." She blushed, and it added this deep rose to her skin.

The top item was a Santa Cruz hoodie, grey with the logo in the middle. I held it against my nose and smelled it. Tony's house. I could almost hear the grandfather clock and the churning and clacking of the dishwasher.

Below the sweatshirt, a pair of framed photos. One of Tony and me, arms around shoulders, bare-chested at eight years old, swim team suits on, me holding a medal off my chest and Tony's hand out with the number one held up. The second, Tony and me, my elbow propped on his shoulder, his arms crossed over his chest, the empty pool behind us, skateboards at our feet. Him in that hoodie, me in a flannel and a G&S t-shirt with a wide rip on the bottom from where I'd flat-faced in the driveway. This time I had my hand out, a sideways peace sign, my chin jerked a bit at whomever was taking the picture.

"We were sober," I said, grinning at the pictures. "Mac sent me the pictures he had of us before we started getting high. Drinking. Being fucking stupid." I laughed and handed Jada the frames, then dove back into the box for more. A stack of Polaroids Tony and I had taken that summer we drained the pool. Chris and Joel and Jason, and goddamn, we all looked so young.

Gavin with Tony in a headlock. Gavin's girlfriend, shit what was her name? In a bikini looking a little pissed for some reason.

I flipped through them and showed them to Jada.

"That's Angel and Marcel," I told her, "Tony's brother, Gavin's, friends from Honduras. They spoke Spanish with me all summer. Fucking great. Learned a ton of profanity."

Jada took in each new picture and held it like treasure, her fingertips on the white borders.

"That's Liza and fuck, what was her name? Meghan? Mollie? I dunno, something with an M. I remember Liza because Tony had a crush on her. The other one, M-something, she was Gavin's girlfriend, so we didn't pay any attention to her."

"Bro code?"

I laughed. "Something like that."

"Liza's got pretty hair. Even in this old-ass Polaroid I can see how bright it was."

"Fake," I said. "But yeah, once she learned Tony loved red heads, it got brighter."

"That was a thing about Tony?"

I nodded. "Yeah, it was a thing."

Out of the box came a CD sleeve with some of Tony's discs on it. Bands I hadn't listened to in forever: Fighting Gravity and Rusted Root and Blues Traveler and Toad the Wet Sprocket.

"Your friend had terrible taste in music."

Then I showed her Jay-Z and Dr. Dre and Tupac, and she grinned. "I gotta like rap?"

"Don't you?"

"Well yeah, but—"

"But not because you're Black."

"Exactly."

"Okay."

"What?"

"Nothing. Just Chris always said the same shit to me. 'It ain't me bein' Black,' he'd say, and then something fucking ridiculous like, 'but this fried chicken is amazing.' And I'd be like, 'fried chicken value isn't a skin color thing, man, it's either good or it isn't.' Ya know?"

Jada held up one of our skateboarding pictures. "This is Chris?"

I nodded.

"All right then."

"What?" I asked this time.

"California and Virginia might be the same like that. Like it doesn't matter so much. But I grew up in Atlanta. It mattered there."

"Chris went to school in Atlanta. He said the same thing."

"You can't grow up being only peripherally aware of your race and then go to Atlanta where that's all you'll ever be."

"It's not all you'll ever be."

Jada shook her head. "In some parts of this country, it is."

I put the pictures I was holding down and reached out for her, just one hand on the angle of her face where her jaw was clenched. She softened into my palm.

"And I thought the heaviest thing in this box would be Tony killing himself."

Jada's eyes widened.

"Yeah, a little over a year ago."

"What happened to you is . . ." She raised her own hand to mine, squeezing it a little.

I felt a tear slip down her cheek and onto my thumb. I wiped it away.

"It's getting okay," I said.

She turned her face into my hand and kissed my palm.

The pizza arrived, and Jada and I delivered David and Abbie theirs without inviting them to come over and share with us. And without collecting payment which was pretty much how it always was with us. When Jada ribbed me about it, I told her there were some relationships in my life where money was all I had to give.

She said she didn't want to be one of those.

I told her she could buy the next pizza then.

She liked Hawaiian pizza with pineapple and ham and we ate most of it, and finished off the bottle of red wine, and then she called her cousin and told him she was fine and he could go on back to East Bay, that she would take the BART home the next day.

I locked the door, cleaned up the pizza mess, gave her a spare toothbrush, and a t-shirt, and she came to bed without pants or a bra.

We lay side-by-side for a few minutes, watching the bay window's streetlights illuminate the ceiling. Jada threaded her fingers through mine and held my hand.

"You miss him?"

"Every day." But that wasn't so true anymore. It was starting to get to every three days or so. Or nights like tonight when I talked a lot about him. Thought a lot about him.

"I wish I'd known you when he was around."

"I wasn't a very good guy."

She squeezed my hand. "You're young. There's time."

I let go of her hand, rolling toward her, framing her in my arms. Face-to-face, I could smell the toothpaste on her breath, feel the warmth of her skin.

"I want to kiss you," I said.

"So, do it."

"I'm going slow here." Tracing my nose up her neck and jaw,

lightly grazing my lips against her skin. "It's a new thing I'm trying."

"Not having one-night stands?"

"Not taking a beautiful woman to bed right away."

"We're in bed."

"But not naked."

"Kiss me, Brian."

So, I did, with my breath held and just the lightest play of my tongue against hers.

"You're good," she whispered. "I'm ready to give you whatever you ask for."

I smiled against her lips.

"You're charmed by me?"

She nodded and dragged her fingertips up my back.

"Good." I kissed her cheek again, her lips, her nose, and lay back on the bed, pulling her into me and holding her close against my side.

"What's happening?" she said, her hips shifting.

"Slow," I said. "We're going slow."

Propping herself up on my chest, she said, "What if I don't want slow? What if I'm staying the night because I want to be naked with you?"

I laughed. "Just be naked? Okay, take off the shirt."

She reached for it and I laughed again, "No, shit, no, Jada—I'll never resist if you're naked."

"Don't resist." She sat up, pulled the shirt off, and caged me in with her arms, breasts against my chest, mouth on mine. She climbed over me, legs on either side, grinding against me.

I groaned into her mouth.

"Stop, Jada, please. It's too much."

"You want me. I can feel you do."

"Yes, fuck yes, I do."

"So . . ." her face in my neck, hot kisses, "what's the problem?"

"I like you. I want to see you again."

"Okay."

"Okay so sex will ruin that."

"Why?"

"Because it always does. Just trust me on this, okay? Let's just sleep. Snuggle."

"Let's fuck."

Then I did laugh, and she bit me, and I grinned at her.

"Enough," I said. "You're perfect. Lay down here with me. Let's be more than a one-night stand."

And we settled in, some more light kisses, some more fingertip-dragging touches, but nothing below the belt and it was like a make-out session with a high-school girlfriend. One I should have waited to have sex with. One I cared about. Who let me care about her. And who cared about me. Jada was new, but I knew this path and I wanted it. I wanted her. I think my Barcelona shrink would have been proud.

"She's a beautiful woman." David was just shy of outraged. "What are your intentions?"

We were walking toward the skate park, my fourth trip in as many days, and I said, "Maybe I just want something sacred."

"Then go to church."

I had been seeing Thomàs regularly at Holy Trinity. Mostly Sundays but the occasional weekday, too, when I just needed a place to feel peaceful. Sometimes it worked. Sometimes it didn't. Sometimes Thomàs wasn't there, but the nice secretary lady would let me in to sit on a pew or if the doors were locked, I'd sit on the steps and smoke a cigarette and think and wait out the urge to pray. Sometimes homeless people waited with me.

Holy Trinity was south of campus and the neighborhood I lived in. I didn't tell anyone about my Holy Trinity habit, so when David suggested church be my something sacred, it seemed easier to just shrug it off rather than admit I'd been edging closer to becoming a member. He and Abbie usually slept well past brunch on Sundays, and if we spent any time together at all, it would be late afternoon.

In addition to church, the skate park, my shrink, writers' group, and Jada, I'd gone back to swimming. Since picking it back up in Spain, I felt the pull of the chlorine and the satisfying muscle exhaustion that only comes from forty-five hundred yards of solitude. My San Francisco life now barely resembled what it had been before. Less drinking. No weed. No unpacked boxes.

Jada helped with the boxes against the wall. We threw out three trophies I was pretty sure I'd never miss and stacked four yearbooks on top of Kacie's scrapbook in the only box that remained closed and hidden in the back of my closet. Jada brought me a poster of a Monet painting, and Abbie and David hung a tapestry they didn't have the wall space for.

Jada said the place now looked lived in. Like it belonged to me, and not just someone passing through.

One night in late April, Jada and I lay entwined in my bed. She'd taken up a Thursday night habit of staying with me since neither of us had class on Friday. We'd linger in bed, sometimes order in food, and stay there all day reading or writing or just talking. We finally had sex about three weeks into seeing each other, and she'd admitted what she called "the wait" had heightened the intensity of that first time. Honestly, though, every time with her was intense. She challenged me and she was sensual and giving, and sometimes it took everything I had not to take her straight to bed when she showed up Thursday afternoon. And sometimes I did take her straight to bed.

Late April in San Francisco is still chilly at night, and we were wrapped up tight, naked but cocooned in my down comforter, and Jada said, "What happened to me was some kind of bro code, too. I was with this guy and his friends didn't like me, and so we broke up."

"Why didn't they like you?"

"Guess I made him want more than them. Like he had real talent. He could really be something. I told him he should go to L.A. and try to make something happen and they all thought I was breaking up their crew."

"You believed in him?"

She nodded, burrowing deeper into my embrace.

"And then?"

"He told me to quit trying to make him something he wasn't, and we broke up. They won."

I pulled her closer, pressed my lips to her forehead, and trailed my fingers down her bare back. Whatever emotion had swelled at remembering the break-up, turned her breath a little bit ragged and wet on my chest. I didn't know what to say. All I could do was wait for her, so I let my fingers stroke her skin and stayed quiet.

"Bet your friends wouldn't hold you back like that," she whispered.

"No, I don't think they would."

"Tell me about them."

She already knew Abbie and David, I told her, and the coffee shop crowd of artists and writers I knew.

"Sara is a friend from my writers' group. After our meetings, I walk her back to her place. It's on the way home for me. And Ed leads the group. Then there's Thomàs from Holy Trinity."

"Monk?"

"Minister. And that pretty much rounds it out."

"What about the skate park?"

"Nah, not really friends there. Just dudes I see when I'm riding sometimes. We don't talk too much."

"And what about Virginia?"

I shifted and she held me tight.

"Don't pull away," she said, a new strength to her voice.

"I'm not."

"You are. You always do. Since we emptied the boxes, you haven't said one word about Virginia. What's going on with that? Have you heard from anyone? Reached out to anyone?"

I sighed. "They're all building their own lives. And I'm doing the same."

"They're your best friends."

"*Were* my best friends. It's been broken."

"Beyond repair?"

I shrugged. "Probably."

"How did you speak to them from Spain?"

"By email."

"Why not try that?"

"It's been too long."

"At least send something to Chris." She snuggled into my side, kissed my chest. "I can't be the only Black person you know."

I laughed and kissed the top of her head and agreed to send Chris an email. Though just what the fuck I thought I'd say, I had no idea. Two days later, I told myself to stop being such a fucking coward and emailed Chris.

April 22, 2000
To: yellowjacketchris@gmail.com
From: captainlisto@yahoo.com
Re: checking in

Hey, man, just checking in to say things in San Francisco are good and see how's things in NoVa? Hit me up, dude, when you get a sec.

B

April 22, 2000
To: captainlisto@yahoo.com
From: yellowjacketchris@gmail.com
cc: joel@planethack.com;
christopherjames@longandfosterrealty.com
Re: checking in

Cap'n! Great to hear from you. Jason said he'd emailed and you hadn't responded? Maybe he has the wrong address? Speaking of which, I cc'd Joel and my work email so you have both. I'm working with Angela these days and doing good. Didn't think I'd like real estate, but it's cool.

Joel and I got that townhouse in South Riding. Moved in last October. Three floors, garage, sweet kitchen, back deck. Joel says since he's just temporary I can decorate. So, you know this shit's da bomb. When you're back here, there's plenty of room for you to crash.

Joel's headed your way next weekend. Y'all should hang.

Chris

Joel replied that he meant to reach out sooner, but the trip wasn't organized yet.

The next day, he confirmed arrival at SFO for the following day and said he had a car service to the hotel, which was way the fuck down in Mountain View, and when I asked why he hadn't flown into San Jose he'd replied someone else made the reservation. He didn't know the difference. We decided to meet on the day before he left. His meetings would finish up before lunch and he'd cancel that last night in the hotel to crash with me. It was a Thursday.

Mine and Jada's ritual had become her arriving by BART, and me meeting her on the sidewalk and us walking to the café to work a while and pretending we weren't anxious to get to bed.

Sometimes we skipped the coffee. And dinner. And everything else.

This time, though, I told her to meet Joel and me at the coffee shop.

He looked good. He'd put on weight and seemed fit. Not as big as Jason had been when I saw him in Barcelona, but big enough to indicate there was some fitness routine. He said he and Chris had a small gym set up on the ground floor of the townhouse and they'd been pretty regular about lifting.

"He's slimmed down," Joel said. "By like thirty pounds."

"Nice," I said.

"You look like you have, too."

"Swimming again."

"No shit? What's that like?"

How to describe the silence of the water? The clean feel of it? The scent of chlorine and the dry papery way my skin had become re-acclimated.

"It's like I'm becoming my dad," I said.

We caught up on how my folks were and his mom, who was dating someone Joel thought she was pretty serious about. We talked about his meetings in Mountain View, and he explained venture capital funding for a start-up and the options they had in terms of taking money to grow or selling the company outright and walking away. It had only been fifteen months since I'd first retained the information about him starting a company. But it had been a little over two years since the company was founded. Joel called it "grow or go" time.

"I love the work," he said, "but I'm not passionate about the product. I'd be fine selling and moving on to the next thing."

"So why look for investors?"

"My business partner. He's more attached than I am, and he thinks we can get to critical mass and raise the price of the

platform before we sell." He spoke with a confidence I remembered from years ago when we skated together.

"So, he thinks you can make more money?" I asked, not really
understanding what he meant by "critical mass" and "platform."

"Get more users, be valued higher, sell for more."

"Make more money," I repeated.

He shrugged. "Nothing wrong with making money."

"No," I said, "As long as you call it what it is."

"Okay, it's about the money." He looked uncomfortable for
a second, and then a wide grin brightened his features. "Tabby
says to stay in. I should have known you'd say cut and run."

"Diametrically opposed, your woman and me. Always have
been."

Joel laughed. "But you're not wrong. It's my instinct, too.
What we've built has value. Let someone else take it to the next
place."

"And then?"

Joel took a sip of his coffee. "Then I can move back to
Pittsburgh."

"And marry Tabby."

He grinned again. "Exactly."

"Have you asked her yet?"

He shook his head. "That's the other thing I need to do. Ring
shop."

"Damn, dude. I've got a girl here. She might get the wrong
idea if we go ring shopping."

"Who's the girl?"

"Jada," she said, appearing nearby, waving at me and
approaching.

I winced, thinking maybe she'd heard what I said before Joel
asked. But she didn't give any indication she had.

She and Joel greeted one another, and she set her stuff down,
kissed my cheek lightly, and went to get a beverage.

"So, she's gorgeous," he said watching her walk away.

I shrugged.

"Like you hadn't noticed?"

"She came after me," I said. "She's in Kittering's undergrad workshop. I subbed one day."

"Hot for teacher then? Nice. You ever hear from Melissa?"

"Nah, she moved to Sacramento and doesn't keep in touch."

"Kacie's in Seattle."

"No shit?"

Joel nodded and then stood again, and I realized it was because Jada had returned. I stood, too, and she sat, and we settled in for some more get-to-know-you stuff.

Joel gave her the basics of how we met and about us skating. She told him I'd been going to the park here. His raised eyebrows suggested he'd like to talk more about that. But we didn't. Jada moved the conversation to him and Tabby and their long-distance relationship. He told her it was tough, but they'd made it work and he was anxious to get back to Pittsburgh and settle down, maybe by the end of the year.

Jada talked about her family and Joel asked her about her studies and plans for the future. She said she was graduating in December and moving to L.A.

That was the first time I'd heard that plan, but I didn't flinch.

When we'd swapped all the get-to-know-you stuff, Jada asked Joel about his trip, and he told us what it was like to stand in front of venture capitalists and try to convince them of the value of your company. He said he was more of a homebody, really, and not nearly the world traveler I was. He didn't even have a passport, he confessed.

"I've been home a while," I said. "Maybe I'll settle down, too."

"Yeah, right. What's the next trip?"

"Six weeks in the Philippines. Summer."

"No shit? Tabby will get a kick out of that." Her parents

had immigrated to the U.S. when they were teenagers and her grandmother had just been relocated to Pittsburgh from Davao, a city on the southern-most Philippines island. "What takes you there?"

"Writing conference. Biggest but cheapest."

"Even the airfare?" Joel asked.

"Six weeks?" Jada asked.

"Kittering is lecturing at the University for a term after the conference. I'm staying on to assist."

Before Jada could ask more about it, Joel suggested we head back to the apartment so he could get cleaned up. As we stood and started making plans for the evening, Jada said she was heading back to her side of the bay.

While Thursdays had become our habit, I wasn't sorry to see her go. Focusing on Joel felt more important right then. We parted on the sidewalk with a hug between she and Joel, who said, "I hope to see you again."

She kissed me and left without looking back.

Joel and I settled into the couch in my apartment. I'd offered him a beer, but he waved it off and we drank water instead. I tried to remember the last time I'd spent this much time sober with him.

"You're not smoking dope anymore?" Joel asked.

I shrugged. "I'm writing and teaching a lot. Joined a critique group, too, so I have these evening meetings."

"Like AA?"

I laughed. "Sure, they keep me sober, so I guess that works." Hadn't really thought about it but I remembered how nervous our drug use had made Joel. He didn't like the possibility that Chris or I might become as addicted as Tony had.

"Kacie's been sober a while now, too."

"That so?"

"Tabby went out to Seattle a couple of weeks back. Said she's got a little flat," he looked around then, "like this, I guess. And a roommate."

"Boyfriend?"

Joel smiled, a gentle softening of his features. "She didn't say."

"I want her to be happy," I said, and meant it.

"She wants the same for you," he replied. "Said she hoped you'd found what you were looking for in Barcelona."

"Fuck, man, all I found in Barcelona were some fist fights, a Mediterranean tan, and a threesome in an outdoor shower."

Joel spit out the water he'd been drinking. "What the fuck, man?"

"I know. It was fucked up. Awesome, but fucked up. Had a shrink there who kept telling me to stop self-medicating with booze and sex."

"And?"

"And I didn't know what the fuck she was talking about." I set my glass on the coffee table, leaning forward, elbows on knees to do it. "I was just living, ya know? Just doing what I always did."

"Except it's after Tony. So, everything is about grief, Brian. Everything." He dropped his head back on the couch and looked up at the ceiling. There was a weight to the room, but it wasn't awkward, it was shared. And familiar. And unresolved.

How long would *After Tony* be a thing? The milestone hung like an albatross around my neck in Spain. Since returning, I thought I was managing without medicating, but it hurt, still, to think about *Before Tony* and now, *After*.

There was no *Before* Tony. I couldn't remember life before he was my best friend.

There was *Before Tony's Suicide*, but that one thing—the suicide—wasn't all of Tony. It was just the end of him.

"She wanted everything to be about healing," I said.

"Who? The chick in the shower?" Joel's eyebrows did that double-lift thing as if he was teasing me or asking for details.

I laughed. "Nah, my shrink. Kept saying I should find a healthy way to process grief and heal."

"And have you?"

"I'm back here. Not hiding in Barcelona."

"So, you admit you were hiding?"

But I ignored that and said, "I'm writing and skating and studying and spending time with Jada."

"And where's that going?"

"Man, she's got me. For real. It's different but awesome. We talk about Tony, but it doesn't hurt as much because she didn't know him. And we talk about writing and the future."

"The future when she moves to L.A.?"

I looked down. "Didn't know about that."

"Tread lightly, Brian. She may not be as invested as you are."

I nodded. "We'll just see what happens, right?"

April 21, 2000
To: playerjay@yahoo.com
From: captainlisto@yahoo.com
Re: your twin was just here

He says you're thinking of quitting hockey. What's going on?

B

April 22, 2000
To: captainlisto@yahoo.com
From: playerjay@yahoo.com
Re: your twin was just here

He's wrong. I'm playing well. Besides, I'm on contract.

What the fuck you been doin'?

J

April 23, 2000
To: playerjay@yahoo.com
From: captainlisto@yahoo.com
Re: your twin was just here

Good to hear. More school. More stories. Like Barcelona. But in English.

B

Joel got me thinking about Spain, so after he left, I pulled the notebook I'd been writing letters in and found the place I'd captured that darkened hallway, the hook-latch on the door, and the surge of blood after fist-met-face. When I'd finished, the piece was 3,500 words long and met a satisfying conclusion in naked limbs and twisted sheets.

The next week, I took the piece to workshop. Ed was supportive of the work. Suggested some places where the sensory details should dominate instead of the action.

Sara said, "This reads like a *Dear Penthouse* letter. 'You'll never believe what happened,' or some other thing. It's hyper masculine, focused on the brutality and animalism of the entire thing. Even the sex act is all physical."

I scribbled notes as she cited specific passages, the phrases and vocabulary.

"Isn't that the point?" Ed asked Sara. "Isn't the physicality of it the entire point? It's very Stanley Kowalski. Like there's no place for emotion here."

"It's one dimensional."

"Unless you're reading the subtext," Ed argued.

"There is no subtext," Sara countered. "But you could add it," she said to me. "How would you tell the reader that what's happening on the surface is a distraction? A farce? Because the real work is happening inside?"

"Or not happening at all," Ed said. "Being ignored in favor of the immediate, the brutal."

And there was the insight I had been looking for: Avoiding the real emotional work with physical distraction. It's like my shrink from Barcelona had called the group and told them what to look for. It was like Joel's observation that Barcelona had just been a place for me to hide.

I scribbled notes, marked out passages, wrote furiously about how to make the scene better.

It wasn't me anymore. I could release it. But it needed to be compelling. And that meant it needed more than one layer.

I walked Sara home like always.

"You knew the piece needed work."

"Yes."

We walked for some time before I broke the silence with, "One of my best friends was in town last week."

"One of the Virginia friends?"

I nodded.

"How was that?"

I shrugged.

"You brought it up. You obviously need to talk about it."

"Yeah, okay, I need to talk about it." I stopped walking. Sara did, too. She waited. Our breath made steamy puffs in the air between us. "I thought I'd feel some peace. Some closure. Something at least."

"And you felt nothing."

"Not nothing. But not closure."

"Did you guys talk about Tony?"

I nodded. "It was ... scabbed, maybe? Like scar tissue? I don't know if that even makes sense."

"It does." She touched my arm lightly at first and then squeezed it.

"And he said Kacie is in Seattle."

"Kacie the ex-girlfriend?" Sara's expression softened.

"She's working up there, he said, and I want to go there. I've been wanting to go there since Thursday. Since he said it. I feel compelled."

"And say what?" She dropped her hand, shifted her weight away from me.

"I don't know. Maybe it'll just come to me when I get there."

"Or maybe you want her to say something to you."

We started walking again.

"She didn't tell you herself she was there," Sara observed.

"She knew he would."

"She didn't invite you there." Her tone had that sisterly thing I loved. It reminded me. Corrected me. Encouraged me.

"I have her address."

"She may not be ready to see you."

"I'm ready."

Sara sighed. "I guess that's all that matters."

We walked a little further, across two intersections, until we stood beneath her building. The evening was cool, and Sara hugged herself inside a thin coat, something from an outdoors label that was probably warmer than it looked. It was purple and the shell was water resistant. She had her hands shoved in her pockets.

"I'm dating this other girl now. She's great and I want to be in love with her," I confided. My own sweatshirt had a hoodie and I thought about pulling it up over my head.

"Why?"

I shrugged. "Seems like the right time. The right girl."

Sara cocked her head and squinted at me.

"It's not the kind of thing you just decide, right? It either is or it isn't."

"But if it isn't, that's because I kept it from being," I said.

The streetlight over my head was shining in her eyes, I realized, and so I stepped to the side, so she wasn't looking right at it.

"The piece you read tonight. About the shelter. Was it true?"

"It's a memoir, Brian. It's all pretty much true."

"Then I'm sorry."

"That I was homeless?"

"That you felt so alone. So helpless."

"We all feel that way at some point." She looked away from me, down the street, into the long row of streetlamps. "Sometimes more than once."

I tugged her toward me and wrapped my arms around her. At some point over shared pages and walks home, I'd earned her trust and she let me hold her in a very brotherly embrace for a few seconds before pulling away, smiling up at me, and saying, "Don't fall in love with this new girl."

"It may be too late for that."

"Then don't say I didn't warn you."

And she went inside.

Summer

I went to Seattle.

After Joel's visit, I couldn't get Kacie off my mind, and when the semester ended, I went to Seattle. It was a fifteen-hour drive, so I booked a cheap flight and Abbie insisted on coming with me so she booked a companion ticket. We left at 2:00 p.m. Friday and landed a couple of hours later.

I'd never been to Seattle and what I noticed first was how green it was.

Abbie had an old roommate who'd fled North, so we crashed at her place. It was small and dark, with too many residents. I wanted to see Kacie first thing. In my head, she'd welcome the reunion and we'd spend the weekend together catching up. Maybe she'd show me her town.

But that's not how it happened.

I entered Kacie's building when a neighbor came out and climbed the two floors to her door and knocked before I lost my nerve.

The person who answered, though, wasn't Kacie. She was a small Filipino girl who looked a lot like Tabby. She said her name was Marlene and offered to let me wait inside since Kacie was expected home any time.

I took in the neat arrangement of furniture, the hangings on the walls, the dishes in the sink. I sat on a barstool and tried to look non-threatening, all the time hoping she didn't have a gun and wondering just what would have possessed her to let me inside.

"So how do you know Kacie?" Marlene asked, reaching into the refrigerator for a pair of bottled beers.

"We went to high school together," I said.

"In Virginia?"

"I'm sorry, where did you say she was?"

"She's got this deadline thing every day. Five o'clock, so if she worked from home, she's running pages to the paper. If she's been there all day, she'll stay until after the deadline." Marlene handed the beer across the bar to me.

"She's a reporter?"

"Copy editor. Lifestyle section. Only gets published twice weekly. The other days she's covering a beat."

"And what do you do?"

"I'm a journalist like her. Been trying to get her to come work with me."

I raised an eyebrow and Marlene continued, "I'm on CNN's website team."

"Website team?"

She nodded and took a long drink. "Basically anything they report on TV needs to be written up and posted. So, I watch a *lot* of CNN."

"You write after they put it on the air?"

"Pretty much at the same time."

Before I could ask her more, the door opened, and Kacie fell through.

"What a fucking disaster," she said. "I don't know how much longer I can put up with..." Then she saw me and stopped talking.

"Kace," I said, and tried to smile but seeing her stung me, unexpectedly, even out of context, even after all that time. Even though she looked so beautiful. Maybe because she looked so beautiful. Her cheeks were flushed, her hair a wild mess, and her eyes bright and wide.

Then they narrowed and she said, "What the fuck are you doing here?"

"Glad to see me?"

"Get out."

"Kacie, let me explain."

"How could you let him in?" This demand was thrown at Marlene.

"What? He said you went to high school together."

"This is Brian!" Kacie all but shrieked it.

Marlene's face went pale. "Oh, shit, like *Brian* Brian?"

"Fuck." Kacie threw her purse and coat on the couch and stood, hands on hips, facing me. She tipped her head at the beer in my hand. "Make yourself comfortable."

"Come on, Kace, don't be pissed."

"Don't call me that. You have ten seconds to say whatever it was you came to say. Then you have to go."

Marlene stepped away from the counter. "I'm really sorry, Kacie," she said. "I'll just give you two some privacy." She slipped down the hall and I heard a door close behind her. I could almost hear Kacie's huffy breathing. Imagined her nostrils expelling smoke. I'd write it that way. Like she was a dragon and I was a reluctant knight.

I took a drink from the bottle in my hand.

"You're wasting time," she snapped.

"I came all this way. Don't kick me out. Let's talk."

"About what?"

"It's been over a year, Kacie."

"Since I saw you, sure," she said, folding arms over her chest,

"But not since your crazy fucking emails and letters. You chased me out of Charlottesville, Brian. I changed my email address. Moved. Told my parents to write return to sender on all the mail they got for me."

"I never sent anything to Colorado."

"How would I know?"

"Kacie, Barcelona was amazing and . . ."

"That's what you're here to tell me? About your European adventure?"

"No, I mean, yes, but that's not all. I went and I saw these places and I wanted to tell you. To tell Tony."

She flinched.

"I'm not doing this right. It's not like I thought it would be."

"What did you think? That I'd hug you?" She glared and her voice dropped on each of the next few fragments. "Hold you? Want to be with you? Want to see you? After the shit you said to me?"

"I was angry."

"And drunk."

"And broken. And missing Tony. And missing home."

"And you took it out on me. Like always."

"Stop, okay, just stop. I'm here to apologize. To explain."

"I don't want you to apologize!" she shouted at me, hands straight to her sides, fists clenched. "I don't want you at all, Brian. I made that clear."

"It's been a long time."

"Not long enough. Get out."

"Kacie, please, just hear me out. For Tony?"

"Don't you dare use Tony to get to me." Her hand came up and she pointed at me. "Don't you dare. I've been hurting, too, Brian. And healing. And part of that was getting the fuck over you. Now here you are in MY town? In MY apartment, and I should give you what? A minute? An hour? The benefit of the doubt?"

I'd stood from the stool and still had a few inches on her, but the distance between us made it seem like we were eye level, so I closed the space. Made her look up at me.

"Stop right there." She was trembling. "Stop." Her hands came up between us.

"Stop what?"

"Moving. Looking like that. You want something. What is it? Get it and get out."

I shook my head. "I don't."

"You always do. You take and take and take. So, what is it this time? My blessing. Go, be with Melissa, be happy."

"I'm not with Melissa."

Something passed in her eyes but was gone just as quickly. "I don't care," she hissed.

"But there is someone."

"Of course, there is."

"And Joel was in San Francisco. He met her."

"I'm sure Tabby can't wait to tell me about it."

Her posture had relaxed a little, but it was more resignation than acceptance. She stared down the hall and then looked back up at me. Her eyes glistened.

"Don't cry, Kace, please." I reached for her, but she jerked back.

"You need to go."

"I came to say something. I need to say it. Just let me, okay? Then I'll go."

Arms folded across her chest again, and a hard bite tightened her jaw.

"Everywhere I went, Kacie, everywhere there was you."

She snorted.

"I'm serious, please, just listen. In San Francisco, the fog sizzles before clearing in a thousand drips like steam. In Los Angeles, the ocean chases up the beach, foaming and rushing. In Montenegro, thousands of pebbles lie under the clear surf like Seurat impressionism. There was water, Kacie, water everywhere."

Her eyes blinked, still wet, and she stood frozen.

"There's an island in the bay in Montenegro with an abbey on it. It looks like Alcatraz. And when we were in Dubrovnik, we stood on the border with Serbia and there were gunshots. Machine guns, Kacie, weapons firing over the border. But in front of me, the Adriatic Sea stretched like a sapphire glacier, shimmering and still. And you. You were there."

She shook her head but when I reached for her hand, she let me take it.

"Why are you doing this?" she whispered.

"The water, it healed me, Kacie. I didn't know it could do that. I've hated it, always, swimming and all that stupid back-and-forth-and-flip-turn shit. But it found me. Everywhere I went, it found me, and I finally felt that spiritual cooling that Tony found."

She tugged her hand, but I held tighter.

"I was healing on the inside. I wanted you to know. In Barcelona, there was a magic fountain and its mists and sprays would cling to my skin. He would have loved it, Kace."

She ripped her hand from mine, the tears let loose, and she shook her head as if in disbelief and ran down the hall.

I chased her, threw myself on the floor at her feet where she sat perched on the edge of her bed.

"Hear me," I begged. "The sun was hot, and it took everything from me. Wore me down. My hands were raw, my back was broken. At the hostel I would strip the work clothes off, stand under the shower in the courtyard, and that cold water would wash me clean. Kacie, it took all of the hurt, the anger, the pain with it."

"Stop, Brian, stop. I can't take any more."

"I lit a candle in Santa Maria del Mar. I prayed, Kacie. I don't even know how, but I did it."

"You're killing me."

"You've been with me everywhere, Kacie. From the Mediterranean to Big Sur. You're in my skin, in my heart. Your voice is the one I hear. It's you, it's always been you." I don't know what made me say it except it suddenly seemed so true.

But her face hardened. "You're a liar," she said. "And a cheat."

"I've seen a lot this year, Kacie, seriously, a lot. But all I've really seen is you."

"Go away," she wailed.

"There is nowhere," I said, softer now, coaxing, "Unless you're there."

"Just go." She choked on a sob in her throat. "We're done, Brian. We're done. Please go."

I reached for her, but she flinched, and when she squeezed her eyes closed and her shoulders shook I wanted to hold her but instead I stood, slowly, and left.

I was wrung out. Staggering the six blocks back to the neighborhood where Abbie's friend stayed, I ran through, again, what I'd said and how she'd recoiled from me. Tears of my own were barely dammed behind my eyes.

She needed to know, I reasoned. She'd been in all those places with me. I'd seen her everywhere, like that Tim McGraw song. She haunted me.

And if she haunted me, I sure as hell oughta be haunting her, too.

But Joel had said she'd moved on. She was happy. She was working. She was in a new place, a better place. And I'd come here to put my mark on this place, too.

Like the selfish motherfucker I was.

I found Abbie and told her we needed to get home.

"Our flight's not till Sunday."

"Then let's get fucking drunk," I said.

I wrote frantically on the way home. Abbie slept in the window seat, and I stuffed earphones into my ears and scribbled for twenty-four pages about how it felt to beg Kacie to forgive me. It was cathartic and exhausting, and my hand cramped more than once but the strokes of my pencil finally slowed, and the words stopped throbbing in my head eventually.

There is nowhere.

Just go.

Like the refrain of a song I couldn't forget. Some kind of fucking ear worm burrowing into my brain reminding me that I ruined the best thing that ever happened to me. She'd loved me and I'd taken it for granted. No amount of time could heal that wound. It felt like it was still bleeding. Maybe because I had just ripped it open.

"You're a real dick, you know that, right?" Abbie had said as we waited in the airport for our flight. "When are you going to stop chasing ghosts?"

"Leave it, Abbs."

A huff, a shift in posture against the vinyl seat and a long exhalation. Then, "At least you didn't take comfort in one of those sluts from the bar last night."

But that wasn't true. I had found myself lip-locked with a pretty blonde with an eyebrow ring and a half-top. I'd had one hand on her ass and lifted her up against me. Only a shot of Sambuca, a black licorice nightmare that made me vomit, altered that course. I found Abbie, told her I needed to go home, and passed out on the couch in her friend's apartment. Lucky I didn't wake up with permanent marker on my face.

"I'm entitled to a backslide now and then."

"Spoken like a true dick."

I scrubbed my palms over my face. "You're not helping me."

"I'm not trying to."

"Then why are you here?"

"Because you require supervision."

"And apparently reprimand. Get it over with."

She squared her hips to face me and I turned to look at her. Expecting anger, hostility, or at the very least disappointment, I was surprised when her face instead showed compassion.

"Your grief is a living, breathing thing, Brian. And you've been living with it for long enough. Everyone else is done with Tony."

I flinched.

"Why aren't you?"

"I am," I said weakly.

"Then stop trying to resurrect him." She placed her hand on my arm and squeezed gently. "And stop trying to live for him."

Once we were in our seats, Abbie turned to the window and slept, and I tore through two dozen pages in a spiral notebook. Sharpening and re-sharpening my pencil as the lead wore down into nubs and my hurt, my loss, my sadness over Kacie bled all over the page.

Abbie and I didn't even say goodbye, just stumbled through opposing doors and shut them behind us. The dark quiet of my flat consumed me and I threw myself on the bed and slept.

By Thursday I'd broken the full zombie mode that consumed me earlier in the week.

Jada arrived at her expected time and we ordered pizza and snuggled into the futon couch to watch a movie she'd borrowed from somewhere. Midway through, though, she paused it and demanded to know what was up with me.

"Long week last week, not much sleep over the weekend, and then another long week this week." I tried to smile but it came out more like a smirk. "Sleep deprivation."

"Why was last weekend sleep deprived?"

"Whirlwind trip to Seattle."

"What the hell? Seattle?"

"Never been. Cheap flight. But it meant an early, early flight home Sunday so Abbie said we should just pull an all-nighter and that was a terrible idea." I scrubbed a palm over my face, slouched deeper into the pillows on the futon and said, "Still recovering."

"You and Abbie went to Seattle. For forty-eight hours?"

"More like thirty-six but yeah."

Jada looked pensive, her eyes studying me.

"What?" I prompted after her staring in silence seemed to go on too long.

"I want to ask, but I shouldn't ask, and I'm trying to decide if I'm gonna ask."

"Ask what?"

"Did you see Kacie?"

That she knew the name, that she knew Kacie was in Seattle, that she connected the trip's fatigue with the drama of the ex-girlfriend, all of these things should have surprised me, but they didn't. I've been caught cheating enough times to know girls are super smart about shit like that.

"Yes."

Jada stood up and took our pizza plates to the kitchen.

More silence. Her moving around, trashing paper, folding the box closed.

I picked up the remote and hit "play." The TV sprung back to life.

Jada didn't return to the couch, and after a few minutes I got the hint and paused the movie again.

"What's wrong?" I called over my shoulder.

"I want to talk about it, but I don't think I should and so I'm trying to decide if I'm gonna."

It was the same cadence as before and I decided to let her figure it out this time. I didn't want to talk about Kacie. About any of them. In my head, Virginia lumped together into one big ball of fucking-painful. I'd gone back to hiding and San Francisco was helping. Once, after a seriously bad New Year's Eve in which I'd alienated all of my friends, San Francisco had given me the perfect escape. Another time, after I buried my best friend and lost the first girl I'd ever loved, San Francisco had taken me in, chewed me up, and spit me out to Barcelona. Now that girl was gone forever and the woman in the kitchen wasn't letting San Francisco do its work.

I waited. She didn't move. In the reflection of the small circle mirrors that hung around the TV I saw fragments of her, in still-ness, by the kitchen's bar counter.

"Bring beers when you come back," I finally said, and hit "play" again on the movie.

Since the thirty-six hours and twenty-four pages I'd done some processing of what happened with Kacie. It was too soon, certainly, for the forgiveness. She needed more time and more space, and she'd tried to tell me that, but I just pushed like I always do to get what I want, what I need, even if it's not what she's able or willing to give.

It was a pattern my therapist had identified. The Barcelona one. Like a petulant child, she told me, Brian thinks if he wants it now, he must need it now and if he needs it someone should give it to him.

"You must grow up." She was so smug when she'd said it, like she cracked the code of me, and I should turn some corner and start changing. Being better. But I hadn't.

I'd gone to Seattle and demanded Kacie give me what I wanted.

Well, not everything I wanted. If I was honest, I wanted her. And that was why I didn't want to talk about her with Jada.

"Did you fuck her?" The question was so quiet I couldn't be sure I'd heard it.

Then she came around the couch, incensed at what she must have thought was me ignoring the question, and ripped the remote out of my hand. She stabbed it in the direction of the TV and the film paused again.

"Did. You. Fuck. Her." She was glowing in the TV light on her left side and the kitchen light on her right. She looked ethereal, like some kind of sorceress.

"No."

"What happened?"

"I don't want to talk about it."

"Did you kiss her?"

"No."

"So, what happened?"

"What part of 'I don't want to talk about it' is difficult for you to understand? The 'I' part? Is it the noun?" I thought my voice must be weary, resigned, emotional. But that can't be what she heard because she said, "You're lying."

"Why would I lie?"

"If you fucked her, you'd lie."

"So, if I say I didn't, it can't be the truth?"

"Is it?"

"She hates me, Jada."

"But you saw her."

"For like ten minutes. Tried to get through to her. I tried to explain. But she wouldn't listen. She threw me out of her place.

She was so—" But I stopped suddenly because I really didn't want to share this with Jada.

"What is it about her?"

Not the question I was expecting.

"Just let it go, Jada. I went. She wouldn't talk to me. I drank a lot with Abbie and her friends. And I came back."

"What am I supposed to do with that?"

"With the truth? I don't know. What do people normally do with the truth? Believe it?" Now I was angry. Things with Kacie were complicated. Things with Jada had been simple. Now the Kacie things were complicating the Jada things.

"I came over here to be with you."

"I know."

"Like *be* with you," she said. "But if you've been with someone else."

"I haven't. She wouldn't even *talk* to me, I told you."

"But there were others."

"Who? Abbie? She's a lesbian, Jada. Jesus, stop being so fucking jealous. I can leave town without sticking my dick in someone else."

"As opposed to sticking your dick in me?"

"Would like to do that, yes. Or I *did* want that but not so much now with you yelling at me. Seriously, what the fuck? Jealousy is childish."

"I'm not jealous, Brian."

"No? Then what's the big deal? So, I went to Seattle. My ex-girlfriend was a raging bitch. I got drunk. I came home."

"It's not what happened in Seattle, Brian. It's that you *went*."

"Now I'm totally confused. You're not jealous, but you're mad I went out of town?"

"That you went to Seattle."

"Specifically?"

"Specifically. What did you think would happen if you went

to see Kacie?" She seethed the name. "What were you *hoping* would happen?"

"I think you just want to fight," I said. "And I really don't want that."

"No, you want to fuck."

"Not anymore."

"Why did you go?"

Because I couldn't stop myself. But I didn't say that. I knew better than to stoke these flames.

"Are you staying?" I asked, standing up. "Because I'm done with this movie, with this conversation, with this day. I'm going to bed."

We were close, near enough I could reach her if I tried. But I didn't. I'd already begged a woman this week. I'd done nothing wrong here and refused to act like I had. Instead, I turned toward the bathroom, stepped inside to piss and brush my teeth, then flipped the light off and crawled over the bed. I checked the alarm was set and collapsed into the pillow.

Jada still stood by the television.

"Are you staying?" I asked again, not looking over at her.

"I want to stay but I don't think I should so I'm trying to decide if I'll leave." Same cadence, same neutral tone as before. Like I was eavesdropping on her inner monologue, not like she was actually communicating with me. A cool distance, a calculation, hung between us.

After a while I heard her eject the movie, put it back in the case, and walk across the room. Some jingling with her purse and keys and then the sound of the lock clicking on the door. It opened, it closed, and she was gone. And I wasn't sure what I felt about that. Disappointed maybe. Pissed that this Kacie thing was still fucking up shit in my reconstructed Virginia-less world. But mostly exhausted. So, I slept. Three days later I left for Manila via Nashville.

May 30, 2000
To: captainlisto@yahoo.com
From: playerjay@yahoo.com
Re: Nashville

Joel and I will be there Thursday night if you want to come
earlier. Cab it from the airport to the hotel. It's the Omni.

See you then.

J

Four days in Nashville and six weeks in Manila and I couldn't
wait to be back in my own bed. I staggered down the hallway of
our building and dropped a heavy duffle bag at my feet.

Abbie's door flew open and she launched herself across the
hall into my arms.

"You're back!" she shrieked into my ear.

"Ow, fuck, Abbie, yeah, and exhausted."

"What did you bring me?" She was bouncing on her toes as I
extricated myself from her.

David appeared over her shoulder. "Let the man get inside,
Abbs, damn."

"For real, and who says I brought you anything?" We all
shoved inside my place, and the smell of home crashed into me.
As I stood looking around, Abbie dragged my duffle across the
floor until she could sit on the bed and dig through it.

"Better let me," I said, "Unless you want to find all my dirty
shorts."

She recoiled with an overdramatic gag.

David laughed behind me. "Would serve you right, nosy
thing."

I knelt beside the bag and turned it over to get at the com-
partment where I had stashed Abbie's gifts. I withdrew two can-
dlesticks, orange wooden cylinders with raffia-like straw tied
around them. I handed them to her and she cooed over them.

"They hold tea lights," I told her. "So you can put any scent you want."

"Thank you, Brian," she said, and leaned in to hug me.

"And the obligatory snow globe." I handed her the box that had made the trip from Nashville to Manila and now back to San Francisco. This time I got a kiss on the cheek and an arm-squeeze around the neck.

I took the third thing out of my bag and stood to hand it to David.

"A book?" he asked me, one skeptical eyebrow raised.

"You said to bring something useful." I pointed at the picture of the author on the cover. "He's the national hero of the Philippines. The one side of the text is English, and if you flip it over," I demonstrated, showing him the other side, "It's the same story, but in Tagalog."

David grinned. "Tell me you didn't."

I shrugged. "I've got some phrases, but I probably couldn't read the entire thing, no."

"You and the languages, it's unnatural, really. And annoying."

"I got candles and David got homework. Seems about right." Abbie laughed wickedly.

"Now get the fuck out so I can sleep."

"Laundry later?" David asked. It was 4:00 p.m. "Date night?"

I laughed. "Sounds awesome. I'll knock when I wake up."

After I closed the door behind them, I took a shower, ignored the blinking light on my answering machine, and crashed on my bed until after dark. I know enough about jet lag to not sleep for days when I return, so I set an alarm and woke up at 8:30, forcing myself out of bed and across the hall to get David for our laundry date.

I hadn't paid for laundry service in Manila. I'd washed what I needed in the sink and hung the pieces over the bathtub to dry. David made fun of me for that during the walk down to the basement laundry room.

"That book you got me is pretty good," he said.

"Really? Using it as a doorstop or a coaster?"

As we separated lights and darks and started loads, I told him about the trip. About working with the university students. About the thriving second shift and the all-night bars that accommodated them. About the best fucking Monte Cristo I'd ever eaten at a place called Heaven and Eggs. About trying to run outdoors and finally settling for the treadmill in the hotel gym because every path I took ended me up in a shantytown with desolate-looking people. I told him about the World War II memorial and the five-story, eight city blocks of a single shopping mall. I told him about the signs with the misplaced modifiers that cracked me up.

"Jesus. Only. Saves," I said.

"He doesn't spend a dime," David responded.

"Exactly. Just these slight things that made it hard to ignore."

"That you weren't in Nashville anymore?" He elbowed me and I nodded, but I decided not to tell him about Nashville, about seeing The Crew, about Jason telling me to leave Kacie alone. Because even after six weeks, I was still kind of pissed.

Instead, I asked him to catch me up on him. He told me about getting back together with his grad assistant boyfriend, Alec, and about the new works he had in a couple of galleries in town. He'd sold three pieces through a dealer to a collector, and he was waiting to see if the collector's agent friends would be impressed and ask about him. He told me about a friend who had tested positive for HIV and about how he and several others went to the AIDS clinic to be tested.

"Had you been with that guy?"

He shook his head. "But one of my partners had."

"Did anyone else test positive?"

He shook his head again.

"I'm glad," I said. "You're careful, right? Always?"

He nodded. "Alec and me are exclusive now, so it's okay."

"It's not," I said. "Stay protected."

"It's not like he can get pregnant."

"Did he get tested?"

David shook his head. "I didn't even tell him about that."

I stared at him. "Partners need to be honest with each other," I said. "It's not worth it to lie. This is a big deal, David. Tell Alec. Get him tested. Don't risk it."

"I know. It's just awkward."

"Better to be awkward than positive, right?"

Another elbow, this one to my ribs. "When did you become the grown-up around here?" Then he grinned. "Can we go skateboarding later?"

"If he's yours, why do you have to stalk him at the park?"

"I'm not there to watch him anymore. I'm there to watch you." He looked a little shy when he said it but then smiled. "You look healthy out there. Confident."

"Yeah, okay, maybe tomorrow."

But the next day I slept until 2:30 and when hunger finally drove me from my apartment, David and Abbie weren't around. I hit the grocery for some basics, started a pot boiling water, and sat on the floor to listen to the answering machine.

"You have thirty-five new messages."

"Fuck me. I wasn't gone that long." I dragged a notebook over and started writing down the various bill collector, student enrollment, and publisher calls. Three journals were confirming receipt of my stories and acceptance with some minor edits. Would I please call them back? Couldn't wait to tell Abbie my long streak of rejection was broken.

Mom twice. Joel once. Chris saying he'd gotten his ticket for New Year's.

Then Melissa.

"Brian. Hi." There was a pause and then, "It's Meli. I'm moving back to the city and thought we could talk. Maybe. Just give me a call or I'll call you back, actually, since I don't know what my new number will be. Okay. Talk soon. Bye."

The air left my lungs. Meli was coming back. The sound of her voice sent me into a panic-stricken flashback. This room, more than any other, was Meli. It was where we took hits of that purple bong and listened to Janis Joplin, Jimi Hendrix, and Pink Floyd. It's where the sunlight dripped through the window onto her bare skin and I trailed my fingertips up over her arms and shoulders and down her back. In this room, Meli held me while I cried over Tony. She pulled me to her in the middle of the night when nightmares stabbed me with memories and regret. Though Jada had made it seem like home—hung tapestries and framed posters, worked through that stack of boxes with me— Meli was still here. As if brought forward by the sound of her voice, a ghost stalking the wood floor. She had helped me pack my funeral suit. She had flipped the lights off behind me when I left for Virginia.

The last time she had been in this room, after I had fucked everything up, she was collecting the things that belonged to her. Music and books and loose pages and a sweatshirt and her favorite wine glass. It was hand-painted with swirls that looked like wisps of snowdrift and tiny asterisk-shaped snowflakes and miniature triangle-shaped trees, like a winter forest. I'd bought it for her at a Christmas craft fair David dragged me to and she'd kept it here for her chardonnay, but that last day she took it, wrapped in a t-shirt and tucked into a wide tote bag bearing the words "Shop Santa Cruz" on it. It had been late March, the last time I'd seen her.

Six weeks after I returned from Herndon and Tony's funeral, I called her. I begged her over the phone to let me explain, to listen, to give me a chance. She had tried but always ended up disconnecting the call before I got the whole story out. The usual paths on campus when I would see her, she wasn't there. She'd altered her routes to avoid me. Abbie and David said she hadn't been to the coffee shop, hadn't left her dorm room really, and wanted to know what I'd done. I told them it wasn't any of their damn business. They pulled away, too.

By that point, I was staggering through the assignments on the syllabi and hoping to graduate in May but truthfully didn't care much. About anything. Only Kittering bothered to notice. He suggested counseling when I confessed what Tony had done. Said it had helped him when his brother hanged himself in 1984. Dad set up Dr. Moses and I'd been to see him twice, and both times he'd made it clear that Tony's death was my fault. At least, that's what I heard.

Meli's cheeks had glistened with tears as she gathered her things. I monologued in cursive, my tongue thick with vodka, my eyes bleary from the last few bong hits.

"He was my brother and he took that from me. Everything we were to each other meant nothing apparently because he just left. Checked out. And I don't know what to do without him. Can't you understand that? He was the best of me, Meli, and now he's gone."

The place was closed up tight, full of smoke, and the bed's dishevelment combined with dirty dishes on the counters and the pulled drapes made it look like a desperate sort of den.

"You're in deep, Brian," Meli was saying. "But I can't help you."

"I don't want your damn help," I'd snapped.

Her breath hitched and she pushed her long auburn hair out of her face. "You're cruel, Brian. That's new." She shook her head and squeezed her eyes shut.

"Nothing is new."

"You're sinking."

"The fuck could youpossiblyknow 'boutit?"

She turned away, looked around the room as if trying to locate anything else she might possibly pack in that oversized bag. Then she headed for the door.

"You gun leaveme, then? Jus' like Tony? Jus' walkaway?"

She hadn't responded. She'd just opened the door, looked around, said, "Brian, seriously, get help." Then she pulled the door closed and her footsteps faded down the hallway.

I kept emailing her. Kept apologizing. For months. Even after I went to Barcelona. Nights when I was so lonely and fucked up. Afternoons when I was so tired and maddeningly sober. I sent Meli emails that tried to explain what was happening to me. Barcelona therapist said I was in shock, even though she insisted there wasn't a pre-determined path or orderly progression through grief. Spring 1999 in San Francisco had been shock. And it lingered. With Meli, it came back to that one day when she'd collected her things and walked out.

Now she was back. And she *wanted* to talk to me. I wondered what I had to say to her. How to sum up over a year? How to condense Barcelona and San Francisco and L.A. and Seattle and Nashville and Manila into a single conversation with someone I had hoped would witness each chapter? Did I hope that? Did I still wish Melissa was witness to my life?

Another message from the university.

Nothing from Kacie. Not surprised. Nothing from Jada. A little disappointed.

Kacie. Meli. Jada. Hunger.

I made some mac and cheese. Flipped through the pages of the notebook I'd taken to the Philippines. Smiled at some of the things I'd jotted down. Wondered when, exactly, Melissa would show.

Startled by a knock on the door, I flipped the notebook closed, set down the bowl I'd been eating from, and sauntered over to open it. Jada stood on the other side.

"Wondered if you'd call. Or if I should call. Decided to just come over. Hope that's okay."

I didn't respond, just reached for her, pulled her into my arms for a long, warm kiss that tasted like sunshine and salt air, and dragged her into my apartment.

"Did you miss me?" Jada asked, when we finally came up for air.

I groaned. "More than you know." I nuzzled between her jaw and shoulder and latched on, kissing and sucking until she went weak in my arms.

"I'm not here to fuck," she said, laughter in her voice.

"Okay, but we can, right?"

More laughter, and she pushed herself away from me. "Tell me about your trip."

"Long flights. Smelly cab ride. Ten-story hotel in the financial district. Bizarre American influence. Some interesting ex-pats. A filthy canal that carried belly-up fish and soggy paper and pushed a putrid breeze over clean sidewalks. Another long flight, and now working to stave off jet lag." It was 4:30. "What are you doing over here on a Saturday?"

"It's Thursday," she said. "I was at the coffee house waiting and when you didn't show, I just thought I'd come by."

Thursday. I thought for a second about when I was expected back on campus, but not till Monday. We had a three-day weekend together.

"You're staying."

She nodded. "So, we have a while for whatever else." She looked down at the floor. "We can eat or something."

"I have gone gourmet in my travels," I said, walking around the kitchen counter and pulling another bowl from the cabinet. "Kraft's finest made with water because there's no milk."

Jada dropped her backpack and followed me into the kitchen. When I'd filled a second bowl and handed it to her, we headed over to the futon couch. I caught her looking me up and down. Travel had been tough, and I'd gotten leaner.

"Catch me up on Jada," I said, sitting and inviting her to follow. "What have you been up to?"

She talked about school and organizing her schedule for this to be her final semester. She had considered a graduate degree but thought she probably needed to work for a while first. I asked if that meant she was headed to L.A. sooner rather than later. She said she may have had a change of plans. I tried to press, but she distracted me by climbing on my lap and kissing me breathless. I'd been forgiven, apparently, for the Seattle trip and the distrust of it. Time and distance had healed us both. We spent the rest of the night and deep into Friday afternoon in bed.

By Friday night I had some cabin fever and convinced Jada to go with David and Abbie to the coffee shop for a poetry open mic. She asked if I would read, and I told her that was a hard pass.

The coffee house was crowded, and we took a table that was meant for two and shoved extra chairs around it, and I pulled Jada close enough so she was nearly on my lap. I tucked my face into her shoulder and kissed along her pretty neck, tugging at her ear lobe with my teeth and whispering dirty suggestions in her ear. She choked on giggles, trying to maintain some composure, but slid her hand over mine and threaded our fingers together with a squeeze that told me she was into it.

We snuggled comfortably together and listened to the readers, lifting our coffee cups for sips. My body felt relaxed, content. The last of the jet lag had been worked off this afternoon in the shower with Jada, and I couldn't remember feeling so peaceful. Like I was exactly where I was meant to be. That feeling lingered as we watched one poet after another take the stage and perform their work.

Finally, Abbie took the mic and delivered a powerful and sexy verse about choosing the person you would follow into the flames, and I squeezed Jada's hand a little tighter. Raising it to my lips, I met her eyes. She smiled, but there was something missing in it. Maybe L.A. really was a thing and she just hadn't been willing to tell me yet. I tried to do what Joel had told me, be careful and respect some distance between us. Eventually I would need to accept her leaving at the end of term. But the fall season every year for me had always been about recommitting to a purpose and this felt like that. Like after all the travel and wandering, I'd found home, and home included Jada.

Until a name over the system broke the earth open inside me like a quake.

Polite clapping and some shifting chairs and then she came, from behind me, and took the stage. She stood in front of the mic and looked out over the room. It wasn't big and there wasn't much distance between us, and when her eyes met mine, I saw scorn in them.

Meli was at the mic.

"This poem is called 'Brian'," she said. Then, she eviscerated me.

If he was warm seaside breezes, I might love him.
If he was laughter and picnic blankets and kites catching
the wind, I might love him
If he was the horizon out on the edge of the sea
Or gull wings gliding
Or the sizzle of waves dissolving into earth.
I might love him.
But I look at him and he is
Sunburn and sand in my Coke and fat men in Speedos.
He reminds me of the beach
And if he was wonderful, I might love him
But I don't.

When the poem ended there were "oohs" and "daaaaahms" and other scorching responses.

I felt the heat of shame on my neck and cheeks.

I deserved it. I wouldn't have argued had it been a fight. I would have simply nodded and accepted that she was right. About all of it.

When she stepped down, she strode past me. The eye contact we'd made from stage hinted that I was the figure in the poem, but her dismissal afterward restored my anonymity.

It occurred to me to grab her hand, to stand and follow her, to cry out, "Meli, wait!"

But I didn't. I sat like a coward and let the shame soak through me.

Abbie spoke first. "That was harsh."

"I deserved it."

"Maybe once," David said. "A year ago. But now?"

I shook my head. "Whenever. She might still be hurting."

"She's not hurting," Abbie said, and jerked her chin toward where Meli had rejoined her friends. "In fact, I'll bet she only decided on that one because she saw you here."

"Saw you happy," David added.

"Another ex-girlfriend?" Jada said.

"From a long time ago."

"How long?"

I looked at Abbie and David. "What's it been? Eighteen months?"

"Since Tony died?" Abbie asked and it didn't sting; it felt like a normal milestone, like graduation or a trip somewhere. "About that."

"She was part of the Tony thing?" Jada asked.

I nodded. "Ancient history," I said. "But yeah. And she's been in Sacramento. I haven't seen her since I got back from Barcelona."

"That was nine months ago."

"Really since before you went," David said, "So, yeah, a year and a half."

"Which is like what in dog years?" Abbie asked.

I raised an eyebrow at her. "Is one of us supposed to be a dog in this scenario?" I said, quoting our favorite movie, *When Harry Met Sally*.

She played along, raising her arms in a shrug.

"Who is the dog?" I asked.

"You are."

"I am? I am the dog?"

David cackled at our reenactment and we all cracked up except Jada, who looked angry.

I slipped my arm around her back and tried to kiss her cheek, but she pulled away.

"Don't be mad," I said.

Abbie and David were polite enough to turn away and face the stage.

"Jada, please?"

She shrugged off my arm.

"It's from a movie. We can watch it when we get back. I own it."

Her eyes narrowed. "You think *that's* the problem."

"Don't be like that."

"I'm not being like anything." But she'd crossed her arms and stared past me.

"Come back." I pulled her to me again, kissed her neck and said into her ear, "I'm not done ruining you for every other man."

She tilted her jaw toward my lips and let me kiss her cheek. "Oh, white boy," she said, smiling, though it didn't reach her eyes, "That was never going to be a thing."

"Then you can ruin me for every other woman," I said, teasing her lips with my own.

"We'll see." She pecked a kiss and sat back again, and we listened to more poets and drank more coffee and at the end of the night we walked back to my place, hand-in-hand.

I never even spoke to Meli.

Thanksgiving loomed and I packed for Tucson with some reluctance, even though we'd been there the last two years. "The new normal," Mom called it. Thanksgiving in Arizona felt unnatural. Thanksgiving should be chilly. There should be a scent in the air of dead leaves and something smoky.

This year the Lincrests were joining us. Joel and Jason's mom had decided to go on a cruise with her new man, and Tabby's family would have their usual big family event. When Mom heard the twins were on their own, she'd invited them to Tucson. I wished we would be going skiing, not golfing, but I'd told the guys to bring clubs and Dad had booked tee times all weekend long.

Abbie came by before leaving to meet her mom in San Luis Obispo for a meditation weekend. David had planned to go home with Alec, Abbie told me, but they'd broken up the night before.

"Apparently when David told Alec he should get tested, Alec took that to mean that David had cheated on him. He wigged. Left saying not to call him because they were done."

"How's David taking it?" I asked.

"He hasn't gotten out of bed yet, so I don't know." She was perched on a bar stool and had taken my water glass for her own.

"It's just initial shock," I said, frowning. "Alec will cool off over the weekend, come back and apologize, and they'll be fine."

She rolled her eyes at me. "I just wish David's broken heart was reason enough to cancel on the Madre. She said to tell him she hoped he'd feel better soon and asked when I planned to arrive."

The phone rang and I heard Marco and Rafael arguing before Marco realized I'd answered and said, "*Hola,* Brian, *como estas?*"

"*Bien, mi amigo, bien. Y tu?*"

Abbie sat up straighter. "If they're coming here," she said in a stage whisper. "I'll stay."

"Oh, you're into dick now?" I said and laughed.

Marco asked what my weekend plans were. Any chance I'd be coming near L.A.?

I said I was meeting Joel and Jason at my parents' place in Arizona and would they like to join us there? Golf and good food and plenty of booze.

Any women? Marco wanted to know.

I laughed. "Negative."

"No, *gracias,* then."

"Abbie says come here and she'll skip meditation with Margo and host you and Rafael in San Francisco. David could use cheering up."

They agreed and I handed the phone to Abbie to make the arrangements. When she hung up, she said I should leave my key so Marco and Rafael could stay in my place. I frowned again and looked around.

"Think of them as house sitters," she said. After she used my phone to call her mom and break their date weekend, Abbie skipped out saying she'd need groceries for the visitors. She took a fifty out of my wallet and my keys with her, kissing me on the cheek before she left. She crossed paths with Jada as she floated through the door, and Jada closed the door behind her, a solemn posture and downcast eyes.

"Abbie's excited for dick this weekend," I said. "Sorry you can't get the same."

She flinched.

"Jada?"

She slunk closer, standing at the end of the kitchen bar and still not making eye contact with me. Her dark hair hung in long roped braids around her face, her skin looked dusted with some kind of sparkling powder. She had a loose zippered sweat jacket on and two tank tops layered underneath.

I started to move closer to her, but she held up a hand to stop me.

A deep breath, then she said, "I want to tell you, but I don't want you to know so I'm trying to decide how to do this."

"What don't you want me to know?" I asked.

"We're done, Brian."

The air left my lungs. Not sure if I expelled it or it simply evaporated, but I could feel a draining, like the deflation of a balloon. Again, I tried to move toward her but again, she held up her hand.

"What does that mean?" My voice was strained, my mind buzzing, a kind of panic burning beneath my skin.

"You were gone for a long time." She lifted her gaze, stared right at me and repeated, "A *long* time."

"But I'm back now. To stay."

She squared her shoulders, tossed the forward braids behind her shoulder. "And I'm leaving."

My throat constricted and I took a breath that barely made it through my lips before I sputtered it back out again, rambling, "I guess we should have talked before I went."

Her brow wrinkled and she said, "About what?"

"Long term. What's next. What this is." I wagged a finger between us.

She glared at me then.

"I care about you," I said. The other three words lingered there, somewhere, just behind my eyes, but I couldn't say them. Not now. Not to keep her. Not to beg her to stay.

"You *care?*" Her voice was mocking.

I was fucking this up. It was a test of some kind and I was failing.

"I'm with you. There isn't anyone else, Jada."

Her chin jerked up and we made eye contact again, but only for a second before she looked away.

"Oh," I said as it hit me. This wasn't about what I'd thought it was about. "You were with someone else?" Disbelief now combined with shock and I had to move, standing wouldn't work anymore.

Jada backed up as I came around the counter and held on to one of the bar stools. Palms flat on the seat that still had Abbie's warmth on it, I leaned into the conversation, trying to make sense of what she was saying.

"What exactly are you doing right now?" I asked her, the hurt deep enough that I couldn't imagine what the next moment would bring.

"I'm breaking up with you," she said. That hard gaze again. No tears, no remorse even.

"But what if I love you?" I could hear the question in my own voice, and I regretted it. Stupid. Fucking stupid to have even considered this a thing.

She actually laughed a bitter sound that emerged from somewhere deeper than her throat.

"You don't," she said matter-of-factly.

"But *he* does?" Not sure why I was torturing myself with this, but I had to know.

Her arms crossed over her chest, the sweat jacket straining on her wrists where she'd threaded her thumbs through small holes. "We were just kickin' it, him and me. It got a little more intense a while back and I got scared. So, I had you. But *we*—" She wagged a finger between us, mocking my earlier gesture with a sneer. "—were *never* going to be a thing."

"Coulda fooled me." Unbidden, thoughts of having her in my arms, underneath me, in the shower, slick and wet and warm and willing rolled behind my eyes like a montage of pleasure and closeness. She'd given herself to me. But not just me. "Maybe you did, actually."

She lifted her chin. "I did care about you," she said.

"Did?"

"Do."

"Then why end it?"

"He's like me. We understand each other."

"I don't follow," I said.

"Because you don't *know* me." She rolled her eyes to the ceiling, shifted her weight at her hips. When she looked back at me, an angry mask had narrowed her gaze and stretched her lips taut. "You don't. You can't."

"It's the guy from before, isn't it? Bro-code guy." I might have deserved Meli's scorn that night so many weeks ago, humiliation even, but I didn't deserve this. "You were having sex with someone else while you were with me?" Outrage took over, a righteous indignation that was more familiar than the heartbreak of her giving herself to someone else. "Do you know the risks of that?"

She took in a quick breath like a gasp. "Not while you were here."

"But while I was gone."

She nodded, finally a little ashamed.

"Just once?"

"Does it matter?" The salt in her voice was back.

Did it? I had once questioned Kacie about the exact same thing. It wasn't hard to draw the lines between how I'd treated the women in my life, even as far back as my freshman-year-roommate's girlfriend. I took her to bed, and when he'd broken up with her over it, I'd ignored her, too. Tony stood up for girls against guys like me. Jason put women on pedestals and worshipped them. Joel had been committed to the same woman for five years, and Chris had renewed a valuable connection with Sarah. But I'd always taken what I wanted from whomever would give it. My Barcelona shrink had tried to unpack that with me. I'd resisted.

I wasn't much older than Jada, and she'd always seemed older than me, but maybe, in this one thing, I was more experienced. Maybe we *had* wanted different things from one another. I thought I was ready for a commitment. Standing in my one-room apartment in San Francisco, emotions raging like a hurricane, I pushed my hand through my hair and held it on the back of my neck for a moment.

"I could forgive you," I said at last, and I think I meant it. My Barcelona shrink would have been proud. "I could forgive you and love you. I could do that."

But she shook her head. "No," she said. "You are who you are."

"I'd be willing to try." But I whispered it, and not even I believed it.

"I don't want you to *try*." Her whisper matched mine and she said, "I thought when I came over that maybe," and her voice hitched, so I seized the possibility that this was a mistake.

"Okay, so let's try to make something work," I said quickly because now I was apologizing. Somehow, though she had cheated, and life was upside down from just twenty minutes ago, I would accept whatever she would give me. *What the actual fuck was wrong with me?*

"Let's try," I repeated.

"No."

But I wasn't expecting to lose. I moved closer and she didn't back away. Reaching for her, I pulled her to me, circled my arms around her, hugged her close. And she let me, she wasn't breathing but she let me hold her for just a second. When I turned my face to kiss her, she jumped back, broke the embrace, and shook her head.

"Are you in love with him?" I asked.

"Maybe." Barely a squeak.

"But either way, you're done with me."

She nodded.

A long minute between us during which all the possibilities of life without Jada streamed through my head like a montage.

"I guess that's it, then."

She finally breathed, like relief that I'd given up the fight and she turned, braids swinging, and started for the door. I watched and waited for her to stop, to look over her shoulder, to say something else. Anything. But she didn't. She opened the door, slipped through, and pulled it closed behind her. And she was gone. And we were done.

TUCSON
NOVEMBER, 2000

The third tee box at El Conquistador Golf Club in Tucson is spitting distance from the fifth-hole green. As we were climbing out of our carts, we heard loud whooping from the nearby finish.

Glancing over, my dad chuckled. "Jay Lowery," he said. "His boys are in for the holiday, too." Then he waved over the cart path at the foursome that was stabbing the flag back into the hole and making their way toward the carts.

"Hey, Alan," the man I assume was Jay called. "Got your boys out with you?"

Dad nodded. "You remember my son, Brian," he said, hand on my shoulder, "And these are my adopted sons, Jason and Joel Lincrest." His pride was evident.

"Dean, Louis, and Evan," said Jay, waiving toward his sons. They looked older than us, but not by much. "Evan's on leave."

After we'd nodded and headed up to our tee box, Dad said, "All he talks about is that younger one being a soldier. Guess he didn't do so great in school, but the army's been good for him.

Every time I see Jay, Evan's written another letter to his mother, sent another set of pictures from overseas." Dad smiled. "*See the world* and all that other marketing stuff."

"That's the Navy," Joel said. "Army guys get all the shit assignments."

"No thanks," Jason said. "I'd rather go overseas Brian's way."

"Hostels and outdoor showers?" I asked.

"Bars, flight attendants, and professional soccer players." Jason winked at me.

"You'll have to tell them about Manila," Dad said. "Not exactly Paris."

I shrugged. "Nah, but it had its *charms*." The last word I said in Tagolig, *bighani* meaning "seductions" and laughed, and the twins laughed with me though I felt certain neither of them knew the word. It probably just sounded dirty enough to imply naked women.

Dad teed up his ball and took a few practice swings.

"You could do something with those language skills in the service," he said, it was an absent observation, not the kind of career pressure he had been so bad about years earlier. I'd gotten used to his recognizing my abilities with an index of how they'd be put to use in the CIA. It was his only point of reference, having spent his entire career at Langley.

The third hole was a par 3 and Dad's shot sailed toward the green, dropping down about three feet from the pin. Joel followed, landed his ball about ten feet from Dad's. Jason's went left and ended up in a bunker and mine followed his, coming up short of the sand, but a chip shot from the green, nonetheless.

It was 9:30 a.m. on the day after Thanksgiving and we had enjoyed a full table the day before. Mom had put Jason and I to work in the kitchen while Joel worked with Dad in the office to upgrade his home network. Jason peeled potatoes and I shelled hard-boiled eggs while we told Mom stories about Barcelona.

The two weeks Jason had stayed with me had been bleary but fun.

We all acknowledged the kind of depths I'd been in just five months after Tony's death. Thanksgiving, a year and eight months later, and I felt transformed. Time really had worked its magic on me. Or so Mom observed. Then she'd cocked her head at Jason and said, cryptically, "Now what are we going to do about you?"

Friday morning on the golf course, Jason and I sharing a cart, I followed him down off the tee box after my shot went left, and as we dropped our clubs in our bags I said, "What was Mom talking about yesterday?"

Jason looked up at me, his brown eyes under the rim of his ball cap, and grinned. "Which part? It was a long day and we talked about a lot of stuff."

"About having to do something about you. You know. Since Tony?"

Jason shrugged.

We walked around opposite sides of the cart and sat down. He had the wheel and pressed the pedal, so we followed Dad and Joel down the cart path toward the green.

"Have you decided how much longer you'll play in Michigan?"

"Nope."

"Any word on a contract for this season?"

"Nope."

"That sucks."

"Yeah."

"Maybe you could take classes online? Get some credits toward a degree?"

"Maybe."

We each grabbed a wedge club and went to try to chip onto the green. Jason did, right out of the sand and between Joel and

Dad. I struck the ball fat and it whizzed over the green and into the rough on the other side.

"Tick tock," Dad called, referring to the shoulders-only movement I was meant to have used for the chip shot.

I waved. "Yeah, I know."

After I crossed the green, they all putted. Then I chipped on from the other side, chased their putts into the hole. As we traveled from the third green to the fourth tee box, I poured a handful of sunflower seeds into my palm.

"Joel's on me about school," Jason said. "Says I should be getting some certifications or credits at least so when hockey's over . . ." He trailed off and shook his head.

"And?"

"And I have no idea what I'm going to do after hockey. Hell, I have no idea what I'm doing now." He laughed, but there was no amusement in it. "Sometimes I'm just tired, ya know?"

"Fuck, I know."

"I didn't think I could be this tired. Not at twenty-three."

By then I had a cheek full of sunflower seeds, so I just nodded.

Jason lifted a canned beer out of the cupholder and pressed it to his lips, taking a healthy pull before wincing and saying, "Hair of the dog."

I laughed and choked on a seed and coughed and spit, and then we had arrived at the fourth tee and he slammed on the brakes, which made me jerk and choke again. Standing, coughing, spitting, I tried to breathe. After struggling for a second, I spit the whole wad out and coughed until my eyes poured sizzling tears and my lungs were clear.

"Just don't hurl," Jason said, spitting off to the side.

"Thanks, dick."

"Everything okay?" Dad asked.

"Guy drives like a maniac," I said.

"Ate too many seeds," Jason replied.

"Just the fourth hole, boys," Dad said. "Let's not get too out of hand."

I wiped at my cheeks. "Noted."

I looked to Joel, who was grinning. "You gonna survive?"

"Asphyxiation on sunflower seeds isn't a thing," I said.

"Yet," Joel said, and nodded gravely.

I opened a beer, downed half of it, and wiped my face with a golf towel. The others teed off and took turns making fun of me for being unable to handle my seeds. Once they established I was in no real danger, the entire thing became a source of comedy. Mostly for them.

We continued to play, Dad and Joel having the better game, Jason and I managing a few good shots per hole, and when we made the turn, we saw Jay Lowery's family again, emerging from the clubhouse as Dad and Jason headed in. It was their turn to stock the coolers, and Joel and I waved off going inside to total our scorecards. As we stood comparing cards, the Lowerys emerged and Jay headed straight for me.

"Your old man said you'd be here this weekend," he said, extending his hand. "Also said you're a damn fine writer earning an advanced degree up in San Francisco."

I returned the firm-clasp-handshake-with-eye-contact and grinned.

"Doing my best, sir," I said.

Joel shook hands with one of the brothers.

"Meant to mention it to Alan inside. We're having a barbeque this evening," Jay said. "Would be glad to have you and your folks, too." He nodded toward Joel. Then looked back toward the clubhouse and back at Joel again, puzzled.

"Twins," I said.

Joel grinned. "You're not seeing double."

"Not yet, Pops," the nearest son said.

Jay Lowery chuckled. "Guess there's time yet for that. Been

doing a lot of golf and the stuff that goes with it since I retired." His raised his eyebrows like arching caterpillars on his forehead. "My wife still teaches at the university so it's not a house party, mind, but we do have four college-aged kids and a pool."

"My sister's sorority will be there," the brother said to Joel.

"I'll run it by Joan and Alan," I said.

"Do that," Jay said. "Hit 'em straight."

Then they were back in their carts and rumbling off toward the tenth tee.

"Sorority girls," I said.

"Swimming pool," Joel replied.

"Jason," we said together.

"And me, too," I admitted. "Jada's done with me, so I guess that makes me a free man."

"I'm sorry for it," Joel said. "I liked her."

"Me, too, but she liked her ex-boyfriend more than she liked me." I tugged my glove back on my hand, folded the Velcro over to secure it, and then clapped my palms together with a satisfying leather *thwump*.

Joel took his baseball cap off and ran a hand through his hair. "Guess I've been off the market for a while. Planning to ask Tabby to marry me over Christmas."

"Good for you."

"I haven't told Jason."

"Why not?"

Joel shrugged. "Things have been moving kind of fast for him since Tony died. He thinks Chris graduating and buying the house, me selling the company and moving back to Pittsburgh, and Kacie out in Seattle..." He drifted off. "He thinks we're all moving on. Shit, you've been on three continents in the last two years." He settled his hat back on his head. "He's struggling, Brian."

"Like how?"

Joel shook his head. "I'm not sure. He won't talk to me about it. Just keeps saying he's fine but he's not."

"Well, Michigan's cold," I said, trying to make a joke. "It might just be he hates where he lives."

"And what he does. And who he knows. And being away from all of us." Joel's brown eyes met mine then. "Talk to him, will ya?"

"And say what exactly?"

"Fuck if I know."

"Tell him you're making plans, Joel. Be honest about it. He'll only hate that you told me first." I grinned. "And congratulations. It's a big deal and good thing. I'm happy for you, man."

Jason and Dad staggered down the club steps then, each carrying a cooler and a pair of shots. We stood in a circle and toasted the shots.

"For the Fridays that feel like Saturdays," Joel said.

"And all the days ahead," Dad added.

"*Salúd*," I said. And we drank.

Two hours later we'd finished the round—my back nine score slightly better than the front nine—and were cleaning clubs and loading the car in the parking lot. Dad offered to buy lunch and we all agreed. He and Joel strode ahead as I lit a cigarette. I said I'd be there after I finished the beer can in my hand. I'd mentioned the barbecue to Jason and Dad, and they seemed interested. Jason in the girls and Dad in forging a stronger friendship with Jay Lowery.

Jason took a smoke from me and lit it, and we stood quietly for a few minutes before he finally said, "Joel's going to ask Tabby to marry him at Christmas. He doesn't know I know."

"Does she?"

Jason shook his head. "Mom told me."

"You okay with it?"

He shrugged. "Guess it's to be expected, right? They've been together forever and it's that time, right? Shit or get off the pot?"

"How very romantic," I teased.

Jason spit toward the gravel edging the parking lot.

"He loves her," I said. "And he's making a life for himself."

"Everybody seems to be."

I took another long drag and waited that one out. He might have something to confess. Something to get off his chest. Or he might be waiting for me to contradict him. I'd known the twins a long time, almost as long as I knew Tony, but I didn't really know how much pressure Jason needed to say what he was really thinking or feeling. Worse, I wasn't sure I wanted to know. Things had been working for me in a certain direction, too. I would defend my thesis next semester and be interviewing for jobs in the spring. It was unlikely I'd stay in San Francisco, but I wasn't sure where I would go, either.

"It's a big world," I finally said, settling on a platitude that would leave the conversation open to anything.

"And he's not in it anymore."

"Who?"

Jason met my eyes.

"Oh. Right."

"You're tied to him for me, did you know that? When I look at you, it's hard not to remember him. To expect to see him. And then to know what he did, and it all comes back around sometimes." He was awkward, that much about Jason had always been true, he was awkward with explanations and the deeper meaning of things and events. He had a kind of film re-enactment style to him, like he was responding the way he thought he should instead of how he might naturally be.

The Arizona sun was casting our shadows across the pavement. I finished my cigarette and tossed it to the ground.

"Maybe we need to hang out more," I said. "Then I won't be a reminder all the time."

Jason nodded.

"Or maybe you've just had too many beers for the middle of the day and you're getting maudlin." If he didn't know the word, he didn't let on.

Another nod, another drag on his own cigarette, and then he tossed it down.

"Come on, brother. Let's get lunch. Go home and nap. Then go to a pool party tonight and find some pretty desert flower to climb all over you." I clapped him on the shoulder. "Maybe this weekend won't be a total sausage fest."

Fed, showered, napped, and afternoon-footballed, Joel and Jason and I piled into the back of Dad's SUV to head over to the Lowerys'. Mom had called Jay's wife, Lisa, to see what we could bring, and we'd settled on a cooler of beer, a bottle of Jack, and a vegetable tray.

Pittsburgh had beaten its rival, West Virginia, in a game Jason napped through. The junior quarterback for Pittsburgh was supposed to be pretty good, and Joel raged each time he threw an incompletion (10) or interception (3). Dad liked breaking down the play of the receivers and the offensive line. Mom and I played Scrabble on the kitchen table. Afterwards, Joel called Tabby and I showered. I wondered what Kacie was doing this weekend. If she was covering the Washington State game. If she was with her parents in Colorado. If she had forgiven me yet for showing up in Seattle.

I guessed maybe we were reminders for one another. I hadn't given Kacie a lot of thought, but being around Jason made me think of her more frequently. When I came out of the shower, he was laying across the bed in the first guest room, the one I used. The rooms were connected by the bathroom, and the door from the bathroom into his room was closed. I glanced at it and then at him.

"Joel's talking to Tabby in there," he said.

"Did you tell him you know about the engagement?"

"In the last five minutes since I woke up and he kicked me out?" Jason blew a stream of air out through his lips, making them vibrate, and turned the page on the issue of Golf Digest he was glancing through. The cover said, "Keep it Simple." I smirked.

"He's worried about you," I said.

"Always."

"Says you're struggling."

"Maybe."

"With what, exactly?"

"Life. The future. I dunno."

"Wanna talk about it?"

"Not really."

"Good. Let's get drunk again and flirt with some pretty girls we'll never have to see after tonight."

"You might see them again."

"Nah," I said. "Sorority girls get over me pretty fast. Faster than exchange students, flight attendants, and fiction workshop writers combined."

"Ladies' man," Jason sung, sitting up and tossing the magazine aside. "Get the fuck outta there so I can shower." He walked past me and turned in the doorway. "I'm glad you're doing better, Brian. For real."

"Thanks, man. And you know if you did need to talk . . . " I drifted off and shrugged.

"I know."

The Lowerys' backyard had lights strung across it, a bubbling hot tub adjacent to a swimming pool, and a set-up for a live band. About three dozen people milled around inside and out, a good mix of college-aged people like us and parent-aged people like Joan and Alan. My parents were enjoying conversation with our hosts when Jason and I followed Joel onto the patio. His conversation with Tabby had been about forty-five minutes long and ended with her extracting a promise from him to "not do anything stupid with Brian tonight." The declaration had me slapping my hand across my heart and saying, "Ouch," in a sarcastic tone.

Jason just laughed it off, saying Joel should have told Tabby I'd grown up some in the last year and could be trusted to enjoy a party full of strangers like a mature adult. Besides, my parents would be there. When Joel said he had tried that defense, Tabby had snorted and replied, "I'll believe *that* when I see it."

"And she didn't mean the part about your parents," Joel said. "In fact, she said to tell you hi," he said to my mom as she crossed the kitchen with the veggie tray.

Thirty minutes later, Joel was in a conversation around the outdoor television screen with a group of guys watching the highlight reel. Jason pulled two Jello shooters off a tray offered to him by an adorable blonde in a half top and cut-off shorts. He handed me one and said, "Let's get fucked up."

The Lowery brothers were excellent hosts. The eldest one, Dean, had staked his claim over the TV area and was leading the discussion over the day's NCAA football action. Another, Louis, I think, was introducing some musician-looking people to a small group gathered near the stage. And the third, Evan, climbed out of the pool dripping wet and came to where Jason and I were standing over the hot tub.

"You're a soldier," I said, after we introduced ourselves again and he welcomed us to the party.

"Yeah, enlisted two years ago when I couldn't get into college and didn't really want to go anyway. Didn't have a skill. Didn't have a job. Needed to get out of my parents' house." He wasn't particularly good looking, but the military service had made him strong, and more than one woman was watching him where he stood dripping on the pool deck.

"Sounds like Jay here," I said. "He's been playing hockey since dropping out of college. Farm team for the Red Wings." I pushed his elbow forward with my own.

"But not Brian," Jason said. "He's one of them grad school freaks."

I grinned. "Not exactly built for manual labor."

"Shit," Jason said. "The docks in Barcelona weren't exactly investment banking."

"You worked the docks in Barcelona?"

I shrugged. "Needed an excuse to stay and a job that didn't let me think too much."

"Man, I hear that." Evan raised a beer, and Jason and I both knocked ours against it. "Y'all bring swimsuits?" He waved toward the hot tub.

"Yeah, man," Jason said right as I said, "Nah, man, thanks."

We looked at one another and started laughing. Evan looked between us and said, "Suit yourselves." Then he turned away from us, told the hot tub occupants to slide over, and slipped into the steaming water.

"Sure you don't want in?" Jason asked. "There's some fine lookin' women in there."

We both watched as the swimmers moved in and out of the hot tub and the pool. The evening had cooled off, but there was a slight steam rising from both indicating they were heated. I glanced at one of the deck chairs on the opposite side and saw a woman curled up under a towel in a guy's lap.

"I'm good," I said, noticing an empty lounge chair on our side of the pool. "Just gonna stretch out I think." I indicated the chair and Jason nodded. He disappeared inside to look for the bag Mom brought that had suits and towels for each of us. I sat down, stretched out my legs, and waited.

Beyond the strands of deck lights, the Arizona sky was black and cloudless. To my right I heard the band members take the stage and a few errant keystrokes and guitar strums. Then the microphone announced, "We're Edgar's Babies," and, to a smattering of applause, the first song began. I listened to the lyrics, to the song, to the melody and musicianship. I heard the construction of a kind of story they were telling and sucked back the rest of my beer just enjoying being out there, available, for the entertainment of the night.

At some point, Jason returned and slid into the hot tub next to Evan, having handed me a fresh beer from the cooler on his way to the spa. I watched them talking and laughing a bit, girls repositioning themselves to be closer to him, learning his name and telling him theirs. I imagined what the conversation must have been. As if my own inner narrative were read-able, I heard, "I'm Candy. What's your name again? Hi, Candy, I'm Mega-Hot-Hockey-player," the first part of the sentence delivered in a squeaky voice, the second part in a deeper, silly voice.

I turned to my right and in the chair beside me, watching the hot tub, sat a woman with a sweatshirt on and bare feet.

"How did you know he plays hockey?" I asked her, amused at her narrating the scene not unlike my internal monologue had been doing.

"Tattoo on his shoulder," she said.

"He doesn't really talk like that. I'm Brian."

"Neither does she. I'm Skye."

"As in Jay-Lowery's-daughter-this-is-your-house-your-brothers-are-scary Skye?"

"As in you-haven't-changed-since-I-saw-you-in-Yeddy's-that-time-you're-still-hot-enough-to-make-panties-melt Brian?"

I laughed, enjoying the back and forth with this woman and wondering why I hadn't placed Jay Lowery as the guy Dad had pointed out to me at Yeddy's. It was Thanksgiving, 1999, when I'd come here from Barcelona and was mostly disoriented by Mom and Dad's new Arizona lifestyle. Dad had said Jay took his daughter there before school every day, but we'd seen them just after ten in the morning. She was in college then, and probably now.

"What's so scary about my brothers?" she prodded.

"Dean has a stockbroker, Louis knows the band, and Evan kills people for a living."

She frowned, pretty lips turned down. "He's not an assassin."

"So, he's your favorite?"

She grinned.

"Sorry I didn't recognize you. Also, I thought you were a lot younger when I saw you last year. Jay said his daughter's sorority was coming tonight and it didn't connect that . . ."

"That I might be old enough for you?"

I laughed again. "Okay, sure. That."

"I know about you. Swimmer, writer, foreign-language prodigy, spent a semester in Spain. My mom wants me to marry you."

"Let's make that happen." I reached out my beer and she clanked hers against mine. We both drank deeply.

"I'm an art history major. Heading to Spain after graduation."

"Plan to restore or curate?"

"Restore."

"Spain's your place then. Lots of old frescos and mosaics."

"And money."

"That, too."

We sat quietly for a bit listening to the band, and I realized we'd been pretty much shouting over it. I slid to the left on my chair and jerked my head to invite her over.

"Come closer," I said.

She stood and Holy Mary Mother of God those legs. Long, tanned, smooth, and emergent from the sweatshirt hoodie like she'd been hiding them as weapons. When she stepped toward me, her thigh was at eye level and it took sucking down another gulp from my beer to keep me from reaching out to touch her. She turned her back on the pool, faced me, and sat down on the end of my chair. I shifted so my legs were on either side, and she did the same, and we were knee-to-knee with a gap of space between us.

She stared at me.

"Are you still swimming?" she asked.

"Three times a week. Do you swim?"

She shook her head. "Not anymore. Too many old wounds."

"Like injuries?"

"Like unmet expectations."

"Scholarships?"

"Olympics."

"No shit."

She nodded. "That's how we got here from Ohio. Didn't Dad tell you? Chasing the coach who was going to make me an Olympian."

"What happened?"

She shrugged. "Not fast enough. Shouldn't everything be that easy? Just not fast enough, and no amount of trying and wishing and spending was going to make it so. A clock said, 'nope,' and it was over."

I noticed then the broad shoulders, long fingers, and slicked-back hair under the hoodie. She was at home on deck. She wore no makeup. Her lips were puffy and pink after having pressed the beer bottle against them. And biting them. As she did now, under my scrutiny.

"I never made it that far," I said. "State champ in high school and left it far behind when I went to college in '95."

"In' 95?" She pretended to gape. "You're so old!"

"Yep," I agreed. "And getting older."

We both glanced at the hot tub. The girl Skye had called Candy was sitting on Jason's lap now as the temperature had dropped, and the pool was abandoned and the hot tub was packed. She had her arm draped over his shoulder and her lips on his ear, talking. Now and then he would laugh and she would frown.

"Failing basket weaving isn't funny!" Skye pretended to pout.

"Aw, baby, you're so much more talented than that," I said, affecting the deep voice she'd used for Jason earlier. "Surely your skills are better in another art."

"Like what?" Skye pouted.

"Interpretive dance?" The question in that funny voice cracked us both up, and Skye and I started laughing. The band's song hit the chorus just then and got louder, and we took a minute to drink our beers and glance around in a comfortable pause of conversation.

The next time I looked at Jason, Candy had her tongue in his ear, and I grinned. He needed that. He needed attention and I was glad he was getting it.

Skye caught me watching and said, "She's a tease."

"And he's a flirt."

"She has a boyfriend."

"Is he here?"

Skye shook her head. "Home for the holiday in Phoenix."

"I'll let Jason know."

She nodded thoughtfully then said, "Would he stop?"

I shrugged. "Maybe. At some point. But a little kissing never hurt anyone, and her boyfriend is her problem, not his."

Skye seemed to consider that for a moment before saying, "Would you stop?"

"Stop what?"

"Stop flirting with a girl if she had a boyfriend?"

The band's song ended and the last word sounded louder than necessary, and I laughed at her and then joined some others in clapping for the musicians. Skye looked embarrassed and pushed a drying lock of hair behind her ear. I reached out and tugged the hoodie back, showing her whole face. Her shoulders came up slightly. She wrapped the length of her hair into a tail and wound it into a bun on the back of her head. Tucking it underneath, she secured it, though it sagged a little, and then bit her lip again.

"Would you?" she asked again.

I cocked my head at her. Did I want this? A flirtation? A make-out session with my parents' friends' daughter? Someone I might very well see again in Arizona? Someone who might be a relationship contender. She was cute. Funny. Interested. And I remembered Barcelona shrink asking me why I was so willing to have sex with these women. I'd said, "Because they are willing to have sex with me."

Skye had sought me out. She knew about me. She was interested.

"That depends," I said.

"On what?"

I leaned in then, sliding my legs wider, forcing her legs wider, too, and drifting my fingertip up over her knee and thigh, to the edge of the sweatshirt. I followed the seam, to her inner thigh, where I could feel heat coming through the swim suit bottoms she wore, and let just my fingertip linger there, as my nose drifted up her jawline to her ear so she could hear me say, "On whether she wants me to stop."

She was holding her breath and let it out, slowly and against my neck and said, "God, you're good."

I pecked a kiss on her cheek and slid back, pulling my hand away, lifting the beer for another drink and grinning at her. We sat for a while just talking about Spain and reasons to go abroad, how long to stay, ways to get someone else to pay for it. Skye said her Spanish wasn't very good, so we practiced a few phrases together and I told her how my Barcelona friends thought I was a redneck because I spoke Latin American Spanish.

Eventually the late games ended, and Joel wandered over and Skye and me—having settled into a healthy but companionable distance—welcomed him in to bring us up to speed on the scores. Jason appeared then, too, fingers pruned and towel-wrapped, and settled into the chair Skye had abandoned with Candy on his lap.

The band took a break, and Mom and Dad finally emerged, asked us how much longer we wanted to stay. Jason and Candy and me and Skye were definitely in the late-night mode. Joel said he'd take them home and come back for us. They said we should all just stay, and they'd come back when we were ready for a ride home. After they left, I told the guys we'd walk it. It wasn't but two miles and fully lined with sidewalks. Skye warned of rattlesnakes and that was when I kissed her for the first time, to shut her up. The band started back up and we cracked another round of beers and at some point, Candy brought a round of shots over, and Skye took mine and I took hers.

Eventually her brothers joined us, and then we were the only ones left—the kitchen cleaned up, the food put away, the band shut down and carried off, and the rest of the sorority retired to wherever they'd come from. Dean offered Joel a cigar and they headed over to the patio to talk about Silicon Valley and venture capitalists. Louis had a girl tucked against his side when he waved goodnight to us all. Evan had two girls with him until the one gave up and told Skye she'd meet her in her room. There were six of us.

"When are you next deployed?" Jason asked Evan.

"I'm halfway through two years in Germany now," he said. "Should be stateside by October. I don't really want to come back. I love it abroad."

"Me too," I said. "My next trip is Paris this spring, two weeks for a conference. Presenting a paper on the unique voice of late-90s realism in the work of Palahniuk and Eugenides."

"*Fight Club* and *The Virgin Suicides?*" Skye asked, and I fell a little bit in love with her.

"He wrote *Fight Club*, yeah, but I'm using *Invisible Monsters.*"

"I would love to see a feminist treatment of *Fight Club.*"

"So, write it," I had pulled her against me at some point to make room for Joel and she hadn't moved away after he followed Dean to the patio. I kissed the top of her head like I'd known her forever and she snuggled in tighter against me.

"For which Art History class?" she asked. "Like I said, I only wish I was an English major. I had to pick something even less useful." She threaded her fingers through mine.

"Not a fan of Paris," Evan said, side-eying me a little as I snuggled with his sister. But his own hand was buried deep between the thighs of the girl on his lap, a towel covering what he was doing to her, but the way her eyes were squeezed tight gave away at least some kind of contact.

Candy stood and said she was going inside for a glass of water. Jason followed. I checked my watch and glanced over my shoulder at Joel. He nodded. Thirty minutes.

Then Evan and the girl gave up the ruse, and were blatantly intimate next to us and Skye turned away from them, whispering, "Should we go somewhere?"

Untangled, standing, and walking away, she led with my hand in hers. We followed the patio around the side of the house and then she pulled me to her, stumbling a little with the effort. I caught her, wrapped my arms around her, and pressed my lips to her jaw just below her ear.

"You should fall in love with me," she said.

"I should, huh?" I kissed down her neck, pushing the hoodie

aside to reach her skin, and breathed against her. "How would your boyfriend feel about that?"

"We won't tell him," she said.

"I think it's better if we just say goodnight."

"And then?"

"And then nothing," I said, pulling back and bringing our hands between us, a slight squeeze on hers. "Then we just stay friends. Our parents will, too. Convivial."

"Convivial," she repeated and bit her lip.

I should have left then. Gathered the twins—one of whom was enjoying a smoke and the other was likely balls deep in Candy's throat—and walked home avoiding rattlesnakes. Instead, I let her kiss me again, this time less sweet and more urgent, and decided her faithfulness was her boyfriend's problem, not mine. Not tonight.

Thirty minutes passed and Joel let out a whistle from the patio. I pulled my hand out from between Skye's thighs as she shuddered around my soaked fingers. I rolled the damp swimsuit bottoms back up over her bare ass. Clutching her to me, pressing the hard length of myself against her—hoping it would subside, not get worse—I thanked her.

"You're beautiful," I said, kissing her softly, and then squeezing her hip, tilting my forehead to hers in that sincere closeness pose, I added, "Can I see you again?"

On the walk home, Joel mused that the streets were empty enough for us to walk on them, away from the brush that crowded the sidewalks and might hide snakes. I told him it was late in the year and they were likely already deep underground. Jason said he didn't trust my knowledge of wildlife. So, we walked down the middle of the road two and a half miles to my parents' house.

"Candy," Jason said. "That was worth it."

"Any chance you'll see her again?" Joel asked.

"Nah, she's got a boyfriend in Phoenix."

"Perfect," I said. "Skye's great, too. She had a very small bikini on under that hoodie."

"Gotta love a pool party," Joel said. "Remember Tony's parents had those barbeques all the time when we were in middle school? All of Gavin's high-school friends would be there." He grinned. "Tony had the biggest crush on that one girl. What was her name?"

"Liza. Crush nothin. She took his virginity."

"No shit," Jason said.

"For real. She was like seventeen, we were fourteen. Her boyfriend dumped her, Tony consoled her, a few kisses, some hands-in-the-pants and Tony was in business."

"That fucker lost his virginity at fourteen?" Joel asked.

"To a redhead," I confirmed. "Never lied about that."

We all kind of soaked in the warmth of the memory, sharing it and not feeling too sad about it. Maybe even feeling glad about knowing him.

"I fucking miss him," Jason said, a little bit melancholier than he had been.

Saturday was more football and late in the day, Skye and Evan came by with mom's platter and stretched out on the couches to watch a game with us. I let her snuggle against me even as Mom raised her eyebrows at me. Then the three of us played Scrabble and Mom won, like she usually does, and Skye asked if I'd ever won, and Mom pulled all the scoresheets out of the box to Skye's incredulous stare. Not once. I had never, ever beaten my mom at Scrabble. Skye cackled with delight and said she'd like to know Mom's secret.

When Evan said it was time to go, Skye reluctantly agreed. I walked her to the door and pulled her into the dark alcove of my parents' front stoop for some heavy making out. Clinging, panting, wild hands, the kind of passion a new thing brings.

"Break up," I hissed. "I'll be back for Christmas. Break up with your boyfriend."

She shook her head, rubbing her lips against mine and said, "We'll see." Then she was gone.

Inside, Mom said, "So?"

And I said, "Jada's done with me. Kacie and Meli are long gone. I'm not a monk."

"She has a boyfriend."

"That's his problem," I said.

Mom gave me a sad look. "Don't you deserve better, Brian?"

"No," I said. "No, I really don't."

December, 2000

Our last writers' workshop of the year was a week before Christmas, and we didn't read—just had some hot cider and cookies and talked about the year.

Sara was planning to travel for a few days over the holiday. She had located her sister, estranged since they were teenagers, and begun a tentative correspondence with her. Being invited to spend Christmas with her in New Mexico was a big step forward. In our walks home and through her pieces in workshop, I had learned Sara's mother's second marriage was dangerous—for her and for Sara and her sister. Though the stepfather had never touched Sara, he hadn't prevented Tony, her stepbrother, from bullying and harassing them both. Sara's sister had run away at fourteen and Sara had endured Tony's brutal attention for five years before finally graduating high school and leaving.

Sara's resentment toward her mother, who was still in Salinas with her husband, was raw and honest. She called the woman by her first name, never Mom, and she judged mercilessly her willingness to expose her daughters to suffering because she was afraid to be alone. Sara's sister's escape was in conjunction with a robbery of a local convenience store and the disappearance of an eighteen-year-old delinquent, whom Sara believed her sister had fallen in love with. We edged around the inappropriateness of that, and Sara seemed resigned that good or bad, he'd offered her sister a way out. Apparently, he was long gone now, but her sister had landed on her feet and settled in New Mexico with a job, a place to live, and a pair of female roommates.

"It's like that Drew Barrymore movie, *Boys on the Side*," she said. "The three of them in some kind of sisterhood."

"That's a good thing, right?"

She shrugged, and I guessed maybe she was a little bit jealous.

"Enjoy the holiday with her," I said. "And try to focus on the now and what's next. Not what came before."

"Oh, okay," she said, a smirk twisting her lips.

"I'm serious. You're an accomplished woman with a job, skills, and a talent for memoir."

"And you're a hypocrite." The tone and her smile took the sting out of the remark. She added, "Any chance you'll take your own advice?"

Staring deep into my cup, I murmured, "It's not that easy for me."

"Which part? The 'now' or the 'what's next'?" Sara stared at me, waiting for eye contact. The room rustled around us: low conversations about shopping and parties and families and gifts, paper plates and plastic cups folded and clasped and emptied and refilled. Below that, a quiet speaker played an instrumental version of "The First Noel."

"Just be yourself," I said at last. "She'll love you." Then I smiled at her in what I hoped was an encouraging way.

"Told you not to fall for her," she said, changing the subject.

"Yes, you did warn me." I'd told Sara Jada broke up with me before Thanksgiving. How she'd cheated on me, confessed, somehow made me feel bad about it, and then disappeared. I assumed she graduated. I guessed she went to L.A. I really didn't know, and it wasn't any of my business.

"Are you sad?" she asked between bites of a Gingerbread cookie. "Also, is this weird?" She held it up and she'd dismembered him so only the head and torso remained.

"Disturbing, really." I drank deeply from the apple cider and said, "You know what this needs?"

"Bourbon?"

"Prosecco."

Sara hummed. "Yes," she whispered. "Bubbly and crisp."

"Except you don't drink," I said.

"No, but you do. And characters do. So, it's worth imagining, right?"

Then Ed wandered over and congratulated me for finishing my MFA coursework. I would present and defend my thesis next term, and Kittering was confident my committee would be pleased with the work I'd done. His health had begun to decline in earnest, and I worried that he would be forced to retire soon. I did not share these thoughts with Ed, but he said, "I hear they'll be looking for a new chair of the program," and I suspected he knew.

"They won't have to look far. Dr. Gladstone is a fine candidate and the next in line. He'll likely get the position."

Ed thought about this for a moment, stroked his beard in a clichéd wizened professor kind of way and said, "That will be a mistake. Gladstone is a traditionalist. The program won't move forward with him at the helm. They should bring in someone new. Someone fresh."

"It's above my paygrade," I said. "But if you have the ear of the Dean, there's a woman I met in Manila who might be a good candidate. She's between positions, or was last summer, and seemed interested in returning to the West Coast after her time abroad. I think she had a year in Portugal and then would be looking. She recommended I check out Maine. I'll be applying for a residency there." I lifted my cup to have another drink, but it was empty and I wasn't sorry. Cider with no booze was disappointing.

"A woman?" Ed said at the same time Sara said, "Maine?"

"Might be just the shake-up the school needs," I said. "And the right change of pace for me." I had only begun to entertain the idea of a cool, dark, wintery place like Maine. Dr. Raquel Morales, the woman in Manila, had suggested University of Maine as a complete departure from my city-inspired work. She had said I could be the next Thoreau, an American Pastoralist with a bend toward rationality. I had been flattered but not convinced. Then Abbie asked if we could visit Bangor together, in the winter, so she might see the frozen river, and the idea started to gain momentum as a contender.

The conversation turned to how we would all be celebrating the holidays.

"New Year's is always a chance to start over," I said. "What could be more worth celebrating than that?"

"It's the true millennium," Ed said. "People who celebrated it last year were wrong. This one is it. Best to find a memorable place to be."

Sara let her hair fall in her face and set her cup down on the table. "I could use some shiny memories," she said. "To fill the pages."

"Like a photo album?" I asked.

"Like a journal. A book of life." She smiled up at me. "The next chapter."

I imagine healing is the kind of thing we can do in pairs and threes and groups. I felt like over the time we'd been reading together, Sara and I had brought the most brutal of our bad memories to the room and worked through them. More than therapy with the useless Dr. Moses, the writing group had helped me tease out those stories of Tony: Radford, the burning valley, losing his virginity, the first time we did heroin. I'd written them, examined them, revised them, and sent them in to publications for acceptance or rejection. And once they were gone, they were gone. I had emptied the box in the back of the closet, the scrapbook and the frames and the torn t-shirts and baseball cap with the script R. I had emptied it, found a home for those things, and put them away.

Sara's own baggage had been opened, unpacked, and re-packed in the way of returning travelers who are not staying long. She had more work to do but had been happier, I could see, over the last few months. I appreciated her more than she knew, and as I walked her home that night, I gave her a small Christmas gift to hopefully let her know how much.

"You shouldn't have," she said, tearing at the paper and grinning.

"It's for a picture," I said, pointing at the top circle that could be removed, and a picture slid inside. The round, plastic music box was from the San Francisco Music Box Company and had a small gold key on the bottom that Sara anxiously cranked to hear the tune. We both leaned in where we stood on the street, cheek to cheek, to hear the tinkling sound.

"'Sound of Music?'" she guessed.

"'My Favorite Things,'" I confirmed. "For when you need a little pick-me-up."

Sara's eyes glistened. "Thank you," she whispered. Then she leaned closer, kissed my cheek, and said again, "Thank you."

My parents' Christmas Card from Arizona had a cactus with Christmas lights wrapped around it. They sent one to each member of The Crew, and Chris called me when he got his and laughed at my dad's weird sense of humor. The card was the first thing we talked about when Abbie and I arrived in Oro Valley two days before Christmas.

Mom had purchased an artificial tree and decorated it with our family heirloom ornaments: the scuba diver from the Caribbean, the silver Mickey outline from Orlando, a miniature wineglass that said, "Cheers!" Mom had received in a white elephant exchange once at work, and a tiny pair of purple goggles the team Dad swam with had given him. I thought of the "Swimmers do it in the water" mug he'd been given at the local diner and smiled. It was something to move across the country and build a group of friends that felt like family.

David had gone home for Christmas, his parents in Big Bear were divorcing and his kid sister had begged him to come make the week less awkward. But Abbie was with me. Her mom had taken a friend who apparently was battling drug addiction to some spa in the desert, and Abbie had planned to stay in San Francisco, veg out with some Christmas movies, and sleep. Mom insisted she come with me and bought her a flight. There were four packages under the tree for her.

I stood in front of the refrigerator reading the cards my friends had mailed back to my parents. Chris's card was a drawing of a Black Santa with a long white beard, red suit, and a glowing candle in his hand. Inside he'd written, "Ho! Ho! Ho! Love, Chris." I had the same card on my fridge back home. Inside mine he'd written, "Ho! Ho! Ho! Motherfucker! Love, Your Only Black Friend." Joel had signed his and Tabby's name to a card with a Nativity scene on the front and a Bible verse on the inside. On mine, he'd only signed his name. Jason hadn't sent me a card, so I pulled his off the fridge and looked inside. He'd written to my parents, "Love you both. See you soon," and signed his name.

"You expect to see Jason soon?" I asked.

"Did you know Kacie's in Seattle?" Dad pointed at the card

with the Space Needle on it. It had been photoshopped to wear a strand of Christmas lights.

"I went," I said, "When I got back from Barcelona. It did not go well."

"And now?"

"Still nothing. Not yet."

"You miss her," Dad said.

I shrugged. "Maybe I miss myself when I was with her."

Dad frowned. "I hope not. It was a pretty wretched time." He meant the drugs and the lies and how Tony and I were struggling, him more than me, but both of us, really. Things were so different now. Christmas two years ago had been a blur of booze and deception. I'd been so afraid to be myself, so afraid of the changes I was making and the change I saw in everyone around me. I'd clung to the past and denied it at the same time. Suffocated, I waited until Christmas Eve to fly back to Northern Virginia from San Francisco, and, even then, I drank on the plane and stayed hammered pretty much the entire time. Except New Year's Eve. The night that changed everything. When the balance shifted between The Crew and me, when they'd accused me of hitting Kacie and lying about it. Even last year the wound would sting when I thought about it. But not now. Now we were different. All of us. As we should be, two years removed from the worst six weeks of our lives. *Maybe they always will be the worst six weeks.*

I was not naïve enough to believe they would be.

Abbie was anxious for me to call Skye. She wanted to know if the Thanksgiving Fling, as she called her, had broken up with her boyfriend for me. I told her my emails had gone unanswered. I only sent her two. One right after I got back to San Francisco, thanking her for the weekend and giving her my email and phone number. Then another one a week ago with my flight and stay information. I wasn't going to chase after her. She was taken, after all, and I'd known that in November. But Abbie insisted.

"Just call her," she said, as I shook the bag of Scrabble tiles.

Mom unfolded the board and patted the seat to her right. "I have her parents' number."

"You're not helping."

"Why won't you call?" Abbie asked.

"What if she blows me off?"

"Then at least you'll know and not be wondering the whole time we're here."

"I'm not wondering."

"I am!" Mom and Abbie said at the same time, and then started laughing. Arranging tiles across the board over the game starting-star, Mom spelled "stakes" and said, "Lisa said Skye was 'smitten.' That's the word she used."

"Did she break up with her boyfriend?" I asked, building on the second S to spell "suspect" vertically.

"Lisa didn't say."

"Only one way to find out," Abbie said, handing me the phone.

"Enough," I said. "I'll call tomorrow if she doesn't call me first." The velvet bag rattled as I reached inside for six new tiles.

"They're going up to the cabin for the holiday," Dad said. "Jay said so yesterday."

"Gotta be tonight," Abbie urged. She played "nuts" horizontally with my U.

I totaled up her score and added it to the scoresheet.

Maybe it was pride, feeling like I'd been blown off after Thanksgiving. Maybe it was that I wasn't that interested in continuing with someone in Tucson. She was graduating this spring and planned to go to Spain. I was done with Spain. Maybe it was nostalgia for Northern Virginia, spurred by the cards on the

fridge. Or maybe after Jada, I was ready for something more serious. An investment of some kind, not just a hookup.

"Could she be the show?" Abbie asked.

I shrugged. "Kinda doubt it."

"What is 'the show'?" Mom played "slick" off Abbie's *S* and hit
a triple letter value on the *K.* I frowned at her, totaling her score
and updating the tally. She wins every time we play. It's what
she does.

"The show," I said, "is the person you're willing to settle in
with. If it's not the show, it's the popcorn. The snacks."

"And you don't want Skye to be a snack?" Dad asked from the
couch, which made me laugh.

Abbie stretched her t-shirt over her knees, pinning them to
her chest in her seat, and peered at me over them.

"You know that stretches the shirt out," I said.

"It's David's." She stuck her tongue out at me and twisted her
hair up into a bun before wrapping the scrunchie that had been
on her wrist around it. The move reminded me of Kacie.

"Carpe diem," Abbie sang.

I lifted the handset, looked at my mom, and she grinned.
"Show or not," she said, "if she's made the right move, you should
see where it leads." Unspoken was the warning that if Skye hadn't
broken up with her boyfriend, I should steer clear.

All those years Kacie and I had been on-again and off-again,
we had both been seeing other people. When she had gone to
bed with Jason, over Thanksgiving in 1998, was the first time
I'd really felt betrayed by her. By then, I was pretty serious with
Melissa. Had spent the holiday with her family. Had decided to
break up with Kacie over Christmas anyway. Then New Year's
Eve happened, and things got so messed up and she told me what
she had done and I'd been so angry. Then six weeks later, Tony
was dead, and we had gone to bed together one last time. To say
goodbye. To mourn our friend. Hell, because it was the natural

fit between us. It was how we were. We didn't know how to be anything else. I'd seen it in her eye, too, in Seattle. She didn't know what we could be if we weren't *that* and we would never be *that* again.

After Jada—after I had committed to her and she had found someone else—the break-up stung more than I was willing to admit. She had cheated while I was in Manila. While I was not having sex with anyone because Jada was waiting for me back in San Francisco, she had found someone else. So, after Jada, I had more respect for the commitment—implied or explicit— that people make to one another. Or I thought I did. Helping Skye cheat her own commitment over Thanksgiving was proof I hadn't really gained respect for anything. Not even for myself.

Skye's mom answered, and I told her who I was and asked to speak to Skye. After a rustle on the other end and a door closing, Skye came on the line.

"I thought you were going to email me," she said instead of "hello."

"I did. Once after I got back to San Francisco and again two days ago."

"I never got them."

I felt relieved. Relieved because if she hadn't gotten them, then she hadn't blown me off.

"Probably sent them to the wrong email." I played my turn at Scrabble, spelling "each" between "suspect" and "slick."

"Some girl named SkyeLowery705 is getting emails from a stranger. Poor thing."

"I honestly don't know what address I sent them to. Maybe I did get the number wrong. What is the number?"

"Doesn't matter now."

"It might."

"It doesn't. You're here."

"Till next Tuesday, yeah." I pulled two tiles from the bag and watched as Abbie played her turn. She spelled "taste" using the *T* in suspect and pluralizing "slick" which gave her the highest single-play score yet. Mom looked impressed.

"We're going to the cabin for the weekend," Skye said through the phone, "What about tonight?"

"I dunno. This Scrabble game just got real."

Abbie grinned.

"Just tell me where to meet you," I told Skye. Then I tried not to remember wandering aimlessly through bars in Barcelona a year ago. It wasn't Christmas Eve. I wasn't drunk. Yet. And I didn't need to think and speak in Spanish.

Abbie and I ate dinner with Mom and Dad and drove Mom's Land Rover to meet Skye at the bar where her middle brother, Louis, was overseeing a live music show. I paid the cover charge for both of us, and Abbie went to the bar to get our first-round while I walked through looking for Skye. I found her standing near the sound set-up at a tall cocktail table, a low-rimmed glass resting in front of her.

Her face brightened when she saw me. In November, I'd gotten the wet-hair-post-pool party hoodie version of Skye, followed by the afternoon grunge gear and ponytail. Tonight was club Skye: long hair flowed over her shoulder in waves of cinnamon strands, glitter eyeshadow and glistening lips made her face shine. A V-neck shirt flared around her wrists but hugged her hips over boot-cut jeans that looked almost like bell bottoms. She could have been a disco queen. The front pockets on her pants had the inverted pentagon shape of back pockets, and I almost teased her for wearing them backwards. But before I could speak, she threw her arms around me and hugged me tight.

"I'm glad you called," she said, her lips moving against my ear.

"Prove it," I flirted, sliding my hands around her waist and pulling her against me.

She leaned back, smiled up at me, and batted those thick black lashes.

"You're hotter than I remember."

"Your mother told mine you were smitten with me."

"She didn't!"

Skye dropped her arms from around my neck and propped her fists on her hips, but I held tight to her. The exposed neckline of the blouse showed glitter on her skin and a perfect cleavage; I let my gaze linger before meeting her eyes again.

"Don't be mad. It's why I called." I meant our moms gossiping, but she took it as I meant the view of her breasts and slapped me gently. Then she pointed to her face said, "My eyes are up here, pal," and we broke apart with a turn of her hip.

We made small talk around how the semester ended up, what her family's mountain cabin was like, what she wanted for Christmas, and her plans for New Year's Eve. Then Abbie joined us, and I introduced them. Skye's face gave nothing away as Abbie handed me a drink.

"Abbie is my neighbor," I said.

"A lot more than that," Abbie snorted. "We're together practically every waking minute." Which was true. Between school, being neighbors, and traveling, Abbie had become my constant companion. The implication, though, was romance.

The music started. I leaned into Skye and said, "She's a lesbian."

When Skye's features softened from concern to confusion, I kissed her jaw and said, "You look beautiful when you're jealous."

She stepped in front of me and we stood watching a few songs, her back to my chest. After the third song, Abbie tugged me toward her and jerked her chin at where my hand rested on Skye's hip.

"Did she break up with her boyfriend?"

I shrugged.

Abbie frowned.

Another song, and I decided we needed a fresh round of drinks. When I asked Skye what she wanted, she grinded her ass against me and tilted her chin back to respond, giving me a perfect shot down her shirt. I leaned into her neck, kissed her tenderly and said into her ear, "No more boyfriend, right?"

She nodded, gave me more of her neck and said, "I'm all yours."

Her lotion smelled and tasted like Christmas, gingerbread or spice cake or something. It was delicious. Everything in me responded to the possibility of feasting on that tonight. I squeezed her hip and stepped away, reluctantly, to get more drinks for the three of us.

At the bar, I got the bartender's attention, placed our order, and gave Abbie's name for our tab. Though I knew I'd end up paying for the check, I liked that she tried to pretend it was hers by giving her card to hold it open. Turning back to step away, I came face-to-face with a guy about my height in a military uniform. For a moment I thought it might be Evan Lowery before realizing I didn't know the guy. He stepped to the side and I pushed past him.

"Crowded, right?" I said.

"Too. Hard to find who I'm looking for."

"Good luck with that."

And then I was absorbed back into the crowd, carrying three drinks and ready for a cigarette. I slid Abbie's drink across the table and stepped behind Skye. She was dancing to the band and shook her ass against me so that I wasn't sure how much longer I would last in this environment. After a few minutes, Abbie put her fingers to her lips to mimic a cigarette, and I leaned into Skye again.

"Going to smoke."

She nodded, then turned, slipped her arms around me and

kissed me, a deep, tongue-heavy kiss. She tasted like pineapple juice and Malibu.

"After you smoke, I might not kiss you," she said, pressing her cheek to mine and nipping at my ear. "It's filthy."

"Right," I said. "I'll remember that." Then I kissed along the edge of her jaw, down her neck, and to that place behind her ear that makes girls' knees go weak. I squeezed her hip again, patted her ass, and followed Abbie out.

"She's pretty," Abbie said, lighting her own smoke and handing my lighter back to me.

"Yeah, and she's leaving the country this summer."

"So, she's perfect for you," Abbie teased.

I shrugged. "Not sure it's gonna be a thing."

"You like her?"

"Sure."

"Wanna fuck her?"

I laughed. "Nice manners, babe."

This time Abbie shrugged. "You don't have to marry her. Just see what happens. Commit to the next step."

"Which is?"

"Learning the color of her panties."

"Is that for my sake or yours?" I asked, teasing her with a wink.

"I do expect full disclosure." She exhaled a long stream, like a dragon blowing smoke against the dark sky. Abbie's really pretty, too. Sometimes I forget because she's not an option, but her funky style and self-confidence had drawn more than one guy's attention inside. She shrugged, and added, "Just don't take it so seriously."

When we walked back inside, Skye was nowhere to be seen. Abbie and I returned to the table we'd occupied before; three new people were standing there, so we hung back. I had greeted Louis, Skye's brother, when we arrived. I searched the crowd for him or Skye, a familiar face, but found first the soldier who had taken my place at the bar. He had found who he was looking for, and it was the Lowerys. Both of them. Skye was in his arms.

Abbie followed my line of sight.

"Maybe he knows their brother," she said. "Isn't he a soldier?"

Maybe. Or maybe this was Skye's boyfriend whom she hadn't really broken up with—only lied about. Maybe he was here to surprise her. Maybe the writer in me wouldn't be surprised by that. I stared until she must have felt my gaze because eventually, she broke away from him long enough to make eye contact with me. Her expression wasn't remorse, though, it was defiance. And I suddenly heard Melissa's poem in my head as if it were replacing the lyrics of the song.

But I look at him and he is
Sunburn and sand in my Coke and fat men in Speedos.

"Pay the check," I told Abbie tersely. "We're leaving."

Then I walked out of the bar.

On the sidewalk outside, waiting for Abbie to appear, I felt Skye pull on my arm.

"Just wait," she said.

"Who is he to you?"

"I wasn't expecting him. I like *you*. This could be something." She wagged her finger between us, but I scoffed at her.

"Bullshit," I said. "Stupid childish bullshit."

The door opened and when we both looked up, the soldier boyfriend was there. He said, "Skye? You okay?"

She nodded, her hair falling across her face, her arms wrapped around her. The bar's front lights made the glitter on her skin and eyelids sparkle.

"Brian Listo, man," I said, stretching my hand out to the solder boyfriend. Pointing at Skye, I said, "Our parents know one another. I'm just visiting from California. Skye and Louis were making sure me and my friend—" And just then Abbie fell out the front door. "—had a good time in Tucson. Good to meet you."

"How long you in town?" he asked.

"Just the weekend."

Skye's small huff pulled my gaze to her.

"Enjoy the holiday," the soldier said.

"Same to you." I managed to smile at Skye. "Thanks."

Abbie came to my side, "Thanks," she echoed. "See you next time."

"Right," Skye said, but her voice cracked, and I shook my head slightly at her. No, there wouldn't be a next time. We were done here.

As we walked away, I heard the soldier say, "Just what the fuck, Skye?"

Yeah, she was his problem. Not mine.

On the day after Christmas, Dad woke me early and we went to the pool. I'd been in two or three times a week since returning from Spain and was in pretty good shape. Dad's workout was around forty-five hundred yards, and I complained about the extensive kick set. I hate kicking and he knows it.

When we finished, in damp sweats, we drove to Yeddy's and ate the calories we had earned in bacon and biscuits. When we left there, with to-go cups of coffee in hand, Dad turned the opposite direction of home.

I didn't ask where we were headed, assuming if he wanted me to know he would tell me. The radio played NPR and we listened to the news and some holiday stories related to celebrations the day before.

"Think your mother liked her gifts?"

"Not as much as Abbie liked hers."

"She was surprised." Dad grinned. "Maybe she thought we didn't know her as well as we do."

"She thinks no one pays attention. She accused me of telling you what she wanted."

"Your mom's just good like that."

"That's what I told her."

Over the years, Abbie's own mother had given her a variety of self-help books, tickets for seminars, and vacation vouchers. She had full collections of healing candles, aromatherapy, incense, crystals, and other new age calming tools and all the pottery to use the various items she was meant to burn, pray over, and breathe in. Abbie had bangle bracelets, Native American talismans and dreamcatchers, and mini Aztec monuments. She would sometimes try to use them, then frown, glare, and declare each one a failure.

"The artifacts of healing for one's self-inflicted wounds," she would say. But she didn't box them up or throw them out. She came back to them, as if trapped in an orbit of hope and disappointment.

My mother gave her three framed black-and-white prints of Robert Maplethorpe photographs. Each had one of Abbie's poems matted with it, and the match of the photo to the print was exquisite. Mom had really connected with Abbie's work and found the perfect photographer to pair it with. Abbie was speechless when she opened them and hugged Mom hard, and for a little longer than I think even Mom expected. Her fourth gift had been from me. It was a collection of Sappho, a Greek poet known for sensual verses. The book was a collector's edition with a leather-bound cover and gold-leaf pages.

"Homework," she said with a sniff and a smile.

Dad had paid someone to cut and combine about thirty-five videos taken of me growing up into one two-and-one-half-hour

DVD. In it I swam, skated, opened Christmas presents, and posed for prom pictures with Kacie. And Tony was in just about every frame. In the pool, I was racing him, on the half pipe he stood nearby cheering me on, Christmas morning we were jammied and slurping hot chocolate together, and at prom, he stood with arms around Kacie and me both, kissed us each on the cheek, and pointed at the camera, said, "Love you guys!" That's where the video ended.

Abbie squeezed my hand. "You okay?" she whispered.

I nodded and met Dad's eyes.

"Thank you," I said.

He nodded. "I was glad to find the videos and wanted something we could save."

"Did you send a copy to Mac?"

"Should I?"

I nodded, a heavy lump in my throat. A single tear dripped, and I flicked it away. "I think he'd like to have it."

Despite two bottles of wine, a filet mignon, and the rich caramel cheesecake Abbie had made to contribute to our Christmas meal, I didn't feel that bad Tuesday morning. The swim had burned off the grogginess and the breakfast had set me fully right. I finally decided to ask Dad why we hadn't headed home.

"Your Christmas present has arrived," he said, and drove through the gates to the Tucson airport.

Standing outside of the Delta arrivals, a backpack on his shoulder and duffle at his feet, was Jason. After watching the video the night before, I'd felt so homesick for Herndon that getting up to swim this morning had felt automatic. Seeing Jason, though, felt like balm on an old wound, something that had been throbbing in me since those images of The Crew skating and horsing around. As the car stopped, I got out of the passenger seat and hugged Jason.

"Man, it's good to see you," I said.

He clapped me on the back and hugged me tightly back.

"This is why the card said, 'see you soon'?" I asked Dad as Jason and I got back inside, and we drove away.

Dad laughed. "When the twins were here Thanksgiving, Jason didn't seem that excited about their Christmas plans. Your mom decided to invite him out here as a gift for you."

Jason leaned forward from the backseat and clapped me on the shoulder.

"You have any idea how cold it is in Pennsylvania right now."

Turns out Joel had not asked Tabby to marry him on Christmas Eve like he planned, but they had left for Pittsburgh the day after Christmas. Mrs. Lincrest had gone to visit her boyfriend's grown children for the week. Chris had gone with his dad and half siblings to North Carolina, so Jason had been alone in Herndon. My parents had rescued him as a gift to me, but really because we were family and real family knew what you needed even when you didn't.

A couple of hours later we were stretched out on the couches in the living room watching football and talking about our gifts. Abbie had shown Jason the photographs and he'd read and complimented her poetry. She beamed.

"Such a waste," she said, stretched between the two of us. "Ridiculously hot men here and me a damn lesbian. If any dick could make me want to be straight, it would be yours." She patted my leg. "Or yours." Jason's leg.

"Good to know," he said. "What about that chick, Brian? What was her name? The one with the brothers?"

"Skye. That's a non-starter."

"Still got the boyfriend?"

Abbie snorted. "As far as he knows. She seemed to take a more liberal view of their connection. But damn, she was hot."

Jason looked over Abbie's head at me. "Was she?"

"Make up, hair, glitter. She was like Arizona Barbie."

"Ginger variety," Abbie added.

"Red head?"

"Kinda auburn."

Jason grinned. "Like Tony would have picked."

"Probably, yeah." I dropped my head back against the couch and closed my eyes. I hadn't shown Jason the video, nobody mentioned it, probably waiting for me to decide if I wanted to watch it again. I knew before the week was over we would. Because it wasn't just my childhood, it was our family story. And Tony was part of it.

That night, though, over dinner, when we told Jason about it, he frowned.

"My dad's back," he said. "Trying to get his life together supposedly."

"Have you seen him?" I asked.

Jason shook his head. "Not sure I want to."

My own parents made eye contact across the table, but nobody asked Jason anything else. Abbie, feeling the tension but not knowing what was behind it, changed the subject by telling Mom and Dad about David's Christmas gift for his sister. They were going camping, in the woods, tents and flashlights and sleeping bags and packaged food. The last part was what made Abbie laugh the hardest.

"Man can't live without his microwave, for real. Lance crackers and bottled water? Please."

"He'll be fine," I said. "It's only three days."

"Three *whole* days?" Mom's concern was funny, too. "Without a shower? Or a hot cup of coffee?"

"You're right," I conceded. "He'll be miserable."

Abbie and Jason and I cleared the table and washed dishes, and Mom and Dad excused themselves to their bedroom. Then Abbie begged off, too, and Jason and I were left to entertain one another. We sat on the patio, a fire blazing in the gas-lit pit between us, and smoked cigarettes and drank red wine.

"You were right at Thanksgiving," Jason said.

"About what?"

"I'm struggling."

"I never said that."

"No, you only asked about it. Joel said it."

The two of them had seemed distant in November, like there were unsaid things between them. I sensed those things remained unresolved.

"I feel like everyone else is moving on. Growing up. Getting their shit together. And I'm just still playing hockey. Still trying to make the team. And every time I go out on the ice, I hope I'll be injured so I won't have to play anymore."

"Shit, dude."

"That's not the worst of it. There's this bridge I drive over every day between my place and the rink and I envision just driving over the edge. Crashing the car. Falling."

"Fuck."

"It's the guy in the passenger seat, my teammate, my room-mate, who keeps me from doing it."

"What does he say?"

"He says he needs a ride to the rink. And he gets in. And we drive. And I can't kill us both, so I don't kill either one of us."

I let the flames flicker, watched them dance shadows across Jason's face. He stared into them and when he squeezed his eyes shut, I knew what was coming. I'd had the exact same thought.

"You think that's what Tony felt, man?" Jason's voice trembled. "Like he wanted to drive right into the concrete barrier?"

"No way to know, man."

"But what do you *think*?"

"I think he thought about ending it every minute of every day until he finally took the dose that gave him the courage to go through with it. Just a little more. Cut a little deeper. Don't call for help. Don't wonder what anyone else will think or feel or say or do. Just make the hurting stop. And I think it was something he couldn't explain. To anyone."

Jason nodded. He leaned forward, elbows on knees and held his face in his hands.

"Are you hurting? Like that?"

He shook his head. "No, man." Lifting his gaze, he met my eyes through the flames. "No," he said again. "I'm struggling. But I'm not hurting. Not like that."

And neither was I. Not even in Barcelona. No matter how much I had acted like the depths of my grief were permanent, I always knew I could swim to the surface and get air. It was all just self-indulgence. Time had thrown into stark relief the difference between Tony's illness and my own self-absorption.

I let my cigarette burn down to my fingers, then stubbed it out in the painted pottery ashtray on the table beside me.

"There's just no way to know some things," I said. "And not knowing sucks."

"So, what, then? What do we do?"

"Fuck if I know. Just go on, I guess." The conversation with Sara came back to me and I smirked a little bit. Without explaining, I said, "Guess we look forward and not back."

Jason shook his head, and the confusion was still there on his face. I didn't know what to do with it and he said, "Not sure what I see in the future, but the past keeps getting brighter."

That I did know. "It'll do that," I said. "And cast shadows. If you let it."

The spark and pop of flames, the spring of the chairs as we gently bounced, the warmth of the wine and the quiet memories of all that had come before, secured somehow, in this safe harbor in the desert.

New Year's Eve 2000
San Francisco

They decided to come to San Francisco for New Year's Eve. Jason traveled with Abbie and me from Tucson and Chris, Joel, and Tabby met us there. Joel got a hotel room for he and Tabby. He'd confided over the Thanksgiving holiday that he planned to ask her to marry him over Christmas but apparently had wimped out. So instead they all flew to San Francisco and we planned a big end-of-the-century party. The hotel Joel booked was having a dance party Sunday night, so we bought tickets to that. We spent our first night together, Friday, at the neighborhood bars.

In addition to The Crew, my Spanish friends came up from L.A. for the holiday weekend. Marco had been my constant companion in Barcelona, and he'd brought Joaquin and Rafael to L.A. with him just over a year ago. Abbie and David and I went down to Los Angeles once to see them back before I started dating Jada. It was down to just Marco and Rafael now, Joaquin having returned to Spain, disappointed over not being cast on a

U.S. sitcom. I loved how they got along immediately with The Crew and how Abbie and David melted in seamlessly, too.

We didn't tell the others about Skye in Tucson. Abbie had apologized for pushing me to call "the skank," but I didn't think of Skye that way. I thought of her as me two years ago. Then I didn't think of her anymore at all. After a month of waffling between begging Jada back, stalking her on campus, and whining to David about how she'd moved on, and a week of getting burned by what might have been in Tucson, I was glad to be focused on my friends.

Our favorite joint was a microbrewery near Sunset Reservoir, and we took up a long table and got loaded, round after round of high-alcohol-content beverages and the occasional round of shots. Then we sent Joel and Tabby off in a cab and staggered home after midnight.

Rafael bedded down at Abbie and David's, and Chris, Jason, and Marco shacked up with me. We had the bed, the futon couch, and an air mattress. Like our weekend in L.A., Marco crashed on the bed with me. When we all stirred Saturday morning pacing through teeth-brushing, coffee-making, and shit-taking, no one seemed the least bit weirded out by the closeness. It was like sharing a dorm with brothers and aside from Chris mocking my Pop Tarts selection and Jason asking for skim milk instead of two percent, we seemed to fit well enough for a long weekend.

"Anyone up for a run?" Chris asked.

Eye contact all around and then nods. We dressed, stretched, and headed out for a four-mile loop around the city. Chris and Jason hadn't been there, so I pointed out a few landmarks to orient them to stories I'd told. Joel's trip, albeit brief, had given them both a picture of my proximity to things like the coffee shop and skatepark. Marco showed them the places he and Rafael had found when they came up for Thanksgiving. He'd finally seen the island prison I described to him when we were in Barcelona.

He said it looked just like the postcards I'd mailed him when I first got back.

"That Abbie is a helluva tour guide," he said between breaths as we ran along.

"All the gayest spots she could find?" I asked. "Nothing but lesbians?"

He laughed and said, "Not at all. Nothing but hot women. It was crazy."

"Man, you gotta get her to give us that tour," Jason said.

When we got back, the apartment across the hall had stirred. Abbie stood in her doorway with an empty coffee mug.

"You have any filters?" she asked.

"Sure thing," I said, unlocking my own door and leading the others inside.

"And coffee?" Abbie said.

I turned around and there stood David as well. Though he was showered, he also had an empty coffee mug.

"Why don't you just have some of ours?" Chris offered, bringing the pot we'd left behind to them.

"Bless you," Abbie said.

"Creamer?" David asked.

Jason laughed out loud. "Man, I love you guys," he said, slapped me on the back, and headed into the bathroom.

We spent the day at the skate park messing around. Jason and I had played golf in Arizona a few days ago, but neither he nor Chris had been on a skateboard in a while. They'd exchanged a look when I suggested it. I told them a day outside would be worth it. They didn't have to ride if they didn't want to.

"What brought you back to this?" Chris asked, waving his hand to indicate the other skaters and the ramps, rails, and curbs of the park.

"David had a crush on a grad student. He overheard dude say

he loved this place. D remembered I skated, dug my board out, and brought me here."

"When was that?"

"Right after Barcelona? Yeah, so a year ago? We made a habit of it. I'm probably here once a week when I'm in town." I handed my board to Chris, who took a turn gliding over a few small crests, tilted into a couple of railslides, and pushed his way back up to where we stood.

"You make sense here," Jason said. "It's like this big city but there's just a little bubble around Brian." He grinned at me, his Frostburg sweatshirt stretched over his chest, sleeves pushed up to his elbows. "Like you've got something that others want to be part of."

"Don't be an idiot," I said. "It's just growing up. We're all doing it."

"For real," Chris said. "Some of us have mortgages."

Jason held up two fingers like a cross. "Please, God, no," he said. "That would mean settling down."

"Like Joel?" I asked.

Jason rolled his eyes. "That motherfucker has wanted to be settled since we were seventeen. We're just lucky Tabby was more sensible. They could be on kid number three by now."

"I thought the whole tech start-up thing was kind of a roller coaster life."

"Not by the time you're choosing the third one you're going to do," Chris said. "People are coming to him for advice now."

My meager efforts at publishing short stories and querying agents for my novel seemed silly. Chris was selling real estate and had his own townhome. Joel was starting companies and getting married. And Jason was . . . well, Jason was Jason. At least he was still fucking around like me.

And Marco. And Joaquin and Rafael and Abbie and David. I did a quick count and the fucking-arounds were the majority.

And Jason was right, this did feel like a Brian bubble. It was easy to be easy about it all. Just taking each day for what it was, not worrying too much about those permanent conditions like retirement accounts and mortgages and kids and marriage.

"You still working that list?" Chris asked after having made a swift run around the edge of the park, and then handed the board back to Jason for another go.

"What list?"

He narrowed his eyes at me. "You're going to pretend you don't know?"

But I did. It was the list I'd started in Barcelona. It was all the things Tony would never get to do. I added to it almost every day for a year or more. And I scratched things off, too. I went to the Philippines. I got into graduate school. I wanted to train for a triathlon. Spend time with Buddhist monks in prayer. See the burning valley again.

"It wasn't healthy," I said. "My therapist in Spain told me to do it."

"So, why'd you quit?"

I laughed. "My therapist here told me to stop."

"Gotta stop living for him."

"I know."

"And live for yourself."

"I know."

"He'd want you to."

"Chris, seriously. What the fuck does it look like I'm doing here? Jason just said it, right? 'Brian bubble,' and Abbie's got me making plans and I stopped with the list. I'm better, man. For real."

Then I looked at him. Away from where Jason was trying a curb railslide for the third time and at Chris. One of my oldest friends.

"You weren't talking about me, were you?" I asked.

He shook his head slightly then jerked his chin toward Jason.
"He's stuck."

The quickest nod, I almost didn't see it.

"His mom sold the house at Nannyglow. Now she's selling
the Herndon house. Joel's gone. Why do you think he went to
Tucson, man? For Jay right now, there's no anchor. Anywhere."
Before he could say more, Jason tugged the sweatshirt he'd been
wearing off, straightened his t-shirt, and skated back toward us.

"I'm all that's left in Herndon," Chris said. "Me and a grave."

I didn't know what to say. I couldn't apologize exactly. I didn't
want to be in Herndon. I was glad for Tucson, as weird as it was,
and glad for west-coast time and my friends here and moving on.
For the first time in a long time, I was feeling a sense of home.
And it was here, in San Francisco.

"Maybe he'll stay here," I said, and it took us both by surprise.

Chris's brown eyes met mine, then he smiled but it was sad.
"Nah, I doubt it. He needs to find his own thing. And he will.
Let's just keep an eye on him, ya know?"

"Okay," I agreed.

Chris slugged Jason on the shoulder as he came to a stop in
front of us.

"What'd I do now?"

"Nothing specific," I said. "But it's good to have you guys here.
I mean it." Then I kicked the board away from Jason and rode
down into the park. This was where I focused on movement,
physics, space and surfaces, not emotions or memories or future
plans. The park was an oasis not a sanctuary. Maybe tomorrow
I'd take Jason to meet Thomás and see what he had to say then.

We had left Marco with Abbie and David. They planned to
watch the entire box set of the Star Wars original trilogy. Some
debate had come up related to the Phantom Menace that could
only be solved by a thorough review of the earlier films. When
we got back to the apartments, they were just about to start

Return of the Jedi. Chris wanted to nap, so we left him at my place and went over to Abbie's to share the limited space but endless supply of microwave popcorn and M&Ms.

"We should have more movie nights," David said. He was draped over the end of the couch with Rafael snuggled against him.

"Okay," I said, taking the empty space between Abbie and the other end of the couch.

"That's it? Just 'okay'?" David questioned.

"Did you expect me to object? Scooch," I told Abbie, air kissing at her.

"No, but wouldn't you want to rule out nights when you have other meetings and veto any movies you think are dumb and know who's paying the rental fees and for all the candy?"

I shrugged. "First and third Mondays, nothing with Sylvester Stallone, and I will."

Jason laughed out loud, taking a seat on the floor and leaning on the couch front of me. "I really do love these two," he said, glancing up at Abbie and David. "They make you a better you."

"Aw," Abbie said, sliding to the floor and sitting on Jason's lap, looping her arms around his neck and kissing his cheek. "He's adorable. Can we keep him?"

David and Rafael seemed content to reignite what they'd started in L.A. and continued over Thanksgiving. They were cute together and overtly sexual, and while the innuendo made Abbie and me and Marco laugh, I kept an eye on Jason to see how he would respond. He never flinched, though, and I wondered about his group of friends in Michigan. Did they look like us? Sound like us? Did he even have friends in Michigan?

We had all committed to keeping The Crew together, and I was the only one who had introduced extra people, except for Tabby. Jason and Chris fit seamlessly in with my friends, and I felt grateful they were willing to get to know the people who had become more present in my everyday life. I also wondered what my Barcelona shrink would have said since she had been hard on me about not introducing Jason to Marco and Paulo when he'd come to Spain. She said keeping my friends separate was another symptom that I was trying to preserve Tony and The Crew as some mythically perfect version of myself that never really existed.

I wanted to call her and tell her I'd fixed that part of me. That broken part that kept Virginia separate from California, that broken part that didn't know it was okay to move forward together as long as we all kept asking the questions and accepting one another's answers.

After Jedi ended, Marco and Jason and I went back to my place to dress for dinner and bar hopping. Chris was sitting on a bar stool at the counter.

"Man, how come you didn't tell me Jada was Black?" he asked.

"Guess I didn't think it mattered," I said, closing the door behind me and following Jason into the kitchen. We stood on the other side of the bar from Chris.

"It matters, man. She got with some other dude? A brother? While she was with you? Come on, man, that shit matters."

"How?" I said, glancing at Jason who shrugged, then back at Chris. "He was her ex. He had her first. She was just killing time with me apparently."

"So, she got with you to make homeboy jealous?" Chris's expression showed outrage. "Man, that's messed up."

"Joel met her. He knew." I turned to the fridge and pulled out four beers.

"Knew she was messed up?"

"Knew she was Black."

"He didn't mention it." Chris stood and finished off the glass of water he'd been drinking.

"Guess he didn't think it mattered either." I used the church key to pry the caps off the beers and slid one in front of Jason.

"So why does it?" Jason asked Chris.

"Because Brian with a Black girl," Chris said, like that was a full sentence, and took the beer I'd held out to him. He took a long swig before saying, "And not just with her, but in love with her? I mean, that's not what I would have expected."

"Why not?" Marco asked, claiming the fourth beer from the counter. "In Spain, he had many women of many different colors and races." He lifted his bottle in salute, then took a long drink.

"Not *many*," I said.

"Sometimes two at a time," Marco added.

Jason's eyes got big and Chris nearly spit the drink he'd just taken from his bottle.

"Thanks, man," I said, and took a long pull off my own beer.

"I knew you flirted with two at the time," Jason said, "But you took them home that way, too?" He shook his head and laughed. "Damn, man. That's game."

"It's not game," I said, "It's a cry for help. I was self-medicating. Then I got here, got better, and yeah, I fell for Jada. And then she played me. End of story."

"I'm sorry, man," Chris said. "I shouldn't have brought her up. I was just surprised."

"How'd you find out anyway?"

"She came by," he said.

"When?"

"Like ten minutes ago. Left this." He pulled an envelope from the chair side of the bar toward the kitchen side.

"Why didn't you come get me?"

"She said not to. I don't think she wanted to be here, honestly. She said she didn't want to leave this somewhere it might be stolen, but she didn't really want to see you, either."

"What is it?" Jason asked.

I finally looked at the delivery Chris had gestured to. The envelope had been opened and resealed. Inside were test results. Jada's. She did not have HIV, and so neither did I and she had made a trip over here to tell me that, but she didn't tell me. She just left this notice.

"What the hell are you supposed to do with this?" Jason asked, looking at it over my shoulder.

"No clue. Haven't seen her or talked to her in weeks."

"Is that what women mean when they say they need closure?" Marco asked.

And then I laughed because just what the fuck was I supposed to do about this? I didn't care that Jada was clean. I didn't even get tested back in November after she'd confessed to cheating. And then later, when Abbie confronted her and she'd said I hadn't mattered to her at all, that she'd played me, I hadn't been angry. I'd just been sad. Because I thought what we'd had was real and it wasn't, and I realized I hadn't really known what love was or should be. Maybe ever. Now this? Randomly?

"One of two things," I said. "She felt guilty and this is her way of apologizing."

"Or?" Jason prompted.

"She's crazy," Chris said.

"Or maybe she wants you back?" Marco offered.

"Maybe she's a little broken hearted, too?" I asked.

"Nah," Chris said. "Crazy girls just don't want to be ignored."

Despite moping, writing some really bad poetry, and metabolizing rejection like it was calcium, I hadn't reached out to Jada at all. I'd seen her on campus. Seen her with him. Seen her writing by herself. At coffee shops. But I hadn't approached her or contacted her in any way. The strategy had worked, apparently, as now she'd come back around. Sort of. As I dragged a notebook out of my bag and flipped to a clean page, Marco slung his own backpack over his shoulder.

"You know, Brian," he said, his Spanish accent still thick after a year in the States, "There is a time for every purpose."

I grinned. "A time to forgive the girl and get back together?"

"Don't hold on to the ones that let you go. Thought you might have learned that by now."

"You'd think so, wouldn't you?" But I hadn't.

The notebook I wrote this scene into took an alternate version. I'd arrived while she was here. I'd confronted her after my friends left the room. I asked her what she was doing, why she was playing, what she wanted. The notebook fictionalized a different scene entirely. One of contrition, forgiveness, and reconciliation. It was fiction, something I'd always used to metabolize disappointment.

I wasn't healed. Not fully. But I was a helluva lot better off than I'd been a year ago.

Los Angeles
One Year Ago

The first long weekend of 2000 had come a week after the first anniversary of Tony's death. David and Abbie decided we needed an epic road trip. It was nearly six hours to L.A. following the major interstates but we decided to ride Highway 1 all the way down, so it took us the better part of Friday. We stopped in Santa Cruz and took pictures on the pier from *The Lost Boys*. Abbie and David competed on movie trivia.

"Did you know the bandstand where Michael first sees Star was destroyed in the earthquake in '89?" she asked. "So was the comic book store where the Frog brothers worked."

"Did you know the nickname 'murder capital' was real in the 1970s because of several serial killers on the loose?" David countered.

"Did you know the Frog brothers' names are Edgar and Allen after Edgar Allen Poe?" Abbie seemed satisfied with this offering until I couldn't resist getting in on it, too.

"Did you know Santa Cruz means 'holy cross' in Spanish?" I

said. "Kinda interesting since vampires supposedly hate cruci-fixes."

Further south, we visited Cannery Row and I bored them with Steinbeck references. Then Big Sur while the sun was high in the sky. We were mostly silent in reverence and awe over the cliffs and waves. We stopped in San Luis Obispo for lunch and crossed from Highway 1 to 101 so we could stay along the coast into Los Angeles. Abbie had a high-school classmate at UC Santa Barbara, so we stopped there for dinner and drinks.

"Tell me again how you two met," the girl said, leaning into her palm, elbow on the table, staring directly at me.

"Brian writes terrible poetry," Abbie said.

"And Abbie tried to help me pass the class," I answered.

The friend blinked at me, glanced at Abbie, and said, "You still like girls, right?"

Abbie rolled her eyes.

"He writes good short stories, though," David said. "Tell her about the one where the Russians kicked your ass."

My eyes got wide. "No one wants that story."

"A bar fight?" the girl asked laying her hand on my arm. "Were you hurt?"

Busted nose, swollen eye, choking on bile. Yeah, I'd been hurt.

"It was fine," I said. "Just a flesh wound." Eye contact with David, who coughed into his drink. "Not much of a story really."

"So, you're a writer?" The girl slid even closer to me, her leg along the length of mine. "Would I have seen anything you've written?"

"Depends on how much time you spend on gay porn sites," David said.

This time I choked on my drink and we dissolved into child-ish chuckles and snorts.

"Morons," Abbie said. "How far is it to L.A. from here?"

The girl invited us to stay overnight with her, but Abbie told her we were expected somewhere else, and we continued south. Eleven hours after leaving San Francisco we made it to Santa Monica around 10:00 p.m.

"We will take highway 5 home," David declared, stretching in the parking lot of the two-storey apartment complex we'd been given as the address. We all surveyed the run-down façade of the building, paint peeling from the railing, that faux-grass carpet beach motels have on the staircases. I led them up the stairs to Marco's door.

"Think they surf?" David asked, nodding to a stack of boards against a wall on the second floor.

When I'd known him in Barcelona, Marco was quick to hop into a fight. He was strong and wide, beefy even, and not much taller than me. He opened the door when I knocked and before I could introduce Abbie and David, he had me in a tight hug.

"You're too small," he said in Spanish. "Haven't you worked at all?"

"It's only been a few months," I said.

"Seven weeks," he said, releasing me and grinning. "Seven weeks since New Year's."

For a completely unassociated reason, the count from New Year's Eve 1999 made me ache, and Marco caught my frown, placed a big palm on my shoulder and said, "One year later. And next year will be another. And another. Keep strong, brother." He'd been the one to take most of my post-Tony's-death downward spiral. Him and the Barcelona shrink. Marco had lost his own brother in an accident when they were teenagers. My grief resonated with him, and he'd dedicated himself to helping me through it. But our activities in Barcelona were what the therapist had called "self-destructive."

"*Hola*," David said, by way of interrupting. "We're still out on the balcony."

Marco dragged us all inside, took the introductions and shared my friends with his, two guys seated on a worn couch. One looked hungrily at Abbie, though she paid him zero attention—this was Joaquin. The other, Rafael, raised an eyebrow at David, which made me smile.

Marco told them, in Spanish, who I was, and they greeted me with knowing smiles and a couple of teasing remarks. I guessed he'd shared a few of our fight stories with them because they seemed to think I'd made Marco the cocky asshole they claimed he was.

"I met him that way," I said. "But sure, a few fights with Russians made it worse."

Some stashing of bags, agreements on sleeping arrangements, a round of shots, and we were off to the bar. David and Rafael hit it off and stayed near one another for the duration. Abbie and Joaquin found a woman and were taking turns flirting with her. Marco asked if I thought Abbie would have a threesome with Joaquin and their new friend. I admitted I wouldn't put it past her.

"We are left to ourselves," he said. "Unless we find a woman to share as well." He raised an eyebrow at me, but I laughed him off.

"Let's just drink," I said. "And try not to start any fights." We ended up being the more sober of the crowd, though, and when the bars closed and we took the others home, Marco nodded as David and Rafe took one room, then Abbie, Joaquin, and their guest took his bed, and I stretched out on the couch in the living room.

After about an hour of playing music for me, he settled into a particular album, leaned back against the couch near my hip, and grinned at me.

"There's a threesome in my bed right now," he said in Spanish.

"If it were anyone but Abbie," I replied, "I'd be into that."

"She is not into men. That is too bad."

"Indeed."

"Tell me how you've been, really, since New Year's?"

One year after the debacle of the Northern Virginia New Year's that had splintered my closest friendships, I'd spent the Y2K with Marco and Paulo in Barcelona saying goodbye to the women and wine. I'd been less of an addict then than when I'd arrived six months earlier, but still insatiable in a variety of categories.

"You seem different," he prompted.

"I've been riding my skateboard," I said. "And going to a writers' group. And church. I found a church."

"Made your way back to God, then?"

"In a manner of speaking."

"And what has he told you?"

"That the wine and the women were easier."

We both laughed.

"I wish you'd stay," Marco said finally. "L.A. sucks really. It's just Rafe and me and Joaquin."

"Like it was me and you and Paulo."

"Yes. Paulo."

"What happened there? Thought he planned to head this way, too?"

Marco shook his head. "He's working in his father's bank after all."

I groaned. "He didn't."

"He did. I fear he's lost to us forever."

"Steady paycheck will do that to a guy."

"And pussy, don't forget the steady pussy."

"Wendy?" Marco nodded. "No shit. Never thought he'd make that stick."

"He's fallen hard for a Lufthansa slut," Marco said, and took a long swig from a beer I didn't realize he was still holding.

"It's fine," I said. "Sloane and Lara will shake her free eventually."

"All women become anchors," Marco said, but he wasn't bitter about it. "They hold you to a place and time. They remind you of who you were and keep you from being what you could be."

"In a good way?"

He nodded. "In the best way."

Maybe that was why I had fled San Francisco. As much as Kacie was Herndon, San Francisco was Meli, and I couldn't see how that would change. Barcelona belonged to Lara, the flight attendant I'd had a recurring affair with. Each city was haunted by a woman except L.A. For a moment, I considered I should stay right there. But it wouldn't be long, I knew, before that place, too, had a woman associated with it. I had another year and a half in the Bay Area. I would need to try to make my own way or else continue escaping.

"When will you come to San Francisco?"

"I'd like to see that island prison."

"If L.A. sucks, then come north."

"And live with you?"

I shrugged as much as I could laying down. "Why not?"

"I have Joaquin and Rafael."

"They have Abbie and David, who live across the hall from me, so we'll be all set."

"Like the friends on TV?"

I laughed. "Sure. Like *Friends*."

"American TV. That's what's keeping us here. Joaquin thinks he'll get famous or something."

"Isn't *Friends* in New York?"

"They film here." He rolled his eyes and chuckled. "But he does not care what show anyway." Marco asked a lot of questions, curious about everything and everyone. That inquisitiveness didn't annoy or invade. It made me feel cared about. Missed.

"Are you writing?"

"Sure," I said. "Stories. Bad ones apparently. Two rejections and counting."

"Make a screenplay," Marco said, and leaned his head back against the couch. "Then we'll develop our own show and get a studio to buy it."

"I don't write for TV," I said. "Come to San Francisco."

"Okay, but let's get laid up there if we're not gonna get laid here."

"Tomorrow night we get the bed," I said. "Sex or no sex. We get the bed."

WINTER, 2001

The first morning in L.A. on what David had called, "Our Annual Trip," Marco and I went for a run along the beach. We'd only slept about three hours, so it was mostly sweating out the booze and shaking off the fatigue. The boardwalk was crowded with Saturday tourists, and we did more stopping and stretching than actual running. But the view was awesome, a shaded beachside town as the sun rose in the east, curiosity sculpting the expressions on the passersby.

We ended back at the apartment with a bag of bagels and a tray of coffees and Abbie saying goodbye to the pretty girl from the night before. They shared a long, lingering kiss before the girl climbed down the stairs and Marco handed Abbie the coffee.

"Good night?" I asked her. She grinned.

Showers and bagels and the slow emergence of first David then Rafe and we all started tossing around ideas about how to spend the day. But it was well after two before we left the apartment in search of photo-worthy landmarks. When we'd been here last year, Marco and the others had only been in L.A. for a few weeks, and so we were all explorers. This year, Joaquin had returned to Spain, Marco had a job at a studio, and Rafael was bartending and auditioning. Marco was with us for the day, but Rafe would go into work at 4:00.

David purchased a folding map in a trinket shop. It supplied dozens of laughs as he and Rafael tried to refold it and store it in one of their back pockets and then the other's. We bought some disposable cameras and were free with lips and limbs through posed embraces. I got cheek kisses from everyone and even a lip-smacker from Rafael before Marco reminded him I was very much straight and he could have David. Then David said I was always his boyfriend first and straight later. Abbie claimed my being gay would be a tragedy for women everywhere. One she'd be glad to help them get over. Marco offered to help her heal the broken hearts. It went on like that, teasing and talking, and swapping stories while walking Santa Monica.

By early evening the play and banter had made me more than a little horny, and I decided I'd find a woman before the night was over. I hadn't been with anyone since the tryst with Skye at Thanksgiving, and a quick hook-up was well overdue.

In the first club a pretty blonde girl worked her way between me and Abbie on the dance floor. Then Marco was there, Abbie was gone, and the two of us worked that girl over pretty good through a few songs. She wore a short dress with biker shorts underneath and let me hold her hips and slide my hand between her legs over her clothes. She was hot and she made me hard, but she bit my ear which stung and then Marco captured her lips in what looked like a sloppy kiss and I'd had enough.

A few more drinks. A few more songs. Sometime after midnight Abbie left with a fancy-looking Asian girl. I was drunk, I thought, or at least buzzed, and the loud music and twisting mass of bodies was working against my restraint. There was no reason I couldn't take someone out of here with me, I reasoned—I was single, attractive, responsible. Then two girls approached

Marco and me asking if we'd pretend to be with them to keep some creepers away.

Marco willingly slid his arm around one and I let the other lean into me.

She said her name was Veronica, which made me think of the redhead Tony had been hanging out with the night he died, and I fought off the memory with a kind of desperation.

"Ronnie," she said. "My friends call me Ronnie."

"Can I be your friend?" I flirted, arching eyebrow.

"Depends on whether that would involve kissing?" Her own form of flirting, I guessed, a forthright proposition.

"I'm going to put my arm around you—" I said, my lips against her ear. "—and pull you against me."

She nodded and I did as I'd said.

"Can you feel how much I want you?" I pressed my hard-on against her hip. "We could leave through the back door and make out in the alley."

"Will you fuck me?" She let her tongue linger below my ear.

"Yes. Against the wall. Where anyone could see."

After the alley happened exactly as I'd narrated it to her, I met Marco back at our table, we paid our tab, and left the bar. My immediate need had been satiated, but I was still unsatisfied.

As Marco and I walked back to the apartment, he asked about the girl in the alley. I shrugged and lit a cigarette.

"You're different this year," he said. "Less predator. More player."

"Predator?" I asked. "Just what the fuck does that mean?"

"Only meaning there was a time you would take without asking. Without waiting."

I stopped walking. "I only fuck women who say yes."

"Of course," Marco said. "You are not a bad guy. But you made them *want* to say yes. Convinced them, like, no?"

I looked around the sidewalk. Who had I been? What had I done? Maybe I was a little too drunk for this conversation.

"They want me." My voice was weak, though, bewildered.

"You seduced them in Spain," he agreed. "Here, though, you wait. You let *them* push *you*."

"Maybe American girls are different?"

He shook his head. "You are different. Reluctant maybe."

"Reluctant to get laid?"

"To *only* get laid. To only fuck. To only know her first name."

"Ronnie," I said, jerking my chin at the bar. "Ronnie Brinks." I held up a napkin she'd stuffed in my pocket. "Says so right here." And her phone number and address in case I wanted to come over later. Or tomorrow.

"Throw it away," Marco said. "You're leaving. You don't need to give a shit about Ronnie Brinks or how much guilt she'll carry for letting you fuck her in that alley."

"What about my guilt?"

"That you have some proves my point. You're different."

I crumbled the napkin and walked it to the nearest trashcan. Finished my cigarette, stubbed it out, and threw it away, too.

"Remorse looks good on you," Marco said. "Makes you more human."

"I had a lot of that in Spain."

"No, in Spain you had regret. There's a difference."

Six hours of sleep later, Marco dragged me out of his bed. I'd passed out under the covers and he'd slept on top of them. We went out for another run. This time it was cooler and overcast, and we worked harder than the day before. We didn't talk, just ran, and the rhythm woke something in me I'd been waiting to feel since we'd left San Francisco. When we got back, I sat down with my notebook and wrote nine pages worth of narration. A night in L.A.: the bars, the women, the music, the dancing, the darkness, the alley, the brick against my palms as I lost myself inside her all like a long stream of consciousness that purged me of the remorse Marco had seen festering.

Then I showered. Jerked off. Packed my bag and led Abbie and David out into the parking lot. Goodbye hugs and some exchanged promises and we were on our way.

"L.A. is fucking awesome," Abbie said. "That chick's house was sick. Hot tub. Glass walls. View. My new career is bedding rich people." Then she passed out in the backseat and slept the whole way home.

PARIS
SPRING 2001

ara from Spain is what I called her, but she wasn't from Spain. She was from Oklahoma. She'd been a flight attendant for six years when we met. After our time together in Barcelona, she'd been writing me letters and sending me postcards from various places in the world.

I wrote her back. Pages of tightly scripted messages that explained the process for getting published, what my current therapist thought of my recovery progress, and the way I'd been building mileage in both swimming and running.

"It's such a big world," she wrote to me. "I hope you'll find a chance to explore more of it."

The last thing I sent her was an email with the flight arrival time and hotel information for my trip to France.

While in Barcelona, Marco and I had taken the train to Marseille for a weekend, but I had never been to Paris. I had two weeks that coincided with the school's spring break but would take me out an extra week, which Kittering said would be time well spent if I could romance a French woman and come back with a broken heart.

I told him last fall had broken my heart exactly enough, and he said, "Good, write about that."

The Jada experience needed writing, so I took it with me to Paris.

Lara couldn't stay the entire time I was there, but she had agreed to introduce me to a group of friends she knew in a literary circle and I felt excited by the prospect of a new city, new people, and a generally new experience. That she was a familiar warm body for my bed only made it that much more inviting.

We reunited in my hotel lobby. She was as tall as I remembered and curvier, too. Her hair was loose over her shoulders, a light brown with auburn highlights. She smiled when she saw me, as if we'd only been apart a short time. But it had been over a year, during which our letter correspondence had become increasingly intimate and honest. Seeing her in person had a warm familiarity but also an edgy vulnerability that I wasn't sure how to navigate.

She walked into my embrace and I held her against me for a moment, breathing her in, realizing I didn't really remember how she felt, and then pulled back to look into her eyes.

"It's good to see you," she said.

"Good to be seen," I murmured, looking at her lips and then back to her eyes again.

She leaned in and let me kiss her, and there was a hint of that reconnection I had expected. Not like in a flashback way, but in the way you feel returning to a place you've been before. Confident and pleasantly comfortable.

We went upstairs to settle in, that euphemistic phrase that means to shower, unpack, and get the lay of the land between the lobby and my room. Lara kept some distance between us as I cleaned up and offered to let me nap or rest before we found food, but I confessed I was starving and would rather eat and have an early night to sleep off the jet lag.

"I rarely get jet lagged anymore," she said. "My body has its own clock that doesn't really care what the rest of the world's clocks say. I eat when I want, sleep when I need to, and in general exist on my own plane of time."

I laughed at the pun. "Literally?" I asked.

She shrugged. "I'm like a savage."

I remembered first being attracted to her because of how easy she made it to simply exist. No expectations, no rules, just an indeterminable stretch of being together and then not.

Rubbing a towel across my damp head, standing in the doorway between the bathroom and the bedroom of the suite, I watched her watching me.

"How old are you?" I asked. "I just realized I have no idea."

"Thirty-two," she said.

"Never considered marriage? Kids? A house in the suburbs?"

"I considered it." She wore a pretty sundress and strappy sandals that may have been ambitious for the cool spring outside. She'd had a button-up sweater on that had since been removed and now lay beside her on the small functional couch. Her legs crossed, showing bare skin, and she was poised but relaxed on the furniture.

I held one towel in my hand, the other wrapped around my waist, and the knot nearly came undone when I hoisted my bag onto the bed. I turned away from Lara and re-wrapped the towel, feeling suddenly awkward about being naked in front of her. Maybe because it had been so long or maybe because when we'd been together in Spain, I was usually drunk.

"So, marriage isn't for you?" I prompted.

"If the right man fell in love with me," she said.

When I glanced at her, she was looking out the window, not at me.

"I haven't decided if I want to stay home yet, and staying put is sort of required. I have colleagues that are married, leave their spouses and children at home, and work this job, and it's brutal. It's lonely."

"Unless you have friends in the cities you travel to?" I asked.

"Friends," she said, and there was a kind of scoff in her voice. "Sure."

I shimmied a pair of boxer briefs on under the towel and then unwrapped it and dropped it, reaching into my bag for a clean pair of jeans. Pulling them on, I glanced up to continue our conversation, but she was watching me, a pensive look on her face.

I grinned. "Bite your lip," I said.

"Excuse me?"

"You're crazy sexy right now. Just bite your lip and I'll probably hit my knees, crawl over to you, and slide my hand up your leg." I meant it, too. The late afternoon light had warmed the room and her skin was amber in it, the highlights in her hair glinting, and the smile on her lips, a pale neutral lipstick staining them. She was beautiful.

Her eyes sparkled when she laughed and said, "Pretty sexy, huh?"

Tucking myself more fully into my jeans, buttoning them, and running a hand through my hair I said, "Are you trying to decide something?"

She shook her head, "It's already decided. You've always been young. And beautiful. And only made for weekends. Which is fine. I wouldn't have it any other way."

She stood and walked toward me, ran her fingertips down my bare chest and clasped the edge of my jeans, tugging just a little.

"Let's go get some food," she said, "Then we'll come back and make use of that bed. And maybe stay there for the rest of the weekend."

I kissed her, a soft, warm kiss that let the breath between us linger, and felt the heat of the light falling through the window and how it made her skin glow.

"I'm good for more than weekends," I said.

"Maybe for someone. But not for me."

Paris was beautiful. Lights twinkled, the river gently lapped its shores, and Lara was charming and affectionate and funny and the perfect amount of sexual energy without the tension. We listened to a sidewalk musician play a violin and I drew her into my arms and danced with her. We bought flowers from a woman with a basket and pulled the petals off one at a time tossing them over the railing onto the water below.

Lara told me about her family and how her siblings had each gone to college, settled down, and got together for holidays and birthdays. She was sort of the black sheep, she said, but her nieces and nephews made her feel like a celebrity anytime she showed up. She always brought them exotic gifts from foreign countries, and they displayed them proudly on their trophy shelves.

By 9:30 I was exhausted, I'd been up for twenty-four hours, and we decided to head back to my hotel. Lara confessed she hadn't yet secured a room of her own and I told her not to. The hotel desk clerk dragged her traveling case out of the closet, and we ascended to the fifth floor together.

I took my time undressing her, peeling off the little sweater, the dress, and her panties one piece at a time, revealing her in the streetlight from the window. She moved slowly, too, removing my clothes, and then leading me to the bed. I liked the strong, intentional way Lara and I came together. It felt more adult than the desperate passion I'd known before. We felt fitted in a temporary but satisfying way. We made love, easy and calm, comfortable and intimate. Like friends sharing the best of themselves with one another.

Holding her while she slept, stroking her back with my

fingertips and watching the Paris night dissolve into rain, I wondered if I was ever a good lover to the women I'd been with. I thought about Kacie and how we fit and Melissa and how she'd held me against her and asked, "Do you love me?" right before the phone rang and ruined everything. I thought about the girls in Spain, two at a time in the outdoor shower, up against the wall in dark hallways, locked bathrooms in noisy bars. All the "slutting" my therapist called it, the physical manifestation of the desperation my grief had driven me to.

I thought about Jada and getting back to what love felt like: vulnerable to where my eyes stung with tears and happy to where I didn't know I could be so fulfilled. The words ran through my mind, descriptions of intimacy that transcended the sexuality of it and got at the connection, the warmth, and the opportunity to be someone special for someone else.

Lara had been a Spain experience. Frantic, urgent, deep in grief and loneliness. Here she was, two years later, the pleasant warmth of friendship, a kind of mutual care that deepened our experience together but also expressed gratitude for the opportunity to connect with another person.

Gratitude. That's what I felt. Like in the church when that kid Taylor played his trumpet.

I pulled her a little closer and she mumbled in her sleep. I kissed her forehead and thought about tenderness. About closeness.

For three days Lara and I teased one another, acted the part of a perfectly matched pair of lovers free in Paris. We wandered through museums and galleries, occupied tables at cafes and restaurants. She took me to Les Philosophes, where we had the most exquisite steaks with mushroom sauce. Lara wasn't a college girl, she was a woman with a career and means, and when she took me into a shop to buy a suit for me, I felt spoiled.

"Are you going to Sugar Mama me?" I teased her.

"Perhaps," she said, with a tender kiss and a swat on my ass. "Or maybe I just want to see what grown-up Brian will look like some day."

She had me in pinstripes, dark shirts with dark ties, even suspenders and a bow tie, standing behind me, on a step stool, in front of a mirror, tying it for me so I could learn how. She walked me through the steps, told me stories of her brothers growing up in Oklahoma and wearing bow ties to church. She tied her prom date's tie and her best friend's husband's wedding tuxedo tie as well.

"I don't trust a man who can't tie a bow tie," she said.

"Why not?"

"Because it indicates he's too lazy to learn. What else might he be too lazy to do?"

We made eye contact in the mirror. I couldn't remember my father ever wearing a bow tie. I wondered if he knew how to tie one and suddenly wanted to call him and ask.

"You watch," she said, stroking my shoulders, eyeing my reflection. "Bow ties will make a comeback. And someday you'll impress the right woman with your ability."

I turned my face up to hers for a kiss. It was gentle, sisterly even, and I knew then that we were done. I was lucky to have gotten a chance to reconnect with Lara, to repair whatever damage that broken me had done in Spain. We spent one more night together and she slipped out of my hotel room before I'd even woken the next day.

I met Joel at the airport later, holding a sign that said, "Biggest American dick in France."

"The sign's supposed to be for me," he said, folding his hand into mine.

"It is," I said, flipping the sign over. The backside read, "And his friend the writer." I grinned and Joel did, too. We hadn't been together since New Year's in San Francisco. He was an engaged man, talking all about wedding plans and bringing news from his brother and Chris who I expected to see on our second trip to Nashville this summer. I didn't mention Lara had been there just six hours earlier. Or that Paris, like so many cities, had already become just another story.

NASHVILLE
SUMMER 2000

Four days in Nashville. That was what Jason pitched and we went for it. Though Joel had been to San Francisco and I'd been emailing with Chris, I hadn't seen Jason since the week he came to Barcelona last fall. He's the one who opened the door. We embraced, a tight hug with no words, and then he turned away from me and I followed him inside. Another tight hug with the other Lincrest twin before I chucked my backpack on the bed and flopped onto my back, crossing my feet at the ankles.

"Who's funding this palace and where the fuck is Chris?"

"I am and he's driving out. Said he'd be here by eight." Joel turned back to the laptop computer he had set up on the hotel room's desk.

Jason stretched across the second bed, two pillows piled under his head and flipped through channels on the TV.

I pulled the book I'd been reading on the plane out of my bag.

"You're gonna read right now, Hemingway?"

"Joel's working, you're looking for hotel porn, what should I do?"

"Go get us some beers, dick," Jason said.

"Why me?"

"Showed up empty handed like some kind of asshole."

"Not the last one here." I laughed. "Besides, I had a buzz earlier. Just didn't think I needed to get wrecked if we're waiting on Chris."

"We're not fucking waiting for Chris," Jason grunted as he sat up and turned the TV off.

"Aren't you playing this weekend?"

"Not till tomorrow night."

"Joeler?"

"Just need ten minutes to finish this," he said, not lifting his eyes from the screen.

I looked at Jason. He had a cut over his eye, maybe four or five days old.

"What happened there?" I asked, pointing to the same place on my own face.

Jason touched the scab. "Took a right hook to the face during a fight."

"On the ice?"

He nodded.

"The other guy fare worse?"

"Sadly, no. Definitely lost that one. Two minutes in the box. Lost the game, too."

"That sucks."

"Coach said I needed to be smarter about the fights." Jason stood and sauntered toward the window. He'd kicked his shoes off and his socks had different-colored seams across his toes, red on left and green on right.

"How many are you getting into? Per game?"

He stretched his arms out wide to either side, arching his back into a restless stretch and expelling a long stream of air, closing his lips into a "pffft" sound at the end.

"Not as many as I used to, but more than I should," he admitted.

"I know that tally." The book was still in my hand, and my thumb pressed the edge and it feathered with the flutter of shuffling cards.

"Probably how you count women." He pressed the curtains wide and looked down on the street below, his forehead making contact with the window.

"Not these days. There's just the one. Didn't Joel tell you about her?"

We both looked to his twin, but Joel didn't respond.

"She's amazing. Beautiful. Smart. Creative."

"Black."

"So Joel did tell you?" I flipped the book over and flattened my palm against it.

Jason turned toward me. "He said you're hooked."

"She's definitely got something."

"But not enough to keep you from going to Seattle to beg Kacie back?"

I sat up. "It wasn't like that."

Jason moved closer, towered over me. "She said you were on your knees."

I shook my head, looked at the floor, at the window beyond him.

"I just needed to tell her what had happened since Tony. Since I'd been gone. I wanted to . . . "

"You wanted to make sure she still missed you." Jason waited a beat until I looked up at him. What was he thinking? Did he still want her? Did he love her as I once did? How often did he speak to her? Had he been to Seattle? But I didn't ask any of those questions. I couldn't bear the answers. I wasn't ready for them.

"You're taunting her."

"I'm not."

"It's fucked up, Brian." Jason turned away from me, retreated to the window. I could see the sun was setting outside, the rose and amber clouds were giving way to the violet bruise of twilight. The room had just one lamp illuminated, and the shadows that crossed Jason's sharp cheeks and jaw made him look dark.

"Just leave her alone," he said.

"I should."

Joel scoffed in the corner as he closed his laptop. "But you won't."

"I can."

"How? I'm going to marry Tabby and Kacie's going to be in the wedding, Brian, like all of you will be. She's still part of our group of friends." He wrapped a cord around his fist and tied it off. Then he shoved it into a nylon bag. "You're going to need to redefine what she is to you." He pushed the computer into the bag and pulled the zipper around the edge. Then he stood up and mirrored his twin's posture, arms folded over chest, feet shoulder width apart. Two soldiers firm in their conviction. "You should make peace with the fact she's done with you."

That stung and I physically recoiled.

"That's our business. Kacie and me." My voice was tight, I knew, but I couldn't help it. "She's moving on. I respect that."

"Do you?" Jason pivoted, looked down at me again.

I stood so we were nearly eye to eye.

"I can. I will."

"I'll believe that when I see it. Five minutes and we can go." Joel strode into the bathroom and pulled the door closed behind him.

"Let's not do this again," Jason said.

"Talk about Kacie? Deal. We've only got three and a half days left."

"Not just this weekend. Let's not talk about this again ever," he said. "You get me?"

I nodded. "Yeah, man, I get it."

Accountability. It's what I was missing in San Francisco.

My friends there all helped me row the boat. Stay in school. Write stories. Workshop. Moderate the drinking. Swim and skate and attend church. There was healing to be done there.

But these fuckers knew me best. They were milestones. Kept me from backsliding. Made sure I was getting my bigger shit together. The past and who I was and who I wanted to be. They held me accountable for releasing Kacie and Tony and all that bad shit.

"Ever been to Nashville?" Jason asked. "It's a party every night. Let's go find some live music."

We wrote the name of the bar we would be in on a pad of paper on the desk and headed out. Joel stopped at the front desk and gave the clerk a message and a key for Chris. We were three rounds and two hours in when he finally caught up with us.

"You couldn't fucking wait for me?" was the first thing he said to Joel.

"Sorry, dude," Joel said. "I was done working and needed a beer."

We occupied a patio table in a beer garden-style alley bar. Jason stood and clapped Chris's shoulder, but Chris shrugged him off.

"Man, it's cool," Jason said.

"Nah, man, it's not," Chris said. "First thing the clerk wanted was my ID to prove I was the friend you were expecting."

"What?" Jason glanced at Joel.

"Yeah," Chris continued, "it's only fun when the manager comes around and suggests we speak away from the desk so the other guests aren't disturbed." He leaned both hands on the back of a chair and I could see he was shaking.

I stood, too. "What the fuck, man?"

"Yeah, well, it's not exactly *natural*," he sneered, "for a guy who looks like me to be going to a hotel room that belongs to guys who look like you."

"What the hell, man?" Joel asked. "Who said that?"

"They didn't have to say it." Chris gritted his teeth.

"But you got it sorted out." Joel raised a hand to flag down the server.

Chris glared at Joel. "Yeah, man, I got it sorted out. Me and the manager and the security guard, we all got it sorted out."

"Jesus, dude," Jason said. "We should have stayed. We didn't think it would be a problem."

"Nah, man, you wouldn't have." Chris squeezed the chair, expelled a long breath of air, and seemed to be trying to calm down.

The server appeared.

"Shots," Joel said. "Five of them. And Chris? What are you drinking, man?"

Chris flipped his hand in the air, and I said, "Dominion." It was what I was drinking. "Lager. Two more please." I pointed at my own and made eye contact with Chris.

He tipped his head just slightly, the nod an assent, and said, "Where's the john?"

A few minutes later, he and I stood on the other side of the beer garden fence and I handed him the one-hitter I carried with me. He took a quick drag, held the smoke in his lungs, and said, "Thanks," in that tight grunt of marijuana smokers that doesn't let any of the smoke escape.

"Wanna talk about it?" I asked.

"Not even a little bit." Another hit from the cigarette-shaped pipe and Chris rolled his shoulders back and shook his head. "Fucking manager probably thought *I* was *your* dealer. Fucking stupid." He tapped the pipe against the rail and shoved it back into the box. Handing it back to me, he said, "Don't ever do that shit again."

"We won't."

"Sucks," he said. "Not gonna be a buzz kill. Let's get over it."

"Two beers on the table. All weekend to misbehave." I grinned. "Might even find you a girl."

Chris smiled then, too. "Sure, Brian. Let's get laid."

Summer 2001

The second time we went to Nashville, it coincided with the World's Biggest Country Music Festival, which wasn't a coincidence. This time it was just Chris and Jason and me, and we were there to plan Joel's bachelor party. Jason said we were auditioning locations. Chris said we hadn't yet decided on Las Vegas (we had). I told my parents I was interviewing at Vanderbilt (I wasn't). Like the year before, I left from there for a three-week stint in Manila.

Without Joel, our accommodations would have been decidedly less luxurious, but Chris's stepmom was from the area and had a cousin, Denean, who put us up in her downtown condo. She was mid-forties, divorced, and answered the door with a glass of white wine in one hand and her phone in the other.

"They're here," she said to whomever was on the other end. "Yes, I told you I did. I don't know. How old are y'all?"

"Twenty-four," Chris said.

"Oh yeah," the cousin said. "They're young."

I grinned at her.

"And too good looking. This could get dangerous. Y'all come on in. I gotta go." The beep sounded as she ended the call and we filed inside.

Chris came last, closed the door behind us, and said, "Let's not let this get dangerous, okay?"

I shrugged at him as if to say, "Who? Me?" and chuckled.

"Good to see you, Chris," she said over her shoulder. They had met at his dad's wedding to Angela, and Chris remembered Denean's husband as being some kind of professional athlete or agent or coach or something. "You were so young at Angie's wedding, I guess I didn't notice you."

We'd been thirteen when his dad had met and married Angela. Their two children, Chris's half-siblings, "thing one" and "thing two" he called them with affection, were now middle schoolers. Chris's mom moved to Atlanta to reunite with her high-school sweetheart and when we graduated, Chris went to Atlanta for undergrad, but he'd found it hard to adjust. His mom agreed and she and Micah had moved back to Northern Virginia, too, not long after Tony died. Angela had been less stepmom-like to Chris and more the older-sister-friend-type. She was who got him into real estate, and he'd learned the ropes in her practice before going out on his own at the beginning of this year.

Now we sat in the kitchen of his stepmom's cousin, Denean, while she told us story after story about them growing up in Tennessee. She had a perfect southern accent and paused for dramatic effect when appropriate, it was as if she'd rehearsed all of these stories by telling them and retelling them hundreds of times.

"Y'all don't want to stay here and listen to an old woman ramble," she said.

"Are you expecting company? I don't see an old woman around here." I winked at her.

"You're a criminal," she said. "Really. It's illegal what you can do to a woman's imagination. Or ought to be anyway." She smiled coquettishly and slid a new bottle of Pinot Grigio across the kitchen's wide island bar toward Chris. He frowned at her and me, but set to the bottle with a wine key, pealing the label away and digging into the cork. Denean added more ice to all of our glasses, and Chris refilled them with a pale pinot grigio that might have been even better if it was sparkling. It was our fourth round.

Chris excused himself to the first guest bedroom. He'd driven out and felt like he wanted to shower before we went barhopping. Jason's flight landed an hour before mine at the airport, and we met up at a bar in the concourse to wait for Chris, so we were a few drinks in before we ever reached Denean's.

She'd turned some music on and cooked us a delicious meal, and it was nearing ten o'clock before Jason followed Chris back into the hallway to clean up as well. I set about helping Denean clean the kitchen. Standing over the sink, I scrubbed suds over plates and pots and rinsed them to hand to her. She loaded the dishwasher, dried pans, put things away, and wiped down the countertops.

"Can I ask you a question?"

"Is it a Black people question?"

"Why would you think that?"

"Usually when white people say, 'can I ask you a question?' it's because they want me to explain something Black to them."

I glanced at her, but she was smiling so I smiled, too.

"Kind of," I admitted. "I dated this woman. Jada. And she cheated."

Denean made a sound like judgment.

"Not saying I didn't deserve it."

"Ain't nobody deserve bein' cheated on, Brian."

"I mean, I've done my share."

"Cheating's never about the person it's done to. It's always about the person doing the cheating."

I shut the water off at the sink and turned to face her.

"I never cheated on her."

"Answer me this." She put her hands on her hips and lowered her chin, looking at me through long, thick eyelashes. "Was she with another white man?"

I shook my head.

"Like I said, that wasn't about you." She shook her hands out, bangled bracelets shimmying and jingling. The sleeves on her blouse, wide and wispy, fluttered like streamers around her arms.

"How can you know that?"

"How can you not?" She came around the kitchen island, bringing both of our wine glasses with her. Handing me mine, she lifted her chin, so I drank what was left in it. Then she smiled. The faintest scent of magnolia emanated from her and it reminded me of something, but I couldn't remember what.

"My ex-husband traveled for his job. He was in sports. Different woman every trip. Took whatever he could get from whomever would give it to him." She smiled but it was a sad, reflective kind of smile. "I thought he'd grow out of it. Like you."

"But some men don't." My voice was quiet. We stood near one another, me leaning against the sink, her leaning against the island.

"Some *people* don't." She tipped her glass up and finished her wine.

"Should I have waited for her?"

Denean shook her head. "Nah, baby. When she's ready she'll find the one who makes her want to grow up."

"But she's the one who made me want to grow up." I could hear the pout in my voice but couldn't stop it. Losing Jada hurt. Still.

"Lord, I know," Denean snorted. "My Marlon did me, too. Don't it just suck how that don't work both ways?"

"What're you two whispering about?" Chris asked, coming into the room from my left.

I turned toward him, flipping my empty glass over into the open dishwasher.

"Brian's ex."

"Jada?" Chris grinned. "Did he ask you a Black question?"

"No," I said.

But Denean said, "Yes," at the same time and they both howled with laughter.

"Damn, man," Chris said. "Leave you alone for one minute."

"I'm gonna go shower."

"Make it quick. Jay's almost ready and I already called a cab."

"You gonna go with us?" I asked Denean. We'd invited her multiple times, naming the places we wanted to revisit from our trip a year ago.

"Not a chance. You boys go find some young women who need romancing."

"More like cougars to pick up the bar tabs," Chris said.

"You just like your daddy," Denean said for at least the third time, and made that noise again, but this time it wasn't real disapproval—it was the affectionate kind.

Two hours later, just after midnight, the three of us were watching a live act in a packed bar. Four women had joined us around a tall table near the stage, and Jason was pinned between two of them listening to them talk about the work they did at a nearby hospital. The third woman, a small, elfish-looking brunette with two mini-buns tied in her hair and a white peasant blouse, sat on a stool next to where Chris stood. Now and then she'd lean toward him and shout some observation or another about what we were watching on stage.

That left the fourth woman to me. She was the prettiest of the set, long hair in various shades of gold and white that lay flat down her back as if it had been ironed, and wide brown eyes and brows that betrayed her natural color. She wore oversized hoop earrings, a pale green baby doll top, and cut-off jean shorts with white frayed edges. Now and then she'd shift and the gap between the shorts and the top would show midriff. I wanted to slide my hand across it and pull her against me. Her name was Leigh, "I-G-H. Not E-E," she said, in a tender accent that melted over her voice and dripped sweet honey into my ears. I wanted to be in love with her. Just for the weekend.

They had also come for the festival. Leigh's brother was a roadie for one of the acts and they had two backstage passes. She didn't say which of the friends she would allow to accompany her. They followed us to the second bar, but when we left that one for a third, Leigh's friends decided to stay behind. She wrote her phone number down on the inside of a matchbook and kissed me. I told her I'd call her tomorrow. But I knew I wouldn't.

They showed back up at bar five and we reunited like old friends. The elfish girl was pretty lit, and she took a seat on Chris's lap. He held her hip to keep her in place but was otherwise a perfect gentleman, despite her flailing and hanging across him. He caught my eye over her shoulder and shook his head as if to say, "Drunk chicks."

Leigh had settled in next to me on the inside of the booth, and though I felt a little trapped and claustrophobic, her lips against my ear as she told me boring shit about school and her family felt nice. Jason kept a studious distance, watching the screens as if international cycling, bull riding, and billiards were the most interesting sports he'd ever seen. One of the girls who'd been chatting with him in bar one had taken a cab home and the other was near the stage dancing.

At last call, we shuffled out onto the sidewalk, and Jason and Chris and I waited while Leigh and her friends made plans for departure. Chris stumbled a bit into me, and when I looked up, I realized he'd been pushed. A couple of dudes about three yards behind him were staring back at us and talking to one another. Chris didn't turn around.

"You okay?" I asked.

"Time to go," he said.

Then the elfish girl draped herself on him and begged him to go back to their house with them. Chris was holding her up, not exactly against him, but within the circle of his arms.

"Let's get you a cab," Chris told her, smiling but starting to get annoyed.

I turned to where Leigh and her other friend were talking with Jason, waiting for the crowd around the street to thin out, cabs pulling away one at the time. We were in some kind of disorganized queue, I realized, and moved closer to them. When I turned to bring Chris with me, the guys who'd been a few yards behind us were now standing in front of him, and his back was to me, hands up, while the girl hung on him like a feather boa.

Without being able to hear what the guys were saying, I called over my shoulder to Jason and we approached Chris together.

"There a problem?" I asked.

Chris shook his head. "No problem, man, just telling these dudes we're getting the girls in a cab." His voice was neutral, no inflection.

I glanced over the girl's head at the guys Chris was talking about. One of them had his eyes narrowed at Chris, another seemed to be sizing up me and Jason.

"Do you know them?" I asked the girl, gesturing so that she turned away from Chris and looked at the others.

She shook her head, "They weren't very nice, were they?" she asked Chris.

"Shh," he said. "It's cool, baby, let's just get you home."

A snort from the nearer of the two guys pulled my attention to him.

"Problem?" I asked again.

"This *nigger* thinks he's gonna take that girl home."

The word singed the air between us, the surprise of it, the weight of it.

Jason lunged at the guy, fist crashing into shocked face with a sickening crack. Dude raised his hands to fight Jay off, but Jason played hockey, and players wail until the whistle blows. Chris and I dove at Jason after he knocked the guy to the ground, and we each caught an arm and hauled Jason toward us. The girl had shrieked when Chris pushed her away to chase Jason, alerting the bouncers from the bar who ran through the crowd.

We'd gotten Jason pulled away before the bouncers arrived, and they stood between us and the other guys looking back and forth to see if it was really over.

Jason's chest was heaving.

"Get this racist motherfucker out of here," Jason said to the guy's friend.

One of the bouncers narrowed his eyes at Jason and looked at me and then at Chris, lingering there as if trying to decide something.

"We didn't do anything," I said. "It was them," and jerked my chin at the guy now climbing back to his feet with the tentative help of his friend.

"Three on two, real brave. Lucky he didn't shoot you," the friend said.

"Someone got a gun?" the second bouncer asked.

Chris's hands went up for the second time that night, "Nah, man."

"Do we need cops?" the other bouncer asked.

"No," I said quickly. "We're just getting the girls in a cab and then walking back to our place."

Chris glanced at me and shook his head slightly.

"Y'all live here?" the bouncer asked.

Before we could answer, though, Leigh was there.

"Brian? Chris? Everything okay?" She put herself between me and the bouncers. The guys on the other side looked her up and down. The one who'd called Chris that word spit on the ground between us.

"Chris?" Leigh asked and waited until he looked at her. "Our cab is here."

"Racist assholes," the elf-like girl wailed from behind us.

"Get in the cab," Chris said, pushing Jason and Leigh toward the other two girls.

The bouncers, looking nearly identical with high-and-tight haircuts and bar logo t-shirts, had their arms out forming a barricade between Jason and the guy he'd hit. They were still looking back and forth between those two and us.

"That asshole assaulted me," the guy said, rubbing the back of his head. "I probably have a concussion. Call the cops," he barked at the bouncers. "I'll sue your ass!"

"Try it," Jason said.

"Jay, shut. The. Fuck. Up, man," Chris said. "We're leaving," he said to the bouncers. "Just a misunderstanding. Seriously. No cops. We're done. It's cool now."

I stepped back as Chris urged, my heart still pounding from the effort of pulling Jason away, from thinking maybe I'd have to throw a punch, too, from wondering if dude hit his head on the concrete and if he was really injured, would we all go to jail?

Fights are messy. I'd been in enough of them. And it had been a while, but I hadn't forgotten. While I'd averted the fight at Radford with Tony, I'd sought the fight with Eric Waters on the night we buried Tony and the one with Christian Heilman the next night. Six months after that, I had tried to talk the Russians out of fighting and got my ass kicked. I wasn't afraid to fight, not really, I just knew it hardly ever solved anything. Even so, I should have hit that guy Jada left me for. And this Nashville motherfucker, the one who'd used that word, he had it coming. I was just surprised Jason had gotten there before me.

Which is what I was saying as we climbed the steps up to Denean's condo. Jason was saying he wished the other dude had tried to get in there, too. Maybe he could have beat the bouncers down, too. I told him one-on-one was hard enough, not to wish for a brawl.

"Hockey fights are different," I said.

"Yeah, skates make it harder to get leverage and dudes slip and fall faster."

"That guy went down pretty quick."

We had piled into the cab with the girls, gone a couple of blocks, and climbed out, sending them on and walking the rest of the way to Denean's. In her kitchen, I fished some ice out of the freezer and wrapped a cold compress for Jason's hand.

Jason and I fell silent. Chris hadn't really said anything.

"You okay, man?" I asked.

"Nashville." He shook his head, sat back, hugged one arm around his waist, propping the other elbow on his fist and cupping his chin in the valley between his forefinger and thumb. "Ain't like Herndon. Or Reston." His hand came off the chin to punctuate each town. "Or South Riding. Racists there, too, you know, but they hide it well."

Jason sat next to him, rolled the ice over his hand.

"I'm sorry, man."

"What for, Jason? Me bein' Black? Or them being assholes?" Chris leaned forward, elbows on the counter. "Or you being willing to throw a punch for pretty much anything these days? What are you sorry for, man?"

He wasn't wrong. A year ago, Jason had told us the coach was on him about fights on the ice. Over Christmas he'd been suspended. Joel told us that. When Chris asked him about it on New Year's, Jason had waved it off. But Joel was worried. In Paris, he told me that Jason had pretty much shut down. Hadn't told him anything, barely talked to their mom, but had told Kacie he was planning to quit playing. Apparently, Jason's roommate and teammate had been fired, and if Jason didn't find a new roommate soon, he'd have to get another job to cover rent. Jason's plan was to work as a bouncer. Joel acted like his twin had said he'd become a stripper.

In Denean's kitchen, I wondered if Joel had told Chris any of this, but then Chris said, "If you quit playing hockey, you should leave Michigan."

Jason looked up from his hand, his face confused. "Why would I quit playing?"

"Play, don't play," Chris said. "But get your head together. What's going on, for real?"

"*For real?*" Jason mocked. "Can't I just be pissed at some asshole calling you a nigger?"

I winced but Chris just stared at Jason, his jaw clenched. "No, man, you can't."

"Why not?"

"Because that's *mine*." He jabbed at his chest with his thumb. "That's why *I* hit a motherfucker, not you."

"Only you can be pissed at racists?"

"You don't see me out there starting fights with all your critics. Sportswriters and coaches and teammates, hell, even your dad's been laying it pretty thick. But I'm not fighting all of them for you."

"Your dad?" I asked, but they ignored me.

"What else has Joel told you?" Jason's voice was low, the betrayal of his twin confiding in us so deep that I decided not to mention Paris.

"Painkillers."

"Of course."

"Says you're buying them off your teammates."

"Once."

"If you'd quit hitting people, you wouldn't need them, Jay."

"It's not the hitting that hurts," Jason said.

The room got quiet. A ticking of a clock somewhere, the hum of the refrigerator, the breath between us, the shift of the ice in the towel.

"It's everything else."

I stepped closer to the counter where Jason and Chris were mirroring one another's posture, elbows on the counter, fingers splayed. Side by side and they both looked like they were hurting. And I didn't know what to do. I tipped a bottle of vodka over the three tumblers I'd pulled down from the cabinet.

Sara once told me that other people had different experiences than me. Even the people who grew up with me. Even the people who knew me best. Their experiences were different and valid, and I didn't have to fix them. Or even understand them.

Thomás had told me just to love them through it. And to extend grace, in all things. In the moment, the only grace I had was vodka.

"I love you guys," I said.

Jason looked up. "You drunk?"

I shook my head. "I don't know what else to say." I took down the shot of vodka. "I miss you when we're not together." I looked at Chris, too, and he was staring up at me.

"Same," he muttered. He took the shot I'd poured for him, then he clapped Jason on the back. "Let's fix this, man."

Jason nodded and swallowed down his own shot.

"We've got all weekend," I said, and poured three more.

"That should be enough to get started," Jason said. The ice in the kitchen towel shifted and Jason rolled it back on top of his knuckles. "Hurts," he grunted.

"Hitting a motherfucker does," Chris said. "But thanks for doing it."

BANGOR

SUMMER 2001

The second time I went to Bangor, Maine, I took Abbie with me.

Years ago, my mom's Uncle Walt died there, and we went for his funeral. It was late January and fucking cold. Four degrees. Like why bother? Just be zero. Mom complained about her aunt wearing too much perfume and showed me Stephan King's house which, she said, was proof only crazy people lived in Maine. It was my senior year in high school and rather than leave me home to misbehave, I'd been Delta'd to Bangor in Dad's place. I did my best impression of him, visiting the brewery, standing close to Mom throughout, and paying one of the front desk guys to scrape snow off the rental car. Uncle Kevin was there, too, and he took a picture of me by the frozen river, the Penobscot, which was flowing wide, wild, and full when Abbie and I got there in the last days of summer, 2001.

"So, it's not frozen all year round?" she asked, snapping pictures from the deck of the Sea Dog Brewery with a Fun Saver disposable camera and frowning.

"Did they not even teach the seasons in California? Like, why bother?"

"Cool it, smart ass. I grew up in Iowa until sixth grade."

"Maine has few weeks of spring, a month or so of summer, and about ten days of fall," I said, taking a long drink out of the pale ale in front of me.

"Are your cousins still here?"

"Mom's cousins run a hippie store downtown."

So of course, we went there, too. I bought Abbie two fish-shaped tea light candle lanterns. They had exaggerated gills and eyelashes and lips, and she adored them. She picked out a tapestry skirt and a shoulder bag with a hand-painted tree.

Strolling through town she said, "I could live here."

We had lunch in an Irish pub and beers in a taproom so new it smelled of wall paint and floor polish. The bartenders all told us about the downtown revitalization underway.

We'd arrived on the Labor Day weekend Saturday, caught some live music on the riverfront, and slept late Sunday morning. Monday, we drove out to Bar Harbor to walk around. By Wednesday, when my interview was scheduled, we'd seen it all.

Abbie drove us up to Orono and the campus of the University of Maine. We split up in the visitor parking lot so she could go find the art museum, and I found the English Department Chair's office.

"You've come a long way," the Chair said by way of greeting.

"I've been here before."

"Stayed all weekend?" He waived me into a chair and sat down behind his desk.

"Enjoyed Bangor and Bar Harbor." I crossed one leg over the other in a figure four and looked past his shoulder to the expansive quad below the window.

"Nice time of year to visit," he said.

"I've disappointed my travel companion. She wanted to see the Penobscot frozen."

He chuckled and said, "Perhaps she'll get her chance if you decide to relocate here after all."

I didn't correct him that Abbie would move with me—she'd threatened such a thing. As far away from her mother without leaving the continent, she said, was good enough for her.

"We're a small department, Brian, but growing. Our creative writing program draws students with talent, and we've enjoyed bringing visiting scholars in for short stints to provide a variety of influences throughout an undergraduate's years here."

"You currently have Arianne Graney," I said. "Her doctoral advisor oversaw my MFA."

"At Penn?" He looked confused.

"They were at Penn. He found me in San Francisco. A few years later."

He chuckled. "I should say so."

Kittering had come home to San Francisco to care for his ailing mother in 1997. He was nearer to retirement than the man across the desk from me, but not by much. There had been rumors around Christmas that he'd be done in May, but he'd confirmed one more year. After I defended my thesis and graduated last Spring, I'd gone to Manila again and decided on one more year in San Francisco to write and try to secure an agent or a publisher. I had considered working for a university press or a literary agency, but Kittering said I could teach a year as an adjunct and look for something more creative.

"What is it you want, Brian?"

"A place to write," I said.

"You can do that anywhere."

"And I have."

"So your application explains. Five continents, sixteen countries."

"But just two published stories," I said. "So, more work to do."

"Two stories that won major awards," he corrected. "You're a rising star. Anyone can see that. Your work is impressive."

I tilted my chin in thanks.

"It's one year only. And one year from now."

"Yes, sir."

"And then what?"

"The next opportunity I suppose."

"You're not looking for tenure?"

I smiled. "I'm too young for tenure."

"And your . . . wife? Family?"

I shook my head. Kittering had warned me that bachelor instructors were not always welcome, given the rate at which undergraduate girls could become infatuated and the number of men who abused positions of authority over them.

"Just my traveling companion," I said, and smiled. "For now."

He nodded and seemed to take the hint that perhaps Abbie was a girlfriend, someone who would keep me from hitting on undergrads but not someone who would require a large salary or medical insurance. Which is what I wanted him to think. It's what Kittering had told me would be the most attractive. No chair wanted a playboy on their roster, but neither did they want a salary negotiated beyond department budget.

"What are your thoughts on our most famous graduate?"

"I liked his early work," I said. "King's a master, to be sure."

I didn't tell him my mother's assertion that he was evidence of *Mainahs* being crazy. It was just as well I keep my remarks professional. The chair could be King's best friend. They seemed about the same generation.

"Kittering was cordial on the phone," he stroked his goatee a bit when he said that. "His letter of recommendation left me with some questions I wanted to clarify."

I had not seen the letter and did not allow my expression to betray concern over its contents.

"He indicated you had experienced a tragedy."

I nodded.

"It's been some time ago?"

"Two and a half years."

We were quiet then. Perhaps he wanted me to tell him what the tragedy was without having to ask. I decided not to. Tony's death had shaped a lot of things for a long time. It was time to stop letting it. I needed to be someone other than the guy whose best friend committed suicide.

"You've done two stints in Manila?"

I nodded again. "Last summer I assisted Kittering and this summer I led."

"Tell me about being the lead."

"There's the easy part, prevalent English language and the friendliness of the culture. But then there are these small irregularities, liked armed guards in Starbucks, and the way they called me 'sir' that kept me ever separate. Different. Apart. It's a dichotomy I've written a good bit about." I used the rehearsed explanation of the Manila experience. Left out the underaged girls with Western businessmen, the misplaced modifiers in signage, and how people were so directive as to be suspiciously compliant. In my notebooks from Manila, I'd scribbled questions like, *What are they hiding? Why are they willing to do exactly as I'd asked without suggesting a better way?*

Had I asked the housekeeping staff to wash my clothes in the bathtub they would have without question. It was disconcerting.

To the chair, I said, "I kind of get this universal-human-experience theme when I'm immersed overseas. It's like living the stories I've studied."

"Foreign travel is good creative material," he agreed.

"I've enjoyed it but am looking forward to staying put for a bit." That may not have been true. My wanderlust had evolved from escaping painful memories into a thirst for exploration. Each new trip energized me and the connections I'd made filled my email inbox with invitations, stories, and photos of lives I had yet to live. This residency was attractive specifically because it was only a year. I had no desire for putting down roots. Only swinging from the vines of others' established forests. I was young, as my father continued to remind me, and now was the time to be everywhere and nowhere all at once. Wherever that was was where I wanted to be.

"What are you working on right now?" He had leaned back in his chair and as it sunk toward the floor, he bounced slightly. I tried to keep my eyes on him and not climbing over the walls of bookshelves two- and three-volumes deep. Loose-leaf notes bled out of worn copies of *Huckleberry Finn* and *Portrait of a Lady*. I knew he was an American Literature specialist with a focus on Realism. My own interest in Dirty Realism of the 1980s and derivations like Rough South bordered his own expertise. I wasn't convinced I was the right fit for the department. But he had published an article on Fitzgerald's use of physical space that aligned with some of my own analysis on Hemingway's sparseness of narrative setting.

"I've been writing screenplays with a friend in Los Angeles," I said. "The dialogue-heavy form is a close relative of my own fiction work. Thought I'd give it a try."

"Television? Not theatre?"

I shrugged. "I'm interested in theatre, but the screenplay, honestly, is my friend's effort in a new production company. He just asked me for a good story."

He chuckled. "Exploratory, then?"

"Experimental." In truth, I'd considered moving to Southern California to collaborate with Marco. I enjoyed him, felt good about the production company he was with, and felt a certain draw toward creating stories that could come to life. But I had little to no training in screenplays and had been unwilling to commit to Marco for any number of unnamed reasons. Two of which were Abbie and David who flat-out refused to migrate to what they called the "cesspool" part of the state.

I had snorted at them. "Snobs." They'd snapped their fingers in unison in response.

"What do you think of our campus?" The department chair jerked his chin toward the window.

"The trees are really great. Lots of shade I bet."

"Indeed." He stood then. "Let us take a tour. We might be able to catch the Dean in his office."

In the lobby, we ran into Abbie. She had returned, as we'd planned, in case there had not been a chance to explain how harmless my bachelorhood was.

"Abbie is a poet," I said. "And her mother is a nonfiction writer of some regard in the personal growth realm."

Abbie's glare at me softened when the chair looked back at her. "Is that so?"

She nodded. "Oh, sure, you know *Californians*. Always looking for alternative remedies for mental health and wellness."

"Ah, yes, Californians," the Chair said. "But I meant about the poetry."

"She's been published more than I have." Before I could add the part about her having an MFA of her own, the chair waived at another older gentleman and motioned he should join us.

"Dean Callahan, Brian Listo, next year's Writer in Residence."

Abbie beamed. The dean stuck out his hand.

"Candidate anyway," I said. "Pleased to meet you."

"Oh, it's yours if you want it, Listo," the dean said. "Kittering was clear we would be, what was it, John? 'East Coast Pricks' if we didn't welcome you aboard."

"And so we shall," John said. "Let California's loss be our gain."

I nodded at them both. "I'm grateful to you."

"We will send an offer letter," the dean continued. "You'll make an exceptional addition. And you, Miss...?" he said to Abbie.

"Nichols," she supplied. "Abbie Nichols. Brian's poetry half."

The dean looked between the two of us, nodded and said, "I hope you'll be returning next summer."

Abbie smiled. "Thank you. We shall see."

As we walked toward the visitor lot, after more small talk around publication and teaching philosophy, firm handshakes, and wishes for safe travel, Abbie said, "They practically had us engaged."

I laughed. "Too bad they don't know I'm not your type."

She shrugged. "Maybe not. But this place will do."

"So, you're in?"

"Let's see if we can talk David into it, too, okay?"

"Not sure I can afford to support you both." But the idea had merit. We were a trio, pals, and I had left my pals behind once before and regretted building a life without them. I didn't plan to do it again.

TUESDAY, SEPTEMBER 11, 2001

HERNDON, VIRGINIA

7:02 a.m.

Through security and still stupid early, I shoved my backpack between my heels and climbed onto the barstool. The sun had just come up, but I'd already had two cups of coffee, and that simply wasn't getting it done.

"What'll it be?"

"Amaretto sour. Lots of cherries."

The bartender grinned at me. "Hangover drink?"

"Getting back on the horse," I agreed. Looking around for an ashtray, I shook a box of Camel Lights out of my pocket, then thought better of it and set them aside until the Amaretto had a chance to reignite my buzz.

"Big night last night?"

"For a Monday, yeah," I said. "We'd been at it all weekend, but this was our last visit till Thanksgiving, so we had to go big."

The bartender's smirk said he knew exactly what I meant. He poured the cocktail into a tall glass and topped it with a splash of Sprite.

"The sugar should be enough," he said, "but the sour mix sometimes needs a little carbonation."

"Thanks, pal."

The bar faced the restaurant, mirrors behind the liquor bottles, and the wall to my right was all windows overlooking the tarmac. Planes glided in and out of the terminal, lights spun as jetways connected and luggage carts bolted in and out with flapping curtains and stacks of bags.

I'd only been here since Friday and hadn't packed much. With the Orioles and the Redskins playing out of town and the Caps season still a month away, we'd settled on a show at The 9:30 Club, a British DJ named Fatboy Slim who won a few awards on last week's MTV Video Music Awards (thank Tabby for that bit of trivia—Joel passed it on to us as she'd asked him to, but it just reaffirmed what a nerd his bride really was, so we laughed at him and then at her).

Since Friday we'd been drinking.

Played some pool at Santa Fe Cue Club Saturday. Chris's girl, Sarah, waited on us.

Visited Tony on Sunday.

Monday, I met with the chair of the English Department at George Mason University. Dad insisted but there was no damn way I was taking that job. Back in Northern Virginia was the last fucking place I wanted to be. Last night, after Joel left for Pittsburgh, Jason, Chris, and I hit Uno hard. I hadn't been there since Tony's funeral weekend. It hadn't changed. I wasn't surprised.

Home around 12:00, I'd made Chris get up at 6:30 to drive my ass to the airport. Just fifteen minutes, ten miles, from the house he owned in South Riding, and before rush hour, but it had made him grimace and cuss me anyway.

"Not much sleep," I said to the bartender. "But it was worth it."

"Good times with old friends?"

I nodded. "It shows, huh?"

He grinned. "Been there." Then he raised a coffee mug to his lips and took a sip.

I could feel the Amaretto loosening my shoulders and chest. Pretty soon it would be working on the tightness I could feel in my forehead between my eyebrows.

"Hey, man," the stool next to me was dragged out, and a sailor in uniform took the seat. "Can I get a beer?"

The bartender pulled a glass from the counter behind him and indicated a draft handle. The sailor waved off the first and accepted the second one from the right.

Once the glass was full, a small white layer of foam topping it, the bartender put it in front of the sailor with a napkin underneath.

"Long night?" I asked my new neighbor.

"Long forty-eight hours," he said. He was young, maybe just twenty-one, with pale buzzed-cut hair and skinny arms. "Left the Philippines yesterday," he said.

"Oh yeah? I was just there over the summer. Manila?"

"I guess. Came off ship, got on a plane. Headed home."

"That's great."

He took a long drink then shook his head. "Not great. It's an emergency. My dad."

"That sucks." Now I did shake the cigarettes out of the pack and offered him one, which he took. We lit them and blew smoke over the bar toward the mirrors, and I waited for him to say what else he had pressing on him.

He drank, inhaled, exhaled, and added, "Motorcycle crash. They're not sure he'll live."

"Fuck, dude, I'm sorry."

He nodded. "Right?"

We both smoked. I finished my Amaretto sour. Asked the bartender for a water.

"Where ya headed?" he asked me.

"L.A."

"Pennsylvania."

"Time's your flight?"

"10:00."

I glanced at my watch. "You got a while."

He nodded again and took a long drink.

"Gotten any sleep?"

He shook his head and I could see, even in profile, his eyeballs were thick with unshed tears.

"Probably should," I said. "In case." In case he got off the plane and his dad was dead and he had a mom and siblings and friends and grandparents that would all want him to comfort them, be strong for them, hug them. If he couldn't stand upright, from booze or lack of sleep, that would make it so much worse.

"You headed home?" he asked me.

"Back to California."

"Were you on vacation?" He sniffed and folded his arms in front of him.

"My best friend Tony's birthday was Sunday."

"That must have been fun."

"Lots of booze."

"You guys get together every year?" Maybe it was a distraction. I was glad to provide one.

"Nah," I said. "The last two years I've been away."

"So why come home this time?"

We'd come back because Jason needed us to. Chris and Joel

and I had planned some acts of remembrance and mourning to get to what Jason had been avoiding. But I didn't share any of that. I said, "Tony's been dead almost three years. At some point the rituals have to stop, ya know?'

"Your best friend is dead?"

I nodded.

The kid waited for me this time. Seemed to be holding his breath. When I didn't volunteer any additional information, he took a drag, blew it out, and gathered his courage to press forward.

"That first year. His first birthday after he died . . ."

"Killed himself," I said. "Tony killed himself."

The sailor swallowed. "What was that first birthday like?"

I told him about Barcelona. Just the highlights. Ten minutes later, I paid both our checks. Told him I hoped the best for his dad. Then I left.

7:45 a.m.

The boarding area for Flight 77 was crowded. Californians bleary-eyed and anticipating the long flight back to L.A. On the other side of all that country: Pacific Ocean, warm weather, surfboards, sand, traffic, and smog. For me and Marco, a few ideas we were going to try out, a meeting with the studio's greenlight team, and then I was back up to San Francisco by Thursday.

Kittering told me to take my time coming back from Bangor, and I had. Sent Abby back to San Francisco, drove down from Bangor to New York and stayed two days in a cramped East Village flat with one of Joel's classmates from Pitt. Then to Philadelphia, where I had lunch with Dr. Raquel Morales, a woman I'd met in Manila. Through email exchanges, she had let on she would be in the States lecturing at a few East Coast schools. She was grateful I'd mentioned her to fill Kittering's role at UCSF and wanted to thank me with dinner. I accepted lunch with wine.

I booked my return flight from Dulles so I could see The Crew for Tony's birthday, minus the girls. Joel drove in from Pittsburgh, Jason came down from Michigan, and we'd taken a bottle of bourbon out to Tony's grave for a round of shots.

Now I'd hit L.A. and put that option to bed. I ought to go through Tucson to see Mom and Dad, but that could wait. We were having The Crew to Arizona for Thanksgiving.

In the boarding area, I squeezed in between an oversized business traveler in his suit and tie and a young mom bouncing a baby on her knee. She gave me a weak smile and I noticed the lines around her eyes. The baby giggled but kept dropping its toy on the ground. I leaned down and picked it up a few times only to have it flung back to the carpet with the child clapping and squealing in delight. The mom tried to smile, too, but I could see she was losing patience.

I kept up the game for a few rounds, and then she shifted the baby to the other side and shoved the toy into a bag.

"Flight's delayed?" I asked.

"We're standby," she said.

"How'd that happen?"

"Missed our 6:50 flight, got added to the list for this one." She rolled her eyes. "My sister couldn't get out of bed to drive us here on time."

I laughed. "My pal struggled, too."

"This one doesn't let me sleep much past 4:30." She frowned.

"Early birds," I said and made a silly face at the baby, so she giggled. "Some of us are just built for 4:00 a.m." I leaned back a little, giving the mom and baby more space, not wanting to be a creeper. Not wanting her to smell the booze and cigarettes on me. "Swam early all my life. Then worked the docks in Barcelona. 4:32 a.m. is my go-to."

"Barcelona, huh?" she said. "Oddly specific. Not just Spain, or just Europe."

"Nah, I'm too Hemingway for that." And I winked at her. I might have been drunk again.

"Hemingway drank himself to death." Her voice was flat, matter-of-fact.

"So I've been told." She definitely smelled the booze on me. "I think I'm like that U2 song." When she looked confused, I added, "Still haven't found what I'm looking for."

She smiled. "Isn't that all of us?"

Before I could ask who "us" was, the gate agent cleared his throat into the loudspeaker and the woman next to me started to ready their things.

7:58 a.m.

"In just a few minutes we will begin boarding Flight 77 to Los Angeles. All passengers please remain in or near the boarding area."

There weren't more than sixty people waiting on the flight. I approached the counter and asked the flight attendant if he planned to move passengers from Standby. He said they weren't sold out and didn't have a standby list.

I waved toward the woman with the baby and said she was waiting for a seat.

He said she should approach the counter herself.

"Come on, man," I said. "She's busy with the baby. Can't you just print her a ticket?"

"I really do need to speak to *her*," he said, his nostrils pinched, and chin raised. "*Sir*," he added and looked past me. Tugging the PA microphone toward him, its coiled cord extending, his thumb depressed the side button and he spoke into it. "Our first-class passengers are now welcome to board."

Which was how I ended up holding the baby for the woman I just met. After I relayed what he'd said to her about there not being a standby, he had crooked his finger at her and she'd stood and gone, as beckoned. I followed for no good reason other than I'd started this thing and wanted to see it resolved—and if he was rude to her, like he'd been to me, I'd have something to say about that.

"You'll need a boarding pass," he said after she slid her standby voucher across the counter. "And a photo ID." As if someone else would be pretending to be her, right? But rules are in place for safety or whatever, so she nodded and complied.

"Passengers seated in rows eighteen through thirty-six in the main cabin are invited to board," the attendant said through the PA. The microphone clicked as he slipped it back into its holster.

The line had formed, and he took their tickets, scanned them, handed them back.

Meanwhile, the mom tried to shift the child around while digging into her bag, then her purse, and then her bag again. Until, finally, I said, "May I?" and held my hands out toward her. If she was skeptical, it was overshadowed by how ridiculously impatient the gate attendant was being. He glared at us and smiled at the lined-up passengers passing the counter and shuffling onto the jetway.

The mom handed the child off and I stood just behind her, my backpack at my feet, my eyes on the baby's. Thirty seconds. Ninety at most. As I was swaying her around, letting her giggles enchant me, her mother was holding out a California driver's license for the flight attendant.

"You have family in L.A.?" she asked me over her shoulder.

"Just good friends."

"Friends can be like family," she said, hand still outstretched, as the agent lay a freshly printed boarding pass and her ID in it.

"The very best ones are." Before I could hand the baby back, she stilled in my arms and then convulsed and spit up all over my shirt.

"Fuck," I hissed, the warmth of the spit-up soaking through my shirt to my chest. "Shit, I'm sorry," I said, and held the baby away from me.

The mom's face showed horror. "Oh my God, I'm so sorry," she said, snatching the child from my arms and digging frantically in her shoulder bag.

"I'm fine, I'm fine," I said. "Is she okay?"

Tiny fists smeared across her lips, but she giggled again, a tiny hiccup, maybe a burp. The cutest damn thing.

"I don't even know your name and you've been so helpful and she just . . . oh my god." The mom's nervous babbling made me laugh, despite the nastiness on my shirt. She flung a towel at me and pressed one to the baby's mouth. "Here, wipe off, I'm so sorry."

I folded the towel and handed it back. "It's cool. I'm just going to step into the men's room," I said.

"But the flight," she said.

"It won't take long."

"I'm so, so sorry," she said again. "But thank you. Anyway." And her gaze slipped to the gate and the others who had already headed down the jetway.

I grabbed my backpack off the ground and grinned at her, one of those smiles Kacie and Meli and Jada had accused me of using for nefarious purposes.

"Jesus Christ," she said. "Now my story is about Emmy throwing up on the hottest guy I've ever met in person."

I laughed. "It's as good a story as any."

I tapped the baby's back. "See ya later, Emmy," and sauntered toward the men's room.

"Flight 77 is now boarding," the flight attendant said into the PA. "All passengers, all rows are welcome aboard."

I had maybe ten minutes until they closed the gate. The nearest men's room was closed for cleaning so I turned right and jogged down the concourse looking for the next sink with paper towels so I could clean up quickly and board the plane.

8:12 a.m.

"You gotta be fucking kidding me."

The jetway door was closed. The flight attendant stood over the counter typing frantically on the keyboard, head bowed like he was praying.

"Excuse me," I said, "I'm back. That's my flight."

"Not anymore." Without looking up.

"It can't have left."

"No, but doors close ten minutes before departure. And departure is seven minutes away. So, they're closed. You'll have to get on the next one."

I slammed my hand down on the counter. He looked up.

"Man, I was just here. I talked to you about the mom and her kid, remember?"

His eyes narrowed. "Of course, I remember. But that doesn't change the fact the plane is leaving."

"And I'm not on it."

"You're not on it."

"The kid puked on me," I said.

His eyebrows rose but he didn't speak.

"And the bathroom was closed for cleaning," I waved lamely down the hall. "So, I had to go further."

"You left the boarding area, and the gate is now closed. Do you want me to rebook you?"

Fifteen minutes later I wandered back into the bar I'd been in an hour before. The sailor was still there. I took my seat at his side, damp shirt and all.

"Man, how did you miss that flight? You left here like fifteen minutes before boarding."

"A woman," I said, grinning.

"Ain't it always?" he said, but he was young enough. I doubt he knew the half of it.

"A little girl named Emmy," I clarified, and laughed because she was pretty cute. "Totally worth it."

The bartender jerked his chin at me and placed a coaster on the bar. I ordered a tall beer. My next flight wasn't for another three hours. I said I'd need a menu, too. Might as well get some food. Shaking a cigarette out of my pack, I slid a glass ashtray toward me.

"Name's Brian," I said. He told me his was Tyler. "Any word from your family?"

"Tried calling from a pay phone but didn't have enough change."

"Maybe call collect?"

He shook his head. "Maybe I don't want to know that bad?"

I nodded. "I can understand that."

We stared up at the TV. Michael Jordan was pictured with the graphic claiming he planned to return to basketball.

"That dude's gotta be like sixty," Tyler said.

"Thirty-eight," I said, reading the graphic. "I mean, why do it? Why keep playing?"

"Nothing else satisfies," Tyler said. "When nothing else will fill that void, you keep playing."

The dimensions of emptiness crisscrossed around me. From the pool, stretching into a streamline, taking those strokes in cycle; from the skate park and the twists and trips and falls; from the church pew and the therapists' couches and the warm sheets of a Paris hotel room. Emptiness, a lost sense of home, the letting go of something essential had been my constant companion for the last three years. Though I'd found ways to fill it, ignore it, and bridge it, the yawning hole remained. It was more than scabbed over now, scar tissue firmly in place, but there, nonetheless. That place where Tony had been. Where I had been before he died. Home. And the myriad craters associated with him. Kacie. The Crew. Northern Virginia. The life we would have had. The life he might have had. But wouldn't.

"Is your dad a good guy?" Tyler asked.

I shrugged. "Pretty much. Faithful to my mom, worked his whole career, doesn't drink or beat me or anything. Just a regular guy I guess." Dad swam every morning like it was his job. Attended breakfast with teammates and regulars at Yeddy's as part of a community.

"A stand-up guy?"

"He loves to introduce people. This one time, we stayed an extra ten minutes at a hardware store because the clerk was interested in technology. Dad got that girl an internship with the NSA." He always looked for how people could help one another. He made connections, introductions, in a way that served people.

"What about your dad?" I asked.

"The best. He's got this way of looking at things, like everything's a long game, ya know? Like whatever is happening will pass and we'll be better on the other side."

"Perspective?"

"As a kid I hated it. You know, 'you'll thank me for this' and 'what you'll learn is' all that crap made me mad. Just be in the moment, ya know? Feel it. Right now. Right here. But not him." Tyler ran a hand over his shaved head, scrubbed it back and forth, then expelled air. "He always looked a lot further out."

I smiled. "Yeah, must be an age thing. My dad's like that, too. Always wants me to have a plan." In Barcelona, back in San Francisco, every holiday in Tucson, hell, even Manila was supposed to be part of some grand plan. Both times. Dad liked to ask, "What's next?" and have me explain the reason and objectives behind every decision I made.

I looked back up at the screen. Took another long drink.

"I keep getting derailed by wanting to live," I said. "You know? Like *live* each moment. Take the most it has to offer. And not just for Tony. Well, maybe it is for Tony." It had been. For a long time, it had been. But now? "Even my friend Abbie is bugging me to make plans. Commit. Choose a future and work toward it." An image of her touring the off-campus faculty housing in Bangor had me smiling. "She's ready for me to settle down."

"With her?"

"Nah, she's into chicks."

Tyler raised an eyebrow.

"California," I said, and shrugged.

Tyler nodded and tipped his glass toward mine. "To living in the moment."

We clinked glasses. I finished my beer and ordered another one.

8:40 a.m.

"Sounds like Jada did a number on you," Tyler said a little while later after I'd overshared. Maybe he'd let me distract him. The bartender had offered the phone next to the register, a free long-distance call, and Tyler had waved him off. Better to not know, right?

I turned my half-empty beer glass around and around on the coaster in front of me.

"She had me tied up. That's for sure. But I had to go through it, ya know? Had to see what it had been like for Kacie. Knowing I'd been with someone else. That would have hurt, ya know?"

The kid shrugged. "I guess. I mean, I've never had a girlfriend, really, so I don't know."

"You will." Kacie's golden blonde curls, Kacie's vanilla scent, Kacie's way of half-singing our Bryan Adams song between kisses. I missed her and maybe it was being back in Herndon, being a little bit homesick, missing Tony again, wondering what took me so long to get here, scabbed over, two and a half years after he left us. All of us. "And she'll be everything to you. Until she's not and you won't know what changed or when."

"But with Jada . . ."

"Oh, yeah," I laughed. "That wasn't a mystery. Fuck. Seems like a long time ago."

"And not yet over it?"

"Every time I think I am, I write another terrible story about it, so I guess I'm not." I caught a glimpse of myself in the mirror behind the liquor bottles.

"You're a writer?"

I nodded and glanced back up at the TV.

"Hey, man," I asked the bartender. "Can you flip that to CNN? This Jordan story's old."

"What do you write about?" Tyler asked.

"Women and bar fights in Barcelona, racism in Nashville, immigrants in Los Angeles, saying goodbye in Paris. All those saved moments that make up life, I guess."

"A memoir?"

"Hardly. I wouldn't be able to protect the innocent. It's all fiction, and good fiction starts as true stories. Then you make them more dramatic with a sharper look at character motivation, stripping away the unessential exposition, and pitting extremes against one another."

"So which parts aren't true?"

"None of it's true. By the time you finish the story, none of it's true."

I pulled another cigarette from the box and got ready to light it.

"How did you get over it? Tony dying?" Tyler had switched to bottled beer, and he was peeling the label away from the glass. We were only two rounds in, but his eyes were already getting that heavy-lidded beer-buzz drowsy that I recognized from drinking with lightweights like David and his boyfriend. Tyler's excuse was that he'd been traveling for twenty-four hours. He needed to go home. He needed to sleep. His dad was probably already dead. He wouldn't get to say goodbye. College graduation, wedding day, first kid, his dad would miss out on all of that.

How did I keep doing what I was doing knowing Tony was no longer my witness?

"I made a list of all the things he'd never get to do because the fucker had given up. At twenty-two, he just gave up. Then I did as many of them as I could." The list was in the kitten notebook. Started in Barcelona and kept a running total of the closure I was achieving. Until I'd decided to stop keeping score.

"My dad's done a lot of stuff."

"And maybe he'll be able to do a lot more," I said. "Like take you to play golf on Christmas Eve."

"Help me restore an old muscle car."

"Hold your child's hand when she walks into church for the first time."

Tyler smiled and it was sad, but sweet.

"You can kind of see her, right? That first sweet little girl?" I thought of the baby, Emmy, who was tucked in her mother's arms right now headed home to California.

"Too young for that."

"Sure, but it doesn't mean it doesn't happen." I lit the cigarette and glanced up at the television again. The scene was New York City, focused on the twin towers and smoke billowed out of one of them.

The graphic pinned to the bottom said, "BREAKING NEWS."

9:50 a.m.

Phones are fixed points. They anchor us to a single place. They promise the person we're connecting to that we are somewhere we can be traced. Safe.

I made my way to a wall of pay phones, the silver cords snaking out to black handsets that hung like unused barbells. It resembled the Reston Town Center Hyatt only those phones had brass plates. Just a few days after Tony died, I had curled one toward me and dialed Meli in California. I was stuck in Virginia and she was so far away, and I was aching and drunk and missing her. Now the voices on the phones, conversations I could barely hear, were scared, sad, and quiet. They told loved ones they were safe. Explained the planes had been grounded. Asked what the other person knew of what was happening.

I looked around at the slumped shoulders, red-rimmed eyes, and confused expressions, as if I might spot the kid from the bar who wasn't going to make it home to Pennsylvania. And how his dad's death would be eclipsed by those burning towers.

When it was my turn, I dialed Arizona.

"Brian, thank God, where are you?"

"Still at Dulles. I missed my flight."

"What time were you scheduled to go?"

"Eight twenty. It was the flight, Mom."

"Which flight?"

"The one that hit the pentagon. That was my flight." I choked on the words, visions of all the Californians who wanted to get home, rolling through my mind like the rotating disc in a viewfinder. I had missed a four-hour flight to L.A., Marco on the other side, and a young mom and her baby had boarded it. The baby. Emmy. I clenched my jaw. There wasn't time to weep, not yet, not now, not here.

"It's a madhouse."

"You want to stay there?"

"They're not going to let me fly out today."

"Your dad says the news is reporting grounded flights." A beat and then my mom said, "I'll call Chris. Tell him you're coming back to his place. Stay with him. Stay in Virginia."

My voice low, I said, "No one really understands what's happening. There are rumors, but nothing confirmed. It's fucking crazy."

"Same on TV," she said, the flow of her tears, sniffs and slurps, choked through her voice. "I'm glad you're safe."

We hung up and I headed toward the airline help desk to see about getting rebooked. The line was crazy long. I decided it could wait and went back to the bar I'd been in before, slid onto a stool, stared up at the TV screen, and ordered another beer.

Tyler was gone.

The mom and her baby, Emmy, gone. Like *gone* gone.

I tried to keep the tears at bay but when the bartender said, "I can't believe this is happening," the tears swelled into my throat and burned my eyes and all I could do was nod, tip the tall glass up, and choke back half the lager.

11:42 a.m.

A traffic cop pointed me from the queue and into a waiting Dulles Flyer. It pulled away into the chaos of cars that had come to retrieve passengers who were no longer flying anywhere. Some were dropping people off, having missed the news that all flights had been grounded until further notice. As we passed, I saw faces with creased brows, swollen eyes from crying, frowns, chewed lips, and bittersweet smiles as they welcomed the non-departed back into open arms.

Twenty minutes of the radio news, speculation on exactly what was happening, announcing the collapse of the second tower, going over the Pentagon story. A sluggish kind of traffic, for the volume of cars on the road and the despondence of life after planes crashed into the World Trade Center and the towers came down.

The towers had come down.

I paid the driver, we made eye contact, a silent gaze that seemed to share our stunned grief, and then I walked up the tall front stoop of Chris's townhouse.

He opened the door, a phone pressed to his ear. When he registered it was me, he threw his arms around me and cried, hard, into my neck.

Through the phone I heard Joel. "What's happening? Is that Brian?"

I held tighter to Chris, nodding. He clung to me, the phone in his hand digging into my shoulder blades, Joel's disembodied voice the only sound.

"It's me," I finally said. "I'm okay."

"That was your flight." The revelation was muffled by my shoulder.

"Yeah, but I wasn't on it."

He cough-laughed and pulled back. "Obviously." Then he lifted the phone to his ear and said, "Yeah, Joeler, he's here. He's safe." A few more nods and grunts and then he hung up. Swiping at tears and sniffing, Chris said, "Joel said to tell you you're an asshole for making us worry."

We climbed the stairs to the middle floor where the kitchen and living room were. Jason stood from the couch and pulled me against him. He smelled like soap and that salon hair gel he used, and we stayed in that hug, hands clasped between us, for a good ninety seconds. I couldn't remember ever hugging these guys for so long. Not even when Tony died.

The TV was on, tuned to the news, and as we broke the hug,

Jason and I followed the sound of the reporting like zombies, sitting down and absorbing the latest bulletins and footage.

Chris's new roommate had been expected to move in the weekend before but was delayed by some unexpected expenses, so the full townhouse was Chris's. Joel had left his sectional couch and a double bed behind. He called it the security deposit he'd never paid. In truth, Tabby rejected what she'd called "a leather L-shaped recliner monstrosity" for their new home. Jason had the bed the night before, I'd been on the couch, and the blankets I'd left behind were still lumped up in the corner wedge. The blinds over the sliding glass doors were open and the midday sun streamed in, warming the beige carpet in a giant rectangle shape. Chris's grey cat, Mr. Jones, stretched out in the warmth, oblivious to the somber news, the smoking imagery, and the urgent red graphics flashing along the bottom of the screen.

The phone rang, and Chris answered it, "Christopher James," in his business tone. He didn't have any appointments scheduled for today and he said that if he had, he would have canceled them. Just what the fuck was happening today was more important than going about daily business.

"Who wouldn't be glued to CNN today?" Jason asked no one in particular.

After he'd hung up with the inquiry call, someone looking to set an appointment for Thursday, he handed me the cordless phone.

"My folks had just woken up when I got in touch with them." The beers I'd had made my head feel swimmy, and the buzz I'd recaptured softened my lips and tongue.

"Call David and Abbie," Chris said.

The line rang three times before Abbie finally answered.

"No one I know would call at this hour," she said, a line from *When Harry Met Sally*. It was just after 9:00 a.m. in San Francisco.

"Abbs," I said. "Turn the TV on. Something's happened."

I waited a few minutes while she found the remote control. Before long I heard David come into the room. In my mind's eye I saw him crawling into her bed and snuggling down and wished I was there, too.

"CNN," I said and then waited, listening to them breathe, while they watched what Chris and Jason and I were seeing again, for the thirtieth time.

Images of the plane crashes: the first into the first tower, the second into its twin, the third into the pentagon, and the fourth into the field in Pennsylvania. Tears swelled in my eyes, burning and the lump in my throat felt like a permanent condition.

"Oh my God," Abbie breathed through the phone.

"That was Brian's flight!" David said. "The one that hit the Pentagon. Wasn't it, Brian?"

"Why weren't you on that plane?" Abbie asked.

"Luck I guess," I said, and looked up at Chris who was standing nearby, waiting for me to tell them all what happened.

The words stuck, though, and I didn't want to share Emmy's story. I didn't want to talk about what I had done just this morning. It seemed like days ago.

"Do they know if it was terrorists?" That question from David, who, apparently had taken the phone from Abbie.

"That's the theory," I said.

"Are there more?"

I looked up at Chris and he lifted one shoulder.

"Fuck if we know."

Jason disappeared into the kitchen. I stroked the cat as he tucked in and out of my legs, finally jumping onto my lap. Jason returned with beers.

We sat in front of the TV. We commented on what we saw. We changed channels across all the networks until the major networks went to daytime TV and the cable news networks were just looping the footage. After a while, Chris went to his office to work and Jason went up to Joel's room to sleep.

I stood at the sliding glass door looking out over the backyard. My heart was broken. I'd felt it before. When Tony died. When Kacie kicked me out of Seattle. When Meli read a poem called "Brian" that I deserved. When Jada said she didn't want me anymore. When Lara had slipped out of the Paris hotel. I knew what a broken heart felt like and this was it, and it fucking hurt.

I hurt for Tyler who wouldn't get to see his dad again.

I hurt for Emmy and her mom who would never reach California.

I hurt for the New Yorkers. The ones buried and the ones digging and the ones who would never be found.

I don't know how long I stood there, hurting, before Chris put his hand on my shoulder and handed me the phone.

"Hello?"

"Brian?" a sob.

"Kacie." And the tears let loose. Choked me. Overwhelmed me.

SAN FRANCISCO
OCTOBER 2001

*P*ackages didn't fit in the mailbox downstairs, so the mailp-
erson left them on a small rickety-legged table. There were
only six units in the building, so it was a kind of honor system
to not take each other's stuff. After I'd opened this one, I kind of
wished someone else had carried it upstairs. The return address
was Seattle and I knew, before ripping the envelope, what it was.

I let it sit on my own entry table for a few more days. There
was no urgency to it. I thought I would need a lot of booze.
Maybe something sacred like an aged scotch or a good bottle of
wine. Midnight and candles, some ritualistic thing like burning
the rejection letters.

Eventually, though, it was just a Tuesday afternoon. Daylight
grey with fog outside, I flipped on the small lamp on the end
table next to the futon couch and sat with the Green Velvet
Notebook in my hands. I read each page slowly and carefully as if
there might be some wisdom in it. As if it wasn't just a collection
of his handwriting and other people's words. Tony had scribbled
down poems, song lyrics, commercials even. He'd taken note of

phrases that struck him as particularly significant for whatever reason.

When we were skating, he dragged a backpack around with him everywhere. It had his pads, his helmet, bandages, deodorant, an extra t-shirt, and this notebook. The front pocket carried his wallet, a half dozen lighters, a pack of smokes, and a half dozen pens. Tony was a lighter thief. He'd ask whomever had one if he could use it to light his cigarette and then drop it in his backpack as if they'd gifted it to him. They hadn't. More than once we'd all be sitting around saying, "Who's got a lighter?" and Tony would unzip that bag—his man purse Chris called it—and we'd see the rainbow assortment he'd collected.

The night he killed himself, Tony left the Green Velvet Notebook on his bed underneath a post-it note with Kacie's name on it. She gave it to me the day we buried him and then took it back on Sunday. And now it was in my possession again. I turned the pages, sliding my finger down the length of each one, tracing his handwriting, listening for his voice.

In my head, the Telemann track played, that quiet but growing crescendo, the aching notes that stretch into openness, and then into closeness. Oneness. I shook my head thinking that Tony had never found the lyrics for that piece. And neither had I.

Dialing Kacie, I waited through the ring, pinned the phone to my ear with a shoulder, and poured vodka straight into a juice tumbler.

"You received it, finally?"

I nodded then said, "Yeah, it's here."

"And?"

"And I can't feel it anymore."

"Me neither."

"Is that why you mailed it to me?"

"It was just time."

I took the vodka back with a swig and poured another one.

"The Salinger book had some underlined phrases in it," I said. "Tony was nothing if not melodramatic."

"Es-ki-mo," Kacie breathed. When we'd first been handed these artifacts, in Tony's parents' house, the day before the funeral, Jason and I had made fun that there would be meaningful phrases underlined, like Heather Duke's copy of *Moby Dick* in the movie *Heathers*. JD, the murderous antagonist, in an overly dramatic scene, attempts to frame Heather for suicide and uses the phrases as evidence of her supposed despair. In one scene, as he tries to convince his girlfriend, the film's protagonist, Veronica, to participate, he selects the word "Eskimo" from the text and rolls it around on his tongue in an absurdly sinister way. It's a dream sequence, and the film is a dark comedy. It's also about suicide. Kacie had snapped at us, bitterly, for bringing it up that day. Now the reference on her breath suggested we had put context to Tony's death. We had categorized it as a node on the timeline. The kind of thing we would jot the smallest of paragraphs for, or a bulleted list, below the dot. February, 1999: Tony's suicide, funeral, break-up with Meli, lose all my friends, alienate my parents.

Except somehow, as if that were the inciting incident over this half decade, my own unraveling had ceased. I had, for a long time, been feeling the end of the Croft poem, "making of the lumber of my life not a tavern, but a temple." In these recent months, I had been building, rather than setting fire to, what had been left for me. Not like then. Then I would have burnt it down, now I built with reverence on the ashes.

"What will you do with it?"

"I'm a writer. We collect these kinds of things."

"Old notebooks with lyrics?"

"Artifacts of a life well lived. Too short, but well lived."

"I can see more than his addiction now."

"More than his hurt," I agreed. "I can remember him laugh-ing. Making fun. Playing tricks."

Kacie chuckled through the phone. "Getting crushes."

"Obsessions more like."

I sipped on the vodka in my hand. My socked feet slipped across the wood floor as I carried the phone and the vodka back to the couch. Crossing my legs under me, I tugged a throw blan-ket from the corner into my lap and propped the notebook on it again.

"I used to play, 'what would Tony do?' as a way of making choices," Kacie said.

"And did you always do the opposite?"

"Not always."

"Give me an example?"

She shifted on the other end, and I heard the brush of mate-rial against the phone and a small noise like a grunt or a hitch in her breath.

"What are you doing?"

"Laying down."

I imagined her in the tiny bedroom in the Seattle flat, the single bed with the hand-sewn quilt and saggy pillows. What I remembered from my observation on my knees on her floor: wood-paneled wall, tiny nightstand with a candlestick lamp crowned with a purple shade. In my head I was back on my knees, beneath her, as she lay above me looking up at the ceiling.

"What would Tony do?" she muttered. "Coming to Seattle was one time, I guess. I thought hard about going back to Northern Virginia after I finished in Charlottesville. I thought about get-ting a townhouse in Chris's neighborhood, finding roommates, waiting tables, trying to get on with *The Post*."

"Did you apply for a job with them?"

"I applied everywhere."

"San Francisco?"

Kacie laughed. "So not everywhere."

"But Seattle?"

"Sports writers take a certain path," she said. "High-school beat to college beat to pros. I needed a high-school gig. Looked in Georgia and Florida, they're big on high school coverage because of recruiting."

"No one wants to live in Florida."

"No kidding."

"Why not Colorado?" Her parents had gone back to Colorado after her father lost his seat in congress in the midterm elections of '98.

"It's harder to travel now," Kacie mused. "Expensive."

"And dangerous?" I asked.

"Feels like it."

"What would Tony have done about September 11th?"

A long exhalation of breath and then, "Given blood."

Sometimes my memories of the day are like paintings Tony would have made. I see the Dulles terminal in smeary grey lines. The wall of pay phones. The distance from there to Chris's place. The bar and the sailor and the young mother and the baby girl. My memories on easels in Tony's parents' basement. Rendered in his vivid style, those lines and grooves, the texture and shapes evoking hurt and confusion and devastation. The burning buildings wearing their smoke like crowns, like souls escaping from the wreckage.

"The stories haven't stopped."

"Nor will they," I said. "Everyone alive that day will have their, 'where were you?' story and they'll all be written. Some imagined, some dramatized, some insignificant. Like footnotes in history. Like scars reminding us that the past is real."

"I can't write mine."

"You're in mine."

"What do I say?" She smiled, and her voice showed it when she said, "What do I do?"

"You comfort me. You ask if I'm okay and I realize, because you asked, that I am." We breathed quietly together, and I wished she could see me. "Your voice is home for me and when I heard it, I felt grounded."

An intake of breath on her side.

"Safe," I added, and exhaled, slowly, in that way we had communicated on that day we'd shared three thousand miles apart but intertwined. As always. Feeling tender and affectionate, wishing I could stroke her cheek, pull a curl to me and let it go, wanting to see her green eyes glitter at me. Since September, all I'd written was my longing for her. The way my heart curled up in hers over the phone, the way forgiveness seemed to rush over me like a tsunami. I wanted to tell her how I'd pined for her, how I'd needed her to tell me she forgave me. How much I wanted to hold her.

"What are you doing for Thanksgiving?" I asked instead.

"Colorado. Audrey is getting married."

"At Thanksgiving?"

"No, in March. But she'll have the ring and fiancé and I'm expected to fawn and be jealous."

"And are you?"

Kacie scoffed and it was a small snort and it made me laugh.

"He's a douche," she said. "So, no."

"But the being connected? Settled?" I may have been fishing for something she wasn't ready to give up.

"Tabby and Joel have that."

"Yeah, they do."

"Are you jealous? You sounded a little wistful just then."

"Now who's writing the scene?"

I knew Kacie was on Tabby's list of bridesmaids along with

her sisters. There were dress conversations and travel arrangements being made for the first weekend in February.

"Another dress?" I asked, thinking about Audrey's wedding.

"No, she didn't ask me to be in the ceremony." Kacie laughed. "I guess she thinks if I don't like who she's marrying, I'm not supportive, so I don't get the privilege of paying too much for a dress I'll never wear again to stand next to her and hold flowers."

"One hundred sixty-five dollars," I said. "Joel said Tabby's bridesmaid gowns were a hundred sixty-five bucks."

"Yep. And that's after we talked her out of the two-hundred ten dollar ones. But I'd have paid two ten. It's Tabby and Joel. I'm willing."

"You know I've never been to Colorado."

"So?"

"So, maybe you'll need a date in March."

"Maybe."

I grinned into the phone. Abbie told me to make plans. To set milestones, and getting Kacie to take me to her sister's wedding was one of those. I resolved to keep asking until she couldn't imagine being there with anyone else.

"I'm told it's fun to go to a wedding as a guest," I said. "Get dressed up, drink someone else's booze, dance to cheesy music, eat those little puffy spinach things."

"Spanikopita?"

"Yes."

"Are you purring? Making 'spanikopita' sound romantic?"

"I didn't even say it. You did."

Kacie laughed and I remembered how much I loved the sound of that.

"Take me with you to Colorado," I said.

"I'll think about it."

We were quiet for a moment and I wondered if she imagined being on my arm at prom, letting me hold her against me in a slow dance, the way I'd been able to gently peel away the straps of her gown in the Marriot Courtyard hotel afterward.

"What are you thinking about?" she asked.

"Can't tell you."

"Then we should probably hang up."

"Thanks for sending the notebook."

"Thanks for calling."

More quiet, and neither of us hanging up, and then she said, "It's a long time until March."

"Less time till February."

"So long since the last February." And she meant 1999. When Tony died. And I could see us writing another timeline where the Februarys are less painful. Where the new memories write over the scars of the old ones. And I was ready. Finally.

After we hung up, I flipped to the blank pages of the Green Velvet Notebook and started writing.

"Dear Tony," I said aloud. "You were right."

New Year's Eve 2001
Tucson

Kacie was covering the Fiesta Bowl in Tempe on New Year's Day because the Ducks were playing, and I tried to get her to come to Oro Valley for New Year's Eve, but she declined. Two days before Christmas I was still hoping she'd change her mind.

Abbie bounded into the kitchen and said, "Did Brian tell you he was offered a job? Like a real one?"

Dad's face lit up.

"It's about time. University Press? Literary agency?"

I nodded. "Nah, still teaching." My thesis was a collection of short stories, many from Barcelona, my L.A. and Nashville experiences, and a few complete fabrications. I'd met with an agent who wanted to publish the collection but in the aftermath of September 11th in New York, he'd reached out and said they weren't scheduling new titles for 2002. Apparently, his office was a block from the World Trade Center and had sustained significant damage.

"So, what's the job?" Dad asked.

"Writer in Residence," I said, glancing at Abbie. "At the University of Maine."

"Well, at least there's family nearby." He shoved his hands in his pockets and looked just a little disappointed. Which I should have expected but was hurt by, nonetheless.

"We won't stay," Abbie said.

"We?" Dad's eyebrow raised.

"I want to see the frozen river. Brian promised."

"The appointment is only a year," I said. "So, we'll be there just a year."

He clapped his hand on my shoulder. "Buy some long johns."

David had refused to go with us, but after I talked Abbie into sending her work to John and he'd shared it with their poetry lead, the English Department at the University of Maine said they'd be glad to have her, too. So, she decided to go with me. The post was set to begin in June to, as John told me, "ease you in," to the seasons.

Abbie had looked up Bangor and Orono and Bar Harbor on the internet, found pictures of icy Christmases and skaters on lakes and declared that would be our future. I liked the idea of seeing the leaves change color, and the scent of a chimney called to me.

I didn't yet feel committed, but telling my parents seemed to make it real. I thought about what Abbie had made me promise to do: make plans. Not too long ago, I'd been living the life I felt I owed Tony. All the places he'd never go, the people he'd never meet, the stories he'd never tell. But since September, that had been amplified. It wasn't just Tony. It was Emmy and her mother. It was that sailor's dad and all the guys on the ship with him who were sailing into combat now. A War on Terror that we could not begin to determine how to win. I hadn't enlisted, but I knew people who had. There was a patriotism swelling that seemed to outweigh reason or logic or even rational thought.

"Kacie's covering the Fiesta Bowl," I said. "She'll be in Tempe next week."

"Why not go see her?" Dad asked.

"He wasn't invited," Abbie said, and laughed.

"I might be taking a break," I said.

"From what?" Dad asked.

"Romance," Abbie sang, and skipped away from the kitchen, into the living room, and threw herself on the couch in front of the Burning Valley portrait.

"I just love that painting," she sighed, pointing up at the canvas.

"Me too," Mom said, emerging from their bedroom on the opposite side of the living area, "That's Tony's painting, but it feels more like a photograph of a certain time of life."

"Like growing up. Being a kid," I said.

"Being young," Dad agreed.

"It's perfect here," Abbie said. "I mean, I know it's a valley in Virginia, but the colors. It's like it belongs in Tucson."

Mom smiled up at the painting and across the room at Dad. "Like us."

The Oro Valley house reminded me of the Santa Fe Cue Club, and later that night, as we sat on the rooftop deck watching the sun set in the west, I remarked that Chris's girlfriend, Sarah, had started managing the Cue Club. She'd been a server there during college, coming home on breaks, and Chris had kept up with her. She was finishing a law degree at Georgetown but couldn't afford to live downtown, so she'd stayed in Herndon with her parents.

"When was the last time you were there?" I asked Dad.

"Not since last spring," he said. "I went for Paul's retirement ceremony." Paul had been my Dad's best friend while I was growing up. He and Sheila had been the couple Mom and Dad played cards with, went skiing with, and watched each other's kids. They had three, Paul, Jr, Kristen, and Stephanie. Sheila had gone back to school when Paul, Jr. and I were in high school and she and Paul, Sr. divorced before we graduated. Their eldest, Paul Jr., had killed himself a year before Tony. During that time, Dad and Paul spent a good bit of time together but once Dad moved to Arizona, I hadn't heard much about Paul.

"What's he going to do now?"

"Connecticut. Stephanie and her kids live up there."

"Grandpa Paul," I said.

A kind of momentum seemed to have overtaken things lately. More of our acquaintances were getting married, having children, buying homes, settling into jobs with healthcare and retirement packages. It felt like 9/11 had sent us into a kind of fast forward.

We referred to Herndon, Reston, Fairfax County, as Northern Virginia as if it were its own state, like West Virginia or North Carolina. The D.C.-area suburbs that made up Northern Virginia also brought the majority of the tax base to the Commonwealth and it differed, widely, from the Western trek along I-81 through the Shenandoah Valley and from the Coastal Tidewater region of Norfolk and Virginia Beach. Northern Virginia, in the years since I'd left, had been swept with change: construction, migration, traffic disfiguring it like a hurricane on the coast.

Chris was thrilled with it all. In real estate, he'd found a good bit of success. Chris had moved two roommates into his town house and now lived rent-free. He was saving money like a miser and investing in land out near Leesburg that he promised would pay dividends. I didn't pretend to know what he did about such things but just hoped he would continue to be successful wherever he was.

Sarah had suggested they move in together, but Chris said he'd told her the finances didn't add up. Which meant she wasn't making enough money for him to kick his roommates out. I didn't blame him but wondered if the choice would cost him his relationship. Women wanted to know they were the most important thing in your life, in my experience, and prioritizing anything over them was an early sign the relationship wouldn't last. Even if the priority was fiscally responsible. When had such things, mortgages and marriage, become our conversation? We were three weeks from Joel's bachelor party weekend in Las Vegas and it seemed like our entire lives had been on fast-forward since September 11th.

After sunset, Dad called me into his study as Mom and Abbie went into the kitchen. He pulled a gallon-sized Ziploc bag from a shelf and handed it to me. Inside was a *Sports Illustrated* from the week of September 11th. The cover read, "The Week That Sports Stood Still." An American flag was draped over a stadium seat. A nameless, unknowable stadium somewhere. Every league in the nation had suspended play the week of September 11th. When we had discussed it, some opponents had said sports should continue on, show the terrorists they couldn't disrupt our way of life.

I'd called Kacie.

"What do you think about sidelining all the games?" I'd asked.

"We can't sit in stands and watch plays and cheer for touchdowns now. Not when there are firefighters and policemen digging for bodies in New York. Not yet." And my eyes burned to hear her say it. She was right. It was too soon. There might still be—God let there still be— survivors under there.

The next week, though, sports had come back. And every league and every game broadcasted the National Anthem and the raising of the colors, and we swelled with pride and let the tears drip down our cheeks for the big black eye we all felt. Goddamn terrorists. I remembered the anger. The anguish. Holding Dad's keepsake, I remembered. My throat felt thick.

"When I was little," I said, "I thought watching the Challenger explode was the worst thing I would ever see."

"Christa McAullife," Dad said, breathing the name of the schoolteacher, "and Ron McNair," the first Black astronaut to die on a space mission. "I remember that day. It was a teacher work-day for Fairfax County schools, and you were home. You and Tony were in the basement. I called you up to watch the launch."

"I had the poster on my bedroom wall."

And they counted down and sent that rocket into the sky and it came apart in flames. Tony and I had just stared, stunned by what we'd seen.

"I didn't know what to say," Dad said. "I think I said something about space travel being dangerous. Maybe shooed you back downstairs. Or maybe you lost interest in the coverage."

"The cameras followed the falling pieces. They showed it over and over trying to figure out what went wrong." We stood in the small glow of Dad's desk lamp.

My fingers felt the flimsy weight of the magazine in its plastic sheath.

"When Tony died, it felt like I was wrong about the Challenger. That then, Tony's death, was the worst thing I'd ever have to go through."

"And now?"

"September 11th is so much more. It's different, obviously, but the same. And so much more. The sheer number of people. The devastation. And then distanced because I didn't know any of them." I thought of Emmy and her mom. "Not really anyway."

Dad took the magazine from me, sliding it back into place on his shelf. "We sold your generation," he said. "We sold you on patriotism. We said 'love your country' because we weren't the communists. We were in the Cold War and we needed you to believe we were right."

"And here we are."

"The Lowery's boy, Evan, has gone into combat," Dad said. "Jay said he's in an infantry division deployed to Afghanistan." His expression was sad.

"He's not alone. I know people who've enlisted. Compelled to defend our country from the terrorists. It's a kind of mania. I guess I get it. But sometimes not really."

"That Cold War chess match," Dad said. "The one that ate up most of my career. Your mom's career. That chess match brought us here. Terror cells. Splinter groups. Guerilla warfare. A global enemy. Us versus everyone."

"Not everyone," I said wryly. "There are allies."

"What's right when everything seems wrong?" Dad asked it, whispered it, and looked skeptical.

In all the urgency, the rush to war, to enlistment, to give blood, to get married, to make everything count, we were a nation grieving. Going through the stages: shock and denial, pain and guilt, anger and bargaining. I knew these stages. Intimately. Knowing them didn't change the pace or correct the behavior, but it helped me put things in perspective.

I pulled my dad into a hug.

"You didn't cause this," I said. "The CIA, the Cold War, the choices you made. None of that caused this."

Dad nodded into my shoulder. "Logically I understand that."

"But it hurts."

"It just hurts," he agreed.

We found Mom and Abbie in the kitchen talking about scented candles which had "change of subject" emanating from it, so I let it go and decided to interrogate Abbie later.

Dad made steaks. Mom made potatoes and grilled asparagus.

"I'm so glad I'm not a vegetarian," Abbie said.

"Anymore," I added.

We were sipping red wine on the back patio, having cleaned up dishes and put Mom and Dad to bed. The stars were perfect in the night sky and somewhere, not too far, Kacie was preparing for her Fiesta Bowl coverage.

"I know you want to call her," Abbie said.

"She knows where I am."

"But does she know how badly you want to talk to her?

"Doubtful."

"For whatever it's worth, you're done with the others?"

"What others?"

Abbie rolled her eyes. She meant the Laras and Jadas and Skyes of the past two years. The ones who had come into my life for a reason or a season.

"Yes," I said. "There's only one woman for me."

"And that's me," Abbie said.

"Exactly."

We were quiet for a while. I knew she was hurting that David had chosen not to go to Maine. She'd say things like, "It's not decided yet," even though it was, and "We still have time," even though he wasn't going to change his mind. I knew, too, that David was hurt she would leave him to follow me to Maine. It helped that he would get my apartment and not need a roommate. Mom and Dad had offered him a very generous rent since I'd been living there without paying anything for about five years. What was between David and Abbie was not mine to organize.

I gave in and called Kacie around 3:30 on New Year's Eve. I thought it was early enough that maybe I could talk her into hanging out but late enough that she could wave me off if she needed to. No harm, no foul. She answered the hotel room phone and seemed to know, even before I said, that it was me, because she was laughing.

"It's not harassment," I told her. "It's me offering a legit alternative to hotel and strangers."

"Aren't you with someone?" she asked.

"Yes!" Abbie called out from the couch beside me.

"No," I said. "That's Abbie. She's like a sister. So, no."

"I thought there was someone in Tucson."

"Goddamn Joel has a big mouth."

"This time it was Jason," Kacie said. "He's usually bro-code about your get togethers. But he had a lot to share about Tucson."

"Like what?

"Like your parents and Tony's painting and how he's thinking about relocating there permanently."

"My dad said he might."

"Jason needs a fresh start, but he also needs a support network. He called it, 'a soft place to land.' I think being in Michigan has freaked him out."

"Twin thing," I said.

"Exactly. Like 'I can't wait to be alone!' and then, 'oh, my God, I'm alone!' so it's been a rough year."

"Did he tell you about Tony?"

"What about him?"

Jason had been mourning Tony more this year than before. It was a weird kind of delayed grief. His posture last Christmas and then in Nashville had worried me and Joel both. Our September trip hadn't exactly provided any of us closure, given the way the weekend turned out. Maybe that was what had made him tell Kacie he needed a soft place to land.

"Tucson might be good for him," I said. "And I can't deny my parents that opportunity either. If I go all the way to Maine, they'll need someone as proxy." I was mostly kidding but also willing to step aside and let Mom and Dad bring Jason in where Tony used to be. Someone like me, but not. Someone who needed them when I didn't. It wasn't that I never needed them, but I knew that when I did, they'd be there, and until then, they could do good work in the lives of others. It was a kind of sharing I wasn't used to, as an only child, but something I'd become more willing to do.

"You should come down tonight," I finally said to Kacie. "We could hang out, talk through some stuff, celebrate the New Year. You've never met Abbie. I promise not to let her hit on you."

"How do you know I wouldn't be into that?" she retorted.

Abbie raised an eyebrow.

"Jesus, now you've given Abbie threesome ideas."

"No, friend. I mean, how do you know I'm not batting for the other team?"

Abbie burst out laughing.

"They say it happens to sports reporters." Kacie was smiling, I could hear it through the phone. "Being around all that testosterone."

"Testosterone is not contagious."

"And manliness."

"Nor is manliness."

Abbie was cracking up, holding her stomach from laughing.

"Kacie, please. You're sending Abbie into convulsions of desire and amusement."

"Desire *and* amusement? Seriously, Brian, have you lost your ability to read a woman's body language? It can only be one or the other."

"Say you'll come to Tucson."

"No."

"Why not?"

"You know why not. It's not time yet."

"What will it take?"

"I don't know. I just know it's not time yet."

After she hung up, Abbie stopped cackling. I finished off the wine in my glass, and said, "This is going to be harder than I thought."

"What, specifically?"

"Winning her back."

PITTSBURGH
THURSDAY, JANUARY 31, 2002

Arrival was what I expected: bumpy air, overcast skies, the jerky motion of landing and braking and careening toward the end of the runway in controlled violence. I collected my things from the overhead bin, and followed the other passengers up the jetway and out into the concourse.

Tabby had insisted I come Thursday so that any cancellations or delays could be managed a full day ahead of scheduled events for the wedding. Being on Pacific time, the earliest flight put me in Pittsburgh at 4:00 p.m.

In baggage claim, I lifted the smallest of the luggage Mom and Dad gave me for Christmas a year ago that had already seen a lot of use. The largest suitcase had gone with me to Manila last summer. The medium-sized one had traveled with me to Paris, and while it was under-packed when I arrived, Lara had made sure to fill it before I returned. She'd been very generous buying me what she called "grown-up clothes" for my interview in Maine and other professional events. The smallest tote had been with Abbie and I in Bangor, and she'd marveled at how I was able to unpack my suit with minimum wrinkles, steam it and wear it like I'd been born to model French couture. Though the department chair hadn't said anything about the suit, I'd noticed more than a few glances indicating that one rarely saw such finery on campus at U of M. In any case, the pockets of the miniature held boxer briefs and toiletries, the shoes were tucked into the bottom, and the clothes were tightly folded to preserve their shape.

I swung the weekender bag off the carousel and reached into the outer pocket for a tightly-rolled but heavier coat. It was a Bangor buy, something on sale during our September trip. One of those outdoors stores that sold winter gear all year round and specialized in ultra-packable lightweight outerwear. Pittsburgh in February was significantly colder than San Francisco. With the coat draped over my forearm, a backpack two-shouldered, and the weekend tote slung over one, I strode from baggage claim to the transportation station to hail a cab.

Since New Year's, I'd been sizzling with anticipation of seeing Kacie in Pittsburgh. So much had changed since Seattle. We'd spoken a dozen times and exchanged a few emails, but we both knew this weekend, today, would be the beginning of something new for us. I wasn't sure what that something would be, but I was hopeful it would include the kind of closeness I'd been living without since Paris.

Like luggage and lakes, all airports are the same. There's a pattern to them that is equal parts usefulness and adventure. The sizes and placement of seating, the bend of secluded nooks, the stretch of corridors. I'm never so at home as in an airport and since September, I have not taken for granted the collective experience we are all having. Travel is a disruption of routine, and passengers are anxious and exhausted in transition. Passing through has its own energy that seems to vibrate around us all. And the people who work here, the store clerks and bartenders and servers and baggage handlers, all seem to be sipping from that same cup of possibility and transitory energy. As if, just by being near those of us actually departing, they might also escape. Or come home.

I liked watching people reunite in baggage claim. Embraces with tightened arms and tear-filled eyes. Laughter and smiles, the way a hand stretched out, pressed against a cheek, and a head cocked and then shook with amazement at what beauty its eyes beheld. I had long since lost the airport greeting experience. Only in Tucson was I ever treated to a tight embrace, a familiar smile. I moved through the families and friends in baggage claim in Pittsburgh and stepped out into the chilly afternoon.

The ride to the William Penn Omni was quiet. The cab driver occupied with his own thoughts, the radio low in the front seat. The stacked townhouses on the ridge of the interstate occupied me, as did the grey sky, the shuffle of traffic, and the various names of exits and landmarks. The Fort Pitt Tunnel closed over us, and I held my breath with anticipation of "popping out into Pittsburgh" the way Tabby had described it. As the light ahead got brighter and the grey sky overtook the ceiling, we emerged onto a bridge, and before us stood buildings whose height had been completely hidden by the mountain through which we'd just passed. The rivers converged far below us, the bridge's magnificent posts and wires seemingly stretched to the sky itself.

To date I'd seen skylines in Paris, New York, San Francisco, Dallas, Seattle, Las Vegas, and Nashville; I'd noted the way places like Bangor, Dubrovnik, and Monterrey lived beside the water in cautious optimism. But Pittsburgh's skyline and its waterfront seemed the kind of dramatic relationship the mountains of Montenegro had with the fjord. As if they couldn't decide what was water and what was shore. As we passed above the waterfront, I thought of Barcelona and the docks on the Mediterranean. The stadiums rose like crowns, great cylindrical witnesses to the city.

For all that I was awe-struck by Pittsburgh, and for as much as I understood Joel and Tabby's decision to remain near family, I felt a stranger, as I had so many times before, and that made me a little bit sad. I wanted to belong to the things that mattered to my friends, and Pittsburgh mattered to Joel. Over the last few years, we'd worked hard to reconnect and understand the world the other occupied. I didn't pretend to know angel investing, start-up costs, or venture capitalists. Joel's work as a mentor to new start-ups, his swift exit from his first firm before the bubble burst and the dot com era petered out, his technical savvy and business acumen were all outside my own vocabulary. But I listened. And I learned.

Moreover, I listened to how he talked to and about Tabby. I hadn't seen her face-to-face since New Year's Eve, a year ago. So not since September 11th. Not since Kacie and I reconciled. Not since everything seemed to pick up speed. But I knew her to be fiercely loyal to both of the Lincrest twins, and her love for them endeared her to me. I found I liked her, liked hearing stories about her, felt amused by them, interested in them, and grateful for them.

Above all, grateful. It was an emotion I'd come to put before every experience I had. Before entering a crowded room, a run-down bar, a class or a campus, before walking into a gallery with David, sitting down at a coffee shop with Abbie, or rolling up to the skatepark with the nameless friends I'd established there. I thought before writer's group and Sunday morning services: *Thank You.* To whomever or whatever had granted me this extended life, this existence, this chance to survive when I'd had a ticket out. I'd had a ticket to see Tony again, and Emmy, that sweet baby, had saved me.

None of this swirled around me in the cab headed into Pittsburgh, though it was pretty omnipresent. It's just this weekend was the culmination of so much planning and discussion that it inevitably carried expectations. I expected to perform my assigned duties and to see my parents, Joel's mom, The Crew, of course, Kacie. To hold her. Even if it was only the short embrace of friendship. But I hoped for more.

While I settled the bill with the cab driver, an energetic bellhop pulled my suitcase and backpack from the cab then led me into the lobby of the Omni. My name was called across the lobby, and I turned to see Tabby's younger sister passing a basket wrapped in cellophane to a woman in the hotel's uniform.

She was small, like Tabby, and thin and pretty, like so many Filipino women I'd met over the years in my journeys to Manila and in the SoMa district of San Francisco. Of the sisters, she was the only one who spoke Tagalog, and I greeted her in it as she moved toward me for a hug.

"You are a surprise," she said.

"A good one, I hope."

"Always. Why so early?"

Then we both said, "Tabby," at the same time. She added, "She worries."

I added, "She's not wrong."

"Just you today?"

"Kacie, too. Us West Coast people."

"Right, she's in Seattle, isn't she?"

I flipped my wrist, read my watch and said, "She's airborne now." Kacie's flight would arrive by eight and we planned to have a late dinner together tonight. Everything in me seized up at the thought of being near her again. What would it be like after so long? Would she feel the same? I knew over the phone she sounded different. Would she look different, too?

"Kacie hates the dresses," Tabby's sister said. "Says there's not a flattering thing about them."

"Is she right?"

She shrugged. "No one will be looking at us anyway, right?"

"That's Tabby's goal."

I asked if she wanted to step over to the bar for a drink, but she said she had more errands to do. We said we'd catch up tomorrow and she ran her hand down my arm before squeezing my wrist.

"Good to see you, Brian," she said. "You're my favorite." Then she was walking away before I could ask, "favorite what?"

It was just after six when I stepped into my room, threw my backpack on the bed, the key on the dresser, and the weekender on the luggage stand in the closet. When I'd checked in, the front desk gave me my tuxedo; I hung it behind the sliding mirror door. Tabby had my measurements taken at a Men's Wearhouse in San Francisco, matched them to a tux in Pittsburgh, and had ordered the suit herself. I was supposed to try it on and let the wedding planner know if anything was missing. She'd selected a silver bow tie and vest combination, and Joel had presented us all with matching cufflinks in Las Vegas. They were black and silver with five small diamonds. One each for our original Crew.

I decided to shower and when I emerged, try on the suit. Maybe once I'd figured out it was fine, practiced tying the tie, and sent the wedding planner an email to confirm, it would be close enough to eight that I could go down to the bar and wait to intercept Kacie in the lobby when she arrived.

Instead, my room phone rang and when I answered it, my mom laughed and said, "I told you he wouldn't miss his flight. Pay up."

"Hi, Mom."

"Your father thought—"

"He's always ready for the drama," I said.

"Did Abbie come?"

"No, she decided to sit this one out."

"Have you eaten?"

The tux fitting could wait. I showered and dressed and went down to see my parents before they left for dinner.

They sat in a corner booth that curved tightly as if to allow close proximity. I slid in next to Mom, gave her a kiss on the cheek and shook Dad's hand across the table.

"I've been meaning to give you something," Mom said, reaching into her purse for an envelope. "I was never sure when was the right time or where was the right place. I might have been a coward about it, truthfully." She's a brave lady, my mom, a no-nonsense contributor in board rooms and situation rooms. She's sharp and funny but smart, too, and she always knew more than anyone else at the table. For her to admit to cowardice had me curious.

I opened the envelope and slid from it a newspaper clipping, *The Herndon Observer*, from February 1999. At the top of the page, "Obituaries," and heading a narrow column: "Anthony Michael Williams, 22."

My throat closed and my lungs stopped. I felt strangled by the impact of this artifact, this remaining piece. Like his dog tags, the burning valley painting, the folded tapestries in San Francisco, and the green velvet notebook, this was a part of Tony. The end of him, really. Seeing it made my eyes well up with tears so that I couldn't read it. I slid it back into the envelope and bowed my head.

"Thank you," I whispered. *Thank you, whoever had deemed it right for me to stay, for me to have this chance, this life.* Gratitude, once again, overwhelmed me.

Dad pushed my drought beer across the table, and I took a long drink.

"You okay?" Mom asked after a while.

I nodded.

"Should I have waited?"

I shook my head. "It's good. It's right. Thank you for keeping it. For saving it. For me."

"You'll share it with Kacie?"

I nodded again. "Just maybe not tonight, okay?"

Mom smiled. "Okay."

Dad broke the conversation away to discuss dinner options, and I told them Kacie and I planned to eat later so I could join them for a snack but didn't want to spoil my appetite.

They had driven here from Tucson. Mom loved a road trip and they'd left Arizona last Saturday to make their way across the country for the second time, this time West to East, and told me about the places they'd stopped, the shows they'd seen, and what pictures they'd taken.

Dad had been anxious to use his digital camera and Mom had been glad to stop at landmarks and national parks along the way. They'd driven the Toyota in case of weather and had stayed on the southern route until they got nearer to the East Coast. Then they'd gone through Nashville, even visiting with Chris's cousin, Denean, who had put us up over the summer for a few days. Dad laughed about Denean taking them to what she called "grown-up bars" and how she described the three of us as tom cats on the prowl.

It didn't seem she'd told my parents about our conversation or about Chris's run-in with the racists, but he'd blown that off when we mentioned it to her the next day, too. Six months later and I couldn't decide what had bothered me more: seeing Chris treated that way, realizing the very real danger he was in for the first time, or knowing it had only been *our* first time, not his. Back together before September 11th and we hadn't talked much about Nashville other than Jason once bringing it up, saying he wasn't sure he'd want to go back.

"A whole city ain't racist, Jay," Chris had said. "But there ain't a whole city that's not, either."

Mom and Dad didn't mention the subject, so I didn't bring it up.

"What qualifies as a 'grown-up' bar?"

Dad said, "Denean told us country music wasn't the only music in Nashville. That the blues lived there, too." He smiled and it was that affectionate look, the one he got when he talked about Yeddy's and the Lowery's, and I recognized it as the feeling I had while telling stories about Abbie, David, Marco, and The Crew.

"I wonder what kind of music lives in Pittsburgh?" I asked, but before we could discuss it, Mom said she was hungry, and they needed to make progress toward food before ordering another drink. They decided to venture out. The server brought us a check and Dad took it, and she recommended a few good places nearby.

It took me less than thirty seconds to decide to run the envelope Mom had given me upstairs. Tonight was about Kacie and me—Seattle Kacie, nomad me, post-Tony, post-9/11—this wasn't a reunion to remember Tony. *Sorry, dude.* We'd done that on his birthday in September. We would certainly raise a shot to him. He had a diamond on our cufflinks. But tonight, this was about me and Kacie being in the same room together again and me trying to convince her I'd changed. In all the ways that mattered, I'd changed. I left the envelope on the nightstand with the cufflinks.

Back in the lobby, Kacie came through the rotating door as I stepped out of the elevator and our eyes found one another like magnets. A thrill shot through me. The strap of her purse had fallen off her shoulder and the bag hung on her elbow, she shuffled her luggage in, a bulky coat compressed where another carry-on hung over the opposite shoulder. I rushed forward to help, lifting the sagging carry-on off her shoulder and the larger case off the floor. Only then did I realize my arms were full and I couldn't hug her.

She pushed a stray lock of hair out of her beautiful face and smiled at me.

"Auditioning for bellhop?"

"Free agent. Only the best hotels in the world."

An awkward moment passed in which we were close enough for air kisses, a half-embrace, or some other more familiar contact. Instead, Kacie stepped around me, murmured, "Thanks," and moved toward the check-in desk.

I followed. Bags in tow.

When she'd given her ID and credit card, received her room key and number, she turned to me. A flick of her wrist and a uniformed bellhop moved toward us. *Where the fuck had he been ten minutes ago?*

"He'll get these," she said. "I'll be right back."

And she was gone. Into the elevator hallway, behind sliding doors, and I stood there, wondering at how I'd wasted it. The first moment back with her and my dumb ass had grabbed her bags like she was a baby-bobbling stranger in the airport. I should have grabbed her, bags be damned. With a groan, I walked toward the bar and ordered a tall beer.

Thirty minutes later, Kacie slid into the seat next to me.

"No vodka?"

The scent of vanilla filled the space between us, and I grinned at her. "Now can I hug you?"

"With a double back-pat like a good platonic friend," she teased.

I slipped my arm around her waist, though, and pulled her against me. We were half standing half sitting in the stylishly curved barstools. She hid her face in my neck and I pressed my lips to her hair.

"I've missed you," I said.

"I talked to you yesterday."

"You know that's not enough." I pulled her tighter, feeling her hips against mine, the way her thighs parted around my leg, her breasts against my chest.

She patted my back and pulled away.

"Slow it down a bit, okay?" Tilting her face up to look me in the eyes, I could see hers were damp. She smiled, though, and added, "I'm tired and it's late and this is a lot."

Nodding, I set her away from me, gently, urging her onto the bar stool.

"We have all weekend." She'd let her hair down while she was upstairs, and its curls bounced and flared over her shoulders. I wanted to dig my hand into them, pull her to me again. The desire felt almost overwhelming.

We talked about her flight, her luggage, the cab ride over, her room. Tabby had sent Kacie's dress ahead, too. I hadn't noticed the bellhop carrying the hanging bag, but it was among her things, she said, and she was supposed to try it on one last time tonight and let Tabby know it fit.

"Did you?"

She nodded. "That's what took me so long."

"And?"

She rolled her eyes. "It's like something out of a Hollywood romcom."

"Laughably hideous?"

"Does your tux fit?"

"Didn't try it."

"Rebel."

I grinned. "Figured I might need another shower after dinner." When she raised her eyebrows I said, "A cold one."

"So, we're flirting now?"

I shrugged.

"You're impossible."

"And you're hungry. Let's go."

We finished our drinks, donned coats, zipped up, and headed out into the Pittsburgh night. The William Penn Omni has an impressive front façade and as we exited, Kacie turned back to look up at the building.

"It's like staying at the Ritz Carlton or something."

"Like in a romcom?"

She hummed in response.

Our hands were gloved but I took hers anyway.

"Where are we headed?"

"Italian," she said and tugged me south toward the restaurant. It was late, but not *that* late, and plenty of people were on the streets, windows bright with commerce and entertainment. It was cold, though, and the few blocks were far enough that the heat of the indoors made Kacie's cheeks flush bright pink when we stepped inside.

"I'm ready to actually eat something. I've been dieting for weeks."

"To fit into the dress?"

"It's rather unforgiving."

Following her to our table, I helped remove her jacket and handed both hers and mine to the hostess who hung them on a nearby coat tree. When the waiter appeared, we ordered wine and the specials and settled in.

"This place reminds me of Da Domenico," I said, naming the restaurant where I'd taken her on our first date. We'd been too young for wine then but had enjoyed a rich, delicious meal and the candlelit ambiance. We had dressed up and it felt special. Afterward, I'd taken the long way home through neighborhoods full of Christmas lights and we'd listened to the Vince Gill album, *Let There Be Peace on Earth*, and held hands. Then, at home, we'd snuggled up to watch *Beauty and the Beast*. After which, as the credits rolled, I'd pulled her off the couch and into my arms and

slow danced with her in the dimly lit living room of my parents'
house. Where they no longer lived. It seemed like a million years
ago.

"You're stuck in a memory somewhere," she said. "Tell me?"

"I'd rather focus on now. And the future."

"Which is?"

"Maine."

"Pardon?"

I chuckled. "I've been offered a Writer in Residence position
at the University of Maine."

"Like *Maine* Maine?"

"Is there any other Maine?"

She sat back in her chair, her expression exasperated. "Main
street. Mainland. Both closer than Maine."

"Closer to where?"

"To . . ." but she stopped, looked away. "Tucson. Your parents.
Your friends in San Francisco. You have a life there, Joel said so."

"It's only a year."

When she looked up this time, her hands folded in her lap,
her brow was wrinkled with the little crinkle she gets when she's
lost track of the conversation.

"Maine is only a year. I can do anything for a year, right?"

"It's cold in Maine."

"Some of the time, yeah."

"A lot of the time."

"Why does everyone go to the weather right away?"

"I didn't," she said defensively. "I went to the distance first."

"You and Mom."

"How are your parents?" And then we were off Maine and
onto another topic, a safer one that wasn't so much about the
future as the right now and the recent past. I had already told
her about Tucson and about Jason moving there. I had told her

about golf and the rattlesnakes, but now I talked about seeing them earlier and left out the fact of the obituary in the envelope.

We drank more wine.

We walked back to the hotel and I led her to the elevators. I let her step in and dropped her hand. She waved gently then the doors closed, and she was gone.

Out on the terrace, I lit a cigarette and huddled deeper into my coat. A quiet drift of snow had started, and I wished I'd kept Kacie with me a little longer. Maybe kissed her. Instead, I hot-boxed the cigarette and headed upstairs. I'd been right about the shower. It was cold enough to do the trick. And the tux. It fit perfectly.

Friday, February 1, 2002

I woke up hard as a rock. All I could think of was Kacie. It was an obsession like I'd only known once before and not for a very long time. I groaned into the pillow, then laughed a little, and promised myself I wouldn't wake up alone tomorrow morning. Whatever it took, today I would convince her we were meant to be.

It was nearly 9:30 and dreary outside. A hard knock on the door dragged me out from under the covers. I threw on a pair of pajama pants and sauntered toward the hallway. When I opened the door, Kacie stood there with a paper bag and a cup of coffee.

She looked me up and down, smirked, and said, "Good morning. Just brought this for you."

"Stay?"

She shook her head and then extended both arms, the breakfast gifts between us.

"Thanks."

A nod, another secret smile, and she was off down the corridor.

I sat on the end of the bed and sipped at the coffee. It was rich and dark and warm, and it made me smile. In the bag was an asiago bagel with vegetable cream cheese. The very breakfast I'd earned from her when we were seniors in high school; I swam every morning, and she met me in the senior parking lot with coffee and a bagel. We would split the bagel. I reached inside. Only half. I grinned.

The TV showed an improved forecast for the day. Sunlight later. Joel and I were supposed to meet for lunch around 11:00. I scarfed down Kacie's gift and tugged my notebook out of the backpack. My pencil flew over the pages trying to capture the surprise of the Fort Pitt Tunnel and the indifference of the sulky cab driver. I wrote about the beer with Mom and Dad and the wine in the warm Italian restaurant. I wrote about Kacie. And the kiss I should have stolen but didn't.

"You gave her my room number?" I asked Joel as we walked down the street toward lunch.

"Nah, Tabby probably did."

"No fucking way your fiancé is helping me."

"How does it help you to get a half-eaten bagel delivered for breakfast?" He laughed.

"The coffee was good."

Joel took me to a sports bar near the stadium for lunch. It was full of white-collar employees with their name badges, khaki pants, and waters-with-lemon. He ordered us beers and said, "I love drinking while other people are working."

"Cheers to that, my friend." Another long drink and I set the tall glass on the table. "Saw Tabby's sister in the lobby when I arrived yesterday. She said I'm her favorite."

"She wants to visit San Francisco. Probably buttering you up."

"I'd be glad to show her a good time." I smirked when he frowned and added, "In that sister-in-law-who's-off-limits kind of way. *Syempre.*" *Of course.*

"She'd better get there quick," he said. "Before you go off somewhere again."

"How about Maine?"

"Like *Maine?*"

"Yes. The state of Maine. Population 1.24 million, about thirteen hours north of here by interstate. Three- maybe four-hour flight. You knew I was up there before Tony's birthday."

"Did I?"

"I was interviewing."

"I swear I didn't know."

"You did. You've just been preoccupied."

"Well anyway, congrats, I guess. But *Maine?*" He shivered and we both laughed. So, yeah, the weather.

Later, in the lobby, we found Chris who had just arrived and Jason who had already made himself at home in the room he was sharing with Joel on Friday but not on Saturday.

"You owe me eighty bucks," Chris said to Jason.

"What the fuck for?"

"Last tab in Vegas."

"I call bullshit," Joel said, but I was already laughing because I knew what bet Jason had lost and why he was supposed to have paid that check. Chris snuck a glance at me and jerked his chin nearly imperceptibly. But Jason saw it and started shaking his head.

"No, no way. Fuck you both."

"What's happening?" Joel asked.

I couldn't contain it anymore and burst out laughing, and Chris and I clasped hands, a kind of brothers' shake, in our mutual mockery of Jason.

"Tell me," Joel said.

"It's a long story," I finally said. "But summary is that Jason claims the woman he was ... um ... *flirting* with was another Vegas visitor like the rest of us."

"Her company had a conference," Jason said.

"And Chris claims she was a hooker."

"And a good storyteller," Chris added with a laugh.

"You didn't," Joel said. "I was there."

"Nah, he didn't take her . . . er . . . home." Chris laughed again. "But let's just say she didn't have a conference badge or even any friends. So, I call it like I see it and she was a working girl." He spread his arms as if he'd presented plenty of evidence.

"And he thinks I couldn't tell the difference," Jason said.

"You couldn't," I said.

"And what's the proof?" Jason asked.

Chris looked at me and I tried to hide the smile and said, "She might have offered me the same package after you went to bed."

"Shut it," Jason said.

"Hand to God," I said, laughing.

"I only told her she should have tried Brian first. He mighta fallen for it." Chris slapped Jason's back and grinned. "Y'all some dumb motherfuckers."

Jason shook his head. "Some shit right there."

"You stepped in it," Chris said. "Now pay up."

Jason handed over four twenties. "Now buy us a round of drinks, asshole."

"Nah, man, I'm going upstairs. Tonight's gonna get here fast enough." He folded his hand into mine for another shoulder-clap-semi-hug. Then Jason.

"I'll go with you," Joel said, and gave us the same folded-clasp hugs before walking with Chris toward the elevator bank.

"On me," I told Jason, and jerked my chin toward the bar.

"Nah, fuck it. Charge it to my room."

"You mean Joel's room."

Jason shrugged. "Wedding budget."

As we took seats side-by-side at the hotel bar I was reminded of that day in September when I'd been shoulder-to-shoulder with a sailor on his way home to hopefully see his father before he died. He came to mind now and then as I expected he would. As the baby, Emmy, did and her mother, too. I remembered them and felt glad to do so. Honored to have known them, for just the smallest piece of time.

I let the rest of September 11th roll through my head like a film reel. Arriving at Chris's. Tight hugs from him and Jason. The couch. Sandwiches. The news. Talking to Kacie. Writing for hours while Jason slept and Chris worked. An early-evening run and a loud-music free-weight workout in the basement with my brothers. Then ordering food. Drinking a few beers. Going to bed early and staring at the ceiling before picking up the phone and calling Kacie again.

"It was heavier than I thought it would be," Jason said, pulling me out of that September day.

"What was?"

"Tony's casket."

And I was in a different day all together. A Friday in February 1999.

We hadn't shouldered it, but gripped the silver handles, the four of us, and carried it from the hearse to the green tent. In the rain. I'd been stoned. Numb. Tony's brother, Gavin, and his best friend had helped. And I could hear the rain splashing on it, sliding down either side, dripping like tears. His mother had wept on her sister's shoulder. His father's jaw had been set like stone. It was a memory I had folded up and put away. Too painful to examine, to relive, to think about. Had I ever processed it, I might have driven myself crazy with mental replays.

"I didn't remember," I said.

"My grip on the handle was slick and I kept thinking I might drop it. And somehow, I got my feet off pace, maybe you all were taking smaller steps and I just wanted to be done, but I was off pace and I nearly stumbled."

"Jay," I said, it occurring to me that he was torturing himself with it. Three years later.

"I dream about it. Carrying him to his grave. Sometimes in

the dream I'm the only one and I'm dragging the thing toward the hole. Sometimes I'm in my hockey uniform and I can't use both hands because I have a stick in the other." He shook his head, ran his fingers through the condensation on the glass in front of him. Late afternoon sunlight came through a window high above the bar and refracted off the carbonation in the glass.

"How often do you have that dream?" I asked and then had to smirk at myself for sounding like that dickhead Dr. Moses. "Have you told anyone?"

Jason shook his head.

"How long have you been having that dream?"

He shrugged. "A few months."

"Before the summer."

He nodded.

"Since the funeral?"

"No. It didn't start right away. It was . . ." He seemed to really think about it, count back. "I think it started after I saw you in San Francisco that first time."

"That's over a year ago." Joel asked Tabby to marry him. We went to the hotel party. Marco, David, and Abbie had come, too. It felt like a long time ago but not as long ago as Tony's funeral. Mom had told me I couldn't delay grief. But that was exactly what Jason had done.

"I knew you were going through something, man, but I really didn't think it was Tony."

"That's what Chris said in Nashville. That he couldn't believe it had taken me this long to deal with it."

"Right." And our September plan had only been a hunch and botched attempt.

"I'd been playing hockey. Trying to make a go of that. It took everything I had to work hard enough to be good enough to compete." He tugged at the cuffs of his sleeves, unbuttoned them and rolled them up over his wrists and forearms. "Nothing fits anymore." It was a casual remark having to do with clothes and dropping weight since he'd quit playing. He was narrower in width, in frame. Even his face was thinner, more like Joel's than it had been a year ago. Seeing them together in Las Vegas had been startling.

"Leaving the game was the right thing to do. Going to Arizona, that's right, too. I'm grateful to your folks."

I edged my elbow against his. "Course."

"Abbie said I had to make plans."

"That's her mantra," I said.

Jason laughed. "She got you set up right."

"She's good people."

"Over New Year's she said I needed to set my sights on what's next. That doing so would help me to stop looking back."

"Her mom's into some serious self-healing, mantra-saying, if-you-see-it-you-can-be-it stuff. Abbie would punch me for saying she sounded just like her." I slid my empty glass forward and let the bartender take it for a refill.

"Being in a new place helps," he said. "Maybe that's how come you got through it so fast? Because Barcelona?"

I shook my head. "It didn't feel fast. It felt like something was sitting on my chest."

"For how long?"

"A year. Longer."

Seems like this was how it would be. Holidays and special occasions and hotel bars and weddings and funerals. All of it together. The Crew. Our family. I felt proud we'd been able to keep *us* intact. That even after Tony, we hadn't completely splintered. They'd held on to one another and when I came back to them, they'd let me hold on, too. Things were changing, and they would continue to reconfigure and reorganize into the next and the next and the next version of us. Since September, those configurations were looking more permanent. Every vision I had of my future now looked like an investment in the kind of life I hoped to lead. I had hope.

I wasn't thinking about the weight of Tony's casket.

Or even that baby girl who never made it back to California.

Or the thousands of lives that were irrevocably changed by that September morning.

I spent most of my time thinking about what would happen next. Looking forward. Making plans. Just like Abbie had told me to. Like Tony never had and never would.

"September put things in perspective for me," I said. "In a way nothing else had."

"Right. Of course."

"No, I mean, it changed everything."

"For a lot of people. For the whole country, right? The world even maybe."

"Seriously, Jason. Listen to me, will ya?" I turned in my seat to face him, had to back up a little or we'd be too close for a face-to-face conversation. "Everything before feels like childhood. And everything since feels like adulthood."

"Okay."

"And adults take action. They get shit done. They don't ask for permission or wait for others to do shit for them. They get to work."

"One would think."

"What choice do we have? We can never go back."

"You think I don't know that?"

"Then why are you still sitting on the bench?"

"I'm not. I said I'm moving to Arizona. Getting a job. I'm making a new life."

"And still thinking about the weight of Tony's casket."

"And you don't?"

"No, man, I don't. Not since I realized he's not worrying about me anymore. The end of him came and went. There was a time I would have given anything to have him here with me, watching Joel get married. In Nashville fucking up those racists in that bar fight. In San Francisco listening to Melissa read that really mean poem about me. And in a way, he was in all of those places. Inasmuch as he can be. Because he's gone from everything but my memory now. And your memory. And Chris's and Joel's. And we can love him. And miss him. But we can't live for him and we can't pretend like we can't live without him. Because we can. And we have to. We have."

He'd been staring at his hands, on the bar between himself and the half-empty beer. He grabbed the beer, drank down the rest of it. When he turned to me, glanced at the very small distance between us, an intimacy maybe we didn't need, he laughed.

Before he could say anything, I clasped his shoulder, stood out of my chair, and said, "Let's go out and smoke."

Jason stood, too, and followed me out to the terrace.

"Melissa read a mean poem about you?"

"It's as funny as you falling for a hooker in Vegas. Wanna discuss?"

Before we could get out the door, I heard my name called and turned to see my parents settling into a pair of conversation chairs near the bar. I jerked a thumb at the terrace and made the universal sign for "smoke a cigarette" only to see my mother frown and my father wave me off. Then Jason and I were outside.

When we came back in, we took the two chairs opposite Mom and Dad and heard about how they'd spent their Friday in Pittsburgh. They planned to go out for dinner and maybe catch some live music. The bartender had recommended a blues club not far from the hotel.

"Your father brought his harmonica and we thought he'd sit in on a set or two." It was the kind of silliness we fabricated like our family's inside joke.

"Use the shared tip money for gas on the way home," Dad said, adding to it.

"I have my ukulele," I said. "Maybe I should come?"

"It's too cold for ukulele," Mom said, and smiled. "Now, a tambourine. That would be something."

I'd once claimed Jason and I would be competing in Flamenco dance competitions in Spain as a same-sex couple. Mom suggested I join the PGA tour if writing didn't work out. Dad had promised to run for Congress in the next election cycle on a campaign promise of outlawing handlebar moustaches. All of these odd stories were part of my relationship with my parents. A kind of acknowledgement that what they kept from me wasn't critical and that I shouldn't feel left out by their intimacy. And a kind of permission to build a story of my own.

"You should get up and run with us tomorrow morning," Jason said.

"You'll have to speak louder," Dad said. "I'm mostly deaf in that ear." He pointed to the one nearest Jason.

"An old war injury," Mom said. "He doesn't like to talk about it."

Jason nodded knowingly. "Something to do with a burning building?"

"And orphans," I said.

"Yes," Mom said. "Fire and children always make a good story."

"Come again?" Dad said, a little louder than necessary.

"Your tuxedos fit?" Mom asked, looking first at me and then Jason. She'd pulled some hand lotion from her purse and now squeezed it into one hand and then capped it, dropped it back in her bag, and rubbed her hands together. A cinnamon scent like Red Hots candy drifted from her. She'd been worried about Tabby's plan to have the tuxedos waiting for us and said she thought a national chain, like Men's Wearhouse, would have had the tux she picked, and we could have each been responsible for our own suit.

The wedding planner, Brooke, appeared seemingly out of nowhere and said, "Well? Did they?"

"Hi, Brooke," Jason said. "These are Brian's parents. Joan and Alan Listo."

Dad stood and shook her hand. Mom waved from her seat.

"Yes, the tuxedos fit," I said.

"The bowties aren't clips," Jason complained.

"All good," I said. "I can tie them."

Brooke nodded and said, "Joel said as much. Upstairs at 6:30." Then she disappeared as quickly as she'd come.

"She's efficient," Mom said.

"And focused," Dad agreed, taking his seat again.

"Like Tabby," Jason said.

Another hour drifted by. Mom and Dad left to change clothes and get dinner. Kacie arrived, catching Jason at the bar. I watched him hug her and saw her place a hand on his cheek and then slide it down his arm. He was smaller, she was probably observing. Then she glanced over at me, looked shy, and nodded at whatever Jason said next.

I stood as she approached, treated us both to a hug, holding her against me and breathing her in, kissing her neck quickly, so slight she might have missed it, and then waving for her to sit in the chair Mom had vacated.

"Saw your parents in the lobby."

"They're on vacay. They tell me being a guest at a wedding is much more fun than being in it." I raised one eyebrow at her, and she shook her head. We weren't going to talk about Colorado in March. Not yet.

Jason brought drinks over and the three of us caught up.

An hour or so later, we went up for the rehearsal, which was tedious and boring. I felt like a lit fuse waiting to get Kacie alone. Waiting to charm her. To hold her. To remind her.

She let me flirt with her. Pull her chair out at dinner and scoot it in gently with her in it.

She let me stare at her. Lingering gazes that felt weighed down with possibility.

She let me tell stories about people and places she didn't know and had never been. And she drank wine. And she laughed. And she told her own stories. And I was enchanted. Again.

We stayed in the hotel bar for an extra round after Chris went up to bed then the three of us, Kacie, Jason, and me, got on the elevator and rode up to the seventh floor. Jason sauntered left down the hall to the room he was sharing with Joel. Kacie and I walked right.

Standing in front of her door, I threaded my fingers through hers and pulled her close enough to kiss her but didn't.

She smiled and said, "This feels familiar."

"It's different," I said. "I'm different."

"I've noticed." She leaned into me, rested her cheek against my chest.

I kissed the top of her head. "Goodnight."

She nodded. Our hands unclasped, she opened her door, and disappeared inside.

I walked the length of the hall to my own room. The phone was ringing when I stepped inside.

"What do you have to give?" she asked.

"Everything that is mine is yours. Everything that will be mine. All of it for you. Only you."

The line went dead.

A gentle knock on the door.

I opened it, reached for her, and pulled her inside.

Kacie and I have always been like magnets. The attraction between us undeniable even when we were angry with one another, frustrated by each other, broken by separation and betrayal, and devastated by loss.

Since September we had been on the phone. She didn't trust herself to be near me. As geographically close as she'd been at New Year's I couldn't convince her to travel down the highway for a night, and I had respected her decision and not gone to her. Though I wanted to. Though Abbie encouraged me to. Instead, I'd let those old coals once dormant start to burn again. And the distance had been like fuel for the fire. Every conversation, every email, just knowing this weekend was coming, had been like a long, slow stream of air, oxygen to the flame.

Unzipping her cocktail dress, peeling it away from her, kissing her skin as it was revealed, that monarch butterfly on her shoulder; I burned for her. As familiar as she was—her taste and shape and the little sounds she made—I felt a thrill at rediscovering her. Beneath the dress a black lacy bra and panties, a garter belt with thigh-high stockings connected to it. I slipped her shoes off, kissed the bottoms of her feet. She rolled my shirt off my shoulders, walked around me pulling it off and tossing it aside, her fingers trailing over my shoulders and down my bare back.

She smiled up at me. I kissed her perfect lips. She sighed my name. I lifted her off the floor and carried her to the bed.

We were back together. We were renewed. And we had all the time in the world.

Saturday, February 2, 2002

On a Saturday morning a long time ago, I woke in a bed beside Kacie and quietly dressed and left while she slept. I did the same in Pittsburgh. This time, though, I donned running gear including a hat and gloves, and met my friends, who looked like cat burglars, in the lobby.

After a morning run and some good-natured teasing, I returned to the room on the seventh floor just before 10:00 a.m. and tossed a bagel in a paper bag on the bed.

"I really didn't think you'd go," she said, shoving the pillow under her cheek and smiling at me.

I crawled up the bed toward her, caging her in my arms and kissed her nose.

"You stink," she murmured.

"Shower with me."

She shook her head.

"Stay until after?"

"Maybe."

But when I got out of the shower, she and the bagel were gone.

Chris, Jason, and I went for sandwiches a block away.

"Seriously, man, how do you eat that shit?" Chris was frowning at Jason's pastrami on rye.

"Rye bread sucks," I agreed.

"Tell Chris what you told Joel about Maine."

"Like cold-as-a-witch's-titty state near the arctic circle?" Chris asked.

"Like Eastern Standard Time home to Stephen King," I said.

"Frozen rivers," Jason said. "Abbie says the rivers freeze."

"But a river moves," Chris said. "How's that manage to freeze?"

"It ain't right," Jason said. "That's too cold."

"Meanwhile, Jay's moving to a place where folks have to stay inside like vampires or risk being burned alive. Where rattlesnakes fall from the sky." I laughed before I could even finish saying it. "Where cactus milk is a menu item."

"Lies. Two of those are lies."

"You moving to Tucson?" Chris asked.

"Think so. Alan's got a lead on an Olympic team pipeline for coaches." He shrugged. "Gonna work a youth league, maybe a school team. See what it gets me."

"That's great, man," Chris said.

"Be near family," I confirmed.

"Family," Jason echoed, and grinned at us both. "Feels good to be with family."

Before we left the deli, I went to the counter and ordered a cookie. Then, when Jason and Chris left me on the seventh floor, I called the Bridal Suite where Kacie had said they'd be getting their hair done this afternoon. One of Tabby's sisters answered.

"Hey there, it's Brian. Is Kacie with you?"

"Perhaps. Why?"

"I found this kind of cookie she likes at the place Chris and I had lunch and I got her one."

"That's so sweet. Why not bring it?"

"Actually, I thought she could come get it. Can she slip away for a minute? But don't tell her why, okay?"

"Okay," she said, a co-conspirator. "I'll just say you have something we need."

"Thanks." I told her the room number.

Then I waited for the knock and when it came, I pulled her inside again like the night before. This time, though, before I could ravish her, I was stunned into letting her go and stepping back.

"What?" she asked.

"That's my shirt," I said.

"Yeah, I wore it out this morning and realized I would need a button-up because, you know, hair and make-up. Hope it's okay I borrowed it."

"Stole it."

"Borrowed it."

"You'll need to pay for it."

"Borrowing is free."

"But you stole it."

She grinned. Her hair hadn't been styled yet, it hung in a messy bun on her neck, but her make-up had been done and her eyelids sparkled like they'd caught snowflakes and her lips glistened with a pale pink gloss.

"I'm going to ruin your lipstick," I said, reaching for her.

She dodged out of my grasp, though, and said, "No you're not either."

"Wanna bet?" Instead of kissing her, though, I took the cookie out of the bag.

"You're evil," she said.

I crooked a finger at her, beckoning her to me.

She shook her head. "I have to get back."

"You don't want a bite?"

She shook her head. "Absolutely not."

"Liar."

"Evil."

I broke the cookie in half and took a bite. It was a white chocolate chip cookie with crystallized sugar baked onto the top. The deep tan color of it and the glint of the sugar were too much for her to resist. I knew that much about Kacie.

"You called me here for a cookie."

"No. I called you here so I can kiss you. The cookie was just extra." She looked perfect in my shirt. It was the one she had taken off me the night before and tossed aside. She'd knotted the front tails of it so it was higher on her waist than it should have been. She wore jeans and flip flops, freshly painted toes wiggling when I looked down at them. That had been this morning's first appointment, she'd told me, even though I'd found nothing wrong with her feet last night as I removed the stockings and kissed them.

"Give me the cookie, Brian."

"For a kiss."

"Cookie."

"Kiss."

She put her hands on her hips and tilted her head. "What if I just leave?"

"What if you do? I'll eat the whole thing myself."

"Evil." She narrowed her eyes and glared at me, but it wasn't real. It was a game, and it was fun, and I wanted her as badly now as I had last night.

"What's this I hear about you knowing how to tie bow ties?"

"I learned in Paris."

"But why?"

"My friend said she didn't trust a man who couldn't tie a bow tie. So, she taught me."

Now the frown was real. "What friend?"

"Flight attendant named Lara. From Oklahoma. Met her in Spain. Stayed in touch."

"And when was the last time you saw her?" Kacie asked.

"Don't do that."

"Do what?"

"Get jealous over women you'll never meet who were with me when you weren't."

"I'm not jealous."

"Good. Because there have been some."

"Some what?"

"Some women. Other women. A few."

"More like a dozen," Kacie snorted. "I wouldn't expect less."

"It's not always like that."

"I don't want to know what it's like. This was a mistake." She started past me, but I reached for her arm and touched her lightly.

"Please don't go. We need to have a vocabulary for this. That's what I learned in therapy. Have a vocabulary for how we talk about uncomfortable things and certainly this, other partners, is uncomfortable."

"For you."

"And you. I can see it. You're not jealous but you're not happy."

"You're mine," she whispered. "So, no, I'm not happy when I think of you with someone else. Anyone else. Any time."

"You threw me out of Seattle."

"Yes." She looked up at me, over her shoulder, and her green eyes shone with tears.

"And ignored me. Told Joel to tell me to leave you *the fuck* alone. You were done with me."

"I was never done with you." She stepped back toward me then. "Understand that, okay? I was never done with you. You are forever to me. Always. But we," she wagged her finger between us, "*We* weren't ready."

"And now we are?"

She crossed her arms over her chest. "I don't know."

"Say yes."

"To what?"

"To all of it. To us. House. Kids. Retirement savings. Anniversaries that don't make us cringe. A dog named Jake Barnes. Milestones that feel like accomplishments, not just the passage of time."

"You're writing a future I don't yet see."

"Then start here. Now. With this." I reached the cookie out toward her. She snort-laughed, that sound of disbelief that was so adorable it really did take everything I had to stand still and wait for her to move closer to me.

"Ruin your lipstick," I teased, and then she did come nearer, and I could smell her vanilla body lotion, and while I thought I'd come completely undone it was nothing compared to how I felt when she leaned forward and let me feed her the cookie.

"You have no idea how badly I want to strip that shirt off you right now," I murmured.

"There isn't time."

"I'll be quick."

She grinned, took another bite of cookie, laughed, and licked her lips to capture a stray crumb.

"You need to go," I said. "Or you're never leaving."

She tilted her face up and let me kiss her cheek.

"Be good," she said.

I tucked my arms behind my back and said, "Beyond reproach." I walked her to the door and opened it.

As she stepped out, she said, "Thanks for the treat."

"You're welcome. Save me a dance?"

"Count on it."

Then she was gone.

I took another cold shower and donned the tuxedo Tabby had picked out, complete with silver vest, silver button covers, and the black-and-silver-and-diamond cufflinks. I tied the tie and headed down the hall to Joel's room. Jason and Chris met me at the door. Chris had his tie in his palm like a sad, floppy ribbon.

"Damn, Hemingway," Jason said. "You wear the hell out of a rental."

"Seriously," Chris said as we stepped inside. "You're such a fucking asshole."

"Who doesn't rent clip-ons?" Joel complained. One by one, I tied their ties.

We married Joel off to the first girl he'd ever loved, and the ceremony was beautiful, and the reception was warm with candlelight and bubbles and champagne. Joel and Tabby shared a two-top table near the dancefloor and the bridal party sat at a round table nearby.

Kacie leaned into me and whispered, "So I guess Tabby's sisters think you're gay?"

I laughed. "Yeah, Joel said she'd told them that."

"Revenge?"

I shrugged. "Amusement?"

Kacie frowned. "Well anyway it made it hard to explain how we dated in high school and some of college."

"Why did you have to explain anything?"

"There was some reapplying of make-up after the cookie thing. And they wanted to know why you had only bought one and not a bag with enough for all of us."

"Fair point," I conceded. "Probably should have been sneakier with that."

I leaned toward her and kissed her jaw, just below her ear. "You're gorgeous by the way."

"No thanks to your attempt at make-up smearing sabotage," she teased.

"Which you very skillfully avoided."

She met my eyes then and said, "It's not because I didn't want you."

"Oh, I know," I murmured against her lips. "Patience."

The music gradually got softer, and the DJ invited Jason to the microphone and when he stood, he looked anxiously at Chris who simply nodded at him.

"You got this," I said.

"Why's he nervous?" Kacie whispered.

"Just working through some stuff."

We turned to face Joel and Tabby, and Jason stepped up to them and smiled at his twin.

"When Joel and I were nine years old," he said, "We met this skinny kid named Tony at a skatepark near our house."

I glanced across the room at Mac who dipped his head. His date's hand was on his shoulder.

"Within a week we were The Crew. Tony, Brian, Joel, and me. We found Chris the next year and we've been family ever since." Jason was smiling but I could see his eyes were shining. "When things got bad. For any of us. There we all were. And I thought our family was stronger than anything. Then Joel went to Pittsburgh and met Tabby. And she saw in him something not even his family, his teammates, our Crew had seen. And she brings out the best in him. In all things. And our family, it's better, because she's in it. So, here's to Joel and Tabby. And to making it official. And to a long and happy life together and a family. *Our* family."

"*Salúd!*" I called out.

"Cheers!" Chris echoed.

And a round of echoes and then we drank. Before Pittsburgh, Joel had been into computer programming and gaming. He'd been the most disciplined skater on our Crew and a helluva competitor. I'd been the cocky captain of our team, but Joel had been its leader. Before Pittsburgh, he had quietly suggested we figure out what we were going to be and try to be that. Then he'd left, he met Tabby, and he'd been on a clear, albeit winding path. And I had been aimless, Jason played at chasing a dream, Chris tried to get by, and Tony slowly went insane. We'd been without a rudder when Joel went to Pittsburgh. On that New Year's Eve in 1999, Tabby had made us an elaborate meal, poured wine, and played classical music. A dinner party. Like adults. We played at being grown-ups. Except Joel and Tabby knew what their adult life would look like and we had yet to figure ours out.

I turned to Kacie. "Dance with me?"

The vision was becoming clearer. Maine, a residency, teaching creative writing and working on a longer work, a novel. Maybe become the editor of a journal. Maybe pursue a faculty position somewhere overseas.

Holding her against me and swaying to the music, I said, "I want you to move to Maine with me."

"I'm not moving to Maine."

"For a year."

"At all."

"Then at least invite me to your sister's wedding in Colorado."

"Why are you so anxious to make plans? Why not just enjoy what we have here, now?"

"Plans are how we promise ourselves we'll survive."

"Can we not promise anything right now?" she asked, and I felt her cheek on my jaw, her nose on my neck, felt her breathe deep. "Can we just be together?"

"Okay," I said. "For now."

After we said goodbye to Joel and Tabby, we closed down the lobby where a pianist had been talked into staying on an extra hour and playing Billy Joel songs for us. Then we were back upstairs in my room, in my bed. Naked and spent, we curled into one another and let our breathing even out, our limbs intertwined.

In the darkness, the only thing between us a deep sense of satisfaction, Kacie whispered, "I'm afraid to trust it, Brian. I'm afraid of getting hurt again."

I didn't respond.

"It feels like we've always been on this path, and even though we lost our way, that we'd get it back. I trusted that. But this," she squeezed my arm around her. "This easy intimacy, this just-like-it-used-to-be, this is hard to trust."

I couldn't breathe. Couldn't speak. Couldn't bear the thought of letting her go tomorrow.

More quiet. More stillness and she said, "Why aren't you afraid?"

"I am." I pulled her tighter against me. "But I'm not willing to let that fear stop me from the life I'm meant to live. The life *we're* meant for." I kissed the back of her neck where she'd pulled her hair aside to feel my breath on her skin.

After a while, the quiet became stillness and we slept.

Sunday, February 3, 2002

I was up before the sun. Maybe it was worry about letting her go, maybe it was wanting more of her and feeling across the bed for her when I realized we'd separated in sleep. Maybe it was the inevitable restlessness of a day of travel.

My flight left at 4:00 p.m. to go back to San Francisco. Abbie and David. My loft apartment. The spring semester as an adjunct instructor for undergrad writers. Packing for Maine.

Kacie was still sleeping, though, so when I figured out I wouldn't get back to sleep, I brushed my teeth, pulled on a t-shirt, a flannel, and some jeans, and went down to the lobby for coffee.

Dad was in the café.

"You're up early," he said.

"Genetics."

"Two coffees?" he asked, nodding at the cups in my hands.

"Overnight guest."

"We'll see you President's Day weekend?"

I nodded. "Bringing down the stuff from the apartment that needs to be stored."

"Safe flight. Call when you land?"

"Call where? You'll be on the road."

"Leave a message at the house. We'll check them when we get to our hotel."

"Enjoy the drive," I said.

"Tell Kacie hi," he replied.

Back upstairs, I used the key card to let me in and faced an empty bed.

Kacie came out of the bathroom, a toothbrush hanging out of her mouth, my tuxedo shirt over her shoulders and down her arms but open down the front. I caught a glimpse of her panties and grinned then held the coffees up. She nodded, stepped back into the bathroom, and finished the chore.

"Care to explain the envelope on the nightstand?" she asked, buttoning the shirt as she came back out. I'd sat down with my back against the headboard, kicked my shoes onto the floor, and crossed socked feet at the ankle. She crawled over me toward the other side of the bed, slid the envelope forward and sat cross-legged in the middle of the rumpled sheets facing me.

"It's Tony's obituary from the Observer."

"Yeah. I read it. Where'd you get it."

"Mom and Dad."

"Joan cut his obituary out and saved it?"

I nodded, handing her the coffee and blowing through the tiny hole in my own cup's lid before taking a sip.

"Thank you," she murmured, accepting her cup.

"They have his painting at their house in Tucson. The one with the burning valley."

"I think Jason told me that."

We sat sipping our coffee in an easy quiet for a bit.

"Yesterday was harder than I thought it would be," she confessed.

"What was hard about it?"

"Being without Tony."

"And?"

"Isn't that enough?"

"Maybe." Over the last three years, I'd been with The Crew quite a few times without Tony. We'd taken shots for him. We'd told stories. But mostly we'd been writing new ones. Other than some wedding prep weekends, and the shower Tabby's family held for them, Kacie hadn't been with any of us. She hadn't seen me since my failed trip to Seattle, and Chris she'd only talked to on the phone on September 11th.

"I forget you haven't been with everyone as many times as I have. We get together a lot actually, for living so far apart."

"I know. Tabby complains."

"She'll get used to it."

"I think she thought Joel would outgrow you guys."

"We're his brothers."

"Jason's his brother."

"And me and Chris."

Kacie shook her head. "Their life is here, Joel and Tabby. How do you and Chris fit into that?"

"Holidays. Vacations. Trips. Same as we always have."

"Not always. Just since."

"What are you saying?"

Kacie shrugged. "That at some point, you're going to have to let go."

"Of my brothers?"

Another shrug.

"Don't fucking do that. Don't shrug like Tony did. He would be so noncommittal about everything. *Que sera sera* and shit. Fuck that."

"Why are you mad right now?"

"Do you understand how long it took me to get to here?"

"Almost three years," Kacie said. "Just about two weeks shy of it, actually."

"Three years of therapy. Writing. Rejection. Travel. Airports and baggage claim and delayed flights and bars with nine-dollar draught beers. The most amazing sunsets. Swimming. Running. Thinking about quitting smoking."

"And women."

"And here I am. With you. Like this. Committed for the first time in my life to a vision of what I want that life to be. And I want you in it."

"But why, Brian? Why me?"

And for a second, I didn't know how to answer that. It was such a simple question, but the response was so not simple. How do you tell someone who has already said she's scared that there is nothing in the world you wouldn't do to please her? To deserve her?

It wasn't that I didn't know the answer, it was that I didn't have the words to describe how everything I'd done had brought me to this exact place and her willingness to forgive me, to accept me, was confirmation that it had all been worth it.

"I'm not a trophy," she said. "You can't win me. I'm a person with my own journey and my own baggage." She waved Tony's obituary in her hand. "My own grief. And I'm wondering if we get back to this. To us. If we aren't just going to end up where we were three years ago. Hating what we were doing to one another."

"We're grown up."

"Aged."

"Matured."

"Time heals all wounds, is that it?"

"Yes."

"Let's just see, okay, Brian? Let's just wait and see if there's a happily ever after for us."

"When?"

"Someday."

"Come to Maine."

"Brian."

"Commit, Kacie. Tell me you'll commit. That you'll get into this thing. You'll give it your best effort. That you won't run away." I narrowed my eyes at her. "Or push me away."

"What is your obsession with getting my commitment?"

"I don't want to be in this alone anymore."

"In what?"

"In this life."

"You have Abbie. And David. And The Crew."

"I want you."

"Why?"

"Because I always have. There has never been anything like this not with anyone else and you feel it, too, Kace, I know you do. So, tell me what I have to do to convince you this is real? And that it's worth going for?"

She shook her head and leaned over to the nightstand, setting both the coffee cup and the envelope on it. Then she got up on her knees and moved toward me. She took my cup out of my hand and set it on my nightstand. Then she climbed over me, straddling my hips, and put her hands on my chest.

"Tell me you love me again, like you did last night."

"I love you," without hesitation.

"I love you, too," she said. "So, come with me to Colorado. Let's date. Let's spend time together like we are together and let's see where this goes."

"It goes to Maine."

"You're impossible"

"But you love me."

She leaned forward and kissed me. "I do."

THE END

THE You—Know—Who—You—Ares (YKWYA)

This book came together a lot faster than *After December*. Over six months of pandemic confinement, I revised the book and readied it for Jodie's developmental edit. The distance Brian felt, the alienation from his core group of friends, his desperation to repair broken things, were all part of my pandemic and election cycle anxiety in 2020. In that way, the timing of this novel did feel as cathartic as *After December*.

I didn't expect to write this book. I thought Brian was done with me. So, first thanks goes to Alexa Bigwarfe who said, "So when's the second one going to be ready?" You believe in these books and in me and I'm grateful to you.

Thanks to the entire team at Chrysalis Press for the encouragement, the enthusiasm, and the work to bring this book forward.

I wanted *Before Pittsburgh* to be an epistolary novel and my writing group hated that idea. You know who you are, same people who hated Brian the first time around. So, thanks for steering me away from a full-epistolary approach. They loved the fight scene with the Russians and had great feedback on the 9/11 exchange between Brian and Emmy's mom. So, thanks, Ginny, Bonnie, Sharon, Sharon, Shawn, Janie, Ruth, and El for your insight and input.

Beta readers are a crucial part of the creative process and this time I had two new ones. Thanks to Agata Chydzinski and John Kirkland for checking that my portrayal of Abbie and Chris (respectively) were accurate and authentic. And thanks to

Stephanie Kirkland for volunteering John and letting him talk out his analysis of the work with you. I'm sure it's made you anxious to read the whole fucking thing. ("There's a *lot* of swear words," he told her.)

Thanks to Jodie Cain Smith who loved the email exchanges between Brian and Meli and encouraged me to use the device more freely. As with *After December*, Jodie piloted the revision of this book and her input, honesty, and hard work are all evidence that we have something special. Stick with me, Jodie. We're going to do more great things together.

My family has always been supportive of my writing and when *After December* was published in 2019, they all *bought* copies and gifted them to their friends. So, thanks to the Whiteners, the Fannings, the Snoots, the Tiedes, the Tessier-Smoot clan, the Apgars, and the Johnsons. Momma, Kris, Dad, there aren't a lot of shared memories in this one, but our adventures in California in 1989 and 90 show up here and there. Maybe you'll recognize them.

My sister who shared her parents and Uncle Kevin with me, shared Tucson with me, and continues to inspire and amaze me, Jessica Thrower. Our paths are always wild and winding, but you've got a forever friend in me. I love you.

As I started *Before Pittsburgh*, I asked Charlie if he thought there was another book for Brian, like Alexa did. He shrugged. He actually *shrugged*. I love you, Charlie, for putting up with this cuckoo-pants writing life I'm building and knowing exactly how much enthusiasm would totally spoil me. Challenge accepted, Shruggy. And to the *real* Shruggy McShuggerson, you're my favorite person on the planet. That will never change.

Take Me to Your Book Club. I can Be Trusted.

I have a great relationship with book clubs. I've been kicked out of three. Twice I've had the chance to speak to Book Club Conferences (Pat Conroy Literary Center and Fairfax County Public Library) and both times I delivered: "Read Like a Writer: How to Get Kicked Out of Book Club." FYI, if you read like a writer, you'll be asking your wine-sipping, John-Grisham-loving neighbors and friends to *go too deep*."

Thanks for picking this book. Contact me at kasie@clemsonroad. com or through the website www.BeforePittsburgh.com to let me know what your group thought. I'm glad to appear via video conference in the meeting where you discuss this book.

Here it is, in gradually-getting-deeper order, the Book Club Guide for *Before Pittsburgh*.

1. Brian is our only point of view for this book. Did that work for you? What other characters might have added a different story or variation on Brian's grief process?

2. The chapters for the book are organized by city and then by time period. How did the progression from month to season mimic Brian's ability to use time to heal the wound of Tony's death?

3. Why does the book start with the Radford flashback? Is it an important scene to set the tone of the book? Why or why not?

4. How does travel help Brian heal? Does his globetrotting seem realistic for the era? Why or why not?

5. Despite the time and the distance and the other women he's had relationships with, Brian remains focused on Kacie as his ultimate goal. Why? What does she represent for him?

6. Brian's parents are generally accepting of him and his friends and enable him to build the life he seeks. How and when does Brian learn to appreciate their role in his life?

7. The L.A. and Nashville sections are back-to-back but one-year apart. Did that storytelling device work? Why or why not?

8. The emails between Brian and the people he left behind provide some missing dialogue from characters we don't actually see (like Mac and Meli). Did the emails add to the story? Why or why not?

9. The 9/11 scene is narrated by time stamp. How does the structure of that scene vary from what came before it? Why is it important that 9/11 be seen in minutes, not days, months, or seasons as the rest of the book?

10. In After December, we saw parts of Joel and Tabby's wedding so we knew Brian had earned forgiveness. Did Before Pittsburgh close the gap? Why or why not?

Get more from www.BeforePittsburgh.com including interviews and blogs with author Kasie Whitener and alternate scenes narrated by other characters.

About the Author

DR. KASIE WHITENER writes GenX fiction. At her core is fantasy romance and not-quite-getting-over-the-90s. This is her second novel, the first, *After December*, has been called "a breakthrough debut" and "outstanding fiction." Her short story "Cover Up," won the Carrie McCray Prize in 2016 and other stories have appeared in Spry, Kairos, and The Petigru Review. She is founder & President of Clemson Road Creative and a lecturer at the Darla Moore School of Business at the University of South Carolina. She hosts the weekly radio show Write On SC, serves on the board of directors for the South Carolina Writers Association and is a member of the South Carolina Council on Humanities Speakers Bureau. Happily married to her best friend Charlie and crazy-proud mom to the one-and-only Hollie, Kasie reads voraciously, plays golf, and cheers for the Clemson Tigers.